WAR WORLD
TAKEOVER

EDITED BY
JOHN F. CARR

Created by Jerry E. Pournelle & John F. Carr

Pequod Press

WAR WORLD VOLUMES
EDITED AND CREATED BY JOHN F. CARR AND JERRY POURNELLE

War World I: The Burning Eye

War World II: Death's Head Rebellion

War World III: Sauron Dominion

War World IV: Invasion!

CoDominium I: Revolt on War World

WAR WORLD NOVELS

Blood Feuds

Blood Vengeance

The Battle of Sauron

New War World Volumes Edited by John F. Carr

WAR WORLD: Discovery

WAR WORLD: Takeover

WAR WORLD: Jihad! (forthcoming)

WAR WORLD
TAKEOVER

A Shared-World Universe Anthology:

CREATED BY

JERRY E. POURNELLE AND JOHN F. CARR

War World: The CoDominium Takeover
A War World Anthology

Printing History

Two of the stories, Coming of the Dinneh and Politics of Melos, first appeared in CODOMINIUM: Revolt on War World, edited by Jerry E. Pournelle and John F. Carr, and published by Baen Books in 1992. The remaining eight stories were written especially for this volume and are new to the War World series.

All Rights Reserved
Copyright © 2011 by John F. Carr
Original Cover Art—Copyright © 2011 by Alan Gutierrez

This book may not be reproduced or transmitted in whole or in part, in any form or by any means electronic or mechanical, including photocopying, scanning, recording, or any information storage or retrieval system, without prior permission in writing from the authors and publisher.

Printed in the United States of America
First Printing 2011

V 10 9 8 7 6 5 4 3 2 1

ISBN: 978-0-937912-13-3

ACKNOWLEDGEMENTS

Once again, thanks go to Jerry Pournelle for allowing me to expand and create new stories in the War World/Empire of Man future history. Secondly, I'd like to thank Don Hawthorne for all his support and enthusiasm for the War World series over the years.

Special thanks go to Larry King, who also maintains a great CoDominium website, for keeping the CoDominium Time Line and for his continuity work on this volume. I'd also like to thank Stephen Shervais for all his help with the War World author's bible. And, to Dennis Frank, Archivist at St. Bonaventure University.

Also, I owe a debt of gratitude to Victoria Alexander for her editorial assistance and proof reading.

I'd also like to give thanks to all the members of the Copyediting and Post-Proofing Team, Dennis Frank, Doug McElwain, and Larry Hopkins.

A big thank you goes to Alan Gutierrez who, as always, did a wonderful job on the cover art.

CoDominium Chronology

1969	Neil Armstrong sets foot on Earth's moon
1990-2000	Series of treaties between the United States and the Soviet Union creates the CoDominium. Military research and development outlawed.
1995	Nationalist movements intensify
1996	French Foreign Legion forms the basic element of the CoDominium Armed Services.
1998	The Church of New Universal Harmony founded.
2004	Charles Castell is born.
2010-2100	CoDominium Intelligence Services engage in serious effort to suppress all research into technologies with military applications. They are aided by zero-growth organizations.
2010	Habitable planets discovered in other star systems. Commercial exploitation of new worlds begins.
2020	First interstellar colonies are founded. The CoDominium Space Navy and Marines are created, absorbing the original CoDominium Armed Services.
2020	Great Exodus period of colonization begins. First colonists are dissidents, malcontents and voluntary adventurers.
2028	Creation of the Humanity League. Sponsored by the ACLU, Sierra Club and Zero Population groups.
2032	Haven is discovered.
2040	CoDominium Population Control under the aegis of the Bureau of Relocation and Bureau of Corrections begins mass out-system shipments of involuntary colonists.
2041	Edwin Hamilton discovers the first shimmer stones on Haven.
2042	Hamilton sells the location to Dover Mineral Development and is paid a fortune to keep secret the location of their planet of origin.

2043	John Christian Falkenberg, III is born in Rome.
2043	The 26th Marines, Company C, Third Battalion is dispatched to Haven to stop criminal gangs from taking over the colony.
2052	The Shimmer Stone Rush. When the location of shimmer stones becomes public knowledge, it leads to a "rush" of shimmer stones miners.
2055	The ConDominium Bureau of Intelligence orchestrates a revolt by a band of imported criminals, which ends in disaster when their attack on Jamesport fails and their leader, Jumo, is killed.

TABLE OF CONTENTS

TO WIN THE PEACE, *Frank Gasperik and Leslie Fish* 15

THE RAID ON PURITY, *William F. Wu* 90

MARCHING ON POLAND, *Leslie Fish* 116

ENOUGH ROPE, *E R Stewart* 129

MORE PRECIOUS THAN RUBIES, *A.L. Brown* 211

COMING OF THE DINNEH, *John Dalmas* 270

BUSINESS AS USUAL, *John F. Carr* 309

POUND-FOOLISH, *Charles E. Gannon* 315

POLITICS OF MELOS, *Susan Shwartz* 333

ATALANTA, *Don Hawthorne* 394

From Stephen Ulrich's *An Informal History of the CoDominium Marines: the Good, the Bad and the Unbelievable.* New Washington Press, 2088.

26th CoDominium Marine Regiment
(Garrison, Provisional)

In the early CoDominium the Marines were an integral part of the CoDominium Armed Services (CAS). They played an important role in keeping peace both on Earth and off-world. The Marines owed their allegiance not to the CoDominium, a vague political entity on distant Terra, but to their Regiment and band of brothers. The CD Marines were the linchpin, along with the CD Navy in keeping the peace on far-flung worlds, as well as at home. For the Line Marines the predominant organization is the regiment, while for the Garrison Marines it's the battalion. "The Fleet is our Fatherland" and "No politics in the Fleet" are the mottoes of the Line Marines.

At the top rung of the CoDominium Marine Corps are the Fleet Marines. Next come the Line Marines and under them the Garrison Marines. The latter come in descending flavors including pure constabulary or police units such as are kept in reserve for use on Earth. However the bottom rung are the Provisional Regiments also known as Transport Units. The nomenclature comes from the French. An ad hoc unit was called a *unit du marche*. In theory they were supposed to be groupings of recruits and replacements formed into temporary units to shepherd them to the front. During war time, higher command would often grab these provisional units as units to meet some pressing emergency. Such units existed for months or at most a few years. Some would find themselves permanently on the order of battle (OOB).

The 26th Marine Regiment took its color and unit's lineage from one such famous French example[5] *Régiment de marche du Thad* (RMT, "*Ad hoc Regiment of Chad*"). It was a proud regiment with a noble history. The same could not be said of the 26th. Regimental HQ is a few aging officers and senior NCO's getting the last few years for their pension on Luna Base. They do the personnel and accounting work for the scattered companies.

The company for the world Haven was formed by this process. The 26th was tasked by Fleet HQ to provide a garrison for Haven. As was usual this was done in response to political pressure with no prior planning and no addition to the Fleet budget for the expense. Sufficient cadre was found by the usual expedients. First officers and NCO's of the appropriate ranks were culled from men between assignments, to minimize transport costs these were men either already on Luna or at Wayforth Station.

Major Lassitre was at the station in transit to a court martial on Luna. The conduct unbecoming charge was silly on its face. Even if he had done everything his commander accused him of it at worst merited administrative punishment. However service politics had no way of protecting a mere major without higher ranking patrons from a colonel's wrath. A company was too small a command for a major in a service with as few officer billets as the Marines but then Lassitre was scarcely in a position to turn it down.

Lieutenant Frasier's crime was even simpler. He was on Luna without assignment and a second officer was needed. Had he been on assignment to anything, however menial, some other soul's life would have been wrecked. Instead he became the other officer for the "company". This was not unusual. The Marine Corps was short of officers both by policy, a high tooth to tail ratio and low percentage of officer slots was part of the mandate of the service, and budget, where units were perpetually under funded with officer slots often going unfilled as an 'economy' move.

Two officers are quite less than a company's worth but then what was sent was only nominally a company. Two officers, some similarly unlucky NCO's and a bit over a platoon's worth of men would be sufficient cadre for something that could be called a company in bad light. The NCO's and men would be warm body requisitions (hit a unit in Luna with a request for two sergeants and two rankers, then live with them sending you the worst troublemakers they had even if they had to pull them off punishment detail to post them).

Over time more cadre would arrive via the same sort of warm body requisitions. There would be permanent requests at Luna and Wayforth from regimental HQ (The battalions of a regiment such as this are purely notional. They have neither commanders nor staff—instead the companies send their reports and receive their orders directly from regimental HQ on Luna for those infrequent occasions where higher command remembers the companies exist at all). These would go into a roster of similar permanent requests from other units almost all of whom had higher priority than the companies of the 26th. Unless a posting was near the bottom of the priority list the 26th would not have been tasked to garrison it. However military personnel systems are nothing if not capricious. There is always some poor soul either unlucky enough or who has offended his superiors sufficiently to be sent on a one-way trip to Haven.

One-way trip it of course was. Again in theory one could be posted elsewhere. However the norm was that when you fell down a career sinkhole sufficient to be posted to the 26th you stayed there until retirement or death. So the growth of the unit to full company size was more a matter of local recruitment. The transports always had a surplus of men with no future and pasts they would as soon forget.

The Marines had recruited such back to when some of these units had actually been part of the Foreign Legion. Pay was not really an issue. The garrison levied on the civilians for food and locally produced products paying in scrip. The officers and men were paid in the same make believe money less any amounts they were sending elsewhere to support dependants or pay fines from past transgressions. The scrip circulated in Castell City (later planet wide). It was money because the stores and bars would accept it as such. They accepted it because to refuse to do so was to incur the wrath of the only force capable of protecting their property. The Marines knew how to make do and the civilians adjusted to what amounted to a form of taxation by fiat currency creation. A Fleet that supported itself in good part by drug sales could not afford to be fussy.

To Win the Peace

Frank Gasperik & Leslie Fish

Haven, 2055 A.E.

A party was obviously called for and Leo Makhno had fueled it, literally. The short olive-skinned, ebony-haired captain had brought in five CoDo gallons of reserve fuel from the Black Bitch—his supercharged, twin Kawasaki-powered, Zodiac built 'baft'—and was presiding over the proceedings, but not taking particular pleasure in them. He had too many problems to think over. Besides, continually being around three-hundred horsepower engines—powered by CH3-CH2-OH at a surface pressure equal to 1,500 meters above Earth sea level—gave one a certain immunity to alch-induced euphoria.

From behind the bar, Makhno noticed that Jane, the winner of the vest-pocket war they had just fought, wasn't drinking either; but Van Damm and Brodski, the two mercs that were responsible for winning it, were sucking it up heavily. Van Damm drank morosely, but Brodski imbibed with as much joy as an ex-Fleet Marine Gunnery Sergeant, of twenty-five years service, who had just acquired a bar and a connection to the best beer, booze, and sandwich makings on Haven—and two adoring charges, (blonde, green-eyed, aged fifteen and seventeen, named Dora and Flora respectively)—could have.

Well, Brodski had earned it. If it hadn't been for him and the shaven-headed Van Damm, Jomo and his Simbas would have consolidated the area around Castell City and with it been able to hold an iron fist over the rest of Haven.

The stories Makhno had heard hadn't boded well for old Harp's daughters either; they were much better off with a man of honor like Brodski than a thug like Jomo.

One of the locals had noticed the changed ownership and they had made a swap: three free drinks for repainting the sign from Simba to Harp's Sergeant (with the insignia of a Fleet Gunny under it). More of Jomo's bullyboys had showed up, after DeCastro left, and been quickly dealt with. The news had spread rapidly around Docktown, and Jomo's goons were having a rough time of it. Several people had told Leo about the Simbas' reckoning. The *justice* in the cribs was downright bloody, while the Simbas at the sweatshops were dealt with more slowly. Leo suspected that there wouldn't be any alive by morning.

DeCastro was a different matter however. It was hard to be a "criminal" on a planet where nothing was illegal. The only restraints were those of social mores and whatever personal code of behavior one had brought from Earth. DeCastro's organization and code seemed to be something right out of the ancient writings of Damon Runyon.

The party was becoming loud; an impromptu "Victory Band" of two guitars, a battery powered synthesizer, a fiddle, banjo, and improvised drums were announcing victory to all of Haven. There were even some Harmonies improvising words to the instrumental jam.

I should feel better, thought Makhno. *Why don't I?*

Maybe it was the understanding that, with the *Last Resort* sunk, his Zodiac was one of the largest river boats on the planet. That did not bode well for trade in the Shangri-La Valley, where the only reliable roadway was the river.

Maybe it was the thought of the Kennicott Mining ship still in orbit around Haven, a shadow of the CoDominium and the future....

Yeah, we won this one, but how do we keep it?

Maybe Owen Van Damm would have a suggestion or two; he'd been around in CoDo space, he'd seen a lot and seemed to know a lot about what was going on—like who was Who amongst the interstellar companies, and who was getting what slice of what pie. Maybe current BuReloc policies? Who better to ask than the far-traveler for news of far-off places? He was off the last ship, too. Not too many people from that ship: only three hundred or so "settlers" from the Bureau of ReLocation, some donations from Earth for the Harmonies and that load of CoDo stunners for Jomo.

"Captain Makhno?" asked the wiry little man with the perpetually stained fingers.

"Yeah, Sam? How's your off-world gear holding up?"

"Better than usual, Leo. I got some replacement parts in trade for some euph from a crewman on the *Kennicott Harbinger* upstairs, and uh, do you know somebody named Van Damm? I got a message and a two-way trip ticket for him. I didn't know somebody up there was a friend of his."

"He's the one sitting next to the big blonde, behind you. How'd you get this? With your ham gear? Or did a shuttle land while I was gone?"

"Off the ham gear. Come on, Leo, who else has the town got as a Comm Tech? Just me, Sam Kilroy: ever since the budget got cut, just one man to keep an off-planet radio watch. I owe you one for the warning about Jomo, by the way."

"You can pay that one off right now if you want. What was in that message to Van Damn?"

"You don't want to know, Leo. I sure don't even want to know; it's in code."

Code? That, Makhno considered, opened up a large can of possibilities. *Van Damm an agent? For who? The Lords of the CoDo? Reynolds Off-World? Kennicott, Dover or Anaconda? BuReloc? Fleet?* It could be anybody. *But then, why did he help us so much?* "See you later, Sam, I need some air." Makhno went outside.

The view from the porch of the bar wasn't particularly inspiring: just the lake and Splash Island, and off in the distance what was called Xanadu River.

Makhno remembered the trip down the river, helping to ferry miners well over a thousand kilometers down river into what could become something next to slavery for Kennicott Metals and Mining, but they were willing to pay for it no matter how much he had talked against that trip. The *Bitch* had towed rafts that could only be considered marginally river-worthy, even during the wind-slack period of Haven's cycle. Some of the miners had been taken by land-gators and cliff lions as they hunted along the river banks. A few had drifted their hands in the water, giving quick snacks to riverjacks, and a couple of the rafts had performed an act of dissolution due to poor engineering and even worse construction, providing the river carnivores with full meals. So had two of the "kit-design" steamboats shepherding the rafts.

No, he wouldn't make such a trip again. If he needed an excuse, it was that the *Black Bitch* wasn't built for such loads, at such distance. Let Kennicott provide more boats, if they wanted to haul more slave labor down river.

And now a Kennicott ship in orbit, and maybe a Kennicott agent as somebody I've come to respect and even to trust a bit. It's hard to say to yourself "I don't know," but the truth is, that I DON'T know. I've been thinking of Jane and Haven, not of the conditions off-planet. We could be pawns in someone else's game—but why not a Knight, a Rook, or even...a Queen?

"No!" *I won't let us be played like this!*

"No to what, Leo?"

He knew that voice.

"I, too, have made a decision, Leo," Van Damm continued out of the darkness. There was a short silence.

"Uhuh." Makhno kept it noncommittal, wondering how much Owen had guessed.

"Will you talk with me, Leo?" Van Damm was drunk enough that his accent was showing. "Are we not comrades? Have we not fought together?"

"Why not?"

Van Damm led the way towards the barrel floats that served as Docktown's Port-of-Entry and reason for being.

"What we have built here is too important to sell out to some company or some government," Van Damm said firmly. "Is certainly too important to be left to the whims of ideological theorists."

"Jane's a practical sort," said Makhno.

"I know that you know…that I have received a message from above," Van Damm plowed on. "I will tell you, Leo. I watched you receive the news and I will tell you what it is about, and confirm some of your suspicions. Yes, I have been summoned to the ship. No, I am *not* an agent of Kennicott Metals. I vork for Fleet."

Makhno could hear the capital letters. He also noticed that Van Damm's Afrikaner accent could have become more pronounced with emotion than drink.

"You may not understand all of what I have to say, Leo; but please listen and remember…and tell Jane everything."

That sounds good. "I'm listening."

"Jomo was a cat's paw. My boss wanted Jomo to win, even provided him with the stunners and sent me to get close to him and make sure that he won. Also make dammed sure that he took slaves and committed every atrocity he was capable of… But they made two mistakes…"

"You were the wrong color," injected Leo.

"That was one, but also they had not counted on Jane and what she represents." He stopped and faced Makhno. "She is a wild card in the deck."

"You mean, nobody took account of a canny farmer!"

"Brodski might have done alone what the two of us did. Not with the same presence perhaps, but, accomplished the same tings and maybe even with fewer casualties. He has fought many kinds of war, that man," Van Damm said with respect.

"Jane had the sense to recruit him." Makhno kept his hand near his belt-knife, but relaxed a little. "She told me what to look for, and I found men who fit her specs."

"Including me."

"True. But why did you fight for Jane, then, instead of Jomo?"

"Leo, I have seen my home and culture destroyed by politicians in Washington and Moscow, and on Luna. Deciding the fates of lands they have never valked over, by drawing lines on maps...."

"I think we've all seen that."

"I vas off-world, Leo, when my people vere killed in vhat the media called 'An exzess of independence' but the result vas the same as if they had called it a 'riot' or an 'insurrection.' The result vas the same, the same...I no longer had a family or a home to return to, except the Fleet—until now."

"Why did Fleet want Jomo to win?" Makhno asked.

"My *job* here vas to make the 'uprising' that happened as bloody as possible, and get the attention of the off-vorld news agencies. They are easy to manipulate and use. The justification for a CoDo takeover vas supposed to be the issue of overt slavery on Haven, and Jomo vas supposed to be the kingpin. But how much outrage can you generate vith a lead-line like *Farmers defeat Slavers, Vid at 11*?"

"Because you joined us, instead."

"Ya."

There was silence between the two men as they watched Hecate pass behind the hub of Cat's Eye.

"Are you going back up, Van?"

"You killed any other option for me, Leo. The message vas delivered to me. I have been called; now I must go. By the vay, my controller is Maxwell Cole. If he ever tries to make a deal vith you...."

"Yeah; don't trust him."

The two men turned and reentered the bar not noticing the child who had listened and learned, literally from sitting (in a barrel) at their feet.

* * *

Sr. Agent (GS14) Max Cole was seething. The reports from Haven pointed to a fiasco. Jomo's head was on a stick outside of his own headquarters. The Kennicott agent who had been Jomo's lieutenant was back in his old establishment, The Golden Parrot, with only one-third the strength he started with. What really rankled Cole was that a bunch of dirt farmers with fowling pieces and other junk had defeated a force of over fifty fighters (thugs and bullies true, but fighters none the less) armed with modern weapons, CoDo stunners. Led by a bloodthirsty egotist, the Simbas should have rolled up the settlers as fast as they found them.

Instead, Jomo and all the troops he'd taken with him were slaughtered. The thugs he'd left behind were being killed or were running out to a hostile wasteland where the odds of survival were ninety-nine to one against, at best.

What had Van Damm been doing? The media would be applauding, not screaming for the CoDominium to take action for 'Pacification.' *If they ever got the news*, he thought. *Chances were slight, since most of the returning ships were bound for Tabletop or Tanith, but still....*

Maybe the farmers can be made to attack the Harmonies and take their land.... Well, I'll find out when he gets up here. If Van Damm doesn't have a plan, he'll stay on that ice-ball until he bloody well comes up with one.

* * *

It was quiet in The Golden Parrot, and Tomas Messenger y DeCastro was disturbed. His bar was the only safe spot for the more overt "criminal" class of the planet, and it felt as if a siege was mounting outside its walls. He had forestalled some of the action by refusing entrance to some

Simbas being chased by a mob—and had killed the one that had broken in through a back window. All the windows were now securely shuttered and barred from the inside. The dead Simba's body was on a hook outside the front door.

That takes care of the present, perhaps even the next week or so, but what happens after that?

DeCastro had seen mobs taken by what they had felt was righteous indignation before, and it had always ended in killings and hangings and looting. He felt no need to dance his final dance at the end of a rope.

Well if one cannot live in one place, one moves to another.

But, how to move and keep things somewhat intact? Well, Capitan Makhno was a capitalist above all else; perhaps he would transport Tomas and his goods down river to the Kennicott camp. DeCastro could bring a few women with him, along with some of his most trustworthy *compadres* and a certain amount of his mostly depleted stock.

Perhaps Capitan Makhno would accept The Golden Parrot and all that remained in it in trade for transportation, including the hydroponic poppy garden in the basement. A pity that: they were just getting ready for bleeding. Opium remained a saleable product anywhere one took it.

He still had to ensure some kind of insurrection to allow Kennicott the rights they wished to steal from the Harmonies who now owned this moon of the Cat's Eye.

The miners downstream might just do to serve his purpose.

He wrote a note and summoned his most trusted girl, Inez, and instructed her most carefully.

* * *

Maxwell Cole pointed his finger at Van Damm as if it was a pistol. "Bottom line, you had a job to do, and you didn't do it."

Van Damm shrugged instead of breaking off the jabbing digit at the root. "I had faulty tools. The gang the previous operatives put together was a laugh. Jomo vas a bloodthirsty tyrant, more interested in pumping his own ego than doing the job. He and his gang of thugs thought they could bully people in submission. Vhen some of the locals put up some resistance, they folded like a house of cards."

"Janesfort, ha! It sounds like the women had some backup, yes?"

"Yes, an ex-fleet gunny named Brodski, gave the ladies some support."

"Why didn't you dissuade him?" Cole asked patronizingly.

"I was busy in Castell, trying to keep control of things while Jomo was beating the bush," Van Damm lied smoothly.

Cole shook his head. "The agency's never going to buy this: a bunch of hicks and women beating off a small army. My ninety days here are just about up; I'm going to have to leave and sell this crock to my boss. Something tells me he's not going to be amused. I know I'm not, and you're the Johnny-on-the-spot."

"I'll take the heat."

"Sure you will. You're going to stay here until my replacement comes."

Van Damm lowered his head as if he couldn't bear the weight. The Velcro patch on his butt kept him firmly anchored to his seat, otherwise he would have floated away. "Not that," he muttered, sounding as if he meant it.

"Yes, that," Cole said. "And you'll stay here until the next agent from BuIntel arrives. We've setup a small post on Wayforth Station to keep an eye on the Tanith Sector. The *Harbinger* will be stopping there first before going on to Newton, so it won't take more than a few T-months to get someone out here. But that doesn't mean you're going to go shimmer stone hunting; I want you to try and light a fire under these hicks."

Cole handed off a satchel which weighed enough to drag his arm down to the table. "This contains 2.5 kilos of assorted gold coins, and some cash. I want you to set up a network to undermine Harmony rule, plain and simple. That shouldn't be difficult for a man of your experience."

Van Damm nodded. "Jomo's payoff for the stunners."

"Yeah, and more. The Agency wants results; they're getting a lot of pressure from higher up."

Van Damm wondered why the Grand Senate was so interested in Haven. Maybe Senator Bronson wanted to reconsolidate his gains on the shimmer stone trade, now that the Company's monopoly had been busted.

"Now, what can you do for us?" Cole demanded.

"It's a difficult situation now that Jomo's been killed." Van Damm shrugged. "The townies and Jomo's competitors used his defeat to clean up Castell City. There aren't a lot of thugs left in Castell, and most of those that are still alive work for DeCastro."

"DeCastro's unreliable. He takes money from both Kennicott and Reynolds. The man's been bought so many times he doesn't know his left from his right. Maybe you can stir up some trouble with the miners."

Van Damm knew that was beating a dead horse. Most of the miners had shimmer stone fever, and couldn't care less about Castell City or who ran it. The rest were indentured serfs working for one of the Companies. Hell's-A-Comin' was like Dawson City during the Alaskan Gold Rush: no place for the timid or the faint of heart. As long as the Harmonies left them alone, they weren't interested in anything but stones, women, getting drunk and gambling. He also knew that he had to give Cole something he could take back to his masters on Luna.

He slapped the leather satchel. "With this, I can buy some serious trouble," he promised. *But for whom?*

"Good, I want you to use that cash to buy the Harmonies lots of trouble: Enough that when my replacement arrives, you can hand him Haven on a gold plate."

"And, if I can't?"

Cole gave him the fish eye. "Then you can stay on this ice-ball for the rest of your life, however long that may be."

*   *   *

The shuttle carrying Van Damm was going to return in the dim phase, and Brodski was getting ready for it. Leo Makhno had delivered six 40-gallon drums of beer, twenty gallons of alcohol and almost a ton of foodstuffs for the bar, along with a selection of weapons and ammo

(Simba salvaged war surplus) for him to sell. Flora, who had grill duty, was cleaning up the kitchen and the ex-Fleet sergeant was bringing a pile of sweepings up to the front door with careful broom strokes, when he heard a sound Brodski had heard all too often in his long career—a child being hurt.

The situation outside was about what he expected. Three men were struggling to hold onto a young boy. The boy was clearly overmatched, but refused to give up fighting for his freedom.

Brodski moved in. A quick thrust with the broom handle to the lower spine of the one with his back to Brodski took the odds down to two. Reversing the broom in a half-spin faced the second with the surprise of assured blindness. He let go.

The child twisted loose of his last tormentor and ran for the door of the bar.

"Pick up your friend and leave," snarled Brodski, "And don't come back for any reason."

"Aww, it's only a Harmony kid. We was just havin' some fun."

Brodski had moved a bit closer while the man was talking. The bristles of the broom ripped open the man's cheek, and the handle end whipped around to break his nose as his head turned. A snap kick to the belly stopped the third man in his tracks.

It pays to advertise, especially when it comes to the kind of custom you want, thought Brodski. "It isn't fun unless everybody involved enjoys what's happening," he said. "You having fun now? No? Then move out and don't come back." He'd remember those faces.

As Brodski entered the bar he sent the sweepings flying out the door with a quick flick of the broom, leaving some blood streaks on the floor, then looked at the child standing well back and holding a heavy clay ashtray ready to throw. Flora backed him with the coach gun from behind the bar.

"It's all finished now, so put up the hardware." Brodski turned to the child. "What's your name, lad?"

"Do you know Captain Makhno?"

"I do."

"I have a message for him, from Charles Castell."

"Why you, lad, and not a beadle?"

"Because Castell doesn't know he sent it." That was stated simply as a fact, with all of the assurance of an eleven-year-old knowing he was doing the right thing.

"What's your message, lad? I'll make sure it gets to him."

"It's only for him, not some sinning bar owner." Disdain was dripping from his mouth when he said it.

"Look kid, you're making me think that I should have left you to your fun-loving friends out there."

There was a look of thoughtfulness on the kid's face. "How did you do that? I mean, with the broom. I never thought of a broom...."

"It's just using what you have at hand to do the job." Brodski thought a moment, "'Being at one with the moment is all; this is the path to Harmony with the universe,'" he quoted a Zen master he had studied under once.

"But...I have been taught that violence is dis-harmonious."

Brodski pulled up the argument he'd used with Harmonies before. "Lad, when you come to think of it, striking a drum with a stick to make a beat is violent. Plucking a string on a guitar is violent. Nobody asks the skin or the string if they want to be treated that way, but what is produced can be music or discord depending on how it's done. Just in case you're wondering, that's called Zen, and is part of a way of defending yourself."

"...I'd like to learn more."

"Well lad, I'm willing to teach if you're willing to learn. You can write your message for Leo and leave it here. It won't get read unless by him, but he won't be back for a couple of days. You can write can't you?"

The look on the child's face told it all.

"Well, I can teach that, too. Flora, bring me a writing pad, some milk and a beer." Looking over the kid, he added, "And a meat sandwich for my student. What's your name, youngster?"

"Wilgar."

"Well, I guess first we teach you to write your name."

*   *   *

Van Damm was still smarting from the dressing-down Max Cole had handed out in his private cabin aboard the *Kennicott Harbinger*, but at least Van was staying on Haven and getting a chance to recover some of his professional pride. With 2.5 kilos of assorted gold coins (the Golden Rand and English Guinea were still the small change of the espionage business), out-system trade units (plastic with embedded holograms), and paper CoDo money in various denominations, it would be possible to set up the kind of network Cole had ordered him to. Using DeCastro's connections wouldn't hurt, and would speed the process.

The question was, did he want to do it?

Seeing the virtues of one's victims: this is how agents get turned, or go native.

As he headed for his temporary cabin in officers' country he noticed a career corporal he'd played chess with on the way out, and the man didn't look all that happy.

"What's new, Heinrick?" he asked.

"Moving out, Mr. Van Damm. Planet-side. Down to that hellhole til God knows when. The Powers That Be have decided to lighten the ship by jettisoning half the ship's guard in forty-eight hours. We go right after the Kennicott stuff drops for Kenny-Camp. You taking passage back to Earth?"

"No," said Van Damm, an idea dawning. "I have part interest in a business in Docktown: one that you might like. A bar run by a friend of mine...an ex-Fleet Gunny named Brodski. Ever hear of him?"

"You mean Hot-Wire Brodski?! We hid him all the way out here! I served with him in Belize and the Sudan, in the old 2nd Division. You say he's got a bar down there?"

"Bar and grill, probably the best food and booze on the planet. Drop in and see us when you hit dirt."

"Sure will, Mr. Van Damm! Say, did he ever tell you about the time in Belize, when the Guat's were kickin' up, and him and me was on this hill...."

Forty-eight hours to wait for the next shuttle, Van Damm considered. *Oh well, I can listen to a combat story or two till then, seeing as I'm to ride down with the troops.*

* * *

"I hereby bring this meeting of the Fraternal order of Hibernians and Caledonians to order," Himself in his green coat announced with three bangs of his fist on a piece of plank. "So all of yahs, shut up."

The motley crowd obligingly shut up.

"First order of business will be a committee of constitution, since we have no committee, with the exceptions of Black Jim who's takin' notes and meself who's the best man of yous all. And we have no constitution so we have no laws as of yet. But since yous here you all seem to think that some sort of law is in order: I appoint the scholarly Robert of the heathen land of Milwaukee as head, and Peter Flowers of Arizona as his Deputy, since he has the best fists of the bunch of all of yah. They can pick the rest.

"I appoint as medical board two others that Doc Schaffer picks, and I want all of yah to go to him wit any hurts that yah got. He's got a good survival rate.

"Some of yahs don't understand what we's about here at Hell's-A-Comin', so I'll explain it to yahs. We help each other...even if yah wasn't lucky enough to come from Ireland, Or Scotland, or Wales. Yah's miners, and we's the older of all miners' unions. We help each other out when we's outside and on surface, yah understand? If ya got food, ya don't let a brother go hungry. Ya help him in a fight. Ya protect his claim when he asks ya, and he'll do the same for yahs.

"All of ya's Brothers now...so as ya line up at the beer, look at each other's faces so ya'll know each odder. And with the tappin' of the keg I call the meeting adjourned."

And he hit the plank once more.

As the others were turning toward the bar, an older miner came limping up to him. "Hey, Irish," he almost whispered. "A word in private, if you please?"

Himself studied the older man for a moment, heart thudding as he recognized him. At last, this was the man he'd waited so long to see. He looked left and right, then strolled out of the dugout and into the windswept street. The old miner followed.

"This should be far enough t' avoid unwelcome ears—Mr. Bronstein," he said quietly.

Bronstein winced, but then smiled. "You've done your homework," he admitted.

"What's left o' the unions on Earth ain't fools," Himself grinned. "We've taken a page from you Wobblies, and learned ta study well—an' keep good records."

"Knowledge isn't exactly power," Bronstein admitted, "But it's way the hell out in front of raw ignorance."

"It ain't power, but it damn-well is survival. That's the mistake your First Union made."

"We had knowledge," Bronstein growled. "It wasn't enough. Why do you think you can do better?"

"First Union had only the one cave-complex," Himself said carefully. "We've got several already, and we're workin' at diggin' more. We've spread further up and down the river, and we're makin' settlements a good ways inland from it. We've already got connections with the farmers, and we make more—and we also help 'em by digging, uh, storm cellars for the lot of 'em, if ya know what I mean."

"It'll take you a lot of work to connect them."

"So we take our time. First Union, well, ya jumped too fast: didn't get enough bolt-holes an' supplies before ya made yer move."

"Hell, we thought we had to make our move before Kenny-Co brought in the next load of transportees for scabs. We didn't think the company could hold out for much more than two hundred days." Bronstein laughed bitterly. "We also thought, miners being rare then, that we were too valuable to shoot. Honest mistake."

"Well, we gotta big population down here now." Himself glanced up and down the dirt street, just making sure. "Aye, and we got no illusions about what the companies will do if we challenge 'em straight out. Nah, we don't just strike; we use a different tactic."

"Such as?"

"First, we don't call ourselves a union. Nobody mentions the Industrial Workers o' the Worlds, nobody quotes the old sayings, and nobody gives any hints the Kenny-Co ears might pick up. By the way, how did ya get alive out o' that cave?"

The old miner winced. "When the survivors saw that the Marines weren't going to follow us into the cave, we put on a little performance for them. They bought it and we kept our heads down afterward. How did you guess?"

"People talk, and I'm good at listenin'. But you get the idea we're playin' at here? We're just the Fraternal Order of Hibernians and Caledonians, and we're just a social an' charitable organization. Ya got that, too?"

"Starting slow, then."

"An' as a charitable organization, it makes sense we should make deals and ties an' all with the settlers. *All* the settlers."

"Even the Harmonies?"

"Especially the Harmonies." Himself fixed Bronstein with an impaling glare. "Who do ya think's got the biggest supply o' seeds an' livestock?"

"The 'Workers' and Peasants' League'," Bronstein laughed. "That used to be a joke, outdated even when we were founded, and that was 1905."

"It wasn't a joke a good half-century earlier," Himself said, straight-faced.

Bronstein frowned. "There are no surviving unions from that far back," he noted.

"Not survivin', no." Himself looked innocently up at the stars. "Reborn, at need. Conditions here are more primitive than they were on

Earth, even in 1905, so we go back to something' earlier."

Bronstein gave him a long look. "Don't tell me," he said slowly, "That your real name is Maguire."

"No," Himself laughed, "An' me mother's name wasn't Molly, eyther, but the ideas are the same. Unify the farmers an' small shopkeepers an' miners—aye, an' even the Harmonies—because there's really only two classes here: the mining companies, with their CoDo troops for harness-bulls—"

Bronstein smiled thinly.

"—an' everybody else. That means we got ta unify all o' that everybody else. Organize everybody who isn't the Ruling Class. Build 'em up so they can run the whole planet by themselves, even if another ship never comes. That's what we got ta do first."

"And now we've got enough population to do it." Bronstein took a deep breath. "Knowledge can be power, after all."

"How d'ye mean?"

"You know, we organizers of the First Union had a couple of good computers with us, part of our 'traveling organizer packs'. When Kenny-Co called in the Marines to smash the strike, they never imagined—and never looked for—anything like those computers. Those jobs had plutonium batteries that can last a century and more if they aren't smashed. Jablonski's long past needing his. You want it?"

"Jaysus," Himself breathed. "What a difference that could make!"

"Come along with me, up to the old cave complex, to the one furthest from the river, and I'll show you a corner that the Marines never found. That's where I've been keeping it for all these years."

*   *   *

Jane paced back and forth across the tower room, chewing her lip. "Is that everything Vann Damm said, Leo?" she asked.

"All I can remember. I'm no expert on politics, Jane, but it all makes ugly good sense."

"Too good. Everybody wants to steal Haven from the Harmonies. Kennicott wants it for the hafnium, Dover for the shimmer stones, the other mining companies want it for whatever they can get, BuReloc wants it for a dumping ground and everybody else wants it for the shimmer stones. That means CoDo has to takeover and run the place itself. The Harmonies won't be able to hold out forever, no matter what we do."

"I never thought I'd feel sorry for the arrogant bastards," said Makhno.

"But there's plenty we can do to slow down the takeover, slow it down until we've got our own population strong enough to deal with the CoDominium. It can be done...." She cast a long look out of the tower window, taking in the view of the island, the river, and the land beyond. "Ever hear of a guy named Thomas Jefferson, Leo?"

"Sure, in basic history. American revolutionary: wrote the Declaration of Independence and a few other things. Why?"

"He also had this idea that if every person has their own turf, their own way of making a living by themselves—and the means of defending it—then they're not dependent on anybody. They're hard to kill, hard to rule, harder to takeover, and...they tend to have this egalitarian attitude. They don't fall into pecking orders. There was another guy, I think his name was Hine-line or something like that, who listed all the things a competent human being should be able to do. 'Specialization is for insects', he said. I don't know who said 'jack of all trades, master of none', but that's our basic strategy, Leo. Whatever their specialty is, we make everybody self-sufficient, then independent. That's how we can beat CoDo, first and last."

"I'm not following you," Makhno replied.

"I'll explain later. Where did you leave Van Damm?"

"In Brodski's bar. He'd brought in a buddy just off the *Kennicott Harbinger* who needed a job, and he figured 'Ski could get him one."

"Did this buddy bring anything useful?"

"Possibly. He had a really heavy duffel bag that he wouldn't let anyone else touch, and it clanked when he set it down."

"Good. When you get back, tell Brodski to keep an eye on him. And have Van Damm radio me, last channel; we have to make some plans together."

"How soon?" Makhno grumbled. "I was planning on getting a little shore time here…with you."

"Not right away," Jane smiled. "Besides, Benny's been working on something else that he'd like to show you."

"Ah, what would that be?"

"You know," she smiled wider, "That thanks to Jomo's stupidity—and some generally poor construction techniques—you now have the only boat on the planet that's fit to run the whole length of the river. That gives you a useful monopoly for right now, but eventually the *Black Bitch* will wear out beyond our capacity to repair and we'll be in real trouble."

"Sooner rather than later if I have to make any more heavy runs the length of the river!" Makhno exploded. "The woodcutters' stations get fewer at every run, and the kit-boats—Damn-it, half of them were made by rank amateurs, and they've been dying ever since. This last trip, I saw the *Putty Princess* sink—no surprise there—but then *Rosie*'s engine blew up. The *Last Resort* was the best built of the lot, and we know what happened to her. And before that… Hell, Jane, The settlers started out with eight steamboats, and now we're down to three. I wouldn't bet on their survival for another year. If I let her take up the slack in the trade, the *Black Bitch* will wear out in another one or two T-years. I won't do it, Jane. I know I've got my share of the fort, but the *Bitch* is how I've always made my living—I won't lose her."

Jane smiled. "Understood. We're going to need more big boats, ones that are built by people who know what they're doing. So, how would you like to become an admiral?"

Makhno pulled his jaw back up and made a good guess. "What will you do for engines?" were the first words out of his mouth.

"Hermaphrodite. Sails, and… Ever hear of a steam-turbine?"

"Wait—waitaminute! Turbines need high-grade steel; we can't make that—"

"Depends on how fast you spin it. Benny has a design he'd like to show you, and he says we can make it out of brass or even crude iron. I do believe we could get that from the miners down river."

"Uh, okay. They're always hot for our crops…Hmm, what will we use for boat-hulls?"

"Steelwood is a real bitch to cut, but that's material for another industry."

"Even so, wooden hulls…. We couldn't make very big boats that way. What kind of design is Benny thinking about?"

"Ever hear of an arrowhead-trimaran?"

*   *   *

DeCastro was beyond impatience and well into desperation. Captain Makhno had taken the *Black Bitch* and gone east up the river and hadn't returned for over a full T-week. The Golden Parrot was out of almost everything, while Harp's Sergeant was doing excellent business. The Fleet troops were groundside, drinking up a storm and spending money, and all DeCastro saw of it came from the women. His bar had become nothing but a whorehouse, and putting all of one's eggs in one basket was bad business. He had to get out of here—and soon.

Subsequently, he was overjoyed to hear from his lookouts that the *Black Bitch* was pulling up at the dock. He almost pulled himself to his feet to run down to the dock himself, but remembered his position in time and sent one of the girls instead.

The waiting was almost intolerable, but eventually Ludmilla returned with the captain in tow. Unexpectedly, that elusive CoDo agent Van Damm was with him. DeCastro invited them into his office, and even shooed out his last bodyguard.

"Well, *Capitan*," he almost panted. "I am most delighted to see you. Have you come to take me up on my offer of last turn?"

"Happy to," Makhno smiled. "I'm about due to head down to Hell's-A-Comin' anyway. I'll be piloting the *Celia*. I'm taking only the light barge, and it'll be slow running, but if you still want to go—"

"Definitely! But why not the *Black Bitch*?" He had heard rumors that Vann Damm had bought the *Celia* from Grubby Marsden for cash on the barrel head. He knew that Vann and Makhno were as thick as thieves and suspected they were setting up a riverboat monopoly. *Hell, that's what I'd do if I was in their shoes.*

Makhno shook his head. "I'd have to fill the barge with fuel instead of your stuff and the rest of the cargo. Some of the woodcutter stations used to distill some alch for me, but too many of them have gone out of business or been hit by river pirates. With a steamboat, worse comes to worse, you can chop your own wood for the firebox."

DeCastro nodded. "Okay. I know we've lost a lot of steamboats lately. I thought Kenny-Co might be behind it."

Makhno laughed. "They don't need to bother. Those boats have barely made enough money to keep the chop-box full. Most of their fees are in barter. Not enough cash for anything but bare maintenance, and certainly no one can afford to scratch-build one anymore."

That explains a lot, he thought. *If things work out in Kenny-Camp, maybe I'll bankroll my own fleet.*

"Now, I'd like you to show me and my friend here that interesting little garden of yours."

"Gladly." DeCastro demonstrated how to open the hidden door, and led them down into the hydroponic garden beyond. "As you can see," he said with an eloquent gesture, "The poppy-heads are ready for bleeding. Do you wish to observe the technique?" *If nothing else, it might give CoDo another excuse....*

"Oh, by all means."

DeCastro picked up a fine-bladed craft knife and shot glass from the nearest table, and proceeded to the planting-bed. "One simply makes a few vertical cuts—like so—and catches the sap as it runs out. One must be careful not to dig too deeply, or the seeds will be injured."

The three men watched as the milky juice dripped out of the cut seed-pod and into the glass. Van Damm looked up at the overhead light. "The growing-lamps must be hard to come by," he noted.

"That is why one must always depend on interstellar trade," DeCastro replied, sweating under the glow lamps. "The lights are especially important. These are tropical plants from Earth, and cannot thrive in dim light, or cold."

Van Damm murmured something that sounded like "Frennel lenz?"

DeCastro ignored him. "As promised, *Capitan*—opium. The only source of morphine on the planet, I believe. All yours, as well as the rest of my establishment, in exchange for taking me, my supplies and my *compadres* to Kenny-Camp. How soon can we depart?"

Makhno and Van Damm exchanged brief looks. "Sign the deed in front of everybody in the bar," Makhno said, "And we can leave right after. How long will it take you to pack?"

"An hour!" DeCastro enthused. "No more than an hour! Come, let's go out to the front room and finish the formalities." With that, he led them back into his office.

"I'll help," Van Damm spoke up. "Meanwhile, I'll get a friend to mind the store while we go down river." He padded out the door and away, looking unhurried but moving deceptively fast.

"'We?'" DeCastro worried as he pulled out the paper and a pen. "He means to come with us? Why?"

"Maybe to guard our backs while we sleep." Makhno shrugged. "Maybe to help make sure that nobody tries to steal the boat. Or maybe he wants to make some deals in Kenny Camp One or Hell's-A-Comin'. Who knows?"

"You understand, I shall be bringing my, ah, employees too?"

"I knew that," Makhno smiled, not prettily.

"Aha." DeCastro guessed that he understood Makhno's precautions now. "Come, let us go sign the papers in front of everybody."

*   *   *

Brodski paced slowly up to the gate of the Harmony enclave, noting with approval that the log walls had been raised to an effective height. Wilgar self-importantly rang the bell and pulled himself up a little taller. The tiny barred window in the gate opened, and a suspicious eye showed in the space.

"Brother Wilgar and Cousin Brodski, come to see the Choirmaster," the boy announced.

The window slammed shut. A moment later the gate creaked open.

"You might want to put a small wheel under the leading edge of that gate," Brodski noted. "Keep the gate from dragging on the ground and pulling on the hinges. It'll move a lot easier and last a lot longer."

The brown-robed gatekeeper gave him an owlish look and said nothing, but closed the gate behind them. Wilgar led the way to the main house, then into the famed library.

Charles Castell, sitting behind the desk, looked older and wearier than the last time Brodski had seen him, which wasn't that many turns ago. He barely raised his eyes as Brodski paced to the front of his desk and took one of the facing chairs without waiting to be told. "Friend Brodski," he asked, "Have you returned to teach Harmonious Defense to more of our brethren?"

"In more ways than you expected," Brodski replied. "Besides Aikido and Tai Chi, I'd like to teach you something of strategy, too."

Castell only raised a suspicious eyebrow.

Nothing for it but to plow ahead. "Are you aware," said Brodski, "That the CoDo government is plotting to take Haven away from you?"

Castell blinked. "I am very much aware of it," he said grimly, "And I confess that I have not found a Harmonious way to prevent this theft."

"Ultimately, you can't." Brodski leaned closer. "What the government wants, the government gets—so long as the only real opposition is a small bunch of folks insisting on their rights. It takes really massive numbers, all of them armed with some kind of real power, to make a government change course—which is what elections used to be about. You don't have that kind of numbers, or anything like that kind of power."

"Have you nothing better to tell me?" Castell asked.

"Yes. You can slow down the takeover. Slow it down while you gain the power to hold off the worst of their control. Are you interested?"

Castell rattled his fingers on the desk. "I do not see a Harmonious way of gaining or using the power you describe," he said slowly. "Can you enlighten me on this subject?"

Brodski smiled. "First, you must extend a Harmonious unity to all the people on Haven. In other words, make everybody your allies—everybody who isn't a CoDo agent or corporate manager. Are you willing to do that?"

"Everybody?" Castell blinked. "Amoral settlers, and sin-loving miners, and...and...."

"Everybody," Brodski said firmly. "Give up your isolation or give up your world. Those are the choices you have."

Castell thought for a long moment, his face crumpling as if it were aging suddenly. Finally he said: "Tell me how you think this unity can be accomplished."

"First," said Brodski, holding up one finger, "Get involved in the economy of Docktown. Trade directly with the settlers, the miners, and everyone else who isn't a company man. Encourage trade: barter, or local trade-standard or any kind of money you can lay your hands on.

"Second, don't antagonize the Marines in any way; that means not leaning on the bars, bordellos or anything else they find amusing. Just smile and ignore them.

"Third, send out more beadles and deacons to throw the real troublemakers out of town. I can help you identify those, and so can other friends of mine. Warn the settlers not to take them in. If they can't reach Hell's-A-Comin' let them make boats and move out onto the river.

"Fourth, make some well-disguised escape tunnels. There's always the possibility that you'll need them. Mark paths not only to your own outlying farms but to settlers' farms as well, and make sure to keep the good will of those settlers.

"Fifth—"

Charles Castell listened attentively, but his face grew bleaker and older with every word.

Wilgar listened even more intently, eyes wide in fascination.

* * *

Kennicott Camp One, or Kenny-Camp as it was more commonly called, had a company dock, a company office-building, company sheds, company housing and a company store, and everything else was a jerry-built slum. The open-pit hafnium mine lay a quarter-mile back from the river, a shameless eyesore with the machines always busy in it: diggers, belts and pumps constantly serviced by the indentured "wage-slaves." Beside it lay the huge artificial mountain of the mine-tailings, being worked by ragged free miners. Beyond it, in the bare hills above the forest, were the numerous man-made caves of the shimmer stone prospectors.

Van Damm frowned at the scene as Makhno made the *Celia* fast at the dock, then turned to DeCastro. "I hope you can make a living from company scrip," he said. "It is plain that there is little else here but barter."

"I will happily deal in whatever my customers can pay," said DeCastro with a smile, as he watched his personnel pull the barge close to the dock. "Besides, the minerals which the company machines cast off can include surprising riches. Do you see that rather shabby assayer's office there?" He pointed. "I have it on good authority that respectable amounts of gold, silver and copper have come through its doors."

"To say nothing of crude iron," Van Damm murmured, fixing the location firmly in his memory.

"They have their own smelter," added Makhno, giving Van Damm a significant glance. "We'll be dropping in there, soon."

"Please, *senores*, assist my companions to unload the barge while I go to seek suitable lodgings for my enterprise." DeCastro hauled himself up onto the dock, automatically patting the filled holster on his hip and cast a calculating look around the near buildings.

"I'll come with you," said Van Damm, climbing up on the dock beside him. "This does not look like a town where it is safe for a man to walk alone."

"Very well," shrugged DeCastro, looking away.

Makhno, watching as the two of them strolled down the dock, judged that Vanny was safe on his own, then turned his attention to unloading the raft and barge. DeCastro's hirelings, he noted—even the women—worked as if they were used to it. By the time Van Damm and DeCastro returned, dragging a handcart, everything was unloaded on the dock and the personnel of the former Golden Parrot were sitting on the assorted crates passing a canteen around.

"Found a good spot, did you?" asked Makhno, eyeing the handcart.

"Most excellent." DeCastro snapped his fingers at his hirelings, who got up and began loading the crates on the handcart. "These hills are honeycombed with man-made caves, and I've obtained a small one for an excellent price."

"For free, to be exact." Van Damm smiled briefly. "Nobody was using it. The place seems to have a bad reputation."

"We shall change that." DeCastro smiled. "Come, *mi compadres*: let us load and move quickly. Chaco, you stay here and wait with the second load. Inez, bring the ladies and personal gear. Move! Move!"

It took half an hour for the personnel of the Golden Parrot to fill the handcart and move out. Chaco sat on a crate in the barge and pulled out the canteen again. Assorted passersby glanced at the barge, glanced at Makhno on the raft, and kept walking.

"I see that the people here know you," Van Damm commented. "Tell me, where and how do you exchange Jane's goods for metals? That assayer's office was careful to deal only in mineral goods, not…ah, Euph-leaf."

"For that, we go a little further downstream, to Hell's-a-Comin', inhabited mostly by shimmer stone miners." Makhno automatically glanced around for anyone listening. "We go to a dugout called The Irish Bar, and ask for Himself."

"Who?"

"Irish Himself. His bar is the local food shop and watering hole, but the serious business is conducted in his storeroom. That's the local pawnshop, barter-house and bank. It's also the information center. We do the exchange there."

"I see. And this is unknown to the Company?"

"Totally. If anyone from Kenny-Camp asks why we go on down river, we say we're making deliveries to prospectors, that's all." Makhno looked around again. "Vanny, this cave that DeCastro picked: is it dug into a ridge that comes down to the river? And is it really close to the riverbank?"

"Yes. Why?"

Makhno heaved a profound sigh. "Traitors' Cave," he said. "The bastard is setting up shop in Traitors' Cave, and I wish him joy of it."

"I take it this has something to do with that first miners' strike, the one that was broken up by the CoDo Marines, yes?"

"Oh yes. Everybody who lives long in Hell's-A-Comin' knows the story, and I'll tell it to you once we're back on the water. Suffice it to say that if DeCastro's looking for info to sell, or trouble to cause, he couldn't have picked a worse spot."

* * *

"So what'm I supposed to do with this place, Brodski?" Heinrick whined, looking around at the emptied half-dugout that had formerly been known as the Golden Parrot. "I can't run it as a bar, or even a restaurant, not with you already monopolizing the trade. I dunno what Van Damm expected."

"True, Docktown doesn't need another bar and grill," Brodski purred, leaning back on the split-log bench against the wall. "But there's plenty else that it needs. An exchange-shop, for instance, or a drugstore, or a repair-shop. Think you could handle any of those?"

A series of emotions played across Heinrick's face in quick order, finally settling on a canny look. "Repairs, maybe. I got…some tools for that."

Brodski smiled, remembering that oversize and clanking duffel bag that Heinrick had brought with him. "Very good. And since a lot of your customers will be dealing in barter, you can't help but run an exchange shop on the side. Hmm, you know anything about repairing—or making—radios?"

"Simple ones, sure." Heinrick shrugged. "You just have to find a frequency that'll work here in the valley, what with all the interference from Cat's Eye."

"I think we've got that," Brodski grinned. "Talk to Sam-the-Ham

Kilroy, just a few doors west. By the way, you know how to make saws that'll cut stone, or steel?"

"Yeah, I think I can manage that. Why?"

"Well, you ever hear of a tree called an ironwood, back on Earth?"

"Think so. ...Uh, its wood was supposed to be so hard that you needed a...metal saw to cut it. You mean, there's a tree like that around here?"

"Even tougher. It's called a steelwood, for good reason. A very useful critter, if only you have the means to saw it."

"I see!" Heinrick's face lit up—then abruptly fell again. "But what'll we do for power? Plutonium batteries last a long while, but you get only so much power out of 'em."

Brodski let his gaze wander to the ceiling. "I believe the miners at Hell's-A-Comin' have dug up something like coal, and there's always wood along the forest. There are ways to work with steam."

"Steam?"

"And if we can set up a water-wheel, there's always the river itself."

*   *   *

"And in exchange for all this foine leaf and upriver brandy," Himself said, peering narrowly at Makhno, "Yous be wantin' what, this time?"

"Brass or good iron," said Makhno. "I know you can swap for it at Kenny-Camp."

"Then why din'cha swap for it there yerself?" Irish leaned forward on the plank table. "Yah know we got nothin' down here but local produce an' the occasional shimmer stone."

"I'd rather the assayer's office didn't know all my business." Makhno grinned back. "They've got too many company men peeping over their shoulders."

Himself smiled broadly, showing crooked teeth. "An' they just might take it into their heads to put an end to the euph-leaf trade, startin' with yerself, eh?"

"Something like that," Makhno agreed.

Irish leaned back, exuding confidence. "Well now, it just so happens that we've got a wee blacksmith's shop, an' a few pigs o' copper an' tin, and summat more o' fine-smelted iron. We was hopin' ta make it inta minin' tools, but for such foine brandy, not ta mention the leaf, I do think we can dicker."

"Coal," Van Damm put in. "We know there's plenty of carbon on the planet, or the forests wouldn't exist. But where can we get usable amounts of it?"

Himself laughed and slapped the table. "From the black-stump tree, o' course! What did yah think it made its black core from? Eh, I suppose yah had ta be a miner ta notice. Ah, but for big loads o' that, ye'll have ta bring us more than just euph an' brandy."

"I think we can come up with something," Makhno grinned, "And in larger loads, too."

As Van Damm watched, the two of them leaned close over the table and settled in for some serious dickering. *Chains of trade routes,* he considered. *Stronger than steel...*

He wondered idly if he could stir up the kind of trouble Max Cole wanted by setting the free miners against the company's slaves, but then decided it wouldn't work. The company "indentured laborers" would desert in a red-hot minute if they knew there was some way they could survive outside the company's town....

And right there, a beautiful idea blossomed.

* * *

When Max Cole heard that there was a coded special message for him coming up from the planet, he practically ran to the radio room to get his transcript, and actually did run back to his cabin to decode it. Yes, of course it was from Van Damm, and high time, too. The ship was due to leave in another two hours.

Have a possibility, the message read. *Can get miners to desert Kennicott. K/Co will then go after them and shoot up local farmers in the process. Is this the atrocity you want?*

Cole swore blisteringly, then coded a return message and carried it back to the radio room himself.

Down on the surface, in Sam Kilroy's establishment on the outskirts of Castell City, the message was received and then relayed to Hell's-A-Comin'. Van Damm got the reply and took it off to the storeroom of the Irish Bar to decode.

Hell, no! Cole's reply read. *Do nothing to make K look bad! Find something else. Stay there until you do.*

Van Damm laughed aloud, drawing Makhno's attention, and he felt obliged to share the news. Both of them laughed uproariously, shared a pitcher of very good Janesfort beer and settled down to some serious analysis and speculation.

Two hours later the ship left orbit and headed back toward Wayforth Station, taking Max Cole with it.

*   *   *

It took a quarter of a T-year for the relocated Golden Parrot to become a successful venture. DeCastro had been obliged to buy raw grains and other seeds from the local farmers, sprout and ferment them himself before he could come up with a passable beer, and his attempts at creating whiskey or brandy had failed dismally. He had built a workable grill and made the Parrot into an acceptable restaurant, and the services of his girls were always a good draw, but for the life of him he could not start a decent drug-trade. A local product called euph-leaf was abundant and popular, but he couldn't find the source, much less get a monopoly on it. The best he could do was extract the active ingredients with alcohol from his failed distilling projects and get a concentrated liquid form, but even that proved no real competition for the natural product. He could not even get the customers to gamble in his establishment, and that was unheard of.

Worst of all, he hadn't been able to contact any of the other company or CoDo agents, or even learn who they were. A bar and grill and whorehouse usually had no trouble collecting information from customers, but for some reason his clientele was remarkably close-mouthed. Some odd reticence seemed to overcome them the minute they set foot through the doorway: a strange solemnity, almost a feeling of guilt, which precluded merriment and small-talk. The relocated Golden Parrot was the gloomiest bar—and the poorest information-source—that DeCastro had ever seen and he had no idea why.

Discreet strolls around Kenny-Camp had told him nothing except that the free prospectors viewed the indentured miners with mixed pity and contempt. Everybody hungrily awaited any out-of-town trade, the settled farmers seemed to be prospering and everyone hated Kennicott Metals.

What he knew from his own sources was that Kennicott had long since made an uneasy truce with Anaconda and Dover, such that they all dug for different minerals, in widely separated and distant locations. Reynolds was left out in the cold, and resented it.

Perhaps it was time to make a personal visit back to Castell City, just to see what he could learn. His excuse would be buying some decent brandy, since he couldn't find or make the product locally. The only difficulty lay in trading company scrip for CoDo creds, since the company's currency-exchange always gave a miserable return and he knew well that nobody accepted company scrip outside of Hell's-A-Comin'.

When he heard the news that Captain Makhno was pulling up to the dock, he took the opportunity. DeCastro left explicit orders with his staff, packed up a sack full of CoDo creds and strolled down to the waterfront.

Instead of the familiar steamboat, there sat the most outlandish ship that DeCastro had ever seen. It had three hulls, all long and narrow, the two outer ones set back from the central—and larger—hull, each carrying a raked mast with double booms and sails made of some thick unbleached cloth. The central hull also sported a paddle wheel at the stern, and the two outer hulls had what were clearly steering wheels attached to rudders hidden below the water. The hulls were joined with angled and arched wings where cargo was strapped. The whole construction was made of a pale gray wood that gleamed with some sort of lacquer. Though smaller than the old *Celia*, this bizarre boat—sporting the name *River Dragon* in what appeared to be metal letters on its bow—looked as if it could carry just as much cargo.

And yes, there was the familiar captain making fast to the dock. Now DeCastro could see that the *Dragon* was towing a homemade barge loaded with what looked like blackened logs, canvas-covered pigs of metal and crates of odd fruit. In the ship itself sat three passengers, hulking miners or prospectors, two of them guarding the third. DeCastro guessed that the third man had made a good shimmer stone strike down river at Hell's-A-Comin' and was taking it to Castell City, rather than the assayer's office, in hopes of getting a better price. *Best leave him carefully alone,* he decided.

DeCastro strolled up to the *River Dragon* with a smile on his face and his hands in plain view.

"Greetings, *Capitan* Makhno," he chirped. "Could you take another passenger up to Castell City?"

"I could," said Makhno, giving him a measured look. "What pay?"

"CoDo creds. Not a penny of company scrip, I swear."

Makhno glanced at his other passengers, who shrugged. "That'll do," he said. "I have some business ashore, but be here in an hour and I'll take you."

"Indeed, I shall be content to wait," said DeCastro, easing himself into the boat.

The miners looked at him, saying nothing. Makhno climbed out, hauling a heavy sack, and one of the bodyguards followed him. The two of them strolled away, in the opposite direction from the assayer's office. The central miner, the one who probably had the shimmer stones, smiled broadly and leaned a little closer.

"Eh, m'good man," he said, showing crooked teeth, "Mightn't you be the fella who runs the Golden Parrot?"

"That I am," DeCastro agreed. "I take it you have sampled my… beer, once or twice?"

"Aye, an' interestin' stuff it is, too. Yah haven't any good whiskey, though."

"That, sir, is precisely why I am going to Castell City. I've heard that a decent brandy, at least, can be purchased there."

"So they say," the miner shrugged. "What with the Kenny-ship gone, folks're cast back on their own resources. Aye, but then, without yon Official People breathin' down their necks, they're free t'experiment wi' the booze, yah know."

"Ah, indeed." DeCastro considered that he might nudge some workable information out of this one. "It is difficult to experiment so with the Company also peeping over one's shoulder."

For some reason, this struck the lucky miner and his hulking companion as extraordinarily funny.

"Oh, aye!" the miner wheezed. "Nobody loves Kenny-Co, not at all. Nor Anaconda, nor Dover neyther." He leaned closer and added in a conspiratorial whisper: "There's some that say Reynolds would love a piece o' the action, and 'twould do us no harm if Kenny-Co had a decent rival. There's another deposit o' hafnium that the Kenny-boys haven't discovered, yah know?"

"Indeed, I did not know." If DeCastro's ears had been mobile, they would have pricked up like a hound's. "And I surely agree that some healthy competition would improve Kennicott's manners, both here and off-world. But how would you pass the word to Reynolds?" *Telephone, telegraph, and tell me!*

The miner leaned even closer, and whispered almost in DeCastro's ear: "There's an off-world-reachin' radio in Castell City. That's one o' the reasons we be goin' there."

"If you can give them the exact location of the lode..." DeCastro hinted.

"That we can, that we can," the miner chuckled. "Ah, but let's say no more 'til we be clear o' the camp, an' any Kenny-Co ears, me lad."

"Oh, to be sure," DeCastro happily agreed, already considering how he could use this knowledge. Yes, Reynolds would dearly love to know the location of a hafnium lode outside of Kennicott's knowledge—and mining-grant. The presence of a rival mine would certainly irritate Kennicott and a battle between those two giants might give CoDo the excuse it needed to step in and take over—not to mention allowing a certain Tomas Messenger y DeCastro an opportunity to profit by playing both sides against the middle.

The voyage upriver would be long, but DeCastro was certain he could wheedle the location of that hafnium lode out of the three miners in that time. He also happened to know that there was usually a Reynolds-loyal ship out near Ayesha, listening for any usable news.

He could hardly wait for the captain to return and start-up the engine.

*   *   *

Brodski, hidden in the shadows of the bar, watched the *River Dragon* coming in with his personal set of binoculars. He noted the surreptitious hand signal from Makhno, and tightened his focus on the passengers. Yes, the first man to get off was DeCastro.

"Bait taken," Brodski muttered, watching.

Sure enough, DeCastro promptly strolled up the dock and turned toward Sam Kilroy's. The three men who climbed out afterward, grinning, were recognizable from their descriptions. The central figure watched DeCastro hurrying off and smirked widely.

"Hook, line and sinker," Brodski chuckled, shoving the binoculars back in their case. He had a few minutes yet before his co-conspirators arrived, and he made good use of them.

By the time Makhno strolled into Harp's Sergeant, with one of the two H&C bodyguards and Irish Himself in tow, Brodski had the drinks poured and the sandwiches ready. He smiled at the lot of them, lifted the tray and led them into the back room where Van Damm was waiting for them.

As soon as the door was shut behind them, Himself—not even waiting to take hold of his glass—delivered the news. "Aye, he fell for it, and he's a-runnin' off to radio the Reynolds boys right now."

"Excellent!" said Van Damm, reaching for his drink.

The others hastily sat down, took their glasses and lifted them in a toast.

"Here's ta playin' 'Let's You and Him Fight,'" Irish intoned.

"Hear, hear," said everyone else, and clicked glasses, and happily downed their contents.

Van Damm, ever the worrier, asked: "Are you certain he got the right coordinates?"

"Now, lad," Himself chided, "Are we miners, or are we not? Aye, we made sure he got 'em right."

"By the way," Makhno added, "We brought in a good load that Jane—and especially Benny—will be happy to see: coal, iron, brass, and a lot of interesting fruit that grows down river."

"Jacko's watching it now," the bodyguard added. "How much do we unload here?"

"Half of everything," said Brodski. "The coal and metal go to Heinrick, as pay for the use of his metal saw. We'll be taking him along, up to the fort again. Little Wilgar, and maybe a Harmonious friend or two, will mind the store til he gets back."

"And the fruit?" Himself asked.

"Ah, that's for the Harmonies to study and take good care of the seeds."

"For a group of miners and prospectors," Van Damm noted, "You Hibernians seem to know much about the local wildlife. One might almost think you had a guide."

Irish paused for a moment before answering. "Aye, we do," he admitted. "Let's say, it's someone with a copy o' the original survey."

"Very good." Van Damm smiled. Then he addressed himself to his sandwich and said nothing further.

"So how long, d'ye think," Himself turned back to Brodski, "Before Reynolds moves in?"

"As fast as they can get a ship here, send a team down and make the claim." Brodski turned to Van Damm. "Where's the nearest station where they've got ships?"

Van Damm took a sip of his drink before answering. "Certainly one at Ayesha, and others…no more than a couple of months out, at most. I daresay DeCastro will be sending his message to Ayesha, and the other company ships will get it soon after. Do you think you'll be ready by then?"

"That depends on just what we're t'be ready for." Himself leaned closer across the table. "Don'tcha think, me lads, that 'tis time yah filled me in on just what yous hopes t'accomplish, besides givin' Kenny-Co a distraction from us?"

"No ordinary distraction." Van Damm's smile was thin and cold. "Kennicott, having gotten here first, got claim to the big hafnium deposit—and thereby raised enough money to buy the right politicians, so as to sway CoDo in its favor. Anaconda and Dover were late-comers, and had to take second-best deposits—and not as many politicians. There's a fragile and uneasy truce between them and Kennicott and it has held in spite of the discovery of the shimmer stones. But add Reynolds to the mix, and the balance tilts; the three of them together could get their politicians to out-vote Kennicott's.

"Now Kennicott will have a real fight on its hands—a fight with other big corporations, not just some fringe church that has nothing but right on its side. That will keep Kennicott too busy to try wresting Haven away from the Harmonies—and also too busy to note how its wage-slaves are escaping into the settlements—for a long time yet. That, we hope, will keep CoDo out of Haven long enough for us to build up a solid, independent, local society with its own government and economy—"

"And army, y'mean?"

"That too. A society too strong for CoDo to squash and rule, no matter how many transportees they dump on us, or how many Marines they land. Do you understand now?"

Himself nodded slowly. "Aye," he said. "Indeed I do."

*   *   *

DeCastro's coded message had received its reply within twenty minutes. Dickering over his fee, in exchange for those precious coordinates, had taken another hour. By the time the arrangements were finished, DeCastro was tired and hungry. A quick visit to his old establishment showed that it had been converted into a repair shop and he knew better than to try for Harp's Sergeant. That meant strolling around Docktown for awhile, looking for a safe hostelry.

The town had changed remarkably in the past quarter-year and he had no idea where to search. The old waterfront had been cleaned up, was patrolled by a dismaying number of Harmony beadles, and there were no brawls or drunks on the streets. There were productive shops everywhere he looked. There were new warehouses, busy and well-filled, with an astonishing number of Harmony brethren delivering, buying and dickering, in peaceful equality with the settlers. There was a new building called the Starman's Inn that was clearly a hotel, with restaurant, currently hosting what appeared to be nothing but local merchants and planet-sided marines.

DeCastro rented a room for the night and got a meal in the restaurant, but found the place too well-lit, quiet and clean to attract the sort of clientele who would be useful to him. For a lawless town, Castell City had become shockingly respectable. He couldn't understand it.

What the hell has happened here? he wondered, while putting away a good-sized dinner of well-cooked lake fish, tasty vegetables and excellent beer. *Perhaps I should go explore in the morning....*

One thing he knew for certain; there would be no clash between Docktown and the Church, not the sort that CoDo wanted. Castell and his minions had somehow made a—feh! Harmonious—working in peace with the settlers.

Disgusting!

* * *

Brodski put an end to the discussion by getting up and announcing that he had a bar to run. Himself and his bodyguard remembered that they had a ship to unload and departed with Makhno in tow. Van Damm likewise got up and strolled into the main room, ordered a beer at the bar and then—as soon as Himself had gone—slipped into a table in a back corner. After serving the next round of customers, Brodski came over and joined him.

"No fool, that Irishman," Brodski said quietly. "I do wonder, though, where he gets all his information. The cargoes we've been getting from Hell's-A-Comin' are, well, surprising."

"...As if he had access to all the original survey records, constantly updated," Van Damm agreed. "He must have his own radio and possibly a computer. I have heard things from the other colonies about well-equipped labor organizers there and someone did organize the miners here ten years ago, so Haven is not unknown to them."

"If so, it's a guard-with-life secret." Brodski shrugged. "Let him keep it, then. We're getting along well enough with what we've got here."

"My friend Heinrick has been recruiting among the landed Fleetmen, and the settlers, who can actually build radios." Van Damm lifted his glass in appreciation. "It's amazing what a glass-blower can do, given the right knowledge."

"I could make a comment about the advantages of 'Harmony'," Brodski grinned.

"And I could comment about your silver-tongued ability to make Castell and his cronies see reason," Van Damm acknowledged. "I would never have thought to see such unity between the miners, settlers and Harmonies. Jane's plans bear fruit with astounding speed."

"Uh-huh." Brodski gave him a keen look. "So, what's gonna happen to you, Vanny, when your bosses learn that you haven't been able to deliver?"

"I'll be exiled here. Oh, woe." Van Damm smiled, and took a long pull of his beer. "Of course CoDo will send a replacement for Cole, probably on the next ship. We must be ready for him. He must see only what we wish him to see."

Brodski thoughtfully scratched his chin. "You know, Kenny-Co won't stop short of a shooting war to keep Reynolds and friends at bay. Will that give CoDo the excuse it wants?"

Van Damm gave a rare laugh. "That is the last thing CoDominium wants! When civilians fight civilians, the civilian rule is at fault and CoDo can move in. Ah, but when company fights company, with company-bought senators as well as local troops, CoDo has no one to blame but its rich friends and itself. Such a war could tear the Grand Senate apart while leaving the tranquil Church in charge here on Haven. Oh, no. CoDo will try to end the fight as speedily as possible—and for just that reason, we must use all our resources to keep it going."

"The miners and settlers they'll be fighting across won't care for that, and won't add to it."

"With the help of Himself, I think we can keep the civilians safe from the battle. And so long as anyone can be bribed for money—gold, trade-coin or CoDo credits—I can keep the pot boiling."

"Hmm, I get the feeling you'll be taking a trip down river again soon."

"I expect to return with DeCastro." Van Damm set his glass down decisively. "I shall need a certain amount of equipment...."

"Aren't you going up to Janesfort with Himself and Makhno first?"

"No, I prefer to keep my eye on DeCastro. I can talk to Jane by CB radio—one of the old portable ones. These new hand-mades are a little too bulky for me."

*   *   *

Jane greeted her guests warmly and sat them down to dinner with the rest of the co-op, after which they retired to Benny's lab for more serious discussion.

"All roight, then," said Himself, looking over the extensive report. "So yer next step is a real factory, not too near yer island yet not too far either, and someplace where neyther the companies nor CoDo will think ta look for it, eh?"

"That's about the size of it," said Jane. "For convenience and concealment, some place along the river between the fort and Castell City would be ideal—some place beyond the forest, since we don't want to cut down any more of that than we have to. I'm already pushing my settlers to go out on the plains, on the grounds that they'll have to do less ground-clearing but can always use the river-transport.

"However, for skilled labor, the best source is Hell's-A-Comin'. Transport would be easy on the river, though time-consuming. What do you think?"

Irish Himself pondered the report, and the map, and a slow smile spread across his face. "Nah, the back end o' Hell's-A-Comin' be yer best bet," he pronounced. "We've got the hills thoroughly tunneled out there, enough ta hide an army—surely enough ta hide a factory, or two, be they small. Aye, an' no worries about the ventilation; we took care o' that from the start."

"And…" Jane leaned forward on the table. "How well could you hide it and all your people, should the squabble between Kennicott and Reynolds-and-allies become a shooting war?"

An unlovely smile spread across Irish's face. "Better than ye'd believe from here. We planned that from the start, too. The population o' the whole town could vanish underground in minutes, an' not even dogs could sniff 'em out."

"Stinkbush sap," Makhno guessed, "Or bluetree."

"So whoever wins will be obliged to import more laborers for their mines," Jane went on. "Of course, they're making plans with the Bureau of Relocation to do just that, anyway. We'll need to have a sturdy enough economy in place to absorb them."

"I daresay we're all workin' on that." Himself gave Jane a keen look. "The key will be river transport. With most o' the old boats all rotted away or sunk, that leaves us all dependin' on just a few ships, includin' the good captain's here. Beggin' yer pardon, me lad, but that's a slender thread ta hang all this on."

Makhno started laughing. Jane smiled.

"That, Mr. Irish," she chuckled, "Is the first thing we want your factory to make. Come along with us; Benny has something to show you."

Benny Donato had, indeed, been practically squirming with eagerness. He now led them proudly to the rear door of his shop, the one that opened on a path down to the river. There, hidden under a low roof covered with living greenthorn bushes, was a large boat-shed. Inside that, as Benny raised his lantern to display, was his completed creation.

Himself dropped his jaw and fervently crossed himself as he saw it.

It was another three-hulled ship, bigger than the *River Dragon* by a good third, made of steelwood planks, caulked and varnished with something that smelled somewhat like bluetree sap.

"I love my old *Bitch*," Makhno murmured, "But oh, you kid!"

"We'll need to make still bigger versions," Jane added, "Which can't be done here. They'll also need more brass and iron for the engines. Benny can give you the schematics and instructions, and I think our friend from the city has come up with saws that will cut steelwood. Can you make a factory close enough to the river to tow the ships out when they're finished?"

"Oh yes," Himself breathed, not taking his eyes off the lovely ship. "In fact... uh, do ye have a crew for this beauty yet?"

*   *   *

A week spent investigating Castell City had not improved DeCastro's mood any. Everywhere he looked were signs of progress, prosperity and cooperation. There was even a new small hospital, and rumors of a school of all things, outside the walls of the Harmony enclave. It was almost as if Docktown, Cambiston and the enclave had merged, making Castell City a single town. In the bar of the Starman's Inn he'd overheard talk of building another dock, out of proper stone and wet-setting concrete this time and he'd wondered where the money for all this was coming from. He couldn't imagine a shimmer stone miner giving a rat's-ass for the town, and the Harmonies didn't seem the types to spend cash on such worldly things. Was there some ingenious banker setting up business somewhere in the city? If so, he was keeping too low a profile for DeCastro to find.

Even the landed Marines weren't causing any trouble! For one thing, he'd noticed, there were signs pointing them toward Harp's Sergeant for food and drink, and for another, he'd also noticed that the remaining whores in the city had all taken to wearing bright red scarves as a badge of their profession, so the Marines had no trouble identifying them and no explosive mistakes were made. The women, however, were all independent operators and each kept her own crib. DeCastro had asked a few of the newer ones—since the older ones were likely to remember him, and not kindly—if they'd care to come work for him, and they'd all laughed in his face.

As for drugs, there was euph-leaf galore—sold mainly at Harp's, but also by street peddlers—and it was cheap. For other amusements, someone had built a "Docktown Theater" that staged live shows and, on an imported big screen, played vids from everywhere along the route from Terrra to Haven. There was a small "Sports Palace" featuring boxers and wrestlers, none of whom—in DeCastro's opinion—were much good, but the Marines liked them.

There was even a dance pavilion off to one side of the Harmonies' walled enclave, where a not-too-bad local band played and sometimes choirs of, if you please, Harmonies got up and sang, and they were surprisingly good. At one point DeCastro saw a trio of drunken Marines parading down the street, singing some off-world song, and damned if the local Harmonies didn't join in, scat-singing in harmony with them.

In short, Docktown had become downright tame. Its vices had become harmless, its factions happily reconciled, its poor settled into ready employment and its business booming. There was no conflict for CoDominium, or unsatisfied desires for DeCastro, to exploit. He was reduced to playing endless card games with the residents at the Starman's Inn while waiting for a boat to take him back down river.

The only high points of his visit were the kegs of good brandy waiting in the warehouse for him to come pick up.

Consequently, he was infinitely relieved to hear that the *River Dragon* had been sighted out on the lake, and would shortly arrive at the dock. With a brief feeling of déjà vu, DeCastro hastened to pay his hotel bill, pack up his gear, send for his barrels and go wait by the dock.

As a couple of dockhands were rolling his kegs into place, he felt something less pleasing than déjà vu at seeing Van Damm come strolling down the dock behind them.

"Ah, *Senor* Van Damm," DeCastro tried to sound enthusiastic. "You are traveling to Kenny-Camp, then. Does your business prosper?"

"It does that," Van Damm said with a smile. He waved to a stevedore behind him who was pushing a hand-cart full of long crates. "And I see yours does, too. I recognize the mark on those barrels; that's an excellent brandy. Congratulations."

"Ah, *si*," DeCastro smiled, trying to guess what was in those crates. "Good beer, even passable wine, I can get locally, but for proper strong drink one must come up here to Castell City. I'm astounded at how the city prospers, this long after the ship has gone."

"Yes." Van Damm heaved a vast sigh. "Peace and prosperity everywhere. No excitement whatever. If all one wishes is to get rich, this is surely the place."

"Ah," DeCastro sympathized, thinking he understood. "Yes, everything thrives in prosperous…Harmony. Have you heard there are plans to build a new dock?"

"So I've heard. At this rate, the city will have a labor shortage before the next ship comes."

"Ah. I can only wonder: Whence comes the money for this new building project?"

"Didn't you know?" Van Damm smiled briefly. "The Harmonies put it up. Old Man Castell has taken it into his head to become an investment banker. He's behind most of the new construction hereabouts."

DeCastro felt his jaw sagging, and hastily pulled it back up. "What in the world made him change his mind so radically?"

"Who knows?" Van Damm shrugged. "Simple greed and common sense, I guess. In any case, it paid off. The Church of Harmony now has the clean, prosperous, peaceful town they wanted—not to mention the increased goodies coming into the church."

DeCastro turned to give the city a bleak look. No, Castell City would not be the source of any conflict sufficient to bring in CoDo rule. "Ah. So, for…excitement one must go down the river, eh?"

"Pretty much." Van Damm gave him a sour smile that hinted much, but promised nothing.

DeCastro nodded absently, thinking of where this would lead. The explosive conflict CoDo wanted must take place in or near Kenny-Camp.

He could imagine possibilities: Prospectors robbing the settlers and the settlers fighting back, a revolt of the indentured slaves, vandalism and then outright shooting between Kennicott and Reynolds… Yes, there was much that a CoDo agent like Van Damm could do. As for himself, he could profit from both sides of whatever trouble Van Damm started.

Just then the *Dragon* pulled up at the dock and cut its engines. She was loaded with sacks and crates, and towing a wooden raft loaded with crates and barrels, but there was room for DeCastro's cargo too. The sight reminded him of his companions on the trip down here; he hadn't seen them anywhere in Castell City. It was unlikely, though always possible, that some greedy thugs in Docktown had killed them for their shimmer stones. More likely, though, they'd holed up in the local lodgings and were keeping their heads down until the next ship arrived. He wondered if they'd ever managed to radio Reynolds and found that their news was no longer new.

Makhno and his bargeman, who looked more like a farmer than a sailor, made the *River Dragon* and its raft fast to the dock and climbed out. "Okay," he called to the assembled men on the dock. "Load up and pay up. We've got to be on the water by dim."

In the resulting scramble, DeCastro noted that Van Damm's crates went onto the *Dragon* rather than the barge-raft. Of course there was no room left on the barge, but knowing Van Damm, there was most likely another reason. The loading was efficient, anyway, and the trimaran and its trailing raft were well out on the water by the time the light changed. Whatever engine powered the paddle wheel, it could make excellent speed.

Everyone had brought their own provisions and as Van Damm settled down to eat a sparse dinner from his basket, DeCastro took care to sit beside him. "Might I inquire," he asked carefully, "What became of the poppy-garden, and its produce?"

"Sold most of it to the Harmonies, for their hospital." Van Damm took a swig from a clay jug. "They got a local glass-blower to make a lens and some mirrors, and set them on the roof of a growing house. It concentrates light well enough that the plants are happy with it."

"Ingenious," DeCastro admitted. "And has their number increased?"

"Quite well. Another few turns, and they'll need another grow-house. The lights in the basement room are holding up well enough for us, but we may need to build a grow-house of our own, soon."

Well, that's something, DeCastro thought, with a slight twinge of jealousy. In time, there might be a flourishing opium trade in the valley. He'd watch and see if he could insinuate himself into it.

It was during truenight that he noticed what looked like a meteor streaking over the sky to the north. *Meteor? No, the Reynolds shuttle!* he guessed. Reynolds had acted fast on his information. Now if the claim only proved to be as good as those fool prospectors had said, another Turn would see a good 20,000 CoDo creds deposited in his account with the Biederbilt Interstellar Bank. DeCastro wrapped himself up in his plastic blanket and lay down to sleep with an untroubled conscience.

* * *

There had been no difficulty finding crew for the newly dubbed *Queen Grainne*. Her shakedown trip around the Janesfort island had uncovered only a few minor problems with the steam engine, which Benny handily fixed. Other than that, her performance exceeded expectations. Himself ritually poured a glass of brandy over her bowsprit, and kissed her polished deck. At next full-light the ship set out on her first serious voyage: trading cargoes along the river shore on the way to Castell City—larger cargoes than the *Black Bitch* could ever have carried. The settlers, forewarned by radio, brought their produce down the narrow roads through the forest and waited eagerly to see the new ship. Trade was brisk and eager, and Himself was gratified by the number of requests for more labor and more finished goods. Janesfort alone, as he remarked to Jacko, soon wouldn't be able to keep up with the demand.

"That's where our little factories will come in handy," he continued. "We'll fill in the gap. Aye, me boy, I foresee a foine future for the lot of us."

"But won't we be runnin' Jane out o' business?" Jacko pondered.

"And what of the trade growin' up in Castell City?"

"All of it different, me lad," Himself purred, filling his pipe with a light mix of euph-leaf and kinnikinnick. "The minerals an' the wildlife vary along the river, and each bunch makes different goods of 'em. We'll turn out large numbers o' simple tools an' large goods—picks an' shovels, hammers an' chisels—and, o' course, ships like this. The boys in Castell City, now, they make high-tech stuff: radios an' power-saws an' such, not ta mention the good glass from the south lake shore sand. Think o' lenses, me boy."

"Much could be done wi' them," Jacko agreed.

"Jane's a rare one," Himself went on. "She an' her mates'll trade farm produce, an' river-clay pottery, an' everythin' that can be made o' the hemp—'scuse me, euph-leaf' plant: cloth an' cordage from the fiber, oil an' flour from the seeds—"

"Say, I wonder if a good beer might be brewed from their sprouts?"

"Heh! I'll suggest it ta her. But also—discountin' the medicines that can be made from the resin, think o' what she an' her chemist ha' done with the wood-pulp. Paper, me boy! Aye, an' simple plastics. She an' Benny an' Falstaff: they also make foine prototypes that factories—such as we'll have—can use ta turn out goodies in job-lots. Oh, aye, we'll be gettin' along splendidly, I do expect. All of us prosperin' nicely, shimmer stones or no."

"Planned economy?" Jacko sniggered.

"If so," Himself glowered, "'Tis planned by us what does the diggin' an' cuttin', plantin' an' harvestin', weavin' an' millin' ourselves—not by some king somewhere bellowin' orders from afar off. Nay, an' not by CoDo bureaucrats, eyther."

"Amen," laughed Jacko. "What would some politician know or care about th' importance of riverjack-proof fishnets, anyway? By the by, did you know that steamed riverjack with yellowsour sauce makes mighty good eatin'? "

"Is that what we're havin' for dinner, then?"

"Right enough. But don't tell anyone down river about eatin' riverjack. Riverjacks have eaten enough people, as they know of, that they'd be a bit queasy about returnin' the favor."

*   *   *

When DeCastro got home, he found the Golden Parrot much changed. In the short time he'd been gone Inez and Ludmilla had—gods knew where—picked up a handmade book of recipes and begun putting them into practice. There were half a dozen fish dishes, all with various sorts of local fruits, an equal number of meat dishes from local land-creatures as well as goat and chicken and nearly a dozen variations on eggtree fruit. Besides the beer and ale, there were three kinds of fruit juice.

One of his guards was serving as doorman, wearing a clean suit and shirt yet, and the other two were busy in the kitchen. All the tables were full, for once, and nobody was pausing to make offers to the girls—all of whom were busy anyway with carrying dishes back and forth.

The Golden Parrot had changed from a moderately-successful whorehouse into quite a successful restaurant.

DeCastro gave orders for storing the brandy, limped off into his private office, sat down and rested his head on the desktop. Of all the changes he might have expected on Haven, this creeping respectability was the last of them. *No conflict, no crisis, no CoDo* was all he could think. The only conflict on the horizon was the inevitable clash between Kennicott and Reynolds-and-allies, and that might not come to a head for, well, years.

Cheer up, he told himself. *In the meantime I'll become very rich.*

He wondered briefly how Van Damm was getting on.

*   *   *

As the *Queen Grainne* made her stately progress down the river, she met the *River Dragon* coming back up. The ships paused in mid-river and tossed on lines so their captains could meet and confer. They had to gather on Makhno's ship, since the wing-decks of the *Grainne* were crowded with cargo—not that there was much room on the *Dragon* either.

"Well, me boy," Himself grinned, "It does look as if the trade has been good for both of us. What're ye carryin', if I might ask?"

Makhno laughed. "Medical supplies, pots and housewares, and… some interesting chemicals, if you must know."

"Eh, blastin' powder, ye mean?" Himself winked.

"More like gunpowder," said Makhno. "Ah, also some useful books. Someone down in Castell City has put together a simple printing-press and Jane's paper was welcome. What've you got?"

"Produce an' timber—and a few homemade shotguns." Himself winked. "Also the ammunition for 'em. Your 'interestin' chemicals' will be welcome; Falstaff said he was nearly out of 'em."

"Ah. I take it all the settlers within miles of Janesfort are well armed, now?"

"Now, how should I know that?" said Himself, piously. "All I know is how many peculiar boxes I swapped for food, timber, furs and…ah, produce o' the euph-leaf plant."

"Lots of fiber, I hope? There's a cloth shortage in Castell City."

"Oh, aye! Enough ta keep the looms o' the Harmonies busy for a Turn or two. …And other things."

"Seed?" Makhno asked quietly.

Himself nodded solemnly. "Jane wants hemp growin' all over the valley by year's end."

"Spread too far for anyone to wipe out. Good idea, though it'll cut into the fort's profits."

"I do believe the lady thinks wider and farther than o' next year's profits."

"She does, at that." Makhno handed over a small wooden box held shut with a crude wax seal. "This is for you, from someone who just called himself The First Organizer. He also asked if I could bring him a workable radio next trip."

"I believe I could get one in Castell City," murmured Himself, studying the box. "Thank ye kindly, me boy."

"I also have a message from Vanny. He says: 'everything's in place', that's all."

"Aye," Himself said thoughtfully, stuffing the box into his shirt.

"Now all we need do is keep on as we've been, an' watch for his boss's replacement."

"We'll also have to watch for incoming transportees. The one thing that could mess up our plans is CoDo dumping more beggars on us than the system can sustain."

"There's more, laddie. All this prosperity in Castell City depends on the continuin' good will an' good sense of Charles Castell, an' he's a man not known for eyther."

"True," Makhno frowned. "Also, watch out for river-trash."

"Eh?"

"When the settlers and Harmonies threw the troublemakers out of Docktown, a lot of them took to the water. They've got small floating cities along the shore between Castell City and Kenny-Camp and they're not above a bit of piracy. Keep your guns ready."

* * *

Brodski returned from his Aikido class in the Harmony enclave happily tired and looking forward to dinner. As he strolled through the door of Harp's Sergeant, though, Flora came hurrying toward him waving a scribbled wax-board. "Mr. Van Damm called on the new radio," she announced, "And wants you to get back to him. Here's the channel; I wrote it down."

"No rest for the weary," Brodski sighed, plodding into the back room. He sat down at the plank desk that contained the clunky new Docktown-built radio, started the whining generator and turned the dials.

Van Damm's voice came across a background of static, but clear enough. "'Ski, the ship is coming. Expect it in another Turn. There'll be more transportees, of course, and Cole's replacement. I mean to stay out of his reach as much as possible. Watch for him."

"I think I'll know what to look for," Brodski replied. "Any idea when Reynolds will make its move?"

"It has already started." Van Damm paused for a long moment. "Another ship landed last Turn, a much bigger one, out beyond the hills. The prospectors report they saw it unloading heavy equipment. All they lack is labor, and—as I said—the transport ship is coming soon."

"I see. Everything's ready on this end; how about you?"

"We've been in place for turns, since before Himself came back."

"Ah. And the new ship?"

"She has a daughter almost ready to launch, already."

"Heh! Those miners work fast!"

"Many of them are miners in name only, by now. I tell you, 'Ski, I am amazed at how fast everyone—the miners, the settlers, Jane's people, even the Harmonies—have put this together."

"Think of the donkey with the carrot in front and the stick behind," Brodski smiled. "Everybody here wants to be prosperous, at least, and nobody wants CoDo to come in."

"That is why I must keep away from my new boss, as much as possible." Van Damm sighed. "Yet I know he'll come here eventually. There's nowhere else he can look."

"Good luck then, Vanny."

"Good allies are better than luck."

* * *

The first sign was the landing of a quiet-running cargo-sized shuttle just outside of Castell City that certain Harmony goatherds saw and reported. The four men who got out of it and began walking down toward Docktown wore sturdy cold weather clothes of an off-world design, with pistol-sized versions of CoDo stunners hidden under their jackets. They also dragged a large fold-up luggage cart, which carried more folded carts. They took up positions at the foot of the old dock, and one of them took out and held up a sign saying: "Jobs Here".

Brodski, watching them with his binoculars from Harp's Sergeant, muttered: "Now it begins," and picked up his old portable radio.

Leo Makhno, waiting at the dock, revved up the engine of the *River Dragon* the moment the shuttle appeared over the lake. By the time it had settled on Splashdown Island and opened its hatch, his trimaran was waiting at the shore. Sure enough, the first people out were ragged transportees. Makhno took as many as the ship could carry in the first load, hauled them back to the new dock and let them off. He noted that the man holding the "Jobs Here" sign stepped forward, smiling.

As Makhno turned the *Dragon* around and headed back to the shuttle for the next load, he picked up his radio and reported what he'd seen.

Little Wilgar, carrying a tray of euph-leaf packets, trotted close enough to the transportees to peddle his goods—and, incidentally, hear all of the sign-holder's sales pitches.

It took hours to finish the unloading, and as Makhno brought the last of the cargo to the dock he saw that most of the transportees—hundreds of them—had signed up with the sign-holder. The other men with him had unfolded the carts, and the transportees were stuffing their luggage on them.

"Who are they, and where are they going?" asked his last passenger, a middle-aged man wearing a better grade of cold weather gear than the sign-holder and his friends.

"Recruiters from Reynolds mining," Makhno dutifully replied. He had to bite his lip to keep from asking: *How well do you know Max Cole?*

"Mmm," said the man. "Tell me, where is the communications center for the city?"

"Oh, that'd be Sam Kilroy's place." Makhno pointed, as he surreptitiously signaled to whomever was watching from inside Harp's Sergeant. "He's got the only radio that can transmit reliably all over the valley when the atmospheric conditions are just right."

"Ah. And the center of whatever government this place has?"

"That's Old Man Castell's office, in the Harmony enclave, inside that palisade." Makhno obligingly pointed—and signaled—again.

"Hmm. And where's the best hotel?"

"That'd be the Starman's Inn." Makhno wasn't about to steer the CoDo man to Harp's, or anywhere near it. "Down that street there."

"Thank you, uh, Captain." The man handed him a 5-cred CoDo bill as a tip, picked up his briefcase and strolled away in the indicated direction.

Makhno watched him walk away in one direction and the gang

of freshly recruited laborers in the other, pulled up his radio and called Brodski.

*   *   *

Word filtered in steadily to the Jane's Alliance radio network. Max Cole's replacement had signed in at the Starman's Inn under the name of Vince Sanchez. After questioning the waitress extensively about the menu, he'd eaten a meal there. Then he'd gone out to Kilroy's place and paid to send a coded message, which received no reply after half a T-day's waiting. Much annoyed, Sanchez had then strolled about Docktown studying the busy warehouses and shops. He'd struck up conversations with the assorted Fleet personnel in town and hadn't seemed too impressed with the results. He had not approached any of the Harmonies, let alone gone into the enclave. At length he made his way to Harp's Sergeant.

Brodski was ready for him.

Sanchez took a seat at the quiet end of the bar and waited until Brodski, moving slowly and leaning heavily on his cane, came close enough to talk to. "So you're the famous Sgt. Brodski," Sanchez opened.

"Retired," Brodski smiled. "And lucked into a fine retirement plan."

"Mostly by defeating Jomo's army, I hear."

"Heh-heh. Well, not all by myself, I admit."

"With just a ragtag bunch of farmers? I'd say that's pretty good strat-and-tac."

"Don't sell farmers short. Anybody who survives here by farming is a pretty tough cookie."

"So I hear, so I hear." Sanchez hitched closer. "So, where's the real excitement in this town?"

"Depends on what your pleasure is." Brodski leaned nearer too. "For booze, euph-leaf and not-bad food, don't move an inch. We also get the occasional music band, but the best place for that is the Dance Palace, up the road and to the left. If it's female companionship you want, well, any lady wearing a red scarf—like that handsome gal over there by the front table—will be happy to oblige you. For a good game of cards, probably the bar at Starman's Inn is your best bet. Cards and dice are about all you'll find here; roulette wheels aren't exactly worth the cost of importing all the way out to Haven. Cards and dice are portable, but they wear out and can't be replaced locally. There's the Sports Palace if you're into watching big goons wrestle and punch each other around. A lot of the Marines like that. There's no racetrack yet: not enough spare horses, and nobody's imported greyhounds. That's about it."

"Hmm. Where do the miners go to blow off steam?"

"Not here to Castell City. They're all over Redemption and Last Chance, or down river in Kenny-Camp or Hell's-A-Comin'."

"Hmm." Sanchez rattled his fingers on his beer-mug. "This is a pretty quiet town for a port. I haven't even seen any drunks on the streets."

"They tend to stay inside, where it's warm." Brodski chuckled. "Besides, there isn't much going on here when the ships aren't in. This is mostly a farming town, with a little manufacturing thrown in. The mining, and most of the shimmer stone hunting, is down or up river. You can follow the Xanadu down to Kenny-Camp or go south up the Alf toward Redemption and Last Chance."

"Hmm. And that 'euph-leaf' doesn't cause any problems?"

"Nah. People smoke it and just bliss out. It doesn't exactly encourage belligerence."

Sanchez frowned briefly and took a swig of his beer. "No problems with the Holy Joes, then?"

"Nah." Brodski loaded his pipe, silently thanking whoever had thought to import kinnikinnick—primitive tobacco—to Haven. "They finally figured out that there was more profit to be made by, ahh, 'harmonizing' with the newcomers. It doesn't hurt that the Church has more off-world money than anybody else—except the mining companies, of course. You need something imported? Talk to Castell. The mining companies aren't nearly as helpful."

"Ah, I take it nobody likes the companies, then."

"No way." Brodski lit his pipe with a little more flourish than necessary. "They're practicing something close to slavery, you know, with their 'indentures'. And everybody knows about how they broke up the miners' strike ten years ago. And any miner can tell you not to trade shimmer stones—or anything else—at those company stores. Everybody knows how they loot the planet and don't give anything back. Take my advice, young fella; don't have anything to do with the companies. You want to hunt shimmer stones? Buy your gear here in town, head off into the hills and do your own digging. You come across anything useful, come trade it here in Castell City. Don't go to Kenny-Camp."

"Still...." A brief grin flickered across Sanchez' face. "It sounds like that's where the money is."

"Money and trouble," Brodski gloomed, inwardly holding back a laugh.

"Hmm. And what's the quickest way to Kenny-Camp?"

Brodski rolled his eyes theatrically. "The *River Dragon* should be coming in soon; she's for hire, and makes regular runs down there. But just remember, young fella; you've been warned."

Sanchez nodded agreeably, saluted Brodski with his glass and drained it. Then he got up and strolled, not too quickly, toward the table near the front of the bar where the red-scarved lady sat awaiting customers, his intentions plain.

Brodski wished him the joy of her. If Sanchez was hoping to pump her for information, he'd be sorely disappointed; everyone else knew that Alzora spoke only Arabic and bad Russian, and her conversation was limited to the list of her fees and services.

Brodski waved a signal to Flora and took himself off to the back room. Once there, he clicked on the radio and cut through the chatter with: "Breaker! Breaker! Heads up, Leo. Codo-Boy's heading for Kenny-Camp as fast as he can get there, and he'll want your boat."

"Got it," Makhno's voice replied. "I'll keep him from seeing the radio."

"Let's keep him from seein' the *Queen*, too." Irish's voice was staticky with distance. "Likewise the *Princess*."

An even more staticky voice, still recognizable as Van Damm's, growled: "Can you stall him for two weeks? We need time to set up the mess with Reynolds' camp, not to mention clearing some of the floating beggars out of your path. We don't want Cole's replacement to see them and get ideas."

"I think I can manage," Makhno chuckled.

*   *   *

The first problem with hiring the *River Dragon* was finding her. The rather large Harmony beadle—if you please!—patrolling the dock had no idea when the ship might come in, though he offered several kindly suggestions as to who might know. Trotting from warehouse to warehouse Sanchez garnered no further information, except that the warehouse managers themselves indulged in a bit of primitive banking, evaluating goods for barter, and changing CoDo creds for gold, goods or out-world currencies.

A visit to the town hospital—likewise guarded by a sturdy beadle—revealed only that it was actually quite a good clinic, employing both off-world techniques and tools and local herbal cures. Another visit around the bars and restaurants likewise revealed nothing new. By the time dim-dark was approaching, Sanchez was beyond impatience and into steaming.

He finally saw a bizarre-looking riverboat approaching, learned that this was indeed the legendary *River Dragon* and took care to be waiting on the new dock when the ship came in. He noticed that her captain looked oddly familiar, enough like the pilot of the ferry-raft to be a close relative. Sanchez bothered to ask the man his name, which he couldn't recall hearing before, and asked when the boat would be heading down river. He was not pleased by the answer.

"Yes, four T-days," Makhno repeated, idly scratching his new beard. "I have a lot of trips to and from the shuttle. There are some shimmer stone miners going home this time, in case you hadn't noticed."

"But four days!"

"That's the least I can make it. The ships come in intermittently, you know."

"And usually stay in orbit for ninety days! Don't tell me you're not taking goods and passengers straight down to Kennicott Camp!"

"Sure, but they usually wait until I've got the full cargo for the town. What's your hurry, anyway? It's not like anything's going to change in four days. Besides, you'll need to collect your own provisions for the trip, unless you want to stop at local settlements every T-day—which I can't guarantee, anyway. I'd say, bring two weeks' provisions—just in case."

With that Sanchez had to be content. He went stomping back to the Starman's Inn, pausing only to buy a cheap packet of euph-leaf and make an offer to another Red-Scarf, one that spoke a civilized language this time. He was already starting to hate this planet. Besides the usual discomforts of gravity that didn't feel right, air that didn't smell right and light that didn't look right, there was something about the people here that turned him off. Even the whores seemed harder and more secretive than usual.

Makhno found work enough to occupy him for the stated four days, but after that he had no further excuses. He arranged for one of Himself's crew to come along as unofficial bodyguard, took Sanchez and his gear aboard, and made a short speech about the time and hazards of river travel.

"Don't trail your hands in the water; plenty of newcomers have lost fingers, and more, that way. Use the chamber-pots under the seats, and then empty them over the side. Do not, under any circumstances, hang your bare butt out over the water; riverjacks can jump. Once on the water, obey my orders instantly. This is a rough world, and there are a lot of dangers on the river. With any luck, we'll reach Kenny-Camp in twelve to fourteen T-days."

"Twelve days!" fumed Sanchez. "With the speed this craft can make?"

"In case you hadn't noticed, it's going to be dim-dark soon. That makes river-traffic risky enough. After that comes truenight, and nobody with any sense travels in that. If we're lucky, we'll be near a settlement by then, where we can pull up and spend the night on shore. If not, I put down anchor and we wait it out on the water. When we get light again

I'll start the boat, but we don't travel fast until full-light when we can see everything around us. That's the way it is on the river. If you've got a problem with that, I'll pull over to shore and you can walk. Got it?"

Sanchez grumbled, but agreed to stay put. The *Dragon* was making fairly good time right now. After a year's travel to reach this benighted ice-ball world, he could wait another dozen days to confront Van Damm.

Besides, there were questions he could ask this ornery captain. The big miner coming down river with them spoke only in monosyllables, but Makhno might be made to yield some useful information, better than the scraps he'd gotten from the Red-Scarf.

"Less than ten years ago, the companies brought in riverboat designs and encouraged building the ships to facilitate river traffic. What happened to them?"

"Well..." Makhno scratched his chin. "The *Rosie*'s engine blew up. The *Putty Princess* just plain sank. The *Rockhammer* was sunk in a storm. The *Elisabet* got her guts ripped out on the rocks near shore, and nobody could agree on how much money and labor to spend on salvage. The *Last Resort*... Well, I expect you heard what happened to her."

"No, I hadn't."

"A thug named Jomo commandeered her to take his army upstream and rob the farms. The farmers shot back, and sank her in shallow water a good ways upstream, and they salvaged her afterward. There's talk of building another boat from the pieces, but I wouldn't hold my breath waiting." Makhno frowned. "Kenny-Co promised it would bring in supplies for half a dozen more, but they never arrived: something about 'production shortfalls' and 'restricted budgets' and crap like that. So anyway, everybody built what they could from their own designs, from local wood and metal-scrap and bits brought in from the off-world trade."

Sanchez fell silent, wondering if the companies could be pressured into footing the bill for a few more boats. It would be a damn-sight cheaper than building roads around the valley, even after the CoDominium took over.

The T-day ended with dim-dark descending. Makhno scanned the shore, found no settlements close, shut off the engine and put out the anchor. The miner emptied out the chamber-pots, washed his hands with what smelled like rotgut whiskey, pulled a wrapped sandwich out of the basket he'd brought with him, and ate silently. Sanchez had no choice but to copy him as the captain seemed to be doing. When Makhno finished, rolled up in a foil-and-plastic blanket and stretched out to sleep, the miner pulled out a battered old tin flute and began playing it. Sanchez fell asleep to the notes of what sounded like *Danny Boy* echoing across the water.

He woke at the sound of the engine starting, raised his head and saw the miner put away his tin-whistle and wrap himself up in a blanket.

"Stay awake," the captain said, obviously meaning Sanchez. "I'll make as good speed as I can, but I'll need you to help scan the river. Some creatures come close to surface during dim-dark, and we'll need to watch for them. And that's not counting tree-snags fallen in from the bank."

Sanchez duly watched, noting that the raft was moving at half-speed now. He also noted that the captain steered away from certain long barrel-like waves that rolled across the water. "What are those—" he started to ask.

Makhno cut him off. "Don't distract me," he snapped, peering at the water ahead. "Just sing out if you see anything approaching from either side."

The next several hours were tense, wet, cold and nerve-wracking. Only twice did Sanchez actually see what the captain was dodging: once the crown of a half-submerged tree, once a snakelike head rearing out of the water several meters off. The miner slept like a log through the maneuvering, and Sanchez wondered how he managed. Half a dozen times he saw small docks along the bank, leading to roads that were barely openings in the forest wall. Makhno didn't stop at any of them, but drove his meandering course onward down the river.

Finally, on a completely isolated stretch of the river, the captain cut the engine and tossed out the anchor. The miner promptly woke up, yawned, stretched and reached for his basket again. Sanchez gratefully made use of the chamber-pot, dumped it and rinsed the pot quickly in the water. He was obliged to ask the miner for the use of his rotgut hand-washing fluid before he dared open his own satchel and bring out a thermos bottle and a pair of Fleet-issue ration-bars. Makhno pulled a hefty sandwich out of his own basket, and kept scanning the river as he ate.

"If we don't reach Chang's landing before Full-Dark," he commented, "We'll have to spend it on the water. That won't be fun, but it's safer than being on land without a roof and walls."

"Why aren't there more fueling stops along the river?" Sanchez wanted to know.

"Bad harvests, nasty wildlife, robbers," said Makhno with a shrug. "A lot of shimmer stone prospectors wind up broke and take to piracy. None of these settlements can survive on river trade alone; they have to farm and that's a risky business. The mining companies have no interest in helping settlers."

The silent miner laughed.

Makhno turned on the engine, and the *Dragon* sailed on.

As Cat's Eye set and the light grew steadily dimmer, Makhno piloted slower and slower. Sanchez noted odd ripplings on the water, and didn't ask about them. Finally, as the last dim light stretched low across the water, Makhno turned off the engine and threw out the anchor. There was no landing, nor even a hint of a path through the forest, visible anywhere.

"All right," said the captain, pulling up a waterproof lantern. "We didn't reach Chang's, so we're stuck here for the duration. I'm taking the first sleep-shift, so both of you stay awake and alert. If you hear anything splashing near the boat, turn on the lantern and shine the light on it; the critters that come up during Full-Dark don't like the light. But don't leave it on all the time, or you'll drain the batteries. You don't want to be stuck out here with no light, believe me. Don't wake me up unless it's important. See you in a few."

With that, he rolled up in his blanket and lay down. Almost at once his breathing grew deep and steady. The miner pulled out his tin-whistle again and began playing. The sweet lonely notes echoed out over the dark water.

Sanchez hitched to the center of the main hull and set the lantern in his lap, wondering if the odd river sounds were growing any louder. He was sure that the noises from the forest were changing. Something far off roared like a lion. *Cliff lion,* he guessed. Everything he'd read about the wildlife on Haven was unpleasant. Even the river smelled of sour spices—gods only knew what caused that.

There was a nearby splashing, then a faint thump and the slightest feel of vibration. Sanchez flicked on the light and turned it to where he'd heard the sound.

For an instant he saw the thing clearly, perched on the port gunwale; it looked like a cross between a boiled crab and a pink octopus, as big as a seat cushion, holding onto the slick wood with its suckers. The light made it retract its eyestalks quickly, and then it slid off the raft and back into the water. It was, Sanchez, reflected, one of the ugliest creatures he'd ever seen.

"What the hell was that?!" he couldn't help saying. "Was that a riverjack?"

"Nah," said the miner, around the mouthpiece of his tin-whistle. "Just a crawler."

That was as much as Sanchez had heard out of him in the past two days of travel. Unwilling to let the chance slip, Sanchez asked: "Do they attack humans?"

"Nah, they can't eat us." The miner shrugged. "But then, we can't eat them, either. Turn off the light. Save batteries." Before Sanchez could think to ask anything more, the miner put the tin-whistle back in his mouth and resumed his playing.

A dedicated musician, Sanchez thought, dutifully turning out the light. It occurred to him to wonder just what the hell he was doing, sitting out here in a wooden boat in total darkness on a river full of unknown dangers, with no companionship but a near-mute primitive and a sleeping sailor who probably doubled as a smuggler. He should have made Van Damm come to him, instead of going there. Why the hell wasn't the man in Castell City, anyway?

But the answer to that was too obvious. The city had been cleaned up; it was prosperous, clean and peaceful. The Harmonies and the settlers were getting along well and there was no chance to stir up any serious trouble between them. The only possible hot-spot was at Kenny-Camp, so of course Van Damm had gone there. Unfortunately, the only space-capable radio in the valley was back in Castell City—except for those in the hands of the mining companies' local managers, who were mostly in Kenny-Camp. For long minutes Sanchez pondered whether it was worth the security risk to send a message through Kennicott's radio—which would necessarily involve the company managers—assuming that the radio staff even knew who and where Van Damm was.

Then another splash and thump drew his attention, and he turned on the light to see another damned crawler climbing up the other side of the craft. Again, it fled the moment the light touched it. The miner played on, not pausing for a second.

Sanchez huddled down in his blanket, clutched the lamp close to him, and settled in for a very long night.

* * *

The attack came in the middle of Full-Dark: A series of explosions that shook the Reynolds' Camp awake, followed by merrily burning chemical fires that wreathed the main digger in a halo of flame. The newly recruited miners scrambled out of their tents and got out of range, stopping only at the edge of the light. The company safety-crew turned out with fire-extinguishers and hosed down the flame-wrapped machine, but it took them nearly half an hour to kill the blaze.

The engineers, searching the smoking metal with hand-lamps, declared that the damage was minimal—nothing that couldn't be repaired in a turn or two—but was definitely caused by enemy action: well-made incendiary bombs, propelled from a distance—by rockets, perhaps. Who, the hastily-wakened managers considered, had the resources to get such weapons and the motivation to use them?

The answer was obvious.

*   *   *

Sanchez was awakened by the sound of the engine starting and a rough hand shaking his shoulder. He pulled one eye open to see the miner shuffling away to his usual spot, barely visible in the faint glow of long-approaching dawn. Captain Makhno sat at the stern, tinkering with the engine, and the *River Dragon* was beginning to move, slowly but steadily, downstream again.

"We should be a quarter of the way to Kenny-Camp by the end of dim," the captain announced. "We won't be able to make any better than half-speed til then, anyway. Go up to the bow and look ahead for snags."

"Right," Sanchez muttered, taking the lantern and shuffling forward. "God, another week of this…."

"And remember," Makhno called after him, "'Port' is left. 'Starboard' is right."

*   *   *

The company loudspeaker at Kenny-Camp censored the news, of course, but it took only a few prospectors coming in from the hills to spread the tale. Within a few T-days everyone knew that Kennicott agents had firebombed Reynolds' Camp, and Reynolds was coming for revenge. It was anyone's guess what form that vengeance would take, but it would be a good idea to stay away from the mine-pit—and the company offices—for a while. Everyone did so, except for the indentured miners who had no choice in the matter. Even they went to work carrying survival-packs and looking around for handy escape-routes. The company engineers, it was noted, clustered around the landing field and spent an inordinate amount of time checking the company shuttlecrafts. dim-day passed with no lessening of the tension, even though nothing obvious happened.

Almost a T-week later, the *River Dragon* came chuffing up to the dock. Word spread quickly, and buyers came down to crowd the dock for deliveries. Not a few dickered for passage upriver. Vincent Sanchez had trouble getting out of the boat past them. The big miner simply got up and bulled his way through the crowd and headed off in the direction of what appeared to be the nearest bar. Seeing no better objective, Sanchez followed him. He didn't look back to see Makhno pulling out a small and efficient radio-phone, nor hear what the man reported.

The bar had the look of old company housing gone to seed, but there was a sizeable crowd inside. Sanchez wondered if the furtive looks and general nervousness of the clientele were the usual state of affairs, settled at the far end of the bar and waited to have a word with the bartender. A few hours of drinking not-too-bad beer and asking questions won him directions to a ramshackle grocery store. Once there, the right words—and a CoDo cred-bill—got him entry to a storeroom that doubled as an office.

At a rickety table behind a wall of crates sat Owen Van Damm, drinking more of the local beer and brooding over a stained and ancient map of the valley. He looked up as Sanchez entered, and said only: "I hear you've been looking for me."

"Long and far," said Sanchez, dropping onto the only other seat, a large and presumably empty crate. "I'm Vincent Sanchez, your new contact from BuIntel." He flashed his ID, along with the expected hand sign. "You're a hard man to find."

"I didn't think it prudent to make myself known to the Kennicott management." Van Damm shrugged.

Sanchez frowned. This wasn't going at all well; he hadn't impressed the man sufficiently with his position, and why this reluctance to deal with Kennicott? "You had a task to do," he growled. "You haven't accomplished it in almost a year and now you say you need to avoid Kennicott. Explain yourself!" He wondered if he'd put enough snap into the order.

Van Damm only gave him a weary look. "The Powers That Be at HQ have very little idea of what the situation is here on Haven. It can't have escaped your attention that this is a very harsh world, where most of the population is struggling for bare survival. The only people who came here well equipped to deal with the environment are the Harmonies, so the settlers depend on them for supplies, construction, medicine and all other assistance. The mining companies haven't exactly provided those things."

Sanchez briefly recalled what he'd seen at Castell City, and on the long voyage down here. "That's why we have to get the Harmonies under control," he growled. "With a CoDo administrator—"

"—the mining companies still wouldn't spend a credit more than they had to on what the settlers need," Van Damm cut in. "The Harmonies finally had the sense to make deals with the settlers and both of them are profiting from it. The settlers won't turn on the Harmonies. End of discussion. The only pot that's likely to boil is right here, in the heart of the mining country. It's likely to be the companies versus the miners, or companies versus the settlers, or the companies versus each other. In any case, the companies will come off being the bad guys. There's simply no way around that, Mr. Sanchez. Believe me, I've looked."

"There must be something you can do! Set the miners against the settlers…."

"It cannot be done. The miners need the settlers for such basic things as food."

"The miners against the Harmonies?"

"Too distant, and the same problem applies."

Sanchez rattled his fingers irritably on the table-top. "The miners against the companies, then—but make the miners look bad. Arrange for them to commit some atrocity, something the Harmonies can't prevent, something to justify CoDo interference."

"That may be taken out of our hands very shortly." Van Damm gave him a hard look. "Had you not heard? Kennicott agents attacked Reynolds Camp a T-week ago and firebombed the machinery, and everyone knows that Reynolds will strike back soon."

"What?! How could Kennicott be so stupid—"

"They're denying it, of course, but the evidence is pretty damning. Nobody else on the planet could have produced those explosives." Van Damm gave a sour smile. "It's no use, Mr. Sanchez. The mining companies are about to go to war with each other and there's no way to blame the Harmonies for it."

Sanchez swore and rubbed his forehead. "There must be some way to spin this, or at least keep it quiet. Keep the damage minimal…."

Right then came the rolling boom of a distant explosion. Van Damm sat bolt upright, listening.

"Was that normal mining operations…?" Sanchez hoped desperately.

"That wasn't from the pit!" Van Damm shoved back his chair and lunged to his feet. "It was nearer—somewhere near the equipment shed or the company office."

Another explosion boomed, closer.

"The company office!" Van Damm shouted, running for the door. "They'll hit the landing-field next, or the warehouses!"

Sanchez jumped up and ran after him. In the main room, everyone else was running toward the front door. Through the open doorway they could see great clouds of dust rolling down the street.

Another explosion, closer yet, shook the ground. Everyone scrambled out the door and began running through the dust in different directions.

"The ore-shed!" Van Damm yelled through the noise. "They could flatten the whole town before they're done!" He grabbed Sanchez by the shoulder and pointed him toward the dock. "Get out on the water," he shouted. "The boat should still be there—"

Sanchez needed no further urging. He ran through the roiling dust, guided more by the smell of the river than by the sight of landmarks, not seeing where Van Damm went. Running bodies loomed out of the dust and vanished. There was another explosion, sounding as if it came from the same distance, as if Reynolds' avengers were determined to destroy the warehouse completely. Shouts and screams didn't cover the ominous sound of crackling flames, and drifts of smoke began mingling with the blowing dust.

Sanchez blundered his way into buildings, down obscured streets, following the smell and sound of the river until the road disappeared, almost under his feet, at the water's edge. He turned to run along the riverbank until he saw the outline of the dock. He hurried down it, searching through the choking clouds, until at last he saw the *River Dragon* huddled against the piers. Yes, thankfully, her captain was still aboard, shoving the last of his cargo up onto the dock. Sanchez practically fell into the craft, shouting: "Get out on the river! Get away from here!"

Captain Makhno needed no further urging. He cast off the mooring lines, ran to the engine and started it. In another moment he was backing the *Dragon* away from the dock, then turning it, then steering out into deep water.

Sanchez looked back and saw, above the dust, the Kennicott company shuttles rising fast into the air. No doubt they were carrying the company managers and engineers to safety, wherever that might be. All else was dust, smoke, flames and confusion.

"Hopeless," he muttered. If the company's office radio still survived, there was no way to reach it. The nearest space-capable radio was all the way back in Castell City.

"What happened?" the captain was bawling at him, like an idiot. "What's going on?"

Quick, put the right spin on this! "Miners' revolt!" Sanchez shouted. "They didn't like the prices they were getting for the stones, so they attacked the company."

"That makes no sense," said Makhno, looking innocently astonished. "Everybody knows that the best prices for shimmer stones are back in Castell City. All anyone had to do was take the supply boat upstream. And I was right here, ready to take on passengers."

That won't work, Sanchez silently cursed himself. "Maybe they were mad about wages, then. They've rebelled before."

"Damn," said Makhno, turning the raft to face the current. "That doesn't make sense either. Everyone knows that Reynolds, inland, pays better wages. All anyone had to do was sneak off to Reynolds' Camp.... Say, do you think Kennicott was locking miners up to keep 'em from getting away? That would qualify as slavery!"

Worse and worse! Sanchez rubbed his forehead. *Think of something...* "We have to get back to Castell City," he announced. "This place is burning down." *And I need to get to a decent communications center....*

"No, look." Makhno pointed. "There're no more explosions, and the fire doesn't seem to be spreading. Besides, I don't have a cargo. Let's wait until the noise dies down and go back to the dock."

And nothing would move him from that decision. They sat out on the water and watched for hours, seeing the fire shrink under the steady work of a bucket-brigade. Sanchez noted that the impromptu firemen all had the look of indentured miners, and wondered where everyone else was. Eventually the cloud of smoke and dust sank down, revealing the extent of the damage.

Yes, the Kennicott equipment-shed was a wreck, as were several machines inside it. Yes, the ore-warehouse had been blown flat, with the burned wreckage lying atop the muddied pile of ore. Yes, there were gaping holes in the sides of the Kennicott office building. Yes, the shuttles were landing again, and the engineers—identifiable by their work uniforms—were coming out and cautiously approaching the office building.

Sanchez groaned inwardly, realizing that the engineers would go for the radio first and call for assistance. If they could cut through the static and interference, they would spread the story all over the Shangri-La Valley and up to the waiting ship, and to whomever was listening in on the ship near Ayesha. Of course, once the shuttles returned to the ship it wouldn't make any difference, whether or not the land-based radio transmissions got through, word of the attack would be broadcast from the ship to Castell City and all interested parties. There was no chance of keeping this quiet, or of blaming it on anyone but Reynolds.

The Church of New Harmony would come out of this looking innocent as lambs and the mining companies would stink to high heaven, no matter what anyone did.

Sanchez felt a twinge of sympathy for Van Damm, wondering if the man were still alive in all this mess.

* * *

"So, where did you leave him?" Van Damm asked quietly, as he and Makhno paced up the path to Traitors' Cave.

"Back at the company guest house, trying to find anybody with a radio." Makhno automatically glanced around him. "As soon as I've got a cargo, he wants to go back to Castell City."

"Good. How long will that take you?"

"Heading upstream?" Makhno smiled. "I can take a good slow three T-weeks getting there."

"Time enough for the story to spread off-world, at least," Van Damm grinned back, "With nothing he can do to stop it."

"By the way…" Makhno paused again to make sure nobody was within hearing range. "How did your guys get the explosives to look like company issue?"

"Much of it *was* company issue," Van Damm whispered. "'Liberated' by the Hibernians, and replaced in the work-orders by the homemade product. That, or bought outright by supposedly independent prospectors, but gathered in tiny amounts over the course of the past half-year. Kennicott, of course, swears they had nothing to do with the bombing of Reynolds' Camp, and Reynolds likewise swears it had nothing to do with the bombing here, but nobody believes either of them—and they certainly don't believe each other. Dover and Anaconda are likewise looking fish-eyed at each other, wondering if either of them set this off."

"Now we just have to keep the pot boiling a little longer." Makhno glanced up the path to the lighted doorway ahead. "I don't know about this, Vanny. I'm not a very good actor."

"Just respond to me, then. I am very good at keeping, as they say, a straight face."

Makhno nodded, and they walked on up the path and into the Golden Parrot.

One of DeCastro's former thugs, now dressed in a downright civilized looking suit, offered to guide them to a table. Van Damm insisted on one in a quiet corner, knowing that was enough to attract attention.

They ordered the red clam appetizer with amber ale, followed by the roast muskylope entrée with green corn and spice-root sauce and began their planned conversation while waiting for the food to arrive.

"I tell you, this is just the beginning," Van Damm was saying, loud enough for the waitress to hear him as she delivered the appetizers. "Kennicott won't sit still for this. Not just the buildings wrecked, or the ore they had to dig out of the ruins, but the personnel losses. A lot of the indentured miners got killed, you know."

Makhno, knowing where a lot of those missing miners had actually gone, managed not to smile.

"I heard from—well, never mind who: a secretary who works for the company," Van Damm went on. "Kennicott's going to try to call in the CoDo Marines for a strike on Reynolds."

The waitress, barely batting an eye, moved out of sight but not out of hearing.

"The Marines?! They'd never do it," Makhno replied, right on cue. "Shooting up strikers is one thing, but deliberately going after Reynolds— No, they won't hit a big company like that."

"If they can't get the Marines, they've got a contingency plan." Van Damm leaned closer, but didn't actually lower his voice. "Those shuttles of theirs: they can use those to fly over Reynolds' Camp and drop, hmm, interesting things on it."

"Bombs?" Makhno did his best to sound shocked. "That's what they did last time. They've got to know Reynolds will be watching for it. They'll have their gear under shelter."

"There are other things that can be dropped from a shuttle," said Van Damm. "Everything from plague-spores to… well, interesting wildlife. They'll try to make it look like a natural accident, if they can. I tell you, my friend, nobody will be safe anywhere near Reynolds' Camp—and, who knows, they may try to steal laborers from Dover or Anaconda, just to make up for their losses? Tell your merchant friends not to make any more runs to Reynolds' Camp for a good while; it's going to be attacked— within five Turns, at most—and it won't be safe. That's all I'm saying."

"I'll pass the word on," Makhno agreed, digging into his red clams.

Van Damm likewise addressed himself to his food and said nothing further. He knew how DeCastro's place worked; a word to the waitress' ears was sufficient.

Before his guests had finished their meal DeCastro was up on the ridge with his CB radio, calling Reynolds' Camp, selling the details of Kennicott's planned revenge for 1000 creds per item.

* * *

Brodski watched with his binoculars from the shelter of Harp's Sergeant while Makhno dutifully took his passengers out to the waiting shuttle. Yes, Vince Sanchez was definitely one of them. Once the man was safely on the ship Brodski heaved a profound sigh of relief, strolled into the back room and turned on his radio.

"CoDo-Boy's gone," he announced into the microphone. "How're things going at your end?"

To his surprise, it wasn't Van Damm who answered first but Himself. "All's well here, me lad. We've got all the refugees well settled, and the factory's doin' just foine, thank ye."

Van Damm cut in over him. "Kenny-Camp is almost deserted, save for the shopkeepers and the company white-collars. The mayor was seen wandering around in a daze, until one of the Red-Scarves gently led him home...."

There was explosive laughter from Himself, quickly smothered.

"...and our scouts are leading the Reynolds serfs away, one by one. Reynolds and Kennicott are no doubt screaming through the radio-relays to their friends back at CoDo HQ, each blaming the other and wanting the Marines sent for protection. This, I daresay, the Grand Senate will be unlikely to do."

"So it has no excuse to yank control away from the Harmonies," Brodski chuckled, "At least not until it's settled the squabble between Kennicott and Reynolds and their shifty allies. How long do you think that'll take?"

"We have bought ourselves safety for perhaps a year, my friends," Van Damm gloomed. "What we have to worry about now is the floating beggars and any refugees from Reynolds who go to work for Kennicott instead, and the next load of transportees that CoDo dumps on us. If there are too many, Castell City will be overloaded no matter what we do. And there's always the possibility that Old Castell will back out of his bargain...."

"Let's put that year to good use, then," said a woman's voice over the radio—recognizable as Jane. "More farms, more factories...."

"Organized as co-operatives," warned a new voice, male. "Let's not preserve the sins of the old society while creating the new one."

"O' course," said Himself, sounding almost offended.

"Who's that?" Brodski asked, worried.

"Ah, just one of me lads," Himself hastened to explain. "An old friend, really. Aye, an' his advice is good."

"That it is," Jane added. "By the way, Jeff's found a local mold that makes a remarkable antibiotic. We'll breed it here and see how it works out before sending packets down to Castell."

"You know," Brodski considered, "We'll be needing a good technical school before long...."

"I don't think you can talk Old Castell into it," Van Damm warned.

"Aye, an' tell me, now that the CoDo boy is gone, can we bring the *Queen* and the *Princess* back upriver? We've a mort o' cargo for the lot of yahs."

As the hopeful voices chattered and planned through the airwaves, in a cave above Hell's-A-Comin' an old miner set down his microphone and leaned back to listen. No one could see him smiling from ear to ear, nor hear him singing quietly to himself:

"...We can bring to birth a new world,
From the ashes of the old,
For the union makes us strong."

2056 A.D., Luna Base

Marshall Wainwright, Assistant to the Director of the CoDominium Bureau of Intelligence, felt like a schoolboy with cap in hand as he entered the palatial office of Grand Senator Adrian Bronson. The Senator's office was four times the size of his own bosses' office and, unlike most of the underground offices on Luna Base, there were no Tri-V projections of Earth's seas, prairies, meadows, deserts or other calming sites to cover up the fact that they were living in a cavern deep underground on a barren moon with a surface that was as completely devoid of life as deep space. Most of Luna's fulltime government employees used the Tri-V projectors to fight off claustrophobia and fears of entombment.

It appeared that Senator Bronson had no such human frailties. Instead his office was paneled with real teak and mahogany wood and filled with bookcases full of legal volumes and lots of hand carved wooden pillars and sconces. He couldn't imagine what it had cost to drag all this wood out of Earth's gravity well.

What Marshall did know was that he was about to be called on the carpet about something, but as far as what—he had no idea. BuIntel had irons in so many hot spots throughout CoDominium occupied space that he wasn't even going to try and guess which particular one this might be. The only thing he was sure of was that it would in someway be related to one of Dover Mineral and Developments off-world holdings, Tabletop, Comstock, Haven, Friedland, Tanith, Markham, New Washington or any of a dozen other planets.

Senator Adrian Bronson Sr. had swept-back wavy silver hair and the smiling visage of a Tri-V pitchman, but his eyes were pure arctic chill. Wainwright knew that Bronson had been a Senator for over twenty years. Grand Senators served for thirty years; new Senators were appointed by both co-option and election from Earth. They could not be recalled only expelled: "The Senate shall be the sole judge of members and qualifications." Answerable only to the CoDominium Council, the Senators were a law unto themselves. No CD bureaucrat, not even his boss, the Director of Bureau of Intelligence was immune to their power.

"Have a seat," Bronson said, using a tone of voice one might use to correct a misbehaving cur.

"Yes, Your Excellency," he replied, trying to keep from tugging his forelock as he sat down.

"I understand you were the man in charge of the Haven Takeover Operation?" His tone brooked no nonsense.

So that's what this is about, he thought. *Max Cole, I'd like to wring your neck for this!* "Yes, sir," he replied, hiding his anger. "We had one of our senior agents, Maxwell Cole, running the operation. *How does the Senator know what happened on Haven when we haven't gotten word one from there yet?* he wondered. *Aha! Their intel must have come from one of the DMD ore ships. Unfortunately, BuIntel doesn't have enough agents to cover every ship because the Grand Senate won't give us the funding we need. However, we will get the blame when something goes wrong that could have been fixed with more credits.*

"Well, if this is the work we can expect from one of your top agents, then BuIntel can expect some funding cuts when the next appropriation bill comes up."

This is not going well. If the Senator cuts our funding—and he has the connections and power to do just that—Director Harrison will have my head. "Your Excellency, we had a well-situated group of malcontents, which we supplied with arms, thoroughly capable of undermining Harmony hegemony—"

"Well, your gang did a terrible job," Bronson said, cutting him off. "According to our people on the ground, they were slaughtered by a bunch of farmers and a gang of women comprised of former convicts and prostitutes." He shook his head in apparent disbelief. "The Harmonies are non-violent and yet your *people* couldn't even hold Castell City!"

"I don't know exactly what happened there because we haven't received our agent's report, but I'm sure there were extenuating circumstances—"

"Enough of your excuses. It seriously worries me that my information is more up-to-date than that of the CD Intelligence Bureau's. It also troubles me that BuIntel can't even run a successful revolt on a world run by pacifists. It might even be amusing, if it weren't so pathetic. We have vital interests on that world. Do you understand?"

"Yes, Your Excellency," he replied, knowing full well that those "vital interests" were not CoDominium related, but Dover interests.

The Senator lowered his voice as if he were taking Wainwright into his confidence. "Thanks to the loss of our shimmer stone monopoly we've taken a multi-trillion dollar hit over the last five years. The man responsible for this loss, my nephew Thomas Ehrenfeld, is going to be sent to Haven to clean up this mess. As CEO of DMD, Ehrenfeld was so busy taking credit for the shimmer stone profits, he forgot to establish effective controls on Haven to see that our monopoly remained uncontested."

Wainwright nodded, understanding full well that the nephew was being sacrificed for his failure to protect Dover's bottom line. If Ehrenfeld had been smart, he would have hired a mercenary battalion to protect the shimmer stone secret. There weren't that many ports of entry on Haven and it could have easily been sewn up tight. After all, dead men tell no tales.

"This blow to the company has meant that I'm going to have to either take a leave of absence from the Senate to run the company again or have my son take the CEO spot."

Taking a leave of absence wouldn't shorten Bronson's term of office, but it would remove him from the hub of power. And very likely make a powerful enemy for BuIntel.

"I'm sure your son would acquit himself well as CEO," he said, trying to placate the older Bronson. By reputation, young Adrian was even more rapacious than the old man.

Bronson nodded. "It'll be good training for him. I don't have that many more eligible years as Senator anyway and I expect him to take my position one day. Still, that's not going to solve the Haven problem."

"Tell me what I can do to rectify this situation, Your Excellency." He would give the Senator all the help he could; otherwise, his career was over and he'd be marooned back on Earth where no one trusted ex-CD officials—especially ex-spooks. His pension would see to his physical needs, but he *needed* to be at the center of power: changing fortunes, building new worlds, moving people and toppling governments were his passions.

"Okay, Wainwright, here's what I want you to do," the Grand Senator said, as he began to tick off points on his left hand with the fingers of his right hand.

The Raid on Purity

William F. Wu

Haven, 2057 A.D.

Chuluun, Second Khan of the Free Tribe of the Steppes, laughed as he rode his mount at full gallop across the hard ground of the northern plains. The icy wind whipped his face, sending his beard and mustache flying like the mane of his sturdy horse. His tight leather hat and his del—the long, broadly cut traditional gown of his people—kept him warm. Up ahead, the yurts of the tribe were scattered near a rocky bluff on the edge of this grassy valley where they had made their home.

Captain Ganzorig of the First Troop, whose name meant Courage of Steel, rode hard by Chuluun's side, grinning even though his mount was a nose behind Chuluun's. Ganzorig was a young man two years older than Chuluun, who also had learned the traditional ways of their people in the historical re-enactment celebrations on Earth. He, too, had taken the ship to Haven to work in the mines. In the rebellion seven months earlier that had brought the miners to freedom far from the mines, he had been one of the many miners to follow Chuluun and fight for their freedom.

As the horses' hooves thundered, Chuluun saw that he was nearing the narrow cleft in the soil they had chosen for a finish line. Eager to win this race with his friend and first officer, he leaned forward even lower and let his mount have his head. Braced against the stirrups, moving in the saddle as though one with his mount, Chuluun sailed over the break in the ground just ahead of Ganzorig.

Moments later, as they reined in together, Chuluun smiled at his companion. "Did you let your Khan win, my friend?"

"Never!" With good humor, Ganzorig grinned and loosened the embroidered hat that kept his head and ears warm. "Our Khan is a fearless rider on a fine horse."

Chuluun knew better than to believe him, but he chuckled and gave Ganzorig a hearty clap on the back. Ganzorig laughed, too, as though they shared the joke.

On Earth, throughout the centuries, the word khan had come to have many meanings, often courteous but mundane. During the rebellion he had led, the title had taken on an exalted meaning among his people. He suspected that out of all them, only his wife Tuya would dare try to outride him, and she might succeed when she was not heavy with child, as she was now.

As Chuluun let his mount walk, cooling down, he looked out over the herd of horses and muskylopes grazing in the distance. His good mood dropped away.

The mining camp near the town of Last Chance from which they had escaped had held roughly a thousand miners in a compound built for only five hundred. They were a mix of ethnic Mongol, Manchu, Korean, and Hui people from the same region of Earth as Chuluun and Tuya. Because Mongols were in a dominant majority, their language was most common among them.

Seven hundred and sixty-one miners had followed him here, while some had fallen while fighting to escape and others had died on the trip of wounds or illness. Others had fled to Last Chance rather than risk the dangers of this life. Now the Free Tribe of the Steppes, as Chuluun had named them to universal agreement, held off starvation only by butchering their limited herd faster than a new generation of offspring was born.

"We must act soon," said Ganzorig, as if being Chuluun's best friend meant that he could read Chuluun's mind. He ran a gloved hand over his narrow, black beard. "If the Americans will join us, we can strike the town of Purity and take their herds. We need their food, their firearms, their mining explosives, everything."

"The people of Purity are much like our own," said Chuluun. "They work hard, but they are mostly poor and desperate." He hated the idea of raiding a town, even of CoDominium loyalists. The son of a miner in Dongbei Province of China, his soul was that of a working man, of many generations of miners, herders, hunters—and, of course, warriors.

"They belong to CoDo," said Ganzorig, his eyes glittering with anger. "They toil in the mines. They tend the herds that feed Dover Mining. A company town! We owe them nothing, Chuluun Khan."

Chuluun did not speak, as he considered the desperate needs of his people. His friend had always wanted to attack Purity. Ganzorig hated the CoDominium and had no love for tending herds. Chuluun had seen the ugly scars of whips on his friend's back, where he had been punished by Reynolds guards for insolence.

The Free Tribe had escaped with mounts and wagons of supplies, from the Shangri-La Valley up through the Karakul Pass to the northern plains. In search of grazing land in the harsh climate, Chuluun had led them east to the Girdle of God Mountains, first through a valley where some Americans had settled, and farther to this valley, which he had named, with both ethnic pride and bitter irony, the Gobi Valley.

"We meet with the Americans soon," said Ganzorig, reminding him. Ganzorig, who had learned Russian on Earth, had arranged the meeting through an American who also spoke Russian.

"I need a moment with Tuya. Then we shall go."

Some of the children and old men were hurrying toward them, ready to tend the mount of the khan and his first officer. Chuluun swung down out of the saddle and handed over the reins to an eager little girl. He gave her a smile as she glanced up at him shyly.

"Chuluun Khan, may I have a moment?" Ganzorig dismounted.

"Yes?"

"I have a gift for the Khan." Ganzorig drew a rifle from his saddle boot. It was not the one he usually carried. He held it out. "This is for you."

Astonished, Chuluun accepted the gift. It was a lever-action deer rifle, the stock old but recently shellacked. The barrel action was in polished blue steel. He checked to see that it was unloaded, then worked the lever, raised it to his shoulder, and squeezed the trigger. It gave a good snap. "A fine weapon."

"It's an antique from America, called a Winchester Model 94. The mark shows it was made in 1961. I took it apart, cleaned and inspected it. They are much prized among Americans. The stock is black walnut from America, a hardwood they like." Ganzorig held out a small pouch. "These are .30-30 shells. I gathered these Winchester cartridges from our people. Their share of the gift."

Chuluun nodded. The tribe's firearms and ammunition were a haphazard collection, whatever they had taken from the mining camp when they had escaped. "Where did you get it?"

"I took it from an officer of the guard at the mining camp—after I killed him. Some CoDo Marine officer probably brought it to Haven and then bartered it—just a guess. It has quite a kick. The original lacquer finish was wearing off the stock, so I stripped it and shellacked it the best I could."

"I'm honored," said Chuluun. "Why do you give it to me?"

"For my Khan." Ganzorig drew himself up with pride.

Chuluun embraced his friend. "Thank you."

"You are welcome, of course." Ganzorig swung back up into the saddle. "Chuluun Khan, we must leave."

"I need only a moment. Tell Naran."

Captain Naran of the Second Troop, whose name meant sun hero, was not as dynamic as Ganzorig, but he was a disciplined, steady commander who had once been a junior CoDominium Marine officer. Naran was the man who had established the two troops with four patrols of twenty-five riders each, and organized the drill for riding and shooting. He had recommended Ganzorig as captain of the First Troop, for his personal dynamism.

"I'll summon the patrol," said Ganzorig, as he reined away. As always, when the riders were not practicing their war arts, they were herding and farming.

Chuluun, broad-shouldered and muscular, strode toward the stony bluff, his leather del flowing with his walk. With the men and women of his tribe, nearly all miners, he had chipped, blasted, and dug a cave in the bluff for his home. Other caves were being carved out, for the greater protection from the cold than yurts or wooden huts could provide. Smoke rose from the chimney built from the rock broken out of the bluff. A wooden door was centered in the mortarless stone wall that fronted the artificial cave.

His wife, Tuya, whose name meant light, sat before the fireplace bundled in her del, made of muskylope leather like his own. Pretty with a petite frame, she was now large in her seventh month of carrying their first child. If she had a son, they would name him Bataar, meaning hero, after Chuluun's mentor. If she had a daughter, she would be named Bayarmaa, after Tuya's mother.

A table full of used brass shells of varied type and size stood near her. She passed her time repacking ammunition for their sizable yet limited supply.

His ray of light, as he thought of her, looked up with a smile, as firelight flickered on her shining black hair.

A young woman attending her withdrew to give them privacy.

"I heard the hoof beats," said Tuya. "He let you win again?"

"He did." Chuluun allowed himself a grin. "I wish he had more trust in me. I'd never be angry about losing a fair race."

"Everyone knows he's your closest friend. It's nothing to anyone else."

Warming his hands at the fire, Chuluun frowned. "He finally arranged that meeting with the Americans. We're about to go."

"What do you want them to do?" Tuya avoided his eyes as she asked, instead gazing into the fire.

"Ganzorig is right," said Chuluun. "We must raid Purity. Our tribe cannot last here without more livestock, tools, and weapons. We need grain and seed. And we need more explosives to blast out new homes. We can't get these any other way."

"Tell me you will not steal the women."

"What?" He turned from the fire to look at her.

"I would not have you kidnapping their women."

Chuluun was puzzled. "Why would we take their women?"

Tuya looked him in the eye. "We have three times as many men as women of child-bearing age. Haven't you thought of this?"

In truth, he had not. The threat of slow starvation overwhelmed his thoughts. He had to keep his people alive now.

"Birthing on Haven is difficult enough," said Tuya. "If our tribe is to live after us, then our numbers must grow."

Chuluun nodded, his mind on Tuya. Whether or not the Americans joined the raid, Tuya and the twelve other women whose time for childbirth was approaching would soon travel down to the Shangri-La Valley where they had a better chance of success and survival in giving birth. He would lead his troops to escort them, and raid Purity if possible on the same journey.

"What is this?" Tuya nodded toward the Winchester.

"A gift from Ganzorig. I'll show it to you when I return."

"And what of the Americans?" Tuya asked.

"They've been good to us. They traded grain and seed for stud service with our stallions. You remember."

"I do. When we arrived, I thought they would fight us. They let us pass through their valley to come here."

"Their colony has been in that valley almost twelve years. They're self-sufficient, herding as we want to do. They hate Kennicott and Dover. The Americans were among the first to flee from the mining companies on Haven. They named their town Independence."

"But why are you meeting with them?"

"The town, and their homes around Independence Valley, have almost four thousand people now. Families live in cabins. Compare that to our two troops of one hundred riders each. We are so few."

"I wish I could ride with you," said Tuya. She had ridden and carried a rifle at his side during the escape from the mining camp. "You want the Americans for their numbers on this raid?"

"We need their help," said Chuluun. "Purity is not far from the Dover shimmer stone mines and the company guards who protect them."

"What do they want from you?"

"I must find out," said Chuluun.

*   *   *

By arrangement, Chuluun rode with his two troop leaders and a single patrol to a place in the open grassland at the south end of Gobi Valley, where a narrow cleft led down to Independence Valley. They and an equal number of Americans all carried their personal weapons. The open terrain ensured that if others of either side approached in a treacherous move, they would be seen from afar. However, it was merely a precaution among cautious neighbors.

The Americans had a big fire blazing in a deep pit.

"Howdy, fellas!" The Americans' mayor was Red Kelter, a short, wiry man whose hair was now gray. In a sheepskin coat and a gray cowboy hat, he was clean-shaven and gave them a big smile.

"Hello," Chuluun said in English. He cradled the Winchester in his arms. "How are you?" He had learned some English phrases from men of his tribe who also knew only a few words and phrases.

Ganzorig exchanged Russian greetings with a tall, young American named Yates Harrow, their interpreter.

"I'm fine, Khan," said Red, shaking Chuluun's hand. "Sit down, everybody."

As they sat on boulders or just the hard ground, Ganzorig and Yates introduced each man by name on both sides.

At Chuluun's signal, Naran brought out a gift for the American leader. Naran was a short, blocky man with a beard along his jawline. Unlike the garrulous and charismatic Ganzorig, Naran spoke little but observed a great deal. If Ganzorig was Chuluun's right hand, Naran was his rock.

Chuluun presented Red with a newly polished, sharpened saber that he had taken in the rebellion from the mining camp. It was a modest gift, but he had little to give.

"Why, thanks, Khan," said Red. He stood up and held it aloft, showing it to his companions. "That's right nice, isn't it, guys?"

The other Americans spoke out, agreeing, and he passed it around for them to see.

"Now I got something." Red opened a leather bag and pulled out a handgun and two boxes of shells. "This here's a Model 1911 Colt .45 semi-auto," he said. "It's an antique, a real source of pride where we come from. And there's some shells, 'cause it won't do you no good without 'em." He held out the weapon handle first. "And it'll go just fine with that Winchester! She's a beauty!"

"Thank you," Chuluun said carefully in English. "Thank you very much. I am honored." He accepted the weapon in both hands, then worked its mechanics to show both his appreciation and his knowledge. "It's a beautiful gift," he said in Mongol, and waited for Ganzorig to translate.

Chuluun was honored but also embarrassed. A clean, polished Colt .45 with shells was a much greater gift than the sword he had given. "Ganzorig?"

In response, Ganzorig brought out jugs of kumiss, their people's traditional drink of fermented mare's milk.

"Hidey-ho! I know that stuff." Red grinned and waved to one of his men. The other man handed him a big bottle of clear fluid. "This ain't exactly smooth. It's moonshine, new and rough." He uncorked the bottle, took a swig, and held it out.

Chuluun accepted the bottle as Ganzorig took a drink of kumiss and gave the jug to Red. The swallow of moonshine burned Chuluun's throat, yet the heat it brought was welcome. He smiled and passed the bottle to Naran.

"This handgun is a treasure," Naran said quietly to Chuluun. "Their gift has meaning. They want an agreement with us."

"Yes, but why?" Ganzorig whispered pointedly.

After each man had tasted each drink, Chuluun and Red were ready to "talk turkey," as Red put it. Even Ganzorig's translation confused Chuluun, but he saw Red take on a solemn demeanor.

"Here's what's on our mind," said Red, pushing his gray cowboy hat back a little from his face. "I know you folks have had a hard time up here. We need more seed grain and livestock and I'm bettin' you do, too. Your man here, Ganzorig, talked to us about a raid. We all hate those Dover Mining bastards. I'm here to tell you, we're all in, if you and I can make a deal."

Chuluun nodded calmly, but excitement raced through him. This was what he needed. "What terms do you suggest?"

"Well, pard, I see it real simple. Ganzorig says you can bring about two hundred men. We got more guys, but we also got more families to protect. So a lot of our guys gotta stay home."

Chuluun waited for the translation. "Of course. We must leave men at home, too." His tribe, however, could only afford to leave behind the young, disabled, and elderly. He chose not to say that, nor that thirty-seven of his riders were hard-riding women.

"So I figure I can bring in four hundred guys," said Red.

Chuluun's excitement dropped. He could not come close to matching that number. His share of livestock and other loot would be proportionally smaller, he supposed. He could live with that.

Red leaned forward, his forearms on his knees. "Khan, I got a problem. I got me a bunch of hotheads, know what I mean?"

Eventually Yates and Ganzorig worked out a translation.

"How can I help?" Chuluun asked courteously. Between the greater gift Red had given, and the bigger numbers of American cowboys, he would be the junior partner in any agreement.

"Did you know a bunch of new livestock is coming toward Purity? It's a month or more off, which is just right for us if we start moving soon. Horses, muskylopes, whatever else. Fact is, we don't need hundreds of men to drive the herd, but we might need 'em to fight our way out if those CD Marines catch up to us."

"We do need livestock," said Chuluun.

"So here's my problem. A lot of my guys want revenge on Dover Mining. They want to attack the mines and free more miners. Trouble is, that's where CoDo's got its troops stationed. I say we ought to stay away from them troops."

"That's wise," said Chuluun. "We should not try to fight CoDo Marines. We must strike fast and return home again."

Red grinned when he got the translation. "Now you're talkin'! So here's what I was thinkin'. First, we do a fifty-fifty split on everything. That way it don't matter who does what. What do you say?"

"That's fair," said Chuluun, though now his spirit soared. He wondered why Red was being so generous. "I agree to these terms. How shall we plan this raid?"

"Here's the thing, Khan. I gotta keep my guys as far from Dover Mining as possible. If I don't, I think them hotheads'll just ride hell for leather on Dover no matter what I say. And the herd is coming toward Purity from the far side, where we could get 'em without goin' too near Dover Mining and the Marines. So, how 'bout you raid Purity, and we hit the livestock outside of town? Each one's a diversion for the other."

When Ganzorig finished translating, he grinned at Chuluun.

Chuluun would have preferred the opposite arrangement. He still hated the idea of raiding ordinary townspeople. However, he also had hotheads among his people, including Ganzorig.

"We raid the town for everything we can take and you bring back the livestock," said Chuluun. He liked the plan more as he realized the two groups would act separately. That would avoid friction between their men. "We will do this."

"So, we got a deal?" Red grinned.

"Yes," Chuluun said in English. He stood up and held out his hand. "We have a deal."

Red got to his feet and took his hand. "Let's drink on it."

Chuluun grinned in return. "Let's drink."

* * *

On the ride home, excitement drove Chuluun's thoughts. The women with child would have to leave soon because the wagons moved slower than the riders. Chuluun and his captains would lead the two troops of riders. The women would stop in a safe place to wait while Chuluun led the raid on Purity.

"We shall destroy Purity," said Ganzorig, as he rode on Chuluun's right. "I've lived for this day."

"The spoils will keep our people alive," said Chuluun. "We just need to get away again."

"That accursed company town. We'll pick them clean."

"Do you trust the Americans?" Chuluun asked.

"I trust no one," said Ganzorig. "I trust their desire for our help. We made an alliance, not a friendship."

Chuluun turned to Naran, who was not likely to speak unless he was asked. "What do you think?"

"They want allies. That's why they let us pass through their land when we first came here. They did not want trouble with us."

"Americans fear no one," said Chuluun.

"Not fear," said Naran. "In earlier times, they were desperate. They understand hunger—and they hate CoDo and the mining companies as much as we do. They have enough enemies."

Ganzorig threw back his head and laughed into the cold wind. "Hatred makes strong alliances, my friends."

Chuluun thought again of the scars on his friend's back from the

Reynolds lash and said nothing.

*   *   *

At home with Tuya, Chuluun watched as she shifted her weight in her padded chair. "You will not take their women?"

"Of course not," Chuluun said angrily. "After we surround the town, I will send an offer for them to surrender."

"What offer?"

"If they surrender the town, we will take what we need, but we will not hurt anyone. No killing, no burning. No dishonoring their women. That will be my promise."

"That's the promise given in olden times by the great khans on their wars of conquest."

"Yes, I learned this from our history."

"And if they refuse?"

"We must take what we need. We will not dishonor the women."

"I hope the townspeople surrender." Tuya sighed. "Now I want to see this rifle Ganzorig gave you. I'll pack more cartridges for it if we have them. It's a good weapon?"

"It's good. I'll show you what my friend gave me."

*   *   *

Chuluun led the way on the long, rugged trip down to the Shangri-La Valley. Each rider led a string of two or three free mounts, each with empty pack saddles, panniers, or manties to carry the loot from the raid faster than wagons could move. Along they way, Chuluun often led hunts, as much to keep the men occupied as for food. He hunted with the Winchester and found that it fired true.

Taking the extra mounts was an act of desperation. Chuluun's order had nearly deprived his people at home of any mounts on which to tend their herds. While he and the troops were gone, the remaining livestock would dwindle even more. If Chuluun failed to return with his share of a big, new herd, his people would starve or go begging, maybe to become enslaved again.

Chuluun's route first took them west from the Girdle of God

Mountains, then south. In the first return since their escape, the Free Tribe journeyed through the Karakul Pass down into the Shangri-La Valley. At last they reached the region where the women would wait for their time of labor. Chuluun sent scouts ahead to rendezvous with the Americans and learn when the Dover Mining herd would approach Purity.

Every day as they waited, Ganzorig and Naran drilled their riders afresh. The First Troop, under Ganzorig, was aggressive and enthusiastic, following the personality of their captain. The Second Troop, in its tight discipline and crisp movements, showed the imprint of Naran's command.

During every dinner time in the long Haven nights, Chuluun walked with his two captains from one cookfire to another, greeting his riders. Their handshakes and shouts of welcome heartened him. They offered him kumiss from their private caches and told ribald stories to pass the time. Ganzorig would tell stories and joke with the riders in his turn. Naran shook hands and asked after the riders' well-being. The thirty-seven women riders, scattered among the patrols of both troops, greeted Chuluun and asked if Tuya was well, knowing she carried the first heir of the Free Tribe.

Every night, he reminded his riders of the offer he would make: If the people of Purity surrendered, the riders would harm no one and leave the town standing when they left with their spoils.

One night as Chuluun completed his rounds and walked away from the troops with Ganzorig and Naran, he thought to himself that he had done little for his people except to lead the breakout from the mining camp. The escape had been arranged by his mentor, the late Bataar, now remembered as the First Khan of the steppes. Chuluun played the role of khan for his people as best he could.

"They love their Khan," said Ganzorig. He clapped Chuluun on the back.

"They do." Naran nodded gravely.

Chuluun said nothing. He desperately hoped the townspeople would surrender.

* * *

One night, Chuluun awoke to the hoofbeats of a single rider approaching the wagon where he slept with Tuya. He rose, drew on his boots and his del, and jumped out to the ground.

A scout drew up in front of him. "Chuluun Khan."

"Speak."

"The Americans are in position and the big herd will be near them soon. They are ready to strike if we are."

"We are," said Chuluun. "At the next dawn, then?"

"That is their choice, too."

"Tell them it will be done."

"Yes, Chuluun Khan." The scout reined away to find a fresh mount and return to the American camp with his message.

Chuluun climbed back into the wagon.

Tuya had lit a small lamp. "My time is coming. I feel it."

He drew in a breath, suddenly cold with fear. "I'll send for the midwife and her helpers."

"I heard the scout. You must go prepare the riders."

Terrified for her deep in his gut, he looked at his ray of light in the glow from the lamp. "I would rather stay here." He knew that anywhere on Haven, women often died in childbirth.

"Go! Just send the midwife."

Chuluun embraced her quickly, then jumped back out of the wagon.

* * *

At dawn on a slope overlooking the town of Purity, Chuluun reined in his mount. He had the Model 1911 Colt .45 stuck in the sash around his del, and carried the Winchester Model 94 in his right hand. The town looked small from here, with two large streets forming a cross in the middle, an open space forming a modest town square. Small streets, crooked and uneven, split from the main thoroughfares.

Ganzorig drew up on Chuluun's right. Naran reined in at his left.

"The town still sleeps," said Chuluun. Somewhere far behind him,

Tuya was in her wagon with the midwife. He shook his head, driving away the thought.

Ganzorig pointed to rising clouds of dust in the distance. "The Americans are on the attack. We must move."

"Forward, Captain Ganzorig," Chuluun ordered. He hoped to finish the raid quickly and return to Tuya as soon as he could. "Stand fast," he said to Naran.

Ganzorig reined away, shouting orders.

Chuluun watched as Ganzorig led the First Troop in a canter down the slope, where he would take a wide loop around the town. They would cut off the back route to the nearest Dover Mines and the guards and CoDominium Marines stationed there. The riders thundered away in a tight line, those at the rear leading strings of pack animals on long leads.

As the column drew small, Chuluun turned to Naran. "Forward."

Chuluun spurred his mount as Naran shouted orders. While Ganzorig's First Troop raced in their arc to the rear of Purity, Chuluun led the charge directly down the slope to block the road where the townspeople expected the big herd to draw near.

His heart raced as the wind blasted his face. Letting his mount have his head with the reins in his left hand, Chuluun held the Winchester high and felt the sheer joy of the ride. Behind him, the riders whooped and shouted.

By the time Chuluun had reached the base of the slope, he could see townspeople running out into the streets. He slowed to a trot, bringing Naran and the Second Troop to the road at a distance of about a thousand paces from the town. The discipline of Naran's troops, drawing up behind him in a wide line, pleased him. Naran had drilled them well.

Behind Chuluun, a huge billow of dust rose into the sky above the area where the Americans had intercepted the herd. He could just barely hear the snap of distant firearms. Chuluun's riders could not waste any time.

"Naran, send the messengers."

Two riders cantered forward, one who spoke some Russian and another who spoke some English.

Chuluun waited as his messengers conferred with a small knot of men standing at the edge of town. He looked over the town while he waited. Now that he was close, it seemed dirty, drab, and slapdash, a place of little prosperity and no hope. He thought again of the mines he had escaped, first in Dongbei Province and later on Haven.

His messengers rode back at a gallop and reined in.

"Speak," said Chuluun.

"They want to know what assurance we give," said one man.

"What did you see when you were up there?" Chuluun asked.

"Chuluun Khan, we can see men and women with rifles in the windows of all the buildings," said the second messenger. "We can take the town easily, but they will die fighting."

"Stand fast," Chuluun said to Naran. He spurred his mount into a canter, signaling for the messengers to join him.

When Chuluun arrived at the knot of men standing together, he found a stout, white-haired white man in a rumpled white shirt and black pants glaring up at him.

"I'm Mayor Fordham Higgins," the man said. "Now why should I believe any damned promise from you?"

Chuluun waited for the translation. "I came forward to give you my sworn oath. I swear it now. If you believe I can't be trusted, have one of your people shoot me." He nodded toward the windows of small, wooden buildings, where he could see townspeople, still tousle-haired with sleep, holding firearms.

Higgins looked up at him and looked at the line of Naran's Second Troop, waiting to charge. His face showed resignation.

"We gain nothing from harming you," said Chuluun.

"Humph. We'll see about that. Hang on, all right?"

Chuluun waited as Higgins plodded back up the big street. Other people came out to speak to him. Then, at last, he took a stick with a rectangle of white sheet and held it up.

"Have his people come down to the town square and drop their weapons," Chuluun said to one messenger. "When we see them in the square, we will move up." He turned to the other. "Ride around the outside of town and tell Ganzorig the town has surrendered. He will stand fast until I send another messenger. Tell him to fire four quick shots when he has this message." He watched as the two messengers rode away in different directions.

Chuluun ordered Naran to send one patrol into the town to supervise the surrender, while the remainder of Naran's troop remained in place as an ongoing threat. Ganzorig's troop would remain in position at the rear of the town. When the surrender of weapons was complete, and the patrols had gathered the unarmed people of the town in the square, Chuluun signaled for Naran's troop to follow him as he rode at a trot into Purity.

At the town square, Chuluun drew up near Higgins. Huddled in a crowd, the residents were angry and afraid as they glared up at him. He saw that they were very much the working people he had heard they would be. Some were tough and strong, while others looked beaten down by their travails. Their clothes were worn and rough. They reminded him of his fellow miners back on Earth.

Naran led his remaining three patrols into the town in a precise column with their pack mounts at the rear, and shouted orders for them to dismount and search for anything of value.

Behind the far side of Purity, four gunshots told Chuluun that Ganzorig had received his message.

The people of the town watched in anger, helplessly, as two mounted patrols stood over them with their rifles and sabers.

Chuluun was startled to hear shouts and whoops from the rear of town in the same moment that the crack of firearms reached him.

"Naran!" Chuluun shouted. "Come forward!"

Ganzorig led a column of riders streaming up the street from the rear of town. He held his rifle in his free hand and fired into the sky, while his men were firing their weapons into the buildings. As Chuluun watched, four riders came into view with women from the town thrown across the withers of their mounts, kicking and flailing. Other riders broke away up side streets whooping and shooting. Ganzorig cantered forward in the lead, grinning.

The townspeople shrieked and yelled. Mayor Higgins's shouts at Chuluun were lost in the din.

Chuluun spurred his mount toward Ganzorig, firing his Winchester into the air. "Ganzorig! Halt!"

Laughing, Ganzorig cantered ahead of his riders and reined in. "What, Chuluun?" He swung out of the saddle and jumped to the ground, slinging his rifle over his shoulder on its strap. "Kill them! Kill them all! Take the spoils and burn it down!"

As Chuluun leaped to the ground, he saw riders up the street dismounting and pulling the captured women off their horses after them.

"Order your riders to stop!" Chuluun yelled. "Order them now! I gave my sworn oath!"

"To these scum?" Ganzorig held his arms out as though embracing the entire town. "Kill them all!"

The thunder of the mounts and the shouts of the townspeople roared in Chuluun's ears. Down the street, he saw riders forcing the captive women to the boardwalk and ripping away their clothes. Behind him, Naran's riders held their reins tight, still under command.

"They are nothing, Chuluun!" Ganzorig laughed again. "They're just slaves to Dover and CoDo!"

"Ganzorig! Listen to me!"

"You like my gift, Chuluun?" Grinning, Ganzorig nodded at the Winchester. "Here, you can kill more of them this way!" He unslung his rifle and tossed it to Chuluun.

Chuluun slapped the rifle away with his free hand as he stomped up to Ganzorig. He took the Winchester in both hands and slammed the stock up under Ganzorig's chin.

Ganzorig stumbled backward but kept his feet. Bloody, his face twisted into a sneer. Behind him, his riders drew up in surprise.

Unarmed, Ganzorig raised his head, still defiant. "Will you be the last khan of a dead people?"

Chuluun brought the Winchester up and jammed the stock against his shoulder. He sighted on the center of Ganzorig's chest, barely one long stride away. His blood burning, he squeezed the trigger. The rifle barked once and Ganzorig jerked backward off his feet with the impact.

Lowering the Winchester, Chuluun stared at his dead friend lying in the street. For a moment, he saw nothing else, despite the shouts and screaming all around him.

The riders of the First Troop stared in disbelief, looking from Ganzorig's body to Chuluun.

"Naran!" Chuluun yelled.

"Chuluun Khan?" Naran reined up next to him.

"Stop this! If they refuse, kill them! Disarm them and bring them here."

Naran called out orders to his riders.

"And stop those men!" Chuluun pointed to the riders dragging women into a nearby doorway.

Naran spurred his mount forward.

In disgust, Chuluun looked down at Ganzorig. Then he turned toward the townspeople, who were still under guard. They were confused and fearful. Higgins caught his eye and spat on the ground.

Chuluun turned away.

* * *

Captain Naran of the Second Troop secured the town of Purity. He reported to Chuluun that half of the First Troop had remained in place outside the far edge of the town. Two patrols, all men, had followed Ganzorig's wild charge into the streets in violation of Chuluun's order to stand fast. They had all been disarmed and taken to the town square. Their weapons were piled with those taken from the townspeople. At Chuluun's order, Ganzorig's body had been dragged to the square and left lying with them, face up.

In the cold morning air, Chuluun stood in the town square before the riders who had broken his promise to Mayor Higgins of Purity. Disarmed, they knelt on the hard ground, a full quarter of the Free Tribe's trained warriors. The people of the town, still bunched together and guarded by riders, had backed up to the far side of the town square. No one spoke.

Chuluun turned and looked into the distance. He no longer heard distant gunfire from the direction of the Americans. However, he could see a low cloud of dust streaming in the air as the herd was being driven homeward.

Naran stood next to Chuluun, waiting patiently. The tight discipline he had imposed on the Second Troop had held. Many of his riders, still mounted, lined the town square.

Chuluun looked at the men kneeling before him. He knew each one from their riding and shooting drills. The Free Tribe might desperately need them in the future. Yet the Free Tribe could not survive at all if they were just a rabble on horseback.

"Execute them all," Chuluun said quietly. "We don't have time to hang them. Shoot them while the townspeople watch." He nodded toward the four men who had taken women. "Bind their hands, strip them naked, and give them to the women of the town. Then load up the pack animals fast. We must get away from here."

"It will be done," said Naran.

Chuluun leaped into his saddle and cantered away from the town.

* * *

Alone, Chuluun rode back the way he had come. At the highest stretch of the long slope, he walked his mount. He could hardly think. Instead, he saw and heard the events of the morning again and again in his mind. Ganzorig's final question returned to him: Would he be the last khan of a dead people?

At the top of the first slope, he turned to look back. A long column snaked out of Purity in the distance, the riders leading pack animals now laden with spoils. He hoped their share, along with their split of the herd, would be enough to give his tribe new life. Yet his real doubt was about himself as their khan.

He mounted up and reined away, anxious to find Tuya. A darkness was growing in the back of his mind, not in words but in a formless desperation. With each step his mount took, he understood that if Tuya and their baby had not survived labor, he would choose not to survive his return to the northern plains. He would lie down next to Tuya's unburied remains and take out the Colt .45. Without his beloved ray of light or the child she bore, the Second khan of the steppes would choose to end his future, but he would choose to end it by her side.

Night had fallen by the time Chuluun neared the wagons of the women. Lamps were burning inside and a big cookfire lit up the sides of the wagons. The riders who had remained to guard and escort the wagons reined up when they saw him approach. Apprehensive yet eager, he rode up to the camp at a walk.

When the women around the cookfire looked up at him with smiles and calls of welcome, relief flooded his being. He swung out of the saddle and ran to Tuya's wagon.

As he climbed inside, he found Tuya watching him from her bed. "Come see your son," she said quietly. "Bataar, meaning hero."

Filled with awe, Chuluun moved forward. Once again, he had a future.

*   *   *

Two evenings later, Chuluun sat in the wagon with Tuya at the next camp. Naran and the column had finally caught up with the wagons, which had started the long trek home on the first morning after Chuluun's return. Of the twelve women who had gone into labor, only four had survived with healthy babies. Three had died. Scouts from the rear of the column had reported no pursuit and messengers from the Americans relayed their success at taking a large herd.

Chuluun had told Tuya of the events in Purity.

Now the riders had pitched camp by the wagons, and the roar of their chatter reached Chuluun. A bonfire had been lit for warmth near Tuya's wagon. The voices of the riders were loud. Many arguments broke out, especially as they drank more kumiss and liquor looted from Purity while the evening deepened. The same comrades who had cheered his arrival, offered their kumiss, and slapped his back in hearty welcome before the raid now spoke in angry, uncertain tones among themselves.

Chuluun knew he had left the riders in confusion by shooting Ganzorig and ordering the execution of those who had followed him. Since leaving Purity, his thoughts had always come back to his own actions as the Free Tribe's leader. Ganzorig's question had become a curse: Would he be the last khan of a dead people?

"You must speak to them," said Tuya, as she sat propped against pillows in her bed. The baby was sleeping in her arms.

"And say what?" Chuluun asked wearily. "Let someone else be their khan. You and I will herd, hunt, and ride together. We will raise our child."

"The women who attend me have asked the riders many questions. They, too, told me their stories of the raid. They have great respect for the women riders, who say you ordered the columns perfectly in surrounding the town. If Ganzorig had not betrayed your trust, the raid would have gone as you planned."

"I killed the only friend I had."

"He was no friend. The women riders are more devoted to you than ever, because you protected the women of the town from those who grabbed them."

Chuluun shook his head, as though doing so would help him find his way.

"The women say the men don't know what to think. Some are angry because you shot Ganzorig and had your own men executed. Many had friends among them. Others say you had to do it. The riders don't know what to expect. They're fighting among themselves. These are the best warriors of the tribe, breaking into factions. If we go home like this, the tribe will split up. Then it will wither and die."

"Tribe," Chuluun said bitterly. "We're a bunch of escaped miners and nothing else."

"The riders have trained well. They are devoted to their people. They farm and they herd. And until the raid on Purity, their loyalty to you was unshakeable."

"Tribe," Chuluun repeated. "We have no society. We're a mob of fugitives trying to herd and plow. So what? We have no laws, no code to live by."

"Give us one," said Tuya.

He looked up sharply. "Let someone else."

Tuya shook her head. "Ganzorig could be inspiring, but he was too impulsive to trust. Naran earns trust, but he has no flair. They only have you."

"For what?" Chuluun demanded.

"For a khan."

"They are nothing! Just barbarians!"

"Instead of what?"

"Instead of a people who believe in something! A people who have a code to live by! People who believe in their own sworn word of honor. We must be as trustworthy as we are tough! Live or die, we have to keep our humanity—"

"Not me, you idiot!" Tuya screamed, pointing toward the crowd from within the enclosed wagon. "Tell them!"

Hot with fury, Chuluun yanked back the flap at the rear of the wagon. He snatched up the Winchester and leaped to the ground. Then he stormed to the bonfire, where two women who attended Tuya happened to pass in front of him, their shadows briefly large and misshapen against the dancing flames behind them.

As he advanced, he was aware that those who saw him first went silent and watched him in fascination and dread. The troops were all on the other side of the bonfire, built in a deep, circular pit. He stopped on his side of the fire, aware of the heat and light on his face.

Little by little, the roar of arguing and shouting grew quiet. The men and women watched him, quietly shifting into a large crescent shape on the other side of the bonfire, removed a respectful distance from the flames.

Chuluun studied those in the front whose faces, dels, and weapons were illuminated by the blaze just as he was. The cold breeze blew his hair back from his face and spread his long, broad del slightly behind him.

Everyone waited, neither moving nor speaking.

The big fire separated him from those he had to reach. Chuluun recalled, then, how the shadows of women passing between him and the bonfire a moment ago had been dark, misshapen and mysterious. He walked briskly to his left around the big bonfire, and saw that the lines of his people drew backward, away from him, as he came closer. Finally he stopped dead center before the flames, throwing a large, shifting shadow on those who stood directly in front of him.

"Who are we?" Chuluun shouted. "Are we barbarians?" He strode from one side of the fire to the other, not many steps, but in doing so he gave them a view of his shadow in profile and let his del swirl slightly as he moved. "Dover Mining and the other company slaves will always hate us! CoDo troops will always look down on us! We know that. It was the same in the mines of Dongbei and the same in the mines on Haven! We are nothing to the rich and powerful, and those who work for them. Shall we prove them right?"

He paused, catching his breath, and heard no one answer, not even a snide comment or angry shout.

"They believe we are nothing but predators! Like animals in the wild! Shall we prove them right?"

Chuluun moved to the center of the fire again. "Live or die, we will keep our humanity! I give you the First Law of the Code of Honor: We keep our word!"

"To our enemies?" A man called out from the crowd.

"To our enemies most of all!" Chuluun shouted back. "They will hate us and fear us—but the next time I give my word of honor, they will believe us. They'll believe!"

He could hear a growing hum of agreement, then, and calls of encouragement. "We will always keep our word! That's the First Law of the Code!"

"First Law!" Someone shouted.

"Word of honor! First Law!" Chuluun called out. "Word of honor!

First Law!"

The riders took up the chant: "Word of Honor, First Law!" He shouted the words and they answered back. While he strode before the fire, whirling in his del at each side, the chants grew louder and louder. Soon the voices were deafening, and changed to "Chuluun Khan! Chuluun Khan!"

Chuluun held up the Winchester and unloaded it before them. Then he smashed the antique wooden stock against a big rock, where it shattered. He threw the rest of it into the bonfire, in a sacrifice that was the final rejection of the man who had given it to him.

"Chuluun Khan! Chuluun Khan!" The crowd roared.

He had their trust again. Before the chants could fade, he whirled one more time and strode back around the bonfire to disappear into the shadows. He was Chuluun, the Second Khan of the Free Tribe of the Steppes.

*   *   *

When dawn broke through the long Haven night, Chuluun Khan took a position on his mount to one side of the route leading back to the Karakul Pass. Once through it, they would again turn east to the Girdle of God Mountains and their home in the Gobi Valley. In a long column, the riders, many of them leading strings of pack mounts, started their long day's march by passing him.

Stern and unmoving, Chuluun held his head high in the cold morning air, looking out over the heads of his riders as they passed. Even while he gazed aloof into the distance, he was aware that each rider, man or woman, looked at him as they rode by. Some gave a quick, furtive glance while others watched him openly. Though many seemed curious, others seemed to hope for the friendly camaraderie he had shared with the riders before the raid.

The column proceeded, but he refused to look at them or even acknowledge their presence.

Chuluun knew he commanded the loyalty of his riders once again. If the tribe survived, he would again share their campfires, exchange stories, and trade drinks with them on raids or wars of survival. With pride and humility, he would be their khan. He understood, however, that he would never again have a friend.

As the cold wind whipped tears from his eyes, his love for Tuya and Bataar warmed his heart.

MARCHING ON POLAND

By Leslie Fish

2057 A.D., Haven

The first hint of disaster came when Brodski, with Wilgar beside him, marched up to the gates of the Harmony enclave to give his usual lessons in Aikido and T'ai Chi, and found the gates barred fast.

"What's the matter?" he asked politely. "Don't the brethren want to continue lessons?"

The man at the gate had the decency to look ashamed. "The Reverend Castell has forbidden all such lessons," he said, adding: "I'm sorry."

Wilgar, who had been growing like a weed this past year, pulled himself up to his full gangling height and said: "Surely the reverend will want to see me."

The gateman, looking even more apologetic, explained: "No, Brother. He considers you…touched by the corruption of the wicked city and will not allow you within the precinct until further notice."

Wilgar gaped at him for long seconds, then backed away shaking his head.

Brodski asked carefully: "Is the Reverend in good health?"

The gateman bit his lip, but didn't answer.

That was all Brodski needed to know. "We won't trouble him, then," he said. "We'll return when the Reverend feels better." He turned and walked back the way he'd come, all but dragging Wilgar with him.

"I never thought he'd turn on me," Wilgar whispered, seeming to shrink by several inches.

Brodski gave him a thoughtful look. "Say, Wilgar, you never told me your last name."

"It's…Castell," the boy whispered, hunching his shoulders higher.

"Ah." *The old fool treats his own son like this? He never even taught his son to read?* Brodski marveled. "It's all right, Wilgar. You'll always have a home at Harp's."

"Yeah, I guess," said the boy, looking only a little less miserable.

Brodski patted Wilgar on the shoulder, thinking to himself that he needed to confer with Jane, Van Damm and Makhno again. If Castell was off on another of his Purity fits, it could ruin the fragile alliance between the Harmonies and the Alliance. That would be hard on Docktown, hard on the rest of Castell City and its burgeoning suburbs, but hardest of all on the Harmonies themselves.

*   *   *

The next warning of trouble to come arrived at the new dock with the *Queen Grainne*. Brodski noticed that the ship carried scars of damage, as if she'd had to fight a battle recently. He also noted that Van Damm was on the ship, along with Irish Himself, both of them looking exceedingly glum, and both of them came marching straight toward Harp's Sergeant as soon as the ship was moored. Brodski simply ushered the two of them into the storage room, set down a bottle and three glasses and let them speak first.

"Motherless spalpeens!" Himself snapped, even as he reached for his glass. "The Floatin' Beggars have turned into bluidy pirates, attackin' any ship that passes. Oh, we fought 'em off with little effort, but look how they scratched up the Queen! And think o' how they're ruinin' river-trade for any smaller ship."

"Between the *Queen*, the *Princess* and the *Black Bitch*, could we clean them out?" Brodski asked.

"We could," said Van Damm, "But that cleaning out, by itself, could give CoDominium the excuse it so badly wants. Can't you see the headlines: 'Castell Merchants Slaughter Innocent Fishermen'? We couldn't keep it quiet enough for them to miss it."

"I get the impression that CoDo is getting close to desperate," Brodski noted. "And I've got to wonder what's pushing them to grab Haven away from Castell so fast."

"A few powerful senators, the mining companies and BuReloc." Van Damm downed his drink in a single pull. "They want the shimmer stones, they want the minerals, and they want a dumping-ground for 'undesirables' from Earth. I get the impression that there's some manner of grand purge developing on Earth and CoDo doesn't want its plans delayed any longer."

"I could almost pity crazy old Castell," Brodski sighed. "If he wasn't likely to ruin the rest of us with him. But anyway, Vanny, why did you come upriver to see me?"

"Because I think I'll be needed here shortly." Van Damm poured himself another glassful. "Besides," he smiled briefly at Irish, "Hell's-a-Comin' is in good hands."

"Aye," Himself beamed, "That it is. Between the mines and the settlements, we can absorb twice the numbers we've got. What's the maximum CoDo could dump on us at any one time, eh? How much do those 'resettlement' ships hold?"

"Ten thousand, easily," Van Damm gloomed. "Less if they use the mining ships. Now that Kennicott and Reynolds have resolved their differences, they'll be happy to get more cheap labor. BuReloc will be happy to send it to them."

There was a long pause as everyone thought that over. "Another five thousand we can take," Himself murmured, "But ten is a bit much."

"And you know they won't be dumped near Hell's-A-Comin'," Brodski guessed. "They'll be dumped right here in Castell City, to make trouble for the Harmonies."

"With all three ships workin' hard and constantly, it'll take several T-weeks to move them down to Hell's-A-Comin' anyway," Himself finished. "Meanwhile, they'll be sittin' around in Castell City with no idea what ta do with themselves."

"I expect Reynolds, Dover and Anaconda will have shuttles waiting as soon as they hear the ship is approaching," Van Damm considered, "But the same problem applies."

"Castell City will be overrun," said Brodski. "The beadles won't be able to contain the robberies and assaults, and the Marines won't be much help either."

"Will you be safe?" Van Damm asked.

"Me? No problem," Brodski chuckled. "The Marines will cluster here, as always, and they'll protect their beloved watering hole. Heinrick's should be safe, too. It's the lesser shops and the clinic I'm worried about."

"P'int the Marines toward the clinic," Himself suggested. "The others… Aye, an' I'm sure I don't know. How's the Lady Jane farin'?"

"She's got the island well fortified, not that anyone's likely to go looking there, anyway. As far as CoDo or anyone else knows, the eastern river shore is uninhabited: nothing of interest out there." Brodski shrugged. "By the way, her settlers have done a fine job of domesticating the muskylopes. We've got ranchers and drovers out on the plains now and lots of meat and hides coming into the city."

"But I doubt if her settlements can absorb all those raw transportees, either," Van Damm sighed. "If Hell's-A-Comin' can't take them, we'll have to get them out to Reynolds', Dover's and Anaconda's camps as fast as possible. Even so, Castell City will become a hellhole no matter what we do."

"If we can just keep that pot from boiling over…"

"Had you heard? Kennicott Mining has given land grants to its various managers, so as to make them officially citizens of Haven. I do not like what this portends."

"Why are they willing to take the jobs?" Brodski asked.

"So that they can become the new rulers, the 'upright citizens' who will become the mayors and governors when CoDo takes over." Van Damm glowered at his glass. "The companies are setting up their own secondary ruling class—who will, of course, have the use of the CD Marines to keep their positions safe."

"Hmm." Brodski gave him a keen look. "Are you in any particular danger, Vanny?"

"Not so far. I was careful to have no further contact with Sanchez before he left; I did my best to let him think I died in the 'bombing'. Still, I do not doubt that the next ship will bring another CoDo agent, seeking trouble to stir. Best I be here, not in Hell's-A-Comin', when he arrives."

"Your old friend, Cole?" Brodski asked.

Van Damm shrugged. "If Cole made it back to Earth, I'm sure he got a not-so-gentle reaming. Besides, not enough time for a return trip to End-of-the Line, which is one of the nicer things they call Haven."

"So, what's ta be done?" Himself interjected. "We'll dig more caves, train more miners ta farm an' work the factories, see what we can do about absorbin' more transportees, but what else?"

Van Damm thought for a long moment. "All I can think of is to make more ships like the *Queen*, and arm them well. And… if you can do it quietly, kill as many of the pirates as you can."

*   *   *

The third warning came from Wilgar, who returned from a morning's rambling to beg Brodski for the loan of some trowels. Brodski, making a good guess, steered him into the storeroom. He noticed the boy's surprise at not seeing the radio there.

"I moved it to the…spare room," Brodski explained. "Three trowels are the most I can give you right now. Didn't Old Castell let you back into the enclave?"

"In, yes." Wilgar shrugged. "I just had to...make my own way out."

"I see."

Brodski opened a crate on a bottom shelf and pulled out three hand-trowels, recently made at Heinrick's shop. "How many are willing to come with you?"

"None!" The boy's face crumpled as he struggled with tears. "Papa had some kind of fit, and he's been getting crazier ever since. He doesn't want anyone leaving the enclave and he's even leaning on our farmers to come stay in the enclave. It's like he's trying to lock everybody up in a storm cellar, except there's no storm."

"There's one coming, but this isn't the way to deal with it." Brodski heaved a sigh, and handed over the trowels. "Wilgar, if you can, warn those outlying farmers to get clothes that don't look like Harmony robes, and tell them to set aside seed and tools they can carry quickly. When CoDo comes, they may have to get away from Castell in a hurry."

Wilgar looked up, eyes wide. "You think it'll get that bad?"

"It'll get bad, son." Brodski chewed his lip for a moment. "And, Wilgar, get hold of your grandpa's book."

"But I don't know where it is," replied Wilgar. "My Papa keeps it hidden."

"Find it and get that book to safety. You're going to need it."

"Me?" Wilgar whispered.

"You. You're the Last Castell and after the dust settles that will be worth something. You'll be needed then. Your grandpa was a smart man, and by rights his wisdom should descend to you."

"I...see." Wilgar thoughtfully stuffed the trowels in his robe and wandered out of the storeroom.

Brodski watched him go, then went to a stack of shelves by the wall and pulled on it. The stack swung forward, revealing a hidden doorway. Brodski went through it, pulling the shelf-disguised door shut behind him. He picked his way carefully down the narrow lightless passage until he came out in a wide underground room, lighted by a solar panel. A narrow pipe coming down from the ceiling brought in a steady breeze, the creak of the windmill far above, and two narrow cables. One cable snaked over to the solar panel; the other attached to the radio on a table directly under the pipe. Brodski pulled out a chair, sat down at the table and turned on the radio.

A moment's fiddling brought the sound of static and a woman's voice saying only: "Yes?"

"Jane," Brodski sighed into his microphone, "Old Castell's gone off the deep end, and there'll be no saving the Harmonies. He's trying to lock everybody up in the enclave and ignore the rest of the world."

"Damn," Jane sighed in return. "Well, the deal was good while it lasted. What'll happen to the rest of the city? It's as wide open and helpless as Poland was before the German troops, and the Russians, and everybody else."

"Next load of transportees will make it a hellhole, and our only hope is to move them out as fast as we can."

"Hmm. If your team can pick out a thousand good ones, we can settle them up here—but it'll have to be done quietly."

"A thousand for you, five thousand for Hell's-A-Comin', maybe another three thousand for the other companies... We just might make it. That still won't save the Harmonies."

"I guess nothing will." Jane paused for a long moment. "Can you save those outlying farms?"

"Maybe, if they'll listen to...my, uh, agent."

"We'll keep trading with them, then, but we may as well cutoff trade with the enclave. If Old Castell won't keep up his end of the bargain, there's no point keeping up ours."

"Keep goods coming into Docktown, though." Brodski paused to think. "Jane, is there any way we could start overland trade? Once the CoDominium takes over, you know they'll be watching the river."

"We're working on it." He could hear her smile through the radio. "Benny and Jeff have a design for a steam-powered truck. If Himself can start manufacturing them...."

"He'll need the tools to make the tools. How fast can you get him the specs?"

"I don't know. Maybe a few T-weeks, maybe more. How's he doing on the next ship?"

"He says he'll have it ready, crewed and armed by the time the shuttles arrive. Cross fingers."

"Fingers, toes and everything else. We're getting braced for the arrival here." Brodski automatically glanced upward. "We're doing everything we can, but it won't be pretty."

"I could almost feel sorry for Old Castell."

"So could I, if he hadn't brought it on himself."

* * *

The beginning of the end came when Sam-The-Ham Kilroy got the first message that the Kennicott ship was entering orbit above Haven. He relayed the word as fast as he could: to Janesfort, to Hell's-A-Comin', and to everyone he could think of in Castell City. After that he duly informed the company offices for Kennicott, Reynolds, Dover and Anaconda.

By the time the first shuttle landed at Splashdown Island, the *Black Bitch*, *Queen Grainne*, *Princess Maeve* and the new *Finn MacCool* were waiting just off the island to take on cargo and passengers. Just outside the last buildings of Castell City, passenger shuttles from the mining companies landed and lined up. Signs sprouted everywhere along Docktown, pointing to "Jobs And Housing Here." Smaller signs, marked with the hand-painted logo of the 26th CD Marines, pointed to "Starman's Inn", "Harp's Sergeant", "Heinrick's", and "Clinic".

Owen Van Damm, watching through binoculars from discreet concealment on top of the main warehouse, took careful notes. The first shuttle, naturally, unloaded a contingent of CoDo Marines. The *Black Bitch* and the *Princess Maeve* duly took them to the Old Dock and let them off near the sign pointing to Harp's Sergeant. The unloaded shuttle took off, and another promptly took its place.

The next shuttle unloaded a lot of large Marine-guarded crates.

Weaponry, Van Damm guessed, making a note. The *Queen Grainne* and *Finn MacCool* took them to the new Castell Dock, from which—Van Damm saw—they did not proceed to a warehouse but waited expectantly. Again, the shuttle took off and was quickly replaced.

Then came the transportees, shuttle after shuttle full of them. The riverboats hurried back and forth, loaded until they rode low in the water, but couldn't keep up with the demand. It was dim-dark before the last shuttle unloaded and left, and full-dark before the river boats deposited the last transportees on land. The shuttles from the mining companies filled early, pulled up their signs and departed. Himself, visible by torchlight, stood up on a stump and urged remaining transportees aboard the riverboats which then pulled out and headed down river toward Hell's-A-Comin. There were still thousands of transportees left milling about on the docks with no idea what to do or where to go.

By the light of his hand torch Van Damm stared bleakly at his notepad. Yes, as bad as he'd feared: a full ten thousand transportees, all dumped on Castell City. Maybe three thousand had gone off on the mining company shuttles. Maybe another thousand were headed for Hell's-A-Comin'. At top speed, the riverboats couldn't return for another two T-weeks; by then the abandoned transportees would have grown desperate and started making trouble.

Oh, and who was that strolling along the docks, studying the bewildered crowd and peering at the local fishing boats, as if he had plans for them. He's familiar....

Hell, it's Simon Shawley! One of BuIntel's Off-World Operation Officers. Shawley was sent out when things were getting dicey. If he was here, there were probably two or three other agents around.

Van Damm turned off his flashlight and flattened himself on the warehouse roof, swearing in three different languages. If Shawley was here, it could only mean that he no longer trusted his various agents to overthrow Castell and meant to do the job in person.

This is the end of the Harmonies.

And another ship would come, doubtless bringing more transportees, in six months.

...And they'll concentrate on Castell City.

For a long moment Van Damm seriously considered cutting out and running upriver to Janesfort, taking up his old homestead and being a farmer for the rest of his life. It took a long moment to banish the temptation and start considering what he could do to help Jane's alliance now and save what could be saved of Castell City.

2057 A.D., Cat's Eye Orbit

Maxwell Cole sighed when he heard his name called out over the space yacht's intercom. Throughout his thirty years of service in the CoDominium Bureau of Intelligence, Cole had visited over twenty different worlds, not counting Earth, Luna Base and Ceres; some multiple times. A few he'd enjoyed, like Tabletop, New Washington and Sparta; others he'd hated, like Folsom's World and Tanith. But even the worst of them were better than Haven, his own personal hellhole.

On the other hand, this was the first time he'd traveled by space yacht with luxury accommodations. *I could get used to this*, he decided. *It sure beats the hell out of that Kenny Co ore carrier I was forced to take on my previous visit.*

"Maxwell Cole please report to the penthouse," the intercom repeated.

Ah, the master calls, Cole thought. He had traveled aboard a lot of different space craft, but never one with a penthouse!

He punched a button, replying, "Tell Taxpayer Bronson I'm on my way." He put down his tumbler of Scotch and rose to his feet. His tunic and trousers were tolerably presentable, not that this was a royal audience. He was a BuIntel agent, not a Dover toady, but orders were orders. Wainwright had said to follow Bronson's orders, but "use your own discretion," so he knew he was going to be walking a tightrope over this assignment. If anything went wrong, he was the fall guy; the upside was that for once he had as many CoDo credits as he needed and military backup.

The space yacht's corridors were better appointed than the best New York hotels, not that he had much familiarity with them. Not a lowly and expendable feet-on-the-ground agent like himself. After that last little fracas they called the Janesfort War, he wasn't likely to come out of this situation with anything much more than his basic pension. Regardless, he'd have to do the job, otherwise he'd either be abandoned on Haven or forced to spend the rest of his life condemned to a Welfare Island back on Earth. Not much payback for thirty years of faithful service to his CoDo overlords.

Entering the penthouse, Cole was directed to a large office where Ehrenfeld Bronson sat behind a big nineteenth-century style partners' desk that did little to obscure his bulk. Bronson wasn't a fat man, just a big mesomorph, like a linebacker with an extra hundred pounds.

Cole pointed to the portal which displayed the blue ball of Haven with a wide brown and black girdle across the center.

"Ultima Thule, at last," he observed.

"Enough of your wisecracks, Cole." Bronson paused to shake his head. "I haven't enjoyed the last year myself. Couldn't they find a worldlet any farther away?"

Cole shook his head. "It's a good place to die."

Ehrenfeld sighed. "You just don't get it, Cole. You're in enough trouble as it is after your last screw-up. If your little revolt had gone off as intended, we'd both be in a better place."

Bronson was wrong, Cole did get it; he knew exactly just how deep he'd sunk into this particular septic tank. He also knew that getting out of it meant taking orders from this fathead, which was something he wasn't going to enjoy. On his last visit to Luna, Assistant Director Wainwright had made it very clear that he was to follow any and all orders of the Bronson scion. Cole's own due diligence had informed him that Ehrenfeld Bronson was in the same cesspool that he was, although at a much higher level; and, knowing just what it was that flows downhill, he knew exactly where he stood.

Thomas Ehrenfeld Bronson had suffered as well, having been cashiered from his cushy CEO position at Dover Mineral Development. He had been sent out to Haven to corner the shimmer stone market and regain the monopoly Dover had lost when some lucky miner discovered the shimmer stones on his own. It was do the job or be stranded on Haven for the next few decades for both of them.

He also knew about Bronson and DeSilva patronage and power. It was no coincidence that the CD cruiser, the *CDSN Invincible*, was scheduled to arrive in a few T-weeks with a battalion of CoDominium Marines. This time the Harmonies were doomed; there would be no rabbits popping out of this hat.

"Just to make things perfectly clear, Cole. This is a joint operation between Dover and Kennicott Metals. For once we're both united in our goal, which is to have Haven declared a CoDominium Protectorate."

"I'm well aware of your joint stand, sir," he replied. *Sure, both companies want to strip the moon of all its resources with the CD's permission and help. Nothing could be clearer, The Masters of the CoDominium have spoken. Who am I to stand in their way?*

"Well, you have about four T-weeks to provide the Marines with a token excuse to clean up Castell City and declare martial law. Is that clear?"

"Yes, sir," Cole answered. "The Harmonies are not the most sophisticated of opponents. This time we'll keep our activities centered on them rather than the farmers and outlying prospectors." *And you'd better hope I succeed, you fat frog. Or we'll both be stranded on this ice-ball for the rest of our lives. And, when it comes to corralling the Haven Shimmer Stone Cooperative and controlling the shimmer stone market, your are on your own, as per Asst. Director Wainwright's orders.*

ENOUGH ROPE

E R Stewart

2057 A.D., Haven

They came from gutters, from hovels and from broken homes. They came from the wrong side of the street and the wrong side of the tracks. They came from sleeping rough. They came hungry, angry and terrified, but they came. From Docktown, Cambiston, and even from Castell City proper they came to the meeting, having heard the whispers, the coded phrases. They came to see, and stayed to hear.

To an undeveloped segment of shore just south of Town Square, where bushes blocked easy access to higher ground, they came, and some helped dig foxholes and trenches amidst the bushes. They came because the son of the man who had led the first settlers to Haven had called them together, all the unwanted, neglected, feral children of Haven. Despite the difficulty of birthing, making each child a kind of miracle of survival, there were many such waifs. Most got by scrounging, stealing, or worse. The rest barely got by. If this preacher's son, this Wilgar Castell, could offer them some better-shuffled deal, then fine, they'd take it under advisement.

"You're all here because there's no other place to go," Wilgar said, his thirteen years of age carried in a tall, lanky frame with a grave face and laughing eyes. And that first time, they'd agreed with his logic, and they'd agreed to help him in his plans to face reality, to find out what was really going on with Haven, and maybe to figure out some way of dealing with matters his father had long since stopped seeing.

* * *

Several months later they dubbed themselves the Irregulars, after a group of street urchins used by Sherlock Holmes for low-level intelligence gathering and running errands. Wilgar Castell had read aloud to them occasionally, but never those dreary Harmony Concordances. He always read exciting stories, stories with elements that made sense to their lives, the way they lived. They learned from Wilgar, and he, in turn, learned from them.

* * *

Wilgar crept on hands and knees from the tunnel, leaving his parents, the Reverend Charles Castell and his wife Saral, sleeping soundly. Activity in the Harmony Compound at that hour consisted of a few bleary-eyed acolytes tending the farm animals or doing other quotidian chores.

Staying low, Wilgar dug up a pouch he'd stashed under a corner of a midden-heap, hurried to his secret exit, then ran away from the Compound, moving first west, then south. He followed a random route on which he decided moment-to-moment, now dashing over yard-fences, then ducking under wagons trundling by loaded with barrels of beer, now dodging barrows stacked high with sacks of foodstuffs from the outlying farms. He hurried, but kept his eyes open. His breathing, even in the thin, cold atmosphere of Haven, remained steady because he'd been born there and his body had acclimated well indeed.

His clothes, dark and nothing at all like a Harmony's usual robes, hid him in shadow and blurred him as he ran to new ones. When he had to run, he clutched the heavy pouch against his chest.

At the trenches he found most of his Irregulars already there. One, Butch, stood up and said, "All set, sir."

"Good. Report."

They told him of strangers. These mysterious souls had drifted during off-times, probably from Splashdown Island. One was definitely from a wealthy, influential family on Earth. Some spoke with off-world accents, and one had a distinctly Earthish accent. Old King Cole, one of the Irregulars called that one. "His name's Cole, I think, and he's always scowling, like he hates it here. He was here a few years ago, smuggling arms for Jomo's gang."

"Find out what he's up to now," Wilgar said.

There were other reports, too, concerning unrest among the miners, rumors of valuable ore-strikes made by lone prospectors in the Atlas Mountains, and even a report of a new strain of venereal disease currently turning various body parts of Haven's whores a purplish-blue. "No other symptom that they can see, so it's kind of getting popular." There was even heavy wagering on who'd come up with the first blue tongue.

Wilgar maintained his connections with all sorts, the better to gather more disparate data. Each datum added to an aggregate mosaic picture which bothered him more and more. His father's church, the Church of New Universal Harmony, owned the settlement charter for Haven, yet dominated the planet less and less: Wilgar wondered how everything fit.

After reports, the Irregulars divvied up the food from Wilgar's pouch, and as they ate perhaps their first decent meal in days, they chattered, sang, rough-housed and generally acted like one big extended family.

Wilgar slipped away when he was able, and made it back home before his father, never a heavy sleeper, awoke and began issuing that day's duties. For him, the world had become the Harmony Compound, but for his son, the world was a much bigger, much more complex, and much more interesting place. It was a place Wilgar intended to affect, and for the better.

*   *   *

"Oh, and get me some rope, would you?" the Reverend Charles Castell asked Wilgar.

"What for?" Wilgar asked. It would be easier to get the right type and length if he knew what purpose the rope was to serve.

His father, however, merely gave a glance to one side and said, "You'll see. I need lots. Any kind. Even odds-and-ends. Just keep bringing me rope."

To avoid sparking another fit of ranting, Wilgar simply agreed to the odd request. In fact, he actually had the Irregulars gathering up bits and pieces of discarded rope, until he saw what it was being used for, and by that time, many other developments occupied both Wilgar and his Irregulars, for Haven, having been settled, was about to be settled again, top to bottom.

2058 A.D., Castell City

"More," the Reverend Charles Castell demanded. He held out his fingers like claws. He motioned with urgency, causing the white robes to flap on his scrawny frame. His eyes stared, and drool escaped a corner of his mouth. His hair formed a white halo behind his shiny, bare face; the walk he'd taken through the fire pit over a decade ago had robbed him forever of his facial hair.

Kev Malcolm, Castell's First Deacon, handed over another tangle of rope, then sat back into a resigned, exhausted slouch. He watched the Reverend Castell work, now and then shaking his head in disbelief, disgust or despair. The lumpy thing on the altar grew slowly but steadily.

"It's got to be perfect," Castell said, crouching over a huge tangle of knots, at the core of which nestled a leather-clad, locked book of some sort. No one but perhaps Castell knew what the book contained.

Kev stood and stretched, joints crackling. "I must see to the others," he said, his tone quiet. When the Reverend failed to acknowledge him, Kev got down and crawled under the curtain, through the zigzag tunnel, and out into dim-day. He glanced at Cat's Eye, which seemed stuck on the sharp peaks of the Atlas Range. His breath puffed, a tiny cloud soon shredded by brisk wind. Kev flopped his cowl over his head, then trudged through the compound, seeking the Deacon's lodge.

Raucous laughter, reports of firecrackers, and other sounds of revelry lobbed over the palisade from Castell City. Such noise fell unwelcome into the Harmony compound, fell as discord into a chorus whose music had already been scattered by too many lone voices.

Cambiston, the section of town adjacent to Havenhold Lake, produced the most noise with the fewest excuses, being the place with the most bars, taverns, saloons, bordellos, flop-houses, gambling establishments, and liquor stores. Between Cambiston and the Harmony compound lay Castell City proper, where merchants cringed behind barred windows, citizens walked the streets only in armed groups, and where the town square once consecrated by the Reverend Castell in the first hours of Haven's settlement lay strewn with garbage and the droppings of foraging animals, some of them featherless bipeds too drunk to make it indoors.

With a raised hand, Kev greeted a group of children, led by three Harmony women. Each woman wore the new garments called Wrappings or Swadlings, to cover all but eyes and hands. Based upon a Muslim burnoose, the clothes stemmed not from Harmony disdain of the feminine sex, but from an impulse of self-defense against the rapacious, lawless males roaming the streets just outside the compound. A glimpse of female flesh often brought rape, even death to the luckless woman, and with no police to enforce restraint, it was best to cover and avoid.

Kev dropped to his knees and crawled into the Deacon's lodge. Smoke stung his eyes. He glanced up, then said, "Someone should clear that smoke-hole," and when no one moved, he snapped, "Is none of you worthy of such a job?"

Three Deacons rose from their pallets and shuffled to find a pole or ladder. The central fire-pit glowed red, and someone had propped a clownfruit against a kettle, to heat both near the embers. Nose-less, the clownfruit had split, and its juices sizzled, giving off a metallic smell.

In one of the study carrels, Kev found Wilgar, nose to a book. From Garner "Bill" had come William Garner, hence Wilgar, a heritage. The boy's dark complexion, flashing eyes, and winning smile echoed his lineage, for as the Reverend Charles Castell's son, thirteen-year-old Wilgar had inherited not only his mother's and father's genes, but those of Harmony-founder Garner "Bill" Castell, and his mestizo wife, as well. The mixture had produced a boy so handsome he was almost pretty, and so charismatic that he could charm his way out of virtually any punishment.

"Writings?" Kev asked, sitting down beside the boy.

Wilgar grinned. "More like readings," he quipped. He watched

Kev's face intently, then shared the laugh the man granted him. After, he asked, "How's Dad?"

Kev glanced at the boy perhaps a bit too sharply. No one impugned the Reverend Castell's health or mental state, not aloud and certainly not to the First Deacon. "He's fine, but very busy."

The boy looked steadily at Kev, saying nothing. He shut his book, then shrugged. "The Concordance should be updated, you know," he said. "It only covers the things my father said in the first year or so. Has he said nothing important or noteworthy since?"

Kev shook his head, a faint grin as good as saying, "And only thirteen."

He said, "I'll appoint a scribe, and have each Harmony submit any wisdom which might have particularly impressed—"

"I could do it." A child's eagerness made the boy bounce. A man's sober assessment of a bleak future made the boy's gaze level and deadly serious; he wanted a part of the grand venture his grandfather had begun.

"You certainly could," Kev said. He stood and slid the book back in its place on the carrell's shelf. "Except that you've got more important things to do. And maybe we should start right now. Feel like doing some body-work, to balance the mind-work?"

"Harmony is balance," the boy said.

Some tiny element in Wilgar's tone caused Kev to frown slightly, but he shrugged off any discomfort and walked after the boy, who had already bounded onto the low wall surrounding the fire pit and who was now walking along with his arms out. Kev opened his mouth to scold, then smiled, noticing how rock steady the boy walked on the narrow wall.

* * *

Max Cole cursed, then kicked. The table toppled, spilling the ore samples all over the shack's loose board floor. "I'm too damned old for this," he said, glaring at the other man, daring him to contradict. "When you tell me you can do something, you'd better be able to follow through, or so help me, I'll kill you. That Janesfort uprising was a debacle, a criminal misadventure. As a rebellion it fizzled, damn you, and now here I am two years later back on this stinking planet facing the same kind of incompetence that almost lost me my fucking retirement—"

"Please, sir," the merchant said, raising his palms to placate this off-world hothead. "It's the best I could do at such short notice, and none better can be had—"

"Do you expect me to pay for this, this mess?" Cole waved a hand at the scattered chunks of rock, clumps of dirt. He then braced himself by placing a hand against a wall. Cole still had transit-pallor and his movements reflected years on ships to and from Earth; he'd only been on Haven little more than the week.

Cole had previously been on Haven two years earlier, delivering arms and otherwise fomenting revolt. He'd gone back to Earth thinking he'd stirred up enough trouble to enable the CoDominium to take possession of Haven, as per his instructions. A few months after Earthfall, however, he'd been given a choice: 'Go back and do it right, or fend for yourself on the streets without your pension.'

The Haven operation had wasted four years of his life thus far and this would be, he promised himself, come hell or high water, his last assignment. At the start, he'd had only six years of service left. That meant spending any more than a year on Haven this time around would end up cutting into his retirement time, and starting one's retirement with a series of Alderson jumps and long months aboard a cramped, stinking cargo vessel held no appeal at all. Thus, impatience dominated his dealings with semi-competent underlings.

The most recent of which now stooped, snatched at an ore sample a few times before snagging it. A huge belly interfered, and he puffed as he straightened and held out the sample for inspection. "You see the glitter in this one? Harmonies love that—"

"You speak of them as if they're simple-minded abo buffoons," Cole said. "It's exactly that attitude which threatens to rouse them into open rebellion: I'm here on Charles Castell's behalf, and I'm telling you, no one knows better than he the need for hammering out a new way of doing business."

"Come off it," the merchant said. He scratched his broken-veined nose, the many rings on his sausage fingers glittering, reflecting the lantern's yellow glow into his baleful eyes. "Harmonies can't get tough, it's not in them. And as for business, we do all right."

"You do lousy. Keep the boycott in mind if you think the Harmonies have no power. They can stop the flow of food."

"Sure, and they can wake up dead, too, if push comes to shove. You tell Castell if he wants to go poking into what the miners at Hell's-A-Comin' dig out of the ground, then maybe he should start digging himself. Dig his own grave is what he'll do."

Cole turned away and marched off as if in a huff, but as he left the shack and splashed through the puddles of Cambiston a glint of glee showed in his eyes, for a moment. He paused to admire a brawl as it spilled from a saloon, then waded through the losers and marched up the slight hill, toward the Harmony compound.

*   *   *

"A visitor?" Kev asked, letting go of Wilgar's hand. At once the boy capered across the compound and shimmied up a brace-pole onto the walkway that ran around the inside of the palisade, which he proceeded to do, also. Glancing back to the acolyte who'd accosted him, Kev shook his head at the boy's energy, then said, "Someone from town?"

"No, First Deacon Malcolm, an off-worlder. He says he represents a contingent of miners from Hel— I mean, uh, Kennecott's Vale."

Kev dismissed the youth, who walked off with relief showing in every line and motion of his body. Dealing with the Reverend Charles Castell's right-hand man apparently required a bit of nerve, at least for the new true believers.

Another glance at Wilgar showed the boy happily battling invisible pirates or other imaginary stormers of the palisade. Kev grinned, but if Wilgar's father had witnessed the obviously-violent game, there would have been penance to be sung for a week. Although not encouraged, such games among children not yet fully indoctrinated as Harmonies served as vents for natural tendencies and, as Kev and a few others thought, might even come in handy later, if actual training in warrior's arts became necessary.

"If ever those walls come down," Kev muttered, walking toward the rickety city-gate, where the sharp tips of the poles which made up the palisade were reinforced with clumps of ugly barbed wire scavenged from farms outside the Harmony influence.

Recently, using small computers and data-chips for which he'd traded food-stuffs not exactly his to trade, Kev had been researching the Shao-Lin and other temples, monasteries, and the like, where men of peace had been forced first to take refuge behind walls, then to learn arts of self-defense and re-directed force, in order to survive in relative peace.

A man slender and tight, with hair cut very short and showing a little gray, with eyes glinting like chips of obsidian, smiled and extended both hands, palms upward. "Peace is mine to offer," he said, voice resonant, pleasant and almost cultured.

Kev replied, "Seek Harmony in all things. How may I join your song?"

"My name is Colin Maxwell, and as you no doubt see quite plainly, I'm lately of Earth."

"We no longer accept stray notes," Kev said, regret in his tone, apology beginning on his features.

Cole smiled and shook his head, the odd combination of expression and gesture giving him, for an instant, a look of innocence.

That look clashed so discordantly with what one usually saw that Kev's brows rose slightly, and his eyes narrowed.

"You misunderstand me," Cole said. "I've been sent here by some of the miners of Hell's-A-Comin', to speak with the Reverend Charles Castell on matters of mutual interest and importance."

"I'm sorry, the Reverend Castell is meditating, seeking harmony with the universe."

"As should we all. But should we not begin by seeking local harmony?" And Cole smiled even wider, all the while staring into Kev Malcolm's eyes.

Without a further word, Kev shut the gate and signaled with a raised hand. At once acolytes appeared, soiled from chores. "Keep an eye on Wilgar, please," Kev told them. "And find a better lock for this gate."

He led the man who'd given him the name Colin Maxwell across the compound, noting that the man's eyes never remained still, but sopped up every sight as if memorizing things meant daily survival. The structures past which they walked mostly rose only to their waists, being semiburied for strength, warmth, and durability. Barns and pens and cribs and feeding troughs stood higher, their floors being shallower.

A group of Harmonies, of both sexes and a wide age range, struggled to run pigs and sheep through a trench full of foul smelling dip of some sort. "From tree-sap, it protects like clothing against cold, radiation, and other Haven hazards," Kev said, when the stranger paused to watch a moment. Kev's voice held a note of begrudged generosity, as if he'd just given away a minor trade secret. Given the demand for succulent Harmony-grown food, perhaps he had.

Kev stopped at his own place, its stone roof glinting with ice from condensation.

"Please," Kev said, gesturing at the flagstone ramp leading down to the zigzag tunnel entrance to the home. When the stranger looked puzzled, Kev dropped to his knees and entered first, to demonstrate.

"Bren, we have an off-world guest," he said to his wife, who nodded and began preparing Hecate tea at the tiny hearth. Her body moved within the robes like sticks, and her face, although younger than Kev's, held many wrinkles and worry lines. Her hair held gray and white streaks and her eyes, when not directly animated by conversation, waned dull. She stirred the tea listlessly as it began boiling.

Kev sat on a pile of muskylope hide, then gestured to another opposite him, where the stranger sat.

"Warm," Cole said, needlessly rubbing his hands. "These places remind me of the mines, they protect against weather."

The man spoke like a book of foreign phrases, Kev thought. He waited until the tea was served, and watched as the man took his first taste.

"Pine-needle tea? No, there's something, I don't know, like cloves or cinnamon or something."

"Hecate tea," Kev said. "A Haven plant, its leaves uncurl only to the light of Hecate, another of Cat's Eye's satellites."

"Of course. Delicious." The man leaned forward, holding his cup of tea in both hands. The plain clay cup, glazed black, warmed his hands even more than rubbing, Kev knew. Already cold weather habits had begun in the man, but Kev certainly didn't believe any tales of mines.

The man said, "The miners want an alliance. They remember the food boycott, and know how effective Harmony help can be."

"Peace is ours to offer," Kev said. "Your words ring with the discord of battle."

"A just cause, believe me," Cole said. "Where is the Reverend Castell?"

"As I said, meditating. He must not be disturbed."

"I see." The man looked up at Kev. "And you are authorized to speak for him, am I right? You're the First Deacon, Kev Malcolm, aren't you? And you've been putting out feelers, trying to create a better form of trade between the compound and Castell City."

Kev held his tongue for a few moments. The man knew much, perhaps more than reasonably possible for a newlie. Kev caught and ignored a look of panic from Bren, who moved quietly through curtains into another room, leaving them to business.

Cole said, "It's nothing violent or in any way harmful or, uh, discordant. The miners want places to put aside some of their ores, that's all. They need secure places, and the only property left more or less alone on this planet are the Harmony farms and compounds."

Kev raised a hand. He took a deep breath and closed his eyes for a moment, seeking harmony, seeking larger chorus. He said, eyes still shut, "Ores mined belong not to miners, but to their employers, Kennicott and others."

"True, but it's in the interest of the entire planet to help preserve the ore. You see, much of it never reaches its rightful owners. Much of it is pirated. And I've been sent here to, well, engineer the capture of those pirates, to stop the intercessions of our lawful trade. And I was instructed by Thomas Erhenfeld Bronson himself to include the Harmonies in any plans."

"You are an agent of secrecy." Kev said this as both quotation and statement, then added, "Or of chaos."

"Nothing but peaceful help is required, First Deacon Malcolm. If you agree, simply spread the word that Harmonies are to, what would you call it, harmonize with the few miners who might contact them. All your people need do is accept receipt of a percentage of the ores normally shipped down the Xanadu River and taken off-world by splashship. We're keeping aside this percentage because it off-sets the ores stolen by the pirates and that means, once we capture them, we'll be able to resume full trade and make up back-log all the quicker. Everyone benefits, by the way; in honor of your help, contributions to Harmony coffers would increase, I am told, amazingly."

"What's the real game?" Kev asked. His well-modulated Harmony tone slid away, revealing a harder, harsher voice.

Surprised, Cole sat back and made a show of taking a twist of tobacco from his pocket and chewing it thoughtfully before answering. "Can't tell you," he said, his own speech automatically becoming terse.

"Render unto Caesar," Kev muttered. Louder he said, "You mentioned a Bronson."

"Thomas Erhenfeld Bronson, yes. He's on Tanith, I believe. Grand tour and all that. He's one of the family gophers, a scion but he's going for more than they realize, I think. And the man has skills and guts to match his ambition, if I'm any judge. Met him a few times."

"And now you work for him."

"Tangentially, perhaps. In point of fact, so do you, if you want to put things in those terms."

Kev grimaced. "Would he..." His voice trailed off, he sought for words this time, not harmony. They came. "Would he become aware, specifically, of the Harmony role in such matters?"

"If you want him to, he'll know your name as well as he knows mine," Cole said, coughing, then spitting tobacco juice into the fire. He ignored Kev's look of distaste and spat again, then said, "Offers to play with the big boys don't come very often. Repeat offers are rarer still."

Kev nodded, then stood. "How soon must you know?"

"As soon as possible, First Deacon," Cole said. "And I'd like a word with the Reverend, if he's—"

"I don't think that'll be possible." He placed a hand on the stranger's shoulder. "Or necessary," he added, as they sank to their knees to crawl back outside.

"Ah," Cole said, standing and refastening his collar and cuffs. He looked once more at the Harmonies dipping the young animals. "I see." He smiled once more at Kev, then shook the startled Harmony Deacon's hand.

"Have you a place to stay?" Kev asked. He glanced toward the acolyte's lodge, where another pallet could always be found.

"Many," Cole said, winking. "Alas, a secret agent is a busy man."

Kev neither smiled nor otherwise acknowledged the jest. He walked him to the city gate and discovered a padlock, then signaled for an acolyte to open it. As Cole trudged back into Castell City, Kev asked, "Where's Wilgar?"

"He went into your house, just after you and your guest," the acolyte answered. "Didn't you see him?"

Kev said nothing, but he was thinking that the real question was whether or not Wilgar had seen or heard, the conversation which had just ended. Not for the first time had the child's precocity created a potential problem. On instinct, Kev turned his steps toward the Reverend Castell's house, hoping he'd find him still alone with his Gordian knots and obsessions.

Instead, he found the Reverend talking animatedly with his long-dead father, or so it seemed. And there, in the corner, taking it all in, sat Wilgar, a half-smile on his lips, eyes staring in fascination.

*   *   *

As he walked away from his first encounter with the Haven Harmonies, Cole laughed again, this time needing no cough to cover his delight at having so easily found the First Deacon's apparent weak spot. So the young man had political ambitions, did he? All the better.

He walked past entreaties from destitute drunks and brazen whores, ignored threats from bullies, and made it through Cambiston into Docktown proper before the two miners caught up with him.

Decking shifted underfoot. Cole paused, then shoved an elbow back and up. It connected with a man's chin, dropped quickly to guard the throat. The man staggered back, while his companion lunged forward, onto Cole's left arm.

Cole went with the inertia, falling and curling into a ball. The miner rolled over him and off the dock. The splash and subsequent thrashing gave Cole a grin.

He rose and glanced at the other opponent. "Well?" he asked.

"You're the one," the guy said, spitting blood. He stuck out a hand. "I'm Forbs. Strippers."

"Make bigger holes," Cole said, completing the contact code. "Why didn't you assholes say something?"

"Gotta have some kind of fun," Forbs said. He walked over to the dock's edge and glanced down. "Hey Jenks, it ain't new-Eye yet, how come you're taking a bath?"

Cole let the two laugh, then punched Forbs in the kidney and grabbed the back of his collar. "Your friend's going to have a bathing partner in about half a second if you don't start telling me things I want to know."

"What, what?" The miner waved his arms as the tips of his toes danced on the edge of the dock.

"Guy could freeze to death," Cole said. "How come you missed the rendezvous?"

"Couldn't help it. Aw, come on, please?"

Cole backed the man away from the edge, mostly to give his own arm a rest. He trained his taser at the man's neck and said, "How much help can I get on short notice?"

"Depends on for what," the miner Forbs said. He stood sullen, shoulders hunched.

Cole explained as much of his plan as Forbs needed to know, then said, "Get him out of the water and into a bar, let him dry off. I'll expect you at the next rendezvous on time, and if you're not, you'd better be dead. That's the only excuse I can tolerate right now."

"We'll be there," Forbs said, grunting as his sopping companion used his arm as a ladder rung.

Cole, meanwhile, walked on. He passed along a dock, then gave a password and was permitted onto the deck of a small houseboat. He walked across it, over the gunwale, onto the deck of the next boat, and so on, until he stood far offshore. A floating village of houseboats housed many of Cambiston's and Docktown's dregs, not to mention refugees and refuse from Castell City proper. Living catch-as-catch-can lives, most of the floating folks crouched ever-ready to snatch, to grab. All Cole had to do was offer them profit of one kind or another, and this he did.

Using promises, he talked a rat's nest of tide-born scum into becoming rag-tag pirates, at least for a time. "And remember," Cole kept saying. "Miners aren't to be harmed unless absolutely necessary."

The boat-people started the hours-long task of unlashing each boat from adjacent vessels. Slowly, from the outer edges, the boat-village dispersed, some drifting down the Xanadu and Alf Rivers, others pulling or motoring up the Jordan.

Cole stepped boat-to-boat ashore. He then went on to his next task, pausing only to grab a quick bowl of heartfruit chili, washed down with foamy, yeasty beer.

* * *

"He speaks with spirits," Wilgar said, gazing up at Kev's face as Bren placed another blanket over the boy.

Kev neither nodded nor shook his head. His face showed only exhaustion. "Sleep now, and we'll seek harmony in such matters later." The boy smiled and closed his eyes, and soon Bren and Kev retired to their room. As he lay down, Kev sighed. Bren reached over and touched him, but he rolled away. She sighed.

A clamor at their door snapped Kev to his feet. He raced through the house, which was illuminated by only a few lamps, well-trimmed wicks turned low. The fire pit smoldered, coals glowing beneath a layer of ash.

On his knees, Kev moved into the tunnel and knocked down the thigh-thick chunk of wood which braced the door, itself several fingers thick and reinforced with costly black iron.

The Reverend Castell thrust his face at Kev and said, "We must consult at once."

Kev nodded, then followed the Reverend Castell from his house. He shivered at once. He walked barefoot through a thin layer of snow to the Castell house. Crawling back to warmth soothed Kev, and he stretched out on a pallet of muskylope hides. "What's wrong?" he asked.

The Reverend Castell, his white robes glowing almost as brightly as the white streaks in his long hair in the fire pits crackling light, said, "So soon my song unravels."

"But we sing harmony in more numbers than ev—"

"We are few," Castell, spat. "We huddle, oppressed as never on Earth. We cower as CoDo Marines march by like strutting conquerors, we quail from strip-miners who rape this planet worse than ever they raped old Earth. Peace is ours to offer, but no one wants peace, and yes, yes, we seek harmony in all things, but must we seek to join a song of utter discord? And now I learn that secret plans are afoot, conspiracies perhaps in the midst of our own communal symphony. Shall this Haven, our home, be lost to us, even before my son can take my place? Will my son have a place to take? Is Harmony at an end?"

Kev sat with gaze lowered. He waited, and when the silence grew past the rhetorical, said, "Harmony is more than a legacy, and Haven more than a refuge for us. There are many new forces on Haven, some of them less evident than others. Some of them cannot be met by your son, no matter his natural state of grace."

Glancing up at the older man, he rubbed his hands. "*Your new role is protector of the Harmonies,* you said to me. It seems ages ago. Two Beads for every acolyte, and even that wasn't enough. We cut poles, built the palisade. We strive to remain self-sufficient." Here Kev frowned, his hands moving against volition to the secular, city-minted coins in his pocket; money, too, was coming to Haven.

After swallowing hard, Kev continued, still not looking at the Reverend Castell. "You said, 'Our church needs a buffer, and the Deaks and Beads shall provide it.' You told me, 'Deaks decide strategy, making sure they harmonize, while Beads deploy tactics, to guarantee compliance among Chosen and Pledged both.' And so I've done, but Reverend, we must change, or—"

"Change what? Our song? Our search for Universal Harmony?"

"Never those," Kev said, voice constricted. He took a breath, and for the first time dared look the older man in the eye. "It's exactly that search which dictates compromise. What you've characterized as conspiracy is, in fact, simple negotiation. Even as your father did, back on Earth, I'm seeking to render under Caesar that which is his, so that we may retain what is ours." Kev opened his mouth to say more, then closed his eyes and sighed and shut his mouth. He slumped, bone tired.

The Reverend Castell walked to the altar, hidden now by the man-sized tangle of knots suspended between the walls on single ropes. He touched the thing, and his prophet's scorn softened to an expression of indulgence. "You've always carried the taint of a warrior," he said. "You do, rather than simply be."

Kev hissed, impatient. "Simply being doesn't help. We're not trees. And remember what happens to every forest man encounters."

The Reverend Castell ran his hands all over the clot of knots. He leaned down and pressed a cheek to it. He muttered something, then hummed one of the many tunes recorded in the Writings. His movements became slow, languorous.

Kev blushed and looked away. He said, "What have you heard? And from whom?"

"My own son, for one," the Reverend Castell said, rising to stand straight and glaring. He took on much of his old charisma in such moments of lucidity. "Secret agents," he said. "Plans."

"We might be of service to—"

"Of service?" Scorn twisted the words like over-heated metal. Charles Castell openly mocked the idea by repeating, "Service?" He slapped his hands together so hard that Kev winced. "Are we mercenaries, then? Do we seek Harmony through the slavery of service?"

Kev's wince tightened. His fists clenched. He scrunched down, as if resisting a physical force. "I'd hoped you'd lead us," he said. "I'd hoped you'd visit those Chosen living beyond our walls. I'd wanted you to walk with me on my next rounds."

"Do you see?" Charles Castell wailed, gazing upward.

Kev's flesh rippled, and he stood as the Reverend Castell continued staring upward, through the smoke-hole, as if he saw something up there, or someone.

"Father," Kev muttered, backing away. He dropped to his knees as the older man began howling semi-coherent laments and curses upward, as if shrieking his betrayal to heaven and beyond, to the very heart of Universal Harmony itself. He shouted as if he wished to shatter the silence at the heart of the note that swells to fill each song; Kev fled, scrambling on hands and knees through the zigzag tunnel, out into the cold.

Only when Bren complained, as he snuggled against her in their warm pallet-bed, did he realize how near-frozen his feet had become.

*   *   *

"No rules," Alwyn Meany said, swiping beer froth from his scraggly mustache and belching with immense satisfaction, proud as a boy. "Shit, Cole, Haven ain't got no whatcha-call Ecology. No damn tree-hugging leaf-lovers. Hell, on Haven a man can just plain dig. Dig right down a pit fit for the devil himself."

"Hence Hell's-A-Comin', I suppose," Cole said, lifting the cloudy yellow wine to his lips, sniffing, then placing the stuff untasted back on the table. He looked at the bartender and snapped his fingers, then held an actual Earth-note aloft. Several sets of feral eyes gazed at the cash, but only the barkeep moved for it. "Take this away and bring me the best whiskey in the house," he said.

When it came, he sniffed it, then shoved it across to Mister Meany, whose facial tattoos stood out much better when flushed with drink.

Slamming down the double shot of rot-gut maize-bourbon, Meany said, "Look," then paused to squeeze water from his eyes and let a shudder shake, rattle and roll through his flab. "Jesus with mayonnaise," he said, "Hold the fucking onions."

Finally able to relate to a wider reality than that found inside a glass, Meany said, "Call me Wyn, everyone does. Call me Al, I'll bust your chops and split your ass, and y'wanna know why? 'Cause my daddy's name was Al, and I killed him when I was fifteen and got just plumb sick of being a whippin' boy, know what I'm saying?"

"Sure do, Wyn," Cole said. He leaned forward and lowered his voice. "So how about it? Can you fix me up with some fireworks?"

"Y'gotta understand," Wyn Meany said. "They keep closer watch on their bangers than a British poufter, but there are times when not every charge in the blasting pattern goes off. Det caps shake loose, wires break, who can tell? Dangerous as jumpin' a puddy-tat, but I know guys who'll grab anything for a buck."

"Money's no problem," Cole said. His back rested against the tavern's wall, just under a crude portrait of sex Haven miner style. The artist had used blue chalk as a medium, and had incorporated several holes and gashes from various fights. Collectors the worlds over might have bid small fortunes to own such genuine, heart-felt folk art, but not if they had to come to the source to get it. Cole flexed his shoulders and kept one hand near a weapon at all times. "In fact, money's the whole point," he added.

Wyn Meany slobbered, wiped most of it off on the back of a hand still dirty from his work unloading Kennicott barges, and said, "So when you want the big kaboom?"

"Any time you can arrange it. Take out the tipple or something, tear up some tracks, that kind of thing. It's got to do damage, though."

"Oh, don't you worry. Doing damage is second nature." He slurped from his empty glass, then slammed it down and bellowed. When a jumpy waiter scampered over to fill the glass, Meany laughed. "What I don't get is how you're going to hang all this on them pussy Harmonies. I mean, hell, everyone knows those folks don't do nothin' to nobody."

"That's the beauty," Cole said. "It's not them doing it, it's the explosives. Just a harmonious chemical reaction."

"I'll be scrogged sideways on a hand-car," Meany said, draining his glass again. "Them philosopher types can explain anything."

"Can't we, though," Cole muttered, grinning on the inside as he tossed down a few more bills and strode from the tavern.

* * *

Wilgar's eyes glittered. "But why do we even want trade? Won't valuables bring exploitation?"

Kev slowed his gait and glanced down at his leader's son. In a hushed voice, he said, "Speak gently of such things."

Dashing around Kev, Wilgar jostled a pair of CoDo Marines. The streets saw such pairs often, but never in force. Only a token company or so were stationed at Castell City, and rumors had it there might be camps or bivouacs in the countryside, but in a city of ten to twelve thousand no one added them up to any kind of official CoDominium presence. If anything, the two-hundred-odd soldiers acted like supervisors, looking after CoDo interests and often sloughing off rougher military disciplines. At least, that's what Haveners had observed; it could all be subterfuge, considering the source.

Glaring, the older Marine walked on, but his younger companion snarled and said, "Kid, come here."

Kev tried to herd Wilgar forward, but the child's curiosity had been piqued: Also, he feared exactly nothing, that Kev had ever seen. "What's up, general?"

"He's a Sergeant," Kev said, adding, "An aspect of respect is the ability to know another's lot in life."

The young Sergeant caught only the word respect, and said, "you'd do well to listen to your father, insolent whelp."

"Insolent whelp?" Wilgar mocked, laughing in a high contralto and bounding back and forth, toward and away from the Marine. "What kind of language is that?" Several street kids gathered, and other, surlier ragfolk, too, at the sound of mockery coming from so small a Harmony.

Kev scratched his forehead with one hand clenched in a fist, thus giving the signal for Beads to gather closer. Some of the ragged folk elbowed in, as if to get a better look at the beating which everyone knew was brewing; Beadles, as first-circle Harmony pledges, could still use violence when necessary, and be absolved. Most knew a pidgin martial art mix as individual, and effective, as each could make it.

"Where are your Deacons?" the older Marine asked, from a distance of several strides. He showed no inclination to actually do anything more than ask questions. He shivered in the light fall of snow, his breath scudding from him in white wisps. His uniform looked new.

Kev snatched Wilgar's arm. "His discord was minor, and an accident. Peace is ours to offer, Sergeant. We mean no harm." When Wilgar struggled, Kev gave him a gentle shake, and the boy settled.

With a nod, the Sergeant walked on, joining his companion with a burst of complaint about scruffy poor-mouthing god-chasers. The crowd dispersed, with it the Beadles, who faded into the background to keep watch and do what they could to protect full-fledged Harmonies.

"Would you have us killed?" Kev asked Wilgar, who shook his head but made no answer. They walked on, and entered a shop selling such delicacies as oranges, bananas, and coffee. Coming in from the cold, their noses gradually opened to the fragrances. Their mouths watered.

Tropical products cost several times the going rate on Haven, and no one's greenhouses had yet managed to produce adequate substitutes in the tough, thin local soil. Photovoltaic energy remained too erratic in Haven's general dimness to allow proper, even heating and insulation had to be improvised, as nothing high-tech had yet been dropped or made available to the general population. On a backwater planet like Haven, making do usually meant doing without.

Kev waited, hands folded across his chest and head bowed, until the shop's proprietor, a Bosnian woman with every other tooth missing, finished serving a Kennicott miner's apprentice all of eleven years old.

"They'll have him walking ledges and setting primers before long," she said as she watched the boy leave the shop. Her battered face, although locked in sadness, somehow conveyed pity of a rough sort.

Wilgar, thirteen, also watched the other boy. In his expression curiosity and empathy mingled with a touch of envy.

"These," Kev said, handing the woman a list prepared by the acolytes and approved by Bren. Pregnant women need nourishment, and growing children, too. Expense could not be counted against the costs of neglect, especially on an unforgiving world like Haven.

As the woman gathered the meager provisions, Kev tugged the sack from his robes. It dangled on a thong around his neck and held Kennicott scrip, CD military scrip, coins from several worlds, one Earth dollar, and even some Haven barter-chips, most made of odd metals or quartz found in trace amounts here and there by displaced engineers and geologists and such forced to become hardscrabble farmers.

Miners bought at company stores; all that cash stayed in a closed loop. For anyone not a company employee, however, there was no such thing as discretionary or disposable income. In the *ad hominem* black market system prevailing then, Haven's supply of money, limited at best, sufficed only to maintain a few high officers and other semi-legitimate officials in relative luxury. Kev sorted his purchasing power carefully.

"Pre-CoDo *Moskva, da*," several forced immigrants commented, remembering long lines, scarce goods, atrocious quality, and free-floating currencies of so many kinds no one ever actually mastered the totality of the city's commerce. Now they had a whole world like that and it neither surprised nor depressed them too much; they'd bottomed out long ago. And the CoDominium linking Russian and American governments had proved to be one more pyramid scheme for enriching the snobbish few at the top. Kev's bizarre, mixed bag of buying-power had no fixed value, no relative rate of exchange, and no fixed amount of work or man-hours behind it.

Taking a breath, Kev gazed down on the bundle the woman made of his purchases, then held out his sack. She rummaged, chewing her upper, then her lower lip, as if they itched. Kev closed his eyes and murmured, "Seek harmony in all things," as a prayer; buying on Haven was a matter of faith as much as a matter of free, unrestricted, unstructured trade.

He accepted his sack, considerably lightened, without examining it. Replacing it, he took hold of Wilgar's hand. The boy's nose pressed up against a jar of peppermint sticks and when the woman noticed, she opened it and presented him with one.

"All this place needs is a pickle jar and a pot-belly stove with old guys playing checkers," Kev said as he walked out. "Frontiers must always echo each other."

"Is that a wisdom?" Wilgar asked, peppermint stick sticking out of his mouth as if it were a cigar. A wagon rumbled by, its muskylope hitched by means of frayed hemp rope. Three women, stark naked, danced in a window, beckoning lewdly to passersby.

Unable to tell if the question mocked him or not, Kev merely said, "Don't step in dung on the way back."

For once, the boy didn't ask how it was possible to avoid it.

They walked in a humble posture, heads slightly bowed. They never made eye-contact. Weapons, most makeshift but some impressively illegal in the CoDominium's eyes, were much in evidence. Most buildings showed bare planks above ground and people walked along the sides of the dirt roads on boards useless for much else, when such boards weren't stolen for firewood. A pallor of smoke captured smells of sweat, shit, and alcohol and kept them near the ground, on which lay the dead-drunk, the dying, and the just-plain dead.

Castell City needed a squinty-eyed, hard-jawed sheriff with a quick mind and a quicker gun-hand, at least, when its condition was expressed in Old Earth Hollywood Western idiom. Comparisons practically jumped one's bones, Kev thought. He'd long since stopped viewing such mental embraces as romantic or attractive in any way. Boomtown meant explosion to Kev now, and he couldn't think of much to recommend being in an explosion of any kind.

"I still think helping that spy is risky. What's in it for them?"

"Our help is passive, peaceful. We may gain a voice in a larger chorus, a part of the grand symphony of worlds."

"And the Alderson drives might stop functioning this very minute, but I doubt it."

Kev rolled his eyes. He walked on, and missed seeing Wilgar's look of quick disappointment as the boy gazed at the First Deacon's back for an instant, before scampering along with his usual overflow of energy.

* * *

Cole handed over Kennicott scrip and grinned. "You're sure you know where this spot is?" he asked the river rat whose skiff he was hiring.

The man shrugged beneath the muskylope cloak he wore. His skin matched the river mud with which his hands and feet were coated. "It's along the river, huh? We go upriver, we find, huh?"

Cole stepped into the small boat, pointed at the front and square at the back. He regretted the loss of the much faster zodiac/raft, *Black Bitch*. This one had no name, at least none he could see. He sat on the middle seat, while the river rat sat at the back, to work engine and skeg-rudder. "Snipers, you know," the river rat said.

"What's your name?" Cole asked, ignoring the comment but glancing warily at the bank as the skiff puttered away from shore.

"Names, huh?" The man spat astern.

"I'll call you Ishmael," Cole said. "Fishing good?"

Ishmael laughed again, this time coughing up blood, or dark bile. He spat some more, scratched his crotch loudly, then said, "Fish okay."

"Okay," Cole said. He twisted around to look back, past the river rat. He watched Castell City recede, then touched a couple of his weapons. The map flapped in the wind under a rock on the seat beside him. It showed a simplistic schematic of the river, with a large, crude X marked on the eastward shore of the Xanadu.

The trip took several hours, and they passed every sort of floating vessel, from skiffs and rafts to complete floating houses. Several barges piled high with ore moved by, each sporting metal turrets at the corners from which armed guards kept watch. Most boardings were prompted by the food and survival gear each barge carried; the ore was of use to almost no one on Haven, with no factories yet delivered, or even promised. Most boardings failed, ended in rout or slaughter. Cole hoped to change all that, if his plan fell into place all along the line.

Haven's water offered better chances at survival than its land, it seemed. Although no one really tried to keep track, it was possible that more people lived on and along the rivers, lakes and seas of Haven's great Shangri-La Valley than on the vast plains of grassland or the higher steppes. The mountains were as sparsely populated as lunar peaks, give or take a lunar colony or two.

Fresh cold air in his face soon had Cole's muscles aching. He used one of his extra sweaters as a scarf. His hood did well when he kept his head turned to one side. Chunks of ice occasionally thunked the skiff, and once Ishmael bounced it over what looked to be a log. "Gator, maybe," was all Ishmael said.

Cole sniffed. He smelled clear water, chill air, and greenery near the shore. Grasses, stalks of reed-trees, and clumps of tanglebush and thornbushes lined the river. Higher trees stood a few meters back in many places, while in others grassy dunes lazed.

Shivering, Cole tried to match the map to the shoreline, but the map was entirely too crude. He folded the map, then burned it by tossing it into the tin can of coals Ishmael kept as a make-shift hibachi between his feet. It not only kept him warm, but cooked his meals and served as a potential weapon when coals were tossed at the gas-tanks of passing opponents.

They came around a bend in the river and Ishmael grunted. He raised a scarred hand and pointed to the far shore. "Barge," he grunted. "Wrecked, huh?"

The letter "K" had been scrawled on the rusted flank of the half-sunken barge. "This is the place," Cole said. "I won't be long."

"I won't wait long, huh?" Ishmael said, maneuvering the skiff so it came alongside the exposed hulk and barely kissed against it.

Cole stood, reaching up to grasp the top of the barge. Rust flaked into his eyes as he pulled himself up. Dark red to begin with, the rusted barge looked virtually black in the orange light of Haven. "Dignity," Cole yelled, the code-word.

"Honor," came the reply. A man's head appeared from behind the canted, twisted remnants of a wheelhouse. "Welcome aboard," the man said, waving Cole toward him.

Inside he found that the man had a pair of thermal beanbag chairs. He sank into one gratefully. "Cole," Cole said.

"Franks," the man said, extending his hand for a manly shake. "You've been active already, I understand."

"Catching heat already?" Cole smiled. It was good to know one's efforts were not in vain.

"My superiors got a couple paranoid memos, yeah," Franks said. His square face, slit of a mouth, and wide, blue eyes gave him a look of conflicting glee and grimness. He waved big hands a lot as he spoke. He wore the standard Kennicott coverall, thermal and quilted, except no tool belt weighed him down and pockets appeared to be stuffed. This marked him as a ground exec, foreman or higher.

"Well, I planted a few false flags with some innocents," Cole said. "So as of a few days ago, some of your people think that the Harmonies want to start buying and stockpiling ore, while other elements think the Harmonies are being paid by Kennicott to hide ore that might be pirated."

"And the walls came tumblin' down," Franks said, hands flapping happily. He belched, then reached around, hauled on a fisherman's gill-chain, and brought up a couple tins of beer, which had been dangling through a hole in the tilted floor, into water. He offered Cole one, and when the agent declined, shrugged and tossed them back into the water, to keep them chilled. "So all I know is I got orders to cooperate with you best I can," Franks said.

"Good. I've set up a couple surprises, explosions. When they happen, spread the word that Harmonies might be behind it. Property damage and delayed explosives might be considered passive, see?"

"You're saying Beadles might'a done it?"

"Exactly." Cole leaned back and snuggled deeper into the warmth of the thermal beanbag. "They ought to issue these things," he said.

"They do. Kennicott's a good comp'ny, you do yer job right for 'em. So hey, here's this." And Franks pulled a thick wad of Kennicott scrip from a pocket. "Funds, they call it in the memo. I call it a wad could choke a horse, only they got more muskylopes than horses here. Choke a muskylope I guess, how about it?" And Franks laughed, appreciative of his own special kind of humor.

Cole took the money and separated it into different pockets of his parka, then said, "I'm going to need some barge crews from you. They've got to deliver ore to various Harmony locations and keep quiet about it, at least long enough for this thing to work."

"No shore leave, then," Franks said, as if making a mental note.

"And we'll need to start spreading a whisper campaign about river pirates, that kind of thing," Cole added.

"Ain't no rumor, no sirree." Franks waved at the river. "There's pirates all over, and rogues, scoundrels, all sorts ah water-scum. Crap floats, Mister Cole."

"I'll remind Thomas Erhenfeld Bronson of that," Cole remarked. "But the pirates I need us to define with our whisper campaign are specifically interested in hijacking ore-barges, cheating Kennicott, and interrupting Haven's trade, such as it is. Remember the food boycott, Docktown's takeover, Janesfort, all that? Well, this is going to be worse.

"Our story is that a black marketeer is getting greedier than usual, and wants a major cut of the legitimate trade. And remember, the Harmonies are in on it, providing sanctuary, hiding places, that kind of thing. Aid and comfort. In short, all legal, valid settlement and trade rights are being abrogated, violated, trashed. And the only way to restore order will be to call in CoDo Marines from Tanith, hell, maybe even from Earth."

"Sounds revolutionary," Franks quipped, smiling broadly.

"It's at least revolting," Cole said. "Meanwhile I'll work on the Harmonies. It seems they may have a rift in their ranks, as well. There's a First Deacon Malcolm who seems somewhat ambitious, in a naive way. If I'm right, then I've got him hooked, and now it's just a matter of playing him into our net. A strong CoDo garrison is just what Haven needs, and it's our job to make sure everyone realizes it."

"You confidential fellas do nice work," Franks said. "I always wanted to be a part of this kind of operation. Seen it done from afar, but always wanted to play a part, you know?"

"Welcome aboard, then," Cole said. He very deliberately took some money from one of his pockets, counted out a few thousands creds worth, and handed it to the other man. "Buy your wife some kids."

"Just might at that."

"Oh, and be thinking of some names. We'll need a half-dozen or so patsies, fall guys. Ostensible revolt leaders. You can either inspire them to do some actual dirt, or just smear them when the time comes, but set them up so they'll satisfy a provisional governor and his field court."

Cole pulled up the left sleeve of his parka and looked at his wrist, where several times, from Haven to Tanith to Earth, glowed when he scratched. Subcutaneous chrono-computers kept a timetable only he understood. "Meet me here in, what, three Eyes? I'm not really used to Haven cycles yet."

"Make it one, Mister Cole. This is Haven. Days and nights get mighty long, and we'll be wanting more talk once things start poppin'."

"And you'll be wanting more kick-back," Cole muttered as he climbed over the side of the barge a few minutes later, back into Ishmael's skiff. Louder, he said, "Home, James."

Ishmael grunted a particularly long fart in reply, then pushed the skiff away from the wrecked barge. "Most ah the ore salvaged way back," Ishmael volunteered as they motored swiftly away, back towards Havenhold Lake and Castell City. "I oughta know, helped wreck the damn thing."

Cole said, "In that case, I might have another job for you." He looked back at the hulk, and there stood Franks, guzzling from a skin. Rolling his eyes, Cole asked Ishmael, "Know any good villains?"

"Thugs, huh? Sure, sure. Dirty deeds done dirt cheap." And for the rest of the trip, the river rat dubbed Ishmael regaled Cole with a raucous, ancient song from another, much older frontier.

"If his friends are as lethal as his singing," Cole told himself in an undertone as he jumped up onto a Docktown wharf, "the CoDo Marines might have a problem after all."

* * *

"Be sure to let me know, though," Wilgar said to the naked woman as he waved to the others, smiled, and stepped outside the place called Cambiston Doxies. He scampered across the mud street and knocked on yet another door, but no one answered, and a man stomping by on the planks called out, "Forget that one, boy, she an' her gals been sent to the miners."

Wilgar nodded. "Last one, then," he muttered. He splashed toward the Harmony compound, careless of the mud. His robes held so much mud already that it doubled their weight. Even his hair was smeared, and he kept tossing clumped locks out of his eyes.

Veering north, he walked past some of the better merchants houses, and raised a hand to several children who appeared in several windows. He called their names, and they called his, and invited him in to play in their walled, guarded homes and gardens. He shook his head, though, and told each one, "Maybe later."

He moved nearer the palisade, and when he came to the juncture of two sewage sluices, he glanced behind himself, then all around. Quick as thought he ducked under the sagging, seeping mess. He ignored what dripped on him as he made his way toward the Harmony compound.

Harmonies used treated human waste as fertilizer, "an old German recipe" as the Reverend Castell called it, but Castell City and Docktown and Cambiston and all the other settlements tended to sluice or pump raw sewage into Havenhold Lake and the rivers, without regard to

Harmony of any kind. Civilization brings its own ambiguities and oxymorons, always; Wilgar studied Earth's many moribund cultures for just such lessons, and he often asked aloud how they could be so willfully stupid. Neither his teachers nor even First Deacon Kev Malcolm had any answer. All of them fell back on Harmony platitudes, emphasizing how truly important a genuine search was for Harmony—for cultures as well as individuals.

It was a hollow only big enough for a small man, or a boy of thirteen. It had been created by water erosion, rare on Haven except where leaky sewers met. And the erosion had exposed the buried ends of seven of the palisade's posts. A ragged square of cloth some might recognize as a Harmony robe, albeit a stained and tattered one, covered a crude hole through the palisade.

Wilgar lifted the cloth and slipped under it, into the Harmony compound. He scrambled on all fours along the small tunnel, touching places his own hands had carved. The tunnel ended about three man-lengths past the palisade, and turned up.

Standing, Wilgar carefully lifted the wood hatch, really just a chunk of board with no hinges: Dirt slid from the board. Wilgar saw nothing but chickens, so he scrambled up into the south-east corner of the coop, where the grain was stored in a locked shed.

Replacing the board so it covered the tunnel hole, the boy used his feet to scrape a layer of dirt back over it. He snatched a handful of grain and scattered it onto the dirt. He studied it for a second, nodded, then turned and moved from behind the shed.

Chickens pecked and clucked around him, and roosters challenged his shins. Wilgar walked through droppings, ungathered down-feathers and swirls of agitated, near-mindless chickens. Haven's orange light had clouded some of the chickens' eyes. Other chickens had developed bigger pupils. Most did nothing unearthly except produce more eggs and more rooster-crowing during Eyerise.

Dashing now, Wilgar crossed an empty space, then came to roost atop the south corral fence. It was split-rail in design, but the fence was altered to fit Haven standards, being made of much shorter, stouter planks, due to the trees available and zigzagging much more than any earthly counterpart, to accommodate bundles of thorn-bush set in each wedge.

Wilgar balanced for a moment, one foot on a post-top, then hopped down, catching his balance by touching a white-faced, mottled Long Angus hybrid. Its stubby horns and husky shoulders gave it a baleful look, but Wilgar simply slapped the beast's rump and moved past it, crossing the corral half-crouched while the Long Angus wandered off chewing cud.

Boosting the fence on the far side, the boy ran hard across another open space, leaping over a dip-trench and vaulting a water-trough. He fell flat and rolled under a wagon, and then for a few minutes simply panted, forcing Haven's thin air to give up more oxygen than it seemed willing to give. As he lay on his back, he gazed up at the underside of the wagon and touched the fingertips of his right hand to those of his left. Snatches of a Harmony prayer-song came from him and as his breathing settled, more of the soft, simple melody escaped him.

"Lazing," came a gruff male voice.

Wilgar rolled out from under the wagon and gazed up at First Deacon Kev Malcolm. "I was seeking Harmony with the horizontal," the boy said.

Kev's face showed pain. "You mock our precepts," he said, but his voice carried fatigue more than exasperation.

Wilgar hung his head and said, "Peace is mine to offer. I'm sorry, First Deacon. My humor has no sense, as you often tell me."

Kev smiled down at the boy's bowed head, but the smile vanished quickly as Wilgar looked up at him. Kev said, "We must prepare for a trek. We must visit some farms."

"It's that deal we made with the spy, isn't it? He's not what he seems, I asked around and he hasn't even visited one bordello. What kind of off-worlder fails to do that? Except Harmonies, and he's not one of us, that's for sure." As soon as Wilgar saw the look of horror on Kev's face, he stopped jabbering and bowed his head again and said, "I'm sorry."

"You'll be coming with me," Kev said. "And as of this minute, it's not a suggestion, but a damned good idea." And he strode away from the boy, back straight and arms swinging stiffly; it was almost the way the Reverend Castell walked when in the grip of a vision.

Wilgar, still gaping from the rare profanity, hurried to catch up. As he walked at Kev's heels, he gazed around at the compound as if to memorize it, or perhaps seeing it for the first time in a new way.

*   *   *

"Tell you what," Cole said, shivering despite the hood, three sweaters and makeshift scarf. "Keep east, and drop me on Splashdown Island."

Ishmael grunted and belched, but passed the buoy and kept the skiff aimed at the island, visible only as a bulk of silhouette in the distance. To their left Castell City and Docktown glittered with a thousand points of light, like some shipwrecked dream. Without neon, streetlights, or anything but private electricity, Haven's first and largest city flickered with frontier fire as gloom gathered. Clotted darkness revealed Hecate and Brynhild, riding low as yet, but still catching Byerlight as Cat's Eye slid into ecliptic.

"We ride trench," Ishmael said, pulling the rudder hard to port which made the skiff slew starboard. City lights dwindled behind them now. The bottom of Havenhold Lake was shallow in many places, due to sandbars constantly shifting in the confluence of the rivers. There were trenches which went down to unplumbed depths and in them navigation was smoother because the surface-water wasn't constantly pushed upward by bottom. Tides could even steer barges when drag-anchors and stabilizer fins were lowered. Only wayward sandbars threatened bigger craft, but pilots knew the patterns better than Mark Twain could have imagined, so accidents were few and due mostly to novices.

In a skiff, however, only exposed sandbars posed a hazard as the boat's draft was so shallow. Cole hunched a bit nearer the can of smoldering coals and warmed his hands. His hired chauffeur hawked phlegm to port and coughed bubbles from his lungs, but seemed otherwise to thrive in the gathering chill.

A sentry boat, swift vee-hull cutting water like a blade, intercepted Ishmael's skiff and Cole rose at once to bellow a code. He almost fell overboard when a random chunk of ice thunked the bow.

A searchlight from the sentry blinded them. "We have you in our gunsights," came a bored Marine's voice through a bullhorn. "Identify and state reason for violating island space."

Cole shouted his codes again, and this time the Marines heard him.

"You're slightly overdue, sir," the bullhorn roared. The sentry's engine revved down, then the boat itself drifted closer and the searchlight flicked off.

In the sudden dark, afterimages danced. Cole blinked them away. His eyes watered, and the tears felt as if they were freezing solid on his cheeks. He hated the breezes wafting around them as Haven settled in for a long Eyeless night.

Ishmael caught a line and tethered his craft to the sentry boat. He cut his engine off and locked the rudder-ratchet in neutral. In a few minutes they'd been towed to a concrete quay at the point of the triangular island which pointed almost due west. On the opposite side of Splashdown Island a long, flat cliff overlooking a pebble beach provided perfect line-of-sight for the north-south splashdown zone, which was wide enough to accommodate the equivalent of three separate spaceport runways. Three separate splash-ships could come down at once, or would be able to, once the floating baffles defined the lanes and blocked hull-wave slosh-over.

Cole hopped up onto the quay, where a grim sergeant in CD Marine uniform glared at him, one hand held out palm up. "ID, sir," the Sergeant said, his shaved scalp and puckered cauliflower ears red in the cold.

Handing over an ID chip the size of his thumbnail, Cole said, "I've got to meet with your comman—"

A gunshot broke the air, interrupting the spy.

Only Cole reacted, by crouching and drawing a weapon. Glancing down at the skiff, he saw Ishmael's body flopped half over the gunwale. One hand trailed into the water, like a tourist idly testing the temperature. Cole imagined the fingers freezing solid, if one of the imported pike didn't snap them off first for an appetizer.

"Tried to escape," a voice called up, and the grim Sergeant nodded.

"Friend?" he asked Cole, who quickly straightened the surprise off his face and said, "I'm not familiar with that term."

Good, the sergeant's expression said. They walked in light provided by kerosene lanterns, the mantels of which glowed blue-white, attracting Haven's few species of moth. "My CO's been waiting for word from you, sir," the Sergeant said, as they entered a corrugated tin building and jogged up a short, dark flight of metal steps.

A door opened, and Cole walked ahead of the Sergeant into a room so overheated and so full of kerosene fumes that he dizzied at once. A tall, rugged man with brown hair, blond eyebrows and flinty black eyes stood and squinted at him, then extended a hand. He wore a plaid lumberman's shirt and jeans, but Cole knew it must be the island's garrison commander, so he took a chance and said, "Colonel."

"Call me Spike." The man did not smile, so it was not, apparently, a joke. When Cole looked puzzled, the man said, "Just Spike. Nickname. Got it on Sauron. Killed a berserker. Railroad spike. Weapon of convenience, just grabbed what was there. Worked good, though. Plain old Spike ever since. You settin' things up for us? Little action be nice, after all this sitting."

He rubbed his buttocks as if they were numb and as if the numbness was at least partly Cole's fault. Glancing at the other three officers, all in uniform, with whom he'd been playing poker, Spike said, "My office," and inclined his head. "Brief me."

Cole followed, his lower lip behind his front teeth and he considered his options and alternatives.

In a plain room with a GI porta-desk, two folding chairs, a file-cube, screen, battered antique keyboard, jury-rigged voice-activated computer interface system, a single lantern and a map on a wall beside the desk, Spike said, "Best billet available. Pathetic. MWR's corrupt and I won't pay, so we get amenities a hermit crab wouldn't want. We even have a hacker on this pig of a jury-rigged network, can you believe? But fuck 'em. Soldiers, damn it. We can take it, tough's what you save up to dish out later, huh?" Spike laughed as he sat behind the desk.

Cole chuckled, then sat in the other chair. It creaked but held. "Okay, first a quick-sketch overview: Pretty soon all hell's going to break loose, uh, sir," he began. His hands, still cold, gestured stiffly. "There should be explosions in a few hours from Hell's-a-Comin' to Docktown, Cambiston and Castell City proper. I might even have one arranged for the Haven Compound."

Spike's brows rose. He said nothing.

Cole continued. "Meanwhile, stockpiles of semi-refined ore are being secreted at various Harmony farms and settlements in the outlying area. That's arranged, and it means that we can catch them with the goods, prove their complicity in what we're going to call the revolt."

"Unrest, violence," Spike said, smiling. "And my boys get blooded."

"At first, but then you call for reinforcements and an official request for an interim governor while CoDominium status for Haven is debated."

"Questions," Spike said, leaning forward, rubbing his hands.

And for the next hour or so Cole answered ever more detailed questions. He found himself elaborating his plan in more detail than he'd done even for himself. After all, as per Director's Assistant, CoDominium Bureau of Intelligence Marshall Wainright's advice, he'd been winging it, applying the Free Hand principle of ad-libbing on the ground. And having been promised Kennicott and Dover help, Cole now found himself grateful for this CD Marine Colonel's unexpectedly trenchant analysis. Between the two of them, the plan coalesced and became layered, almost intricate, but subtle enough to respond to the inevitable changes first contact with any enemy causes to all battle-plans.

"Those poor harmless Harmonies," Spike said.

And for once, Cole himself almost felt pity. Almost.

* * *

He had no way of knowing that a dozen or so hours before Cole had met with Spike on Splashdown Island to plot against him, but Kev Malcolm concentrated on discords just the same. Walking in the dark on Haven provided interesting challenges, but Kev had long since mastered them all, or so he thought. What he'd never experienced before was the frustration a parent must feel when a child simply scampers off and refuses to remain in hand and in control.

"Wilgar," Kev called, pausing on the path, glancing up at the stars in silent beseeching. "Wilgar, come back to me this instant, there are slush swamps and firegrass and all sorts of—"

"It's okay, First Deacon," Wilgar said, materializing out of the dark to one side of the path. "I didn't see any cliff lions or frenzied muskylopes."

His tone mocked. "Besides, nature called."

"That's the seventh time since the last homestead," Kev said, reaching out to grasp Wilgar's arm. He pulled the boy close and spoke directly into his face. "You'll stay strictly with me, do you understand? How many times must I tell you? Haven is no place for mindless solos. Try to remember that you're the alien here, and—"

"You might be an alien here," Wilgar said, "but this is where I was born, and it doesn't frighten me the way it—"

Kev knew as soon as he did it that he'd broken all manner of precepts and constraints, stepped over a thousand cultural and social bounds, but his hand simply drew back from the boy a few spans, then whooshed back to slap the boy soundly on the side of his face.

Wilgar fell back, more in surprise than in pain. His hand rose to touch the now-warmed cheek. "You," his eyes watered. "You struck me."

"Dear Universal Harmony, forgive me," Kev said, distraught and falling to his knees. In the dark, on the thin bare-dirt path, with a hill to the right and trees clumped to the left and a farm somewhere behind them, the man and the boy faced each other like two actors on an otherwise empty stage. Secrecy tempted them. "No one need know," Kev muttered, thinking of the distances involved, how far away was anyone of authority.

Looking at the First Deacon kneeling before him, Wilgar sniffed a few times and wiped away the tears. He shivered as a brisk wind found them, touched them, swirled on. "I've been hit before," he muttered. "In the city. I've even won fights with new beadles."

Kev gaped, his mouth opening as if to scold, but then he closed his mouth and let his head drop. He moaned in emotional pain. "Peace is ours to offer, and if we drop the fragile vessel, it shatters, leaving our hands empty, meaningless."

A tiny sound, almost like a bell, jingled in the near distance.

"First Deacon, please get up. We've got a schedule to keep." Wilgar went to the older man, placed a hand on a shoulder. "It's nothing." He smiled and patted the man's shoulder. "Really, it was me. I tested your patience and I, I failed to harmonize."

"You don't have a feel for things harmonic," Kev said, quietly. He got to his feet. "You mouth platitudes without conviction. And yet, as the Reverend Castell's only son, you'll one day take his place as leader of us Harmonies. Can't you see how much I've tried to help you, bring you along? I know what you're like, I really do. I was like you, more than you know. I've even been reprimanded for war-like, disharmonious thoughts. Can't you understand how I've worried, how I've—"

A muskylope snuffled somewhere close, and again a tiny jingle of metal on metal came to them, and for the first time the sounds registered; someone lurked close by, in the dark. Thuds sounded.

Kev grabbed Wilgar's robe and dragged him off the path just as two riders crested the hill and rode down upon them. Making for the trees, Kev shoved Wilgar away, to split the target. The salty smell of muskylope clogged the air.

One of the riders raised a farm implement of some kind. In the dark, it might have been a hoe or a rake or a shovel. Kev, glancing back, saw the thing swinging down at his head, and moved quickly backwards, toward the attack, into the arc. He came in under, catching the opponent's weapon hand as it came down.

Bracing his arms, Kev let inertia and momentum pry the weapon from the opponent's hand, as it completed its arc. After that, it was a simple matter of changing the hold's emphasis, and the muskylope's rider fell from the beast. A grunt of lost breath came just as Kev's right foot came down with all his weight on the man's sternum.

Turning, Kev squinted in the dark. The muskylopes huffed and puffed and pawed the ground. A big silhouette loomed, and Kev fell and rolled from it, then got to his feet and called, "Wilgar?"

"Over here," the boy cried, from the fringe of clownfruit trees. A weapon spat fire, and slugs flew.

Kev ran, zigzagging, and got to the trees. He tumbled into cover and lay as still as possible, covering his panting with both arms. Only infra-red goggles might betray him, and the attackers seemed more the farmer type.

Kev frowned. Farmers in this region were all Harmonies and Harmonies attacked no one, particularly not their First Deacon and their leader's son. "Imposters," Kev said.

A rustling preceded Wilgar's arrival. He seemed to have better eyesight in the gloom, for he said, "They're riding away. Both on one muskylope. The other 'lope wandered off. Maybe we can catch it."

"Did they hurt you?"

"Never had a chance, First Deacon. How can we seek harmony with this? Why did they try to kill us?"

Kev said nothing, but shrugged in the dark. He said, "If memory serves, these trees should give us cover for most of the trek back to the compound." They stood to the north of Castell City and the Harmony Compound, where it was mostly the high plains of the Shangri-La Valley, but irregular swaths and stands of Haven's few species of trees marked arroyos and other low-lying areas, and were thought also to mark underground streams. Some farmers swore on the latter, many settlers swore about the latter being a lie.

"Do you think there's an uprising?" Wilgar asked. His voice held neither terror nor despair, just a pragmatic level tone bespeaking maturity beyond his years. "The Harmonies are in minority, and no one much likes us these days. And then there's that spy, Cole...."

Kev heard that tone and, referring to the early days of Harmony founder Garner "Bill" Castell, said, "You know, Wilgar, your name may yet prove your heritage, if your grandfather's many scraps and battles mean anything to us now."

"My grandfather's one of the mysteries."

Kev acknowledged the quoted Writings by a quick gesture, drawing the staff and notes in the air. He rose and began walking. "We must convene the Beads, see if they've heard anything. I'm beginning to trust your distrust a bit more."

A glow appeared on the horizon before long, showing through the trees. It proved to be the next Harmony farm, still burning even as animals squealed and squawked in terror. Kev and Wilgar checked for people but found only one dead man. "Women and children were taken for the mines," Wilgar said.

Kev glanced sharply at the boy, but said only, "Perhaps." Then, under his breath, he said, "Saloons, more like."

Wilgar grinned in the dark for an instant, then looked again at the burned homestead and started to cry. He cried silently, and began walking stiff-jointed and mechanical, the way his father often moved when in the thrall of visions or when riding herd on his own surging emotions.

Kev found himself following Wilgar back to the compound, even though the boy had never been on this particular circuit route before. And when they arrived, they found the Reverend Charles Castell in his brightest white robes standing atop a watchtower, staff raised as if to direct a sky-symphony, singing in a slip-shod baritone a song about voices joined in concert defeating lone singers in a contest of harmony.

"What's going on?" Kev asked.

Wilgar, glancing at him as he began running the final distance, said, "Father's sealing the compound."

And that's when Kev noticed the extra light coming from the city, where flames leapt upward in flares dozens of man-heights high. It looked as if Docktown now burned, even as the homestead had burned.

"Not war," Kev gasped, dashing forward to catch up with Wilgar.

*   *   *

Cole lowered the infra-red binoculars as Lieutenant Ibansk said, "But Harmonies are not supposed to fight."

Ibansk, infantry, carried Colonel Spike's blessings and sealed orders, as well as Cole's need-to-know confidence. Cole said only, "We were supposed to do the roughing-up."

Standing, Cole waited until the two men on the remaining muskylope got back to the rally point, a stand of pine-like trees, the resin of which accumulated on the outsides of trunks, giving older trees a lumpy, bloated appearance. The resin could be peeled and used as adhesive, melted and used as glue, or employed in many other useful ways.

Just then, however, Cole hated the stuff. He said, "We should've taken cover in the oak-like trees." They'd been too far from the ambuscade, however. As the muskylope's original rider helped his wounded comrade down, he glared at Cole and said, "They're sitting ducks with teeth, damn your eyes."

At once Ibansk, a slender, gray-eyed man with a slit mouth and the beginnings of jowls, whose eyes peered at the world from the depths of wrinkles, snapped, "Insubordination may be punished in the field with summary execution, Sergeant. And may I remind you that Mister Cole is ranking officer on this mission, despite his lack of overt insignia."

"Can I get these damned farmer's clothes off? They stink of manure and worse," the healthy ambusher asked. His partner, groaning from a bruised neck and cracked ribs, nodded weary agreement.

Cole scowled. "We've got to follow them. They'll make their way back to the Compound, of course. If we vector toward the city gate, we should be able to parallel First Deacon Malcolm and the Castell brat without running across their path. They'll move wary, anyhow."

"But please," Ibansk said, his English carrying both Russian and quasi-British accents, depending upon the words or the tone he used.

This betrayed his origins; he'd no doubt been pulled from British Isles garrison duty, probably for some infraction involving politically-unsavory types, or the black market, still the most potent economic force on Earth, "Why did this Kev Malcolm fight?"

With a shrug, Cole said, "In his eyes, it wasn't fighting. He was just accepting what life offered with as little harm done to anything as possible. See, in the Harmony philosophy, force can't be met by opposing force, but it can be misdirected, deflected, absorbed, and, well, other passive things. Use the enemy's strength against him is their philosophy. The tougher the enemy, the tougher the Harmony. They don't see things as conflict or competition. In fact, there are no enemies, only melodies. It's all music metaphor. They seek to harmonize. So if a forceful, dynamic tune comes along, they try to add it to their drone, or weave some harmony onto it or let it come and go without affecting their song much."

Cole squinted at Ibansk in the dark; the Russian's face showed impassive boredom. "Come on, let's hike."

They left the muskylope riders to return to their bivouac. Cole followed Ibansk, who knew the land. Both wore low-light goggles with IR overlay, in case something warm-blooded entered the scene.

The First Deacon and Castell's son moved with surprising stealth, and left little spoor, especially in the dark. It helped to know their eventual goal. As Kev and Wilgar examined and investigated the burned-out farm, Cole and Ibansk lay at the crest of a hillock, shivering but placid.

Cole had his IR overlay turned low, to eliminate interference from the ruins' residual heat. "Look at that," he said, indicating Wilgar. "Kid's shoving a chunk of ore into his robes."

"They have no pockets, Harmonies," Ibansk said.

Cole smiled. "One does, apparently. Or else he's got remarkable muscle control somewhere." After a few more moments' watching, Cole said, "I'll be vented. Kid never mentioned the ore to the First Deacon."

Ibansk caught the possible significance and said, "This place has an agenda for every soul, it seems."

"We're each of us alone," Cole agreed, sardonic tone lost on a keening wind which brought sleet for a few seconds before whooshing upward again. Haven weather defined surprise. When the wind had passed, he said, "It's better, anyway. I couldn't quite figure out how to plant ore inside the Harmony Compound, if I ended up needing to. As a contingency, I was planning to carry it in on our raid, so we could 'find' it on them even in their sanctum sanctorum. This way, though, maybe I won't have to cheat so flagrantly."

Ibansk snorted. "A snatched sample of ore hardly constitutes criminal possession of stolen—"

"A trace of drugs suffices, when necessary."

With another, louder snort, the Russian said, "Da," and turned away for a moment, perhaps nursing an exposed nerve. "Laws of letters and laws of spirits. We used to say, 'In the evil spirit of the law.'"

They moved along, the pace difficult on Haven.

As Kev and Wilgar entered the Harmony Compound's northernmost gate, the portal nearest the Reverend Castell's lodge, Cole and Ibansk crouched on flat ground, in sawgrass. Stillness, shadow, the night, and the Harmonies' lack of low-light or IR scanning kept them unobserved from the ground, even though a fist-sized satellite probably noted their positions to the micrometer, for CD convenience.

"Look at the old man," Cole said. He had his goggles off entirely now, as fires from the town back-lit the Harmony Compound.

Atop the watchtower, the Reverend Charles Castell waved his arms, flapped his white robes and howled his bare head and face to the stars as if conjuring heaven's mighty host of spirit warriors. Despite distance and cross-breezes, Cole and Ibansk caught snatches of Castell's voice, although they could make out no words.

"Directing defenses," Ibansk said, lowering his own binoculars after taking a few digital pictures for later inclusion in a report. "He's very dynamic and forceful."

"Must've come out of his fog for a while," Cole said, voice low. He lay prone, then began moving forward by walking his elbows. Ibansk followed, Cole stopped, however, and said, "This is no good, we're leaving a trail of pressed grass. Better if we stand up and run." And he suited action to his own advice, dodging closer to the Harmony Compound.

Cole veered west and unknowingly ran past Wilgar's tunnel. His easy stride soon stuttered, staggered, and then he fell flat, gasping for breath, curing Haven's thin air. "This," he snarled, "is," his fists pounding in frustration, "ridiculous."

Ibansk, not winded, leaned down and applied a pen-sized bottle of compressed oxygen to Cole's lips. He squeezed off a couple hits, and the muscles in the spy's body un-kinked even as his lungs gained the upper hand over breathing. "Thanks," Cole said.

"Standard issue, I'll make sure you have some." And he handed over five small cylinders, which Cole placed in five different pockets of his parka before rising. They made their way a bit slower into the edge of Castell City, taking refuge behind a garden wall. They settled back into shadow cast by flames. Explosions, ranging from dull thumps to sharp reports, sounded behind them, as some of the fun Cole had arranged came to festive fruition.

"Whole city'll burn," Ibansk said. "They've no fire brigade, you know."

"Only the above-ground wood shacks'll burn," Cole said. "Fire won't spread to the underground, stone neighborhoods. Got to give the Reverend credit on some points. Can't burn or flood the Harmony structures out."

"What are we watching for?" Ibansk wanted to know after a while.

Cole, with one eye on the Reverend Charles Castell as he conducted his orchestral defenses from the tower, and the other eye on the fires glowing in the sky to the south and east, said, "Rebellion."

*   *   *

"Come down," Kev shouted, "please, please." He gazed up at the Reverend Charles Castell, who stood not on the watchtower's observation deck but on its roof.

"Those, there," the Reverend shouted, gesturing to barrels of water and slashing his finger toward a woodpile with a dramatic flourish.

"Peace is ours to offer," he screamed, and then, voice lowered but every bit as resonant, "In Harmony is strength."

Kev stepped toward the ladder, but a sow and three of her piglets knocked him down. Wilgar helped him up as three acolytes raced after the sow. Chickens fluttered everywhere, running as if pursued by foxes. Dogs barked, cows offered plaintive moos, and oxen kicked at stalls. People ran everywhere; the compound contained chaos but just barely.

The Reverend Castell bellowed, "There, form a bucket-line," and pointed to a flower of flame which had blossomed near the base of another watchtower. Splashing water onto it, volunteer Harmonies soon had the fire extinguished. The dewpond had been close enough, and they had responded quickly enough, that time.

"They're lobbing in torches and Molotov's," Wilgar said.

Kev nodded, took a few steps, then paused. "How do you know about Molotov cocktails?"

But Wilgar raced ahead, and scampered up to the platform which ran around the inside perimeter of the palisade. Already manned by worried Deaks and Beads armed with buckets and skins and pots and pans of water, the palisade swayed here and there. Ropes creaked, wood crackled.

Kev paused between the north watchtower and the Reverend Castell's lodge and waved wildly. He caught his leader's attention and called, "Come down," and gestured the same message. This time Castell nodded.

"What's going on?" Bren, Kev's wife, asked, rushing to him and hugging him tight. Her long dark hair moved in the crosscurrents of flame-swirled air like tendrils in water.

"It's madness, I don't know any more yet." Kev kissed the top of his wife's head and said, "See to Wilgar, he climbed up there."

As Bren moved away, Kev spotted Saral, the Reverend Castell's wife. He rushed to her, and helped her move. "My tapestry," she wailed, tears streaming: Her life's work, at least, her Haven's work, gone to flame's mindless greed.

"I was waiting," Saral said, grunting under her breath as she hefted the wood walker one of the Beadles had crafted for her. "It had been on our lodge's roof, so I could enjoy the sun, and when night fell, I wanted it moved inside, but no one came to help me, and Charles flew into one of his visions and I was waiting, Kev."

"I should have visited you before I left the compound," Kev said, looking down so as to avoid stepping on her twisted feet.

Someone cried out, and a wagon without a driver rattled by, its twin goats pulling as if in competition. Kev had time only to grasp Saral and lift her out of harm's way. Her walker shattered, as did one wheel of the wagon, which lacked metal bands. Pine-like resin made the ride somewhat smoother, but added little to the structural integrity of the wheel.

Kev lay on his back, Saral on his chest. He panted, she sobbed. Struggling to his feet, Kev carried her back to her lodge, then discovered that her rolling sled had been left inside the lodge. That meant he had to either leave her to fetch it, or drag her in through the zigzag tunnel. He chose the former, and so entered the Reverend Castell's lodge for the first time with the knowledge that it was empty.

The huge knot hovered between its wall-anchors like a clot of nightmare. Fire from the hearth offered erratic light. The smells of cooking, incense, much-used bedding, muskylope hides and wood smoke permeated the place.

A furtive movement in a corner drew Kev's attention. "Who's there?" he asked, voice sharp. Was it an intruder?

Wilgar's voice said, "First Deacon?"

"Where are you?" Kev squinted around the room in the dark, one hand on Saral's roller sled, the other on the fire-pit's wall. "What are you doing in here?"

The boy stepped out from behind the huge knot. He held a knife, and a small book. "It's almost time," he said, voice calm and assured and deeper than usual. "I've come for what I'll need."

Kev's face showed doubt and a slight cast of terror. Then he snarled, using anger to wash away uncertainty. "What have you done?"

"I've discovered the heart of the matter, the core of the knot, and the silence in the note which swells to fill the song."

Kev inched back. He gazed at the boy's eyes, the stiff motions. In a whisper he asked, "Who are you?"

And Wilgar smiled. "I am my grandfather's grandson," he said, and slipped both book and knife under his robes, where obviously he'd fashioned pockets of some sort.

"Pockets are against the Writings," Kev said. "What you cannot carry you cannot use, and in use lies ownership...."

"But special needs arise," Wilgar said. He pulled something from his pocket, held it out. It was a lump of ore. "There were several small mounds of this at the burned-out farm. And I saw tire-tracks, tread-marks, which means trucks, which can only mean Kennicott."

Wilgar hurled the ore into the fire-pit, where it burst in a shower of yellow, blue, and green sparks. "Harmony is the response," he said then, voice a monotone brimming with intensity, "But melody is the start," and with that he brushed past Kev and left the lodge.

Grabbing the sled, Kev hurried after the boy. He bumped into the Reverend Charles Castell half-way down the tunnel, and at once Kev backed up to let his leader enter. "Wilgar," Kev said, "I've got to find him again."

"Last I saw him he was on the palisade, helping drape the drenched quilts," Castell said, his gaze steady.

"But he just—" Kev began. "You didn't just see him?"

The Reverend gave his First Deacon a searching look and said, "I've just seen him, yes. On the palisade. Helping with fire prevention." He reached out and clamped a paternal hand onto Kev's shoulder. "What is it, Kev? Has the madness shaken you out of Harmony?"

Kev shook his head. He closed his eyes for an instant of inner assessment, then opened his eyes and said, "I'm fine." Holding up the sled, he added, "I'll get Saral in here, then we can—"

"She is gone. I have sent her for medical care. She's been burned, a brand fell from the sky. Two of the Deacons offered to carry her."

Kev blanched. He'd left her sitting there, exposed to harm. "I'd better make sure they make it across the compound."

"As you wish, First Deacon Malcolm, but may I remind you that our compound must achieve Harmony once more and maintain it against the cacophony surrounding us." The Reverend Castell heaved a sad sigh. "I've worked so hard, and so long, and now this crescendo of discord crashes upon us: And yet, everything takes longer and costs more, as one of our Writings teaches. But I'd thought of costs as money. It is not so. Cost can be counted in lives, too, and most often there is no fair rate of exchange."

He looked into Kev's eyes. "Our work must go on," he said, again placing a hand on Kev's shoulder. "Our song must transcend the loss of single notes."

Nodding, Kev wriggled out from under the touch which once he would have craved. "What can be done?" he asked, sounding suddenly much younger, much less assured. His voice had gone weak.

"Seek Harmony in all things," the Reverend Castell said. "Harmony cannot be achieved in a lifetime. Certainly not in mine."

Kev closed his eyes and tears escaped, but he managed to nod and kneel as if he meant it. "We must sacrifice to the greater harmony," he said, and when the Reverend Castell hummed a note, Kev hummed a chromatic tone which blended well, and created a third note heard only in the ear; streaming was an ancient musical anomaly which Harmonies had long since mastered: "Our Harmony is manifest once more," Kev said, having heard the third yet unsung note. Taking it as confirmation of blessing, both men raised their gazes to the imagined heavens.

Kev shuddered then. He grabbed the sled and crawled out of the lodge even as the Reverend Castell turned toward the knot, which was by now the size and weight of the notoriously-corpulent Kennicott VP forced to dwell in free-fall lest gravity of even the slightest intensity overstrain his bloated system; for a nauseating instant, Kev saw the knot as a tangle of intestines, and the stench of death radiated through him.

He backed out of the lodge tunnel and stood, finding himself at once obliged to duck as a chunk of flaming wood whooshed over his head.

Running, he caught up with the Deaks who carried Saral, and with their help and the rolling sled they got her to the Birth and Medical Lodge where for the first time Kev saw, as a doctor performed triage, the ugly blistered burn on Saral's left arm.

"We're under attack," Kev said then, in a wondering voice. It wasn't just mob churlishness, it wasn't only a rampant fire, it was a concerted attack. "That farm, burned and ruined," he muttered. "And now Castell City, and our compound." He gazed over the palisade at the fiery glow.

A Bead ran up, wearing only a rough tunic made of several sacks. Despite this and the cold, he glistened in the firelight with sweat. "Please, First Deacon. Our acolytes need guidance, and several of the Beads want to abandon the compound, and there's a stampede brewing in the western corral, and—"

For the next few hours, Kev stayed in constant motion, pausing only to catch his breath and gulp mouthfuls of water when possible. He asked many questions and offered few answers. He made decisions, but fulfilled his function mostly by rote as his mind stayed with other, larger problems than those currently creating such secular disharmony around him.

* * *

"I'm going to recommend this planet as a vacation spot," Cole said, getting to his feet and stamping to get the circulation going. He kept his gaze on the Harmony Compound's city gate. A wagon, pulled by two weary men, trundled up to the gate on wobbly wheels. One of the men knocked, then quite distinctly sparked a cigarette lighter's flint three times.

"That's the signal," Sergeant Ibansk said, also getting to his feet. "Our quarter ton of cayenne pepper is in place." The cold bothered him less. Between Siberia, his birthplace, and Blighty, his personal downfall, his blood had learned to take cold lightly.

Cole was already snapping IR and low-light pictures of the wagon, which bore a mark that fluoresced when Ibansk shined a darklight on it; this provided continuity in the chain of evidence and demonstrated that the wagon had been delivered from Cambiston to the Harmony Compound intact. That much red pepper could only mean that the Harmonies were making ersatz mace, which was considered a defensive weapon only when deployed by CoDo authorities. Like most colony worlds, even those not *officially* protectorates of the CoDominium, the Haveners were forbidden advanced weapons and high technology. Obviously the CoDo prohibitions didn't always work, but they kept the gun runners and interstellar weapons dealers somewhat in check.

When anyone but Marines or cops used mace, it became highly offensive indeed. And those photographs would prove one more part of the mosaic which added up to rebellion. When added to stockpiles of ammonia, derived from urine, for example, or the photographs showing pongee sticks in covered trenches smeared with feces, such evidence would be damning. It would demand a stern, decisive CoDominium response or, if evidence followed action, justify same.

That, at least, was how such dubious evidence would be interpreted by the powers that be when it came time to justify taking Haven by force. Cole's function was being fulfilled step-by-step and quite smoothly and the poor Harmonies wouldn't know what hit them.

"Not much happening yet," Ibansk observed.

With a shrug, Cole stashed the special camera and said, "I hope the satellites are getting this." BuIntel had authorized the expenditures necessary to put several satellites into geo-synchronous orbit high over the Shangri-La Valley, including Castell City and Hell's-A-Comin'.

Ibansk scratched his left wrist, then held it up. A low-intensity blue light blinked there. "Satellites are a go," he said, adding archaic American astronautisms to his patchwork speech-patterns. He scratched off the indicator light, then mused, "We're slowly becoming cyborgs, you know."

"Speak for yourself." Cole moved southwest, following the curve of the compound's palisade as he moved deeper into Castell City. "It's my idea that machines are becoming more human."

"Ah, an optimist."

"I've studied expert systems, is all," Cole said.

Ibansk laughed. "I've been studied *by* them. Look where it got me."

"Could be worse," Cole told the Russian. "You could be on the receiving end of this party we're arranging."

Ibansk, as Cole looked away, let his smile drop away, and nodded as if to himself as if hearing whispered warnings.

They walked through streets in which children and women scurried like rats flushed from sewers. Pain and panic kept sounds loud and harsh. Fires flared where wooden structures stood and while some tried throwing water on the fires, other people simply looted or ran.

Stone and semi-underground structures offered shelter for some, but the portals into such places were guarded by armed people with desperate faces: They would not lose easily the small hoard of life they'd scraped from exile and Haven's hardscrabble environment.

Now and then Cole raised a hand or brow in recognition. Informants, contacts, and low-level agents dashed to and fro, stirring havoc and tossing in confusion like mad chefs.

"Some people are made for this kind of work," Cole said, as they stood watching a group of men and boys demolish a building made of green, warped oak-like planks. "And I've never found it much of a challenge to rile people to riot, either. It's controlling things afterwards, that's where skill enters into things."

"You're certainly an education," Ibansk said. "Even to me, a rabble-roused Russian."

A man dashed up to Cole, his arm raised. His hand gripped a board with several nails through it. Cole smiled, then hit the man with a blur of elbow. Cole side-stepped as the man fell and walked on, ignoring him.

A woman lurched toward Ibansk and threw her arms around his neck. She wore only a torn brown dress. She kept yelling about rape and doctors and then she began clawing at Ibansk, who rolled her off him by ducking at the waist. He kicked her smartly in the face, then danced away as she tried to grab his feet. "Am I so irresistibly handsome?"

Cole hurried them along, leaping from stone roof to stone roof when able, ducking past flaming, spark-tossing wrecks when necessary. At the heart of Castell City, they came to a low mound of dirt surrounded by sandbags. A Waltimire sand-tank stood at the center of the mound, its flank-sacks empty just then. Several military types stood around it, some smoking, some spitting, all jabbering. None paid any attention to the arrival of Cole and Ibansk, who proceeded to the sunken door.

"Wood?" Ibansk asked, knocking on the door. "Not armored?"

"Metal's costly around here," Cole said. "Besides, it's probably filled with compacted dirt. Stop shells better than Nemourlon, I'm told."

"Outposts are always told such optimistic things," Ibansk said. He sounded quite sure of himself, and considering his background, probably knew about such things in personal detail.

The door opened and three armed guards in body armor trained three different types of weapons on Cole and Ibansk, each of whom raised his hands. ID's were checked and cross-referenced by blip and portable computer and finally by eyeball. "Okay, sorry gents," the guard carrying the flame-thrower said.

The other guards parted, and Cole led the way into the bunker. He walked down a slope for twenty meters, then veered left. "You've been here before?" Ibansk asked, his face showing how impressed he was by what he was seeing.

"Good briefing, is all," Cole said. "This is new, we call it The Egg. Rebels don't know about it, yet."

"Rebels?"

Cole ignored the other man's sardonic tone. He turned into yet another corridor, then stopped at an unmarked door, this one metal, probably Dover Mineral Development's best steel. Before either man could even think of knocking, the door slid back, revealing a carpeted office complete with a huge desk standing before what appeared to be a window. The scene apparently outside the window, however, belied the fakery, for it showed Washington, D.C. on a snowy evening, cars and pedestrians moving amidst the remaining stately architecture, the remaining pre-CoDominium monuments.

Beside the Washington Monument, a second obelisk, this one neither tapered nor pointed at the top, rose to half again the older structure's height. In contrast to the white marble of the Washington Monument, the CoDominium Block was made of black marble. Its corners were embraced by polished brass. An airplane beacon flashed on its top, where it was said the CoDo presidents met to discuss mutual benefits.

"That beacon's no longer operating," Cole said. "With all the airspace restrictions, it wasn't necessary. Birds can't even get to it."

"It's an old holo," said the man behind the desk. Only when he stood and leaned into a recessed spotlight's cone of illumination did his craggy features become clear.

Ibansk snapped to attention. "General, sir," he said, saluting and remaining ramrod stiff. Cole, on the other hand, merely gestured to the leather swivel chairs and said, "May we?"

"Please," said General Lassitre, whose black-sheep nephew, a Marine major, had delivered the first cargo of transportees, along with a second wave of Harmonies, to Haven, following the Reverend Charles Castell's Harmony settlement. "Oh, and at-ease, Lieutenant"

"Sir," Ibansk said, his Russian accent thickening, chasing away any signs of American or English influence, as if taking orders and maintaining military formalities came easier to him in native tones.

And as Cole and Ibansk sat, a fourth man entered the room, moving on cat-like feet with a fleeting look of surprise on his face. And before the general could introduce anyone, Cole extended his hand to the fourth man and said, "Taxpayer Thomas Erhenfeld Bronson," in an impressed tone.

Everything about Bronson was cubical. His head, his massive torso, his double-breasted suit, his legs, his big hands. "So we meet," Bronson said, taking Cole's hand in his like a child accepting a bite-sized candy.

Ibansk muttered, "I'm honored to meet you, sir."

Thomas Erhenfeld Bronson's eyes, hooded by folds of flesh not quite fatty, not quite ethnic, flicked to the Russian, then blinked and came back to Cole. A smile twitched the big man's face, but only for an instant. In repose, his features seemed sullen and calculating. "It's going well?"

"As planned," Cole said. He and the others sat when the general made a show of arranging chairs. Brandy was produced, consumed, and commented upon, then Bronson asked, "So when can we take command?"

Cole said, "It's been ten hours since full night fell. That means we've got twelve hours of full darkness left. We ought to be able to have everything mopped up by dawn, if—" and he paused, looking first at Taxpayer Bronson, then at General Lassitre, the latter of whom nodded.

"Good. Then let's do the Hand Trick," the General said.

To Ibansk's puzzled look Cole only winked as the four men rose and left the room through a door to the left of the holo-window. They entered a conference room: A long table big enough to seat fifty took up the center of the room. A briefing screen had been adhesed to the wall, but it showed only a mini-sat view of the Byers' System, probably from the vantage of the Alderson Jump Point and magnified many times.

Nine men and three women sat at the conference table. Each wore the grim look of people out of their depth, away from their support, yet each radiated power. "County commissioners meeting the federal congress for the first time," Cole whispered to Ibansk, who reacted with a blank look but said, "*Da*, dead souls. Read your Gogol." A tone of pity crept into his voice, but his eyes glittered with nothing but good old Russian ice.

What they really were only they knew, but each represented a district of the Shangri-La Valley, a map of which now appeared on the screen. Twelve districts, and one rep per each. A neat planetary quorum was thus instituted, whether the general population knew it or not. Through this carefully-selected instrument the CoDominium would rule, following the put-down of the Revolt of course. Legal niceties were thus observed in adherence to detail and in breach of intent, which, as always, was convenient to all participants—if not to all concerned.

"Gentlemen," said General Lassitre, a slender man with gray hair combed straight back in classic British Empire manner, After an appreciable pause, he added, "And ladies."

One of the women snorted, as if to indicate there wasn't any such animal, especially in places like this.

Thomas Erhenfeld Bronson sat at the head of the table, The General sat to his left, Cole to his right, and Ibansk beside Cole. A military man sat beside the General, and he kept one hand flat on the table between them, as if holding down his note-box.

"We must never waver in our resolve," Taxpayer Bronson said. "My family means to have dominion, and so we shall."

"Hear," some of the men said, until cut off by a glare from Bronson. "Sycophants bore me," Bronson said. "What I want is results." Here he regarded Cole with a look of tenderness, like a glutton surveying the inside of a melon just before devouring it.

That's when General Lassitre stood. He pulled his short sword from its scabbard. The ceremonial blade, half its length covered with scrollwork engravings, flashed as he emphasized his words with it. "We are poised to take Haven back from the leaders of the revolt, and they will be rounded up and dealt with according to martial law. You, as district reps, will cooperate fully and completely in this process, and in any other processes we, the legal military authority, may ordain or decide."

He paused, glared at each rep in turn. "This is not a negotiation," he announced, slashing the blade down with a whoosh. He stopped it inches from the polished table, and its reflection hovered downward even as he lifted the blade again.

One of the men winced as the sword swept and slashed. A few stared at it as if hypnotized. Others pointedly ignored it.

"An under strength regiment of the 77th CD Marines are even now in orbit, twelve-hundred souls, and it can descend to restore order at a moment's notice. They've been quietly assembled from Levant and Adyta, our two nearest Alderson neighbors." Again the sword flashed, but this time the Sergeant sitting beside the General said, "But sir," and made a move as if to rise to his feet.

The sword came down hard, thunking into the table, and the Sergeant screamed. He raised his arm, now a blood-spurting stump. His hand lay on the table, twitching in a pool of blood.

Lieutenant Ibansk half-rose, his face clenched harder than his fists. Thomas Erhenfeld Bronson showed no reaction at all, and Cole only smiled a little.

"You see how we deal with nay-sayers," General Lassitre bellowed, frightening the reps to their feet. "Now get out of here and get back in place and wait for your orders. Dismissed."

The reps filed out quickly, some gagging back vomit, others pale and shaky. None seemed unaffected and all would not only carry the image with them always, but all would spread tales of ruthlessness and unpredictable violence.

When the last rep was gone Ibansk rushed around the table to help the stricken Sergeant, who howled a few more times in the direction of the fleeing reps before bursting out laughing. To an astonished Ibansk he held up his stump, then pulled it off. It was fake. A bulb-bladder was squeezed to effect the spurting, and the blood itself had come from a cow freshly slaughtered that morning for the evening's steaks at the officer's mess.

Cole held up the hand, which proved to be rubber. From it he shook a couple fish, which continued to twitch. "Nice touch, the fish," he said to the sergeant, who shrugged an Aw-Shucks and said, "Hand-jobs come easy to the average soldier," which was the standard joke.

"Just remember," Thomas Erhenfeld Bronson said then, voice low and slow and as certain as stone. "Politics is theatre, and the best politics is Grand Guignol."

Ibansk looked puzzled again, but Cole explained the reference, particularly as it related to the French Revolution, as they walked back into the General's office for the real meeting. "Short horror plays," Cole said. "Theatrically macabre, meant to shock. By-passes the intellect, you see."

"Ah," said Ibansk. "Surprising they'd bother by-passing what little intellect can be found around here. They're taking things quite seriously, aren't they? I mean, after all, it's a *Harmony* planet."

"Do you know the definition of non-combatant? According to Ambrose Bierce: it's a *noun*, means *a dead* Quaker—meaning pacifist.

Change Quaker to Harmony and you've up-dated the Devil's Dictionary nicely. And you've also pretty much defined the CoDo's stance, I suspect."

They sat down and drew on other traditional Earthish parallels, from Entebbe and Murchison Falls to Dusa Marreb, from vertical insertions into Panama for Operation JUST CAUSE to the orchestrated 'salvation' of Grenada and even the stage-managed confrontations between the UN Forces and Iraq. Ibansk even knew about Central America.

The plan Cole had ad-libbed, from dropping off arms with Jomo and other Docktown rubbish, to the Janesfort War and its taste of organized resistance in the form of the food boycott, to the later machinations with the purloined ore, pirated barges, social revolt in Castell City, and the frame-up of apparent Harmony complicity; the plan made sense in retrospect: That was all that counted. "And then I'll retire," Cole said several times during the meeting. It was his goal, his dream, his cherished hope.

He might not have mentioned it had he glimpsed the cold glitter it caused in Thomas Erhenfeld Bronson's hooded eyes.

* * *

One watchtower burned where it stood, two toppled and burned where they fell. Two chicken coops on the Compound's east side and the barn on its northwest side burned flat, but with minimal loss of stock. Crews of resourceful acolytes salvaged carcasses, and completed cooking the meat in huge pots hung over the Common Lodge fire-pit. Loose animals were gathered by children, some of whom had to wade into icy dewponds to fetch recalcitrant oxen and Long Angus cattle. The city gate had held, but a wagon of cayenne pepper had been dumped there, then set on fire. The stench drove everyone back, and it continued to smolder. "If we could've mixed the pepper with the meat we would've had a nice base for curry," one of the Deacons observed.

Mud froze where water had sloshed. Scorched gaps along the top of the palisade resembled cavities in an otherwise healthy smile. Some lodge roofs had burned, one had collapsed. Survivors wandered dazed, helping as much as possible to restore harmony, the kind found in order. The injured lay in the Birth and Medical lodge and only one was expected to die, a young woman who'd braved the burning barn to set free oxen from their stalls. Her robes had caught fire just as she ran out and she'd burned until a Bead, unable to wait for someone to fetch water from the north side dewpond, dropped to his knees and rolled her, smothering the flames. His hands required salve, but others, who'd done nothing but gape, needed balm for their consciences.

"It's a mess," Kev said, "but it's still here." He surveyed the Harmony Compound from atop the Reverend Castell's lodge. Ice coated the stone where water had splashed. Kev watched his footing, uncertain in torchlight, as he climbed down.

"All's discord," Castell said. He sat just inside his entranceway, hands on his ankles, face resting on his knees. "And my father's journal's been stolen," he added, sobbing: "All the secrets, all the tricks."

Kev squatted down beside his leader. He reached out a hand, placed it on a scrawny shoulder. "Saral wants to see you," he said.

"Her place is here. With me. Where I can look after her, get her healthy again." Castell looked up. "Maybe the echo of a miracle's been planted by all this noise." He gazed with desperation into Kev's eyes. "Maybe I can cure her legs, have her walking straight and proud again."

Kev looked away. "Maybe," he said. He dropped his hand. "Just remember that polio is a song of its own, as tuneful to some as a child's happiness."

"You learn too well," Castell said. He placed his forehead on his knees. He shuddered a few times.

Kev stood, moved away, letting the man cry in privacy.

To the first Beadle he encountered, Kev said, "Saral Castell must be bundled in blankets and carried with care to her own home. Can you get some help?"

"Yes First Deacon." The man made the sign of the staff and eight notes, then scampered off, eager to please. He wanted now more than ever to be accepted, to qualify as a full-fledged acolyte and thus have a chance at becoming a Harmony. In such people Kev had placed his darker faith, for Beadles were the outer edge of the Church of New Universal Harmony, the ones who could still use violence when necessary, the ones whose easy transgressions and sins would be just as easily forgiven, as long as what they did served the interests of the kirk.

Kev's eye saddened as he watched the man run off. "Enthusiasm is Harmony's greatest danger to itself," he said, quoting the Writings. Then he added, in his own tone and words, "And I've manipulated it shamelessly."

"First Deacon," Wilgar said, running up, leading Bren by the hand. "We saw the fire, from the palisade."

"Much of Castell City is gone now," Bren said. "The rickety places all fell down and burned."

Kev began to smile and nod, then gave a sober look and glanced at Wilgar who had taken it all in. "There will be people needing help," the First Deacon said, in a First Deacon kind of voice. "We must go to them."

"Should we not administer to our own needs first?" Wilgar asked. "The better to be able to help others?"

Bren grinned and glanced away, still viewing Wilgar's precocity as cute and relatively harmless.

Kev, however, knowing now what the boy had stolen from the core of the massive knot, but not knowing how cynical or manipulative or Machiavellian or useful the advice it contained might prove to be, said only, "Your heritage must serve others to be worth anything."

Wilgar's eyes glinted. He grabbed a torch from a sconce and said to Kev, "Let's go, there's something you should know about," and ran off.

Kev kissed Bren, shrugged and smiled in ignorance and apology, and dashed off after Wilgar whose reserves of energy and lung capacity easily let him out-distance the older man.

They went from the Reverend Castell's lodge past the dewpond and a fallen, burned watchtower. There Wilgar paused to examine the damage, seeming to look for something in the smoldering planks. He poked with his feet, risking the muskylope-hide boots which Bren had crafted for him last Eye-cycle.

Wilgar led the way around the back of the burned barn. Carcass-mining still went on, and wagons and barrows trundled back and forth, carrying slabs of scorched, bloody meat to the Common Lodge. Wilgar skirted the corral's fence, went behind the unscathed chicken coop, then approached the palisade through thorn bushes and mounds of reinforcing dirt. He slapped an upright pole and said, "I think it's this one."

"This one what?" Kev asked.

Wilgar only grinned and returned to the chicken coop. They entered, and he led the way to the rear corner. He moved some supplies and showed Kev the trap door. "A tunnel. My secret entrance and exit, leads to a sewer nexus."

Kev said, "Why show me now?"

And Wilgar said, "Because we have a few things to do and we'd better do them right away. Come on." And with that, he jumped down into the tunnel and vanished.

Kev glanced back at the coop's door, which he'd closed. It was warm in the coop, from the body heat of the chickens, and it stank as only chicken coops can stink. Clucking, ruffling of feathers and pecking were the close sounds, while outside the coop people worked, shouted, even laughed and sang. Kev sighed, shoulders slumped from fatigue. He brushed at the smears of soot and scorch marks and just plain dirt which soiled his robes. "Our balbriggans don't suffice," he quoted, citing one of the Reverend Castell's first pronouncements regarding the Harmonies' advent upon Haven.

With that, Kev climbed down into the tunnel, dropped the trapdoor over himself, and crawled after Wilgar, who was whistling a fugue softly at the far end, as a guide. Echo, stench and blind faith defined Kev's next few minutes, and then he came to the sewer which offered secret escape from the Harmony Compound.

*   *   *

"Pre-positioning," Cole said, "is essential in normal raids, but Haven doesn't exactly have a communications network needing cut." He surveyed the office. He sat at one battered collapsible field desk, while Ibansk sat at another. Each had before him a field-issue note-box, and each processed his report in his own way. As they worked, they chatted.

Cole continued. "Vertical insertions usually involves paratroop units, but we're not bothering here on Haven, because there's not only no professional military, there's also no expected resistance, outside the usual mob-scenes stuff and, hell, police can handle that. Our soldiers should slam down like a cast-iron toilet lid. And, as I said, without effective real-time communication, word of the presence of CoDo troops won't spread much faster than the troops themselves."

"I know about Haven's static, Byers is mostly too active," Ibansk said, "but during lulls the indigs have used radio, for example."

"Sheer luck. Unpredictable. Hell if I'd want to lug around CBs or field-pack radios on the off-chance of being able to use them."

"What do the shuttles use during splashdowns?"

Cole grinned. "Line-of-sight lasers," he said. "They're almost perfect. No side-band bleed, which means you can't passively monitor it, and you can't decipher a laser transmission unless you directly intercept it. Try doing that on a battlefield sometime. You're infantry, aren't you? If you were a tanker, or artillery, you'd know about such basics."

Ibansk pretended to be insulted, but smiled as he said, "Well, at least my family never had to sell a son into the slavery of spying." He paused, made a note, then said, "But tell me, what do they do in heavy fog, for example?"

"They have problems," Cole said. "And if necessary they can resort to burst-repeaters. They call the system MOSAIC, just to be cute. It's not an acronym, I mean. Same as a normal squirt radio, compresses the message, but it repeats at random and the receivers build up the complete coded message from multiple scans of what ever punches through the interference each time."

"Then why not issue those to field units?"

Cole shook his head. He lifted his fingers from the keyboard long enough to spread his arms wide, palms facing each other. "Hardware's too big, you'd need about an APC and a half just to haul them to the transceivers. Shuttles can carry them, but only a few bother."

Ibansk grunted, impressed. "Should've opted to fill in my professional military education gaps," he muttered.

Cole said, "Forget that. PME doesn't cover this kind of stuff. Fact is, no one does. You just sort of learn it if you ever need to, and if you don't, then you'll probably never hear about it."

"You're saying this information is classified?" Ibansk looked both startled and slightly frightened at the possibility.

Cole put him at ease with a shrug. "Damned if I know."

Both men laughed, then continued processing their reports. Cole occasionally asked Ibansk for help with local nomenclature or map specifications.

"That's a quern," Ibansk said, "it mills grains, hand-cranked." He pointed to the diagram, then said, "Obviously not the one you're seeking, eh?"

"It's these access binaries. Somebody's got them scrambled. " Cole clattered a few keys and tried another, then sighed and slumped back as a diagram of a roller coaster came on screen.

"What is it you want?" Ibansk said. "Perhaps my access is better."

"I'm arranging the evidence we'll use against the Harmonies to revoke their settlement rights. We'll find piles of ore on Harmony farms, proving they were in on the pirating. I got Kennicott and Dover miners to help with that, and they even pitched in some equipment, trucks and shovels. We'll find a stockpile of cayenne pepper at the Harmony Compound, proving they intended to make pepper mace, an illegal weapon. I got that from the Docktown and Cambiston restaurants; good thing BuReloc's sending out so many ethnic types these days.

"We'll find a rebel map, showing both the compound and Castell City and its environs. Drew it myself, with details to be added by the rebels we round up. And then that Janesfort thing shot my smuggled-arms wad; what a waste of good surplus. Old sonic stunners, experimental and not much good to combat soldiers trained in hand-to-hand, but still too fancy for this bigger provocation. What I wanted to add to this Harmony evidence package were a few weapon systems schematics, catapults and napalm and that kind of thing."

"Weapons feasible in this environment and culture."

"Exactly." Cole leaned forward, watching Ibansk tap the keys this time. Again, they came up with inappropriate files.

"Someone's substituted these," Ibansk said.

"Well, we've got enough. The hell with schematics, I'll just toss a few references into the confessions."

Ibansk stood up. His eyes twinkled as he asked, "And have you written them in advance, too?"

But Cole, perhaps thinking of his retirement, returned weariness for his colleague's mirth as he answered, "Why leave things to chance?"

"If there's always hope, then there's always a chance," Ibansk recited as he walked back to his desk. "And if there's always a chance, then the unexpected can never be eliminated. And if that's true, then plans are the folly of man."

"Gogol? Tolstoy? Zinoviev?"

Ibansk sat down. "My father's last letter from the Gulag, just before they stripped him of rank and made him a *zek* for having compassion for a young mother and her daughter. His crime? Giving them milk. Guards could give only watchfulness and bullets, you see."

"Those post-Unified years were shameful times," Cole said, sympathy in his tone.

Ibansk, however, only smiled sardonically. "Oh, indeed. And we've come so far since then, with this CoDominium." He paused and looked at the room as if all of Haven could be seen in the dingy walls. "In distance, at any rate," he added in a quieter, flatter voice.

* * *

"Here, wear these," Wilgar said, handing over coarse, crude trousers, a tunic, and a smock, all made of un-dyed burlap from Janesfort hemp fibers. It smelled of marijuana and scratched like a hair shirt.

The boy changed from Harmony robes to nondescript city-garb in no time, demonstrating much practice. Kev held his new garments for a few moments, hesitant. Then he smiled and muttered again, in a new tone of justification, "Our balbriggans don't suffice, after all."

Although many Harmonies wore trousers beneath their robes to combat Haven's cold, it had been years since Kev had even seen trousers. He fumbled them on, having to remove his boots despite the utter lack of tapering or tailoring which distinguished the pants. "Why are we disguising ourselves?" he asked, almost dressed.

"Our robes, out there," Wilgar gestured with his head, meaning everywhere on Haven outside the Harmony Compound, "serve only discord. They draw ire and disharmony results."

"When in Rome, eh?" Kev asked, as if to himself, as if trying out a new idea. "Well, I'm ready. What is it we must do?"

Wilgar led, his motions confident, his manner stealthy. Kev followed through streets and alleys where rubble smoldered, where corpses lay abandoned, where stray pets claimed vengeful meals. From every doorway and lodge entrance baleful gazes watched them pass.

They worked their way first southwest from Wilgar's tunnel, then southeast, toward the Town Square, which they skirted on its north side. A minor construction project was going on in the square, and they paused to squint through the dark, to try to figure it out.

"Looks like CoDo Marines," Kev said, and Wilgar nodded, face sober, and moved on.

Where Docktown, Castell City, and Cambiston meet, at the southeast corner of the Town Square, the biggest bordello/saloon/casino on the planet towered four stories high. It featured three underground levels, as well, and was called Cambiston Doxie's, after the three-hundred-twenty pound woman who ran it, who called herself Doxie. No one knew her real identity: The place was notorious and when Wilgar moved as if to enter, Kev grabbed his arm and said, "What are you doing?"

"We've got business—"

"In there? I don't think so."

Wilgar yanked his elbow from the older man's grip. "Stay out here if you must. Act drunk, sit in the gutter. If anyone bothers you—"

"Wilgar, what's going on?" Kev stepped closer, looked at the boy closer. He frowned and backed a step away. In a quieter voice he repeated, "What's going on?"

Wilgar's face showed no emotion as he said, "I've got a pretty good idea we're about to lose Haven. An under strength regiment of the 77th CoDominium Marines are due any minute now, to put down the rebellion. This is one of my best intelligence spots." And with that, he turned and strode up to the guards who smoked and guzzled booze at the main entrance.

Kev hurried to catch up to Wilgar, and heard the boy mutter, "He's with me," and was surprised when both were permitted entrance. A huge lobby, lit by flaming braziers and sconced torches, gaped like pre-Harmony ideas of Hell. Craps tables, pool tables, blackjack, baccarat, poker and roulette tables strained under heavy use. Drunks shouted, laughed, or wailed. Women sauntered, some nude, others dressed as exotically as if there might be an interplanetary costume ball going on.

Kev's eyes never stopped moving, but Wilgar walked through it all nonchalantly without even a side glance. He marched to an unmarked brass door, touched it near the middle, and said, "It's me."

The door slid back, revealing an elevator big enough to haul a yoked team of muskylopes to the roof. Kev jumped in after Wilgar, then said, "This place takes away my breath."

Wilgar, not looking away from the door, said, "Only after it's taken everything else."

Pausing in its vertical ascent, the elevator seemed to sway for a moment, then twisted widdershins. Clamps and clunks sounded. The door opened, and Wilgar led Kev into an office.

Behind a huge desk sat Doxie, chomping her cigar stub, one hand around a mug of ale. She belched, her froggy eyes glistening with the effort, then barked, "Who's your shadow?"

"First Deacon Kev Malcolm," Wilgar said, and when Doxie's eyes widened in pleased surprise, the boy added, "He doesn't know."

"Ah," Doxie grunted. She shifted weight and slurped some ale, letting the foam mustache it deposited upon her upper lip linger for an instant, before lapping it off with a quick, splotchy tongue.

"We'll ignore him, then," she said. "Your instincts were right, kid. This planet's in for a change of management. My people tell me there's talk of a battalion or more, poised to strike even now. That's confirmed. Irregulars are standing by, implementing phase one." Doxie laughed, which sounded like someone trying to start an Earthside lawnmower under water and failing. "How's that for jargon?" she asked, pleased.

"We'll be ready," Wilgar said.

"Hell we will, boy," Doxie barked. "We'll be swallowed whole like the cherry in a Shirley Temple."

Wilgar stood in front of the desk, while Kev stood nearer the elevator, unable to stop gaping as he shifted from foot to foot. In the shadowy corners of the office, several people of indeterminate sex, size, or function lolled or leaned, only their watchfulness evident. From other rooms both above and below the office came the sounds of revelry and debauchery. Kev winced at particularly loud squeals and whoops and thuds, and under it all music hammered like smithies in a factory forge; harmony seemed only grudgingly tolerated in the songs.

"Will you do something against it?" Doxie asked, adding, with much heavy sarcasm, "Phase one?"

Wilgar nodded. "Small things, token protests. We can do little more, but survival allows some room for resistance."

"Good." Doxie scratched her shoulder, which sported a rainbow-hued tattoo of a guillotine, from which bounced a laughing head resembling nothing so much as a younger version of Doxie herself. She wore a sleeveless shirt patched together from other garments and her hair grew wild and tangled, with streaks of gray in its Stygian black tresses.

Kev looked pointedly away from the huge woman, but jumped as she struck a sulfurous match with her thumbnail to ignite the tip of her cigar stub. Wilgar walked over to him, and whispered, "That means our business is over," and practically pushed Kev into the elevator.

They left Cambiston Doxie's through a side door and made their way down to lakeside. As they faced south, gazing at Splashdown Island, the last of Docktown's quays offered silhouettes on their right. On their left, Cambiston glittered with fires, most contained, some flaring into the dark sky. Starlight offered the slightest respite from the illusion of blindness, but Kev and Wilgar, acclimated to Haven, could see fairly well.

A shout of surprise escaped from Kev, however, when several ragged children suddenly leaped into their path from lake's edge bushes. "Hail," one said, while the others tensed for trouble.

To Kev Wilgar said, "My Irregulars," then asked the children, "Are the turtles in place?"

"They're ready," one of the children said.

Kev asked what was going on, but Wilgar simply led the way into the bushes, which offered cover as well as any Earthbound laurel. The leaves smelled of lemons. Tiny blue berries left stains.

At water's edge they came upon a trench. It was hidden by branches and living bushes and once down in it, Kev found familiar building techniques evident. "Your irregulars learn well," he said to Wilgar, who nodded. "They have to or they're out," he answered.

"So why are they called irregulars? They look normal enough."

"Sherlock Holmes stories." Wilgar paused, just long enough, then said, "Yes, more of that useless Earthish fiction I'm always reading," in a sassy tone. Then he smiled. "None of these kids has a home, or much chance, without me. The only school on Haven is the one in our Compound and we only take Harmony children. That leaves them doubly orphaned, first by death and then by neglect. I offer them hope and structure. We work as a team, and get things done."

Kev said, "Your father would be proud." He knew that the school had only been opened because Wilgar had nagged his father into it. Charles Castell had resisted until the boy had volunteered that the outsider, who ran Harp's bar, had been teaching him to read. That had been all the goad necessary for the establishment of Haven's first school; Castell had then forbidden the boy to associate with Brodski or his companions.

"My father wouldn't acknowledge these people," Wilgar shot back. "He ignored them as infidels; tell me how that's harmonious?" The boy sneered that last word, making it a term of opprobrium. Softer, he added, "I may not have the feel for things Harmony, but I know what's right and what's not, and I know how to pay attention, and how to get things done."

And here he pulled something from inside his shirt. It was the leather book he'd stolen from the tangle of knotted ropes in which his father had hidden it. He held it up to Kev, the way a convert often thrusts a bible into the face of a nonbeliever. "Garner 'Bill' Castell's diary," he said. "My grandfather's story in his own words, how he accomplished everything, all the practical advice and hard-nosed truth. He would have kicked my father's sanctimonious ass if he had lived to see what a holier-than-thou fanatic the great Reverend Charles Castell became."

Kev gasped and leaned back against the trench's wall. "What are you saying?" he asked. He frowned as indignation gathered in him.

But Wilgar shoved the book back into its pocket and shoved a hand upward and said, "Look."

A trail of fire, then another, and then a third, marked re-entry for three shuttles. "They're coming," Wilgar said. To the children around them, he said, "The turtles are deployed?"

"What are these turtles?" Kev asked.

"Waterlogged logs," one of the kids answered. "They float, but just barely. Can't be seen, not even from a boat."

"But jeex when they hit one," another boy said, smacking his hands together and kiting one high over the other in parody of a flaming crash.

"My God," said Kev. "What are you doing? That's an act of war, Wilgar you can't—"

"Passive tactics," Wilgar said. "It's not our fault if they decide to come swooping down on our turtles. We have our own right to float what we will in Havenhold Lake and they have the right to wreck their splashships if they want."

They watched as the bright specks in the sky grew. The splashships extended wings, and sonic booms echoed as they approached in formation. As all re-entries took place west to east, the final maneuver necessary for coming down in Havenhold Lake's splashdown lanes was a dogleg to north or south, depending upon cross winds and other ground conditions.

This dogleg usually took the shuttles over the Harmony Compound, or over Shorewood Forest to the south. This time they banked over the forest, which was preferred, due to the lack of settlements there. Dropping salvageable shuttles and/or cargo on populated areas was avoided; no use making scavenging any easier for the Haveners.

Kev tensed. He found himself holding his breath. He couldn't take his eyes away from the shuttles coming down, even though he couldn't see them all that well in the dark sky. Mostly they looked like shadows, and except for their relative motion against stars and their blinking lights, they would not have been visible at all.

The three splashships seemed to be coming directly at the trench now, and the irregulars collectively hushed. "The turtles are near the middle," someone whispered.

The first splashship kissed water, sending up spray which looked fluorescent. It settled on the water, plowing a trough of wave, its speed slowing considerably. And then, just as the second shuttle touched the water's surface a few seconds later, in another lane, the first splashship struck several semi-submerged logs.

It canted sideways and entered the third ship's lane even as the second shuttle veered due east in a standard emergency right turn which took it out of harms way.

Lights and sirens came on at Splashdown Island, and rescue boats deployed. The first shuttle rolled almost gracefully onto its right wing, which was still extended for atmosphere. The wing dug into the water like a paddle and the shuttle, now perpendicular to its motion, rolled onto its back and completely blocked the third shuttle's lane.

Screaming engines drowned out screams and sirens for a moment as the third splashship tried to pull up and out. It failed, and so the third splashship came down virtually on top of the first, nose up, engines roaring.

When water entered the suddenly-reheated engines, steam formed, tearing the engine compartments apart. Explosions illuminated the night.

"Two out of three, anyway," one of the irregulars muttered, seeking approval. Another muttered, "Four hundred pissed-off soldiers left," and shuddered. "Yeah," a third realized, "their buddies all got killed; they'll be after revenge for sure."

The irregulars discussed where to hide, or whether or not to split up into smaller groups.

Kev and Wilgar gazed at each other, their faces visible now as fuel burned on the lake's surface. "Murder," said Kev.

"Accident," said Wilgar.

Kev blinked first.

*   *   *

"Eight-hundred and four Marines killed," Ibansk said, face sad. Cole shook his head. "Never expected this," he muttered, making notes. "Come on, I'd say it's time to activate Operation: ROPE."

But General Lassitre and Thomas Erhenfeld Bronson were way ahead of him, and from The Egg and other, smaller bunkers placed all over and around Castell City and Environs and as far west as Hell's-a-Comin', as well as from the surviving splashship, CoDo Marines swarmed like angry wasps, to put down what was now looking like an actual rebellion.

Furious squads jumped from ship to dock even before the lucky shuttle got tied down by dockhands. They fanned out, moving from a wharf just south of the Town Square. At each building flash-bang grenades were tossed, and trained, angry soldiers with weapons set on automatic cleared each successive building with quick, merciless bursts.

No quarter was asked or given; Haveners met the attacking soldiers with axes, hammers, stones and fists; they were mauled, mowed down, routed. Nothing stood against the Marines, who channeled their fury into professionally disciplined tactics. Choreography could not have gone smoother, and it became difficult for squad leaders to control their men's wrath. "Take no prisoners," was a frequent refrain.

Corporal Jenges waved his squad forward. He crouched behind a boulder some indig had used for a front door. The dwelling had been full of cowering people; it was now empty, unless you counted fresh corpses, which they didn't.

Jenges growled, "Clear that next pile of shit," and fell in with his Lieutenant, Mazziolli, who said, "Fuckers killed Bobby's squad."

"Two ships gone," Jenges agreed. He inhaled deep, to chase tears. His face hurt from all the frowning he'd been doing the past hour or so. When a torso appeared from behind a rickety wood-slat shack, Jenges raised his rifle and squeezed off a quick burst. The Havener fell, howling, and Mazz finished him off. "Loud, ain't they?" he said.

Corporal Jenges saw the all-clear signal and moved out, rounding a building and leading his people directly into an ambush.

A rock bounced off his helmet, another off his right shoulder. He fired his rifle in reflex even as he dived flat. A stick fell across his arm, and he brushed it aside. His squad had all fallen flat, too, and now systematically crawled forward in staggered movements, a pair at a time.

A hail of pathetic makeshift hurlants fell on the soldiers. One sergeant, tired of the bullshit, stood up and sprayed his weapon. "Hose 'em down," he called, and a few of the others stood to do the same. In about ten seconds the ambush had been defeated, all indigs chased or dead.

"And this one's for Jay-Jay, you holy scum," a monitor yelled, administering a coup-de-grace to a wounded Havener with his pistol.

Corporal Jenges shuddered. The Havener had been a little girl no more than ten years old. For throwing a rock and for being there to catch the flack from two wrecked shuttles, she'd been blown away.

"Up for it, sir?" Mazz asked, moving out.

With a nod, Jenges followed, his moment of regret over, his hunger for more payback returning with a vengeance.

APCs bulled through crowds and the ruins of burned buildings. Squads of Marines cleared and secured areas with mechanical efficiency. Field commanders enjoyed excellent communications using tethered balloons to take line-of-sight laser-relays aloft. A couple of tanks offered bluster and boom. Unit after unit reported resistance as light to non-existent. "It's harder securing our barracks," one report asserted.

There were guns on Haven. Most were wielded by one-time hunters, who had expended most of their ammo on muskylope slaughters. Still, occasional shots rang out in response to the overwhelming fire-power of the CoDominium Marines.

Chuck Wittbeck, a private, slogged under a laser radio pack. He heard the shot which knocked out his comm-gear. When the slug hit, it not only trashed the radio, it slammed Wittbeck to his knees. "Damn, I'm hit," he said. He lay right in the middle of a street, between two-story buildings, not far from the wharf. They could still smell Havenhold Lake, but they could smell Castell City gutters a lot better.

"Medic," his pair-partner Ed Kaufener called, firing a wild burst that tore apart a wood building, almost knocking it over.

"I'm not wounded," Wittbeck said, pushing out from under the radio which, despite advanced technology and all that slap-happy stuff, still weighed over twenty-eight kilos, even on Haven. Helium leaked from the pack; no more comm-balloon line-of-sight relays. They'd be off-lasernet. "It was my radio that took the hit."

Pulling his sidearm, Wittbeck spotted a glint in a window on a second story. "Hey Ed, up there." He pointed. "Let's go get 'em, huh? Damned if I'm going to be pinned down by some Have-Not."

They zigged and zagged toward the building. More shots dug into the ground around them.

Ed slammed into the door and hit the stairs as if he'd known where they'd be. Wittbeck followed, panting in the thin, cold air, his gun carried at the ready, barrel raised. Training on the transit ship hadn't prepared them for the change in atmosphere, but CoDo Marines can cope, and they'd prove it, no problem.

Footsteps sounded in a room ahead of them, to the left of the top of the stairs. Ed signaled, then they flanked the door. On three, Wittbeck mouthed, and when Ed nodded, he counted.

They hit the door, which broke inward as they kicked. Ed fired a clear-the-room shot, then rolled in, with Wittbeck spinning around the doorframe just behind him. They covered the room in standard two-man vectors, each aiming their weapon at the old man who wore nothing but a kind of diaper rigged from sheets. "You ain't gettin' it," the old man said. "Ain't getting what, old man?" Ed asked.

"Ain't getting m'gold map, so go ahead and shoot."

"Gold map my ass," Wittbeck laughed.

"Might as well shoot," the old man said, his rifle lying at his feet, having fired its last bullet during the soldiers' charge toward the building. "What do you think?" Ed asked.

"Not much," Wittbeck said. "Almost insulting to be fighting these losers."

"So shoot, already, I'm tired of your waffling," the old man said one last time, snarling without teeth.

Ed plugged the old man in the head. Brains flew out the window from which the old man had sniped. They ruined the ancient rifle and left it for scrap, then checked the rest of what appeared to be a run down hotel. The boards had never been painted in some rooms. They found no more people, got sick of being separated from their squad, and rejoined their comrades a few blocks north, where the killing continued.

What little fight some of the rougher elements of Haven offered got knocked out of them with their first exposure to professional weapons and tactics. Discipline beat desperation every time, and coordination smashed the few contradictory poses struck by recalcitrant saloon owners and the like. It was harder for field commanders to keep their people from looting than to gain control of the assigned zones and, with all the bars and lowlifes, temptations could not always be avoided. Gang rapes, organized theft and other insubordinations were inevitable, but few.

"Gridlocked," came report after report, code for mission accomplished, area secure, awaiting further orders. And then came the calls from outlying farms. "Stockpiles of stolen ore found," they said, and "Obvious rebel activity," and "Resistance nil."

Ollie Sheed was in on one of those farm raids. They used an APC to get them out there fast, then waited for the good-to-go signal in a no-fire bivouac, just thermals to keep them warm. When word came of the sabotaged splashdown, tempers ran high, and it was about all Corporal LaMonte could do to settle them down. "Farmer's daughters," someone started chanting.

By the time the Corporal's implant chirped, they'd creepy-crawled to within a few meters of the farm's central building, which was a Harmony style mound of sod, covering a three-quarters sunken home made mostly of wood-slats and stone. Ollie got to flash-bang the tunnel, which zigzagged as he crawled into cordite and magnesium residue.

Choking, Ollie flash-banged the place's main room for good measure, and only then did he rise up and train his weapon on the people lying blind and deaf here and there.

Ollies' pals were forever grateful that he'd resisted his first urge to pull the trigger; only women occupied the farm, their menfolk having been called down to the Harmony Compound to help with all the discord.

Harmony women are demur, on average, but those raised in Haven's harsh environment could hardly be called beauties, even by horny soldier standards. They did, however, provide sport for those in the squad who believed, as Ollie himself observed, "All cats are gray in the dark."

Corporal LaMonte didn't participate, and didn't condone, and didn't much like what happened, but he didn't report it, either. After all, these Harmonies had proven treacherous, and had apparently killed over eight-hundred fellow Marines. If they wanted war, then fine. Wars got rough right from the start, and they'd learn that, if the soldiers had to teach the lesson over and over and over.

"What's the matter, Corporal?" Ollie asked, crawling out of the tunnel tired but satiated for the nonce.

The squad leader said, "Nothing," but what he meant was the women's screams, and the men's laughter. He told his radioman to report the mission a complete success, with no casualties.

*   *   *

A single Haven night was all it took to create, then crush, a rebellion.

Cole and Ibansk rode with General Lassitre and Thomas Erhenfeld Bronson in an Armored Personnel Carrier from a wharf in Docktown to Town Square, where the gibbets had been built. "Remember," Ibansk said, upon seeing the apparatus of death. "No gallows humor, please."

His oxymoron was not appreciated by Taxpayer Bronson, who grunted in disgust and looked away.

The interior of the AFC had to be air conditioned, even on icy Haven, because its engine was an old fusion model which built up excess heat. It smelled of stale sweat from the thousands of soldiers who'd ridden in it to battle over its years of service. The plain metal was scored with layers of initials, probably scratched with bayonet tips by doomed soldiers bored with the hours of waiting between the instants of terror which defined their lives. Cole touched the layered names and letters and numerals and muttered, "Palimpsest."

"Don't worry," General Lassitre said, eyes twinkling. "You've left your mark on this place."

Ibansk placed a hand on Cole's shoulder, but said nothing.

They came to the square. Cutting diagonally from the middle of the north side to the middle of the west side, a long stage had been built. It stood three meters high. At its center, ten cross-beam gibbets had been erected, and an eleventh was even then being finished. A military band warmed up on a grandstand near the southwest side of the stage. Lights were hoisted and lashed to remaining above-ground buildings. Loudspeakers squawked as technicians adjusted them. Other calibrations caused other sounds of preparation.

"Reminds me of a political rally," General Lassitre said.

Thomas Erhenfeld Bronson snorted and said, "What else is it, then?"

"I thought it was to be a public execution of the rebel leaders. The CoDominium Marine commander demands it, as do I. Examples must be set, and the deaths of our people must not go unanswered."

Taxpayer Bronson merely chuckled, a sound as quiet and unpleasant as a slice through an abdomen.

When the APC's safety was ensured by a phalanx of soldiers, the VIPs were allowed to get out of it. Cole and Ibansk let the general and the businessman/politician go ahead of them. As they came down the ramp, guards crushed in on them. "Crowd's raucous," one of the guards said. "Threw some rocks, that kind of thing."

In the harsh glare of klieg lights and mantle-lanterns, Cole saw a sea of faces just beyond the ropes separating square from stage. All eyes seemed riveted to a spot just past the gallows and Cole tried to step up onto a crate to get a better look, but a guard knocked him down. "Don't expose yourself like that, sir," the soldier said, face sheepish but voice quite sincere. He seemed willing to knock his charge down as often as necessary, so Cole just nodded.

A clear plastiflex barrier had been built on the northeast side of the gallows; behind this the VIPs were herded. "As if they expect snipers," General Lassitre said in contempt, and a soldier said, "SOP, sir, that's all."

Observing the niceties and doing everything by the book meant, as usual, that most of the off-the-books maneuvering was over. Thomas Erhenfeld Bronson sat heavily, then offered the General a single baleful look.

Now that they were on stage, Ibansk and Cole could see the prisoners, each suffering fate in his own way. One man, short and skinny, danced a hellish mockery of the pomp and circumstance surrounding them, and jabbed at guards in mock-boxing stance. He jumped around like a leprechaun and put up about as much squawk and derision as a banshee. He even wore mostly green, and he refused a hood as the hangman passed along the line of condemned prisoners. "That's Fineal Naha," Ibansk said, "Governor of Hell's-a-Comin'."

"And that," said Cole, pointing to the tall, wild-haired figure in the torn, soiled robes, "is the Reverend Charles Castell. I'll be damned."

"So will he, apparently, at least by human standards," Ibansk said.

He and Cole took seats behind the general and the politician. Neither thought of Anwar Sadat, but some of the security procedures currently making them so uncomfortable and bored owed much to that Earthside warrior's demise as each layer of protection covered the others.

Finally the lights, their colored gels like swollen stars in the middle distance as viewed from the stage, mixed into brilliant white and illuminated only the stage. The crowd was left in silence usually said to be awe-struck by the lighting designer in his after-action reports.

A plastiflex podium was carried on stage by two armed Marine sergeants, who fell in to either side of it once it had been placed properly, and then General Lassitre rose. "Ladies and gentlemen of the fair planet of Haven, outpost of CoDominium's grand design and eternal glory, welcome to this sad, this festive occasion. Sad because we must face the fact that some of your brethren, yes, even members of the gentle, peace-loving Harmony sect, have conspired and committed acts of rebellion against the greater order.

"Evidence has been gathered and presented to a tribunal, which returned a unanimous verdict. Such evidence shall become public soon. Also be it known that it wasn't sheer luck that saved you. A formal request for military help in putting down the rebellion was made through channels, and it met with the response you have, in the past few hours, experienced. Professional, restrained force has been applied to the problem, despite the dastardly sabotage of a splashdown, and the problem is no more. And that's why this is also a festive time."

Here the General paused, as mixed applause, probably from claques, backfired through the crowd. He raised his hands as if to still a thunderous ovation, then said, "And to further our civilized ends, we have found it necessary to revoke the Harmony charter of settlement rights, which, upon examination, has been lawfully found to have been granted in error and undue haste. Public pressures must not be permitted to victimize an entire planet's population, and certainly a single religious sect must not be allowed to hold sway over what promises to be a population of millions in the very near future.

"And let us remember those brave, unfortunate soldiers killed earlier by rebel terrorist activities on Havenhold Lake. Expecting an orderly implementation of legal orders, they found only watery graves. They shall be missed, but more, many more shall follow. Perhaps living well shall be, for the survivors, the best revenge."

Here Ibansk leaned over to Cole and said, "On Haven?"

Cole nodded, staring past the stage at a group of robed figures just barely visible in reflected light to one side of the crowd. He was biting his lower lip and did not grin at Ibansk's typically cynical jest.

"First," General Lassitre said, drawing his ceremonial sword and flourishing it once more, perhaps to alarm the dozen representatives now seated around the VIPs, "we must have done with an unpleasant but necessary task." He gestured toward the gallows, his sword catching a golden spotlight's beam perfectly. "Having been duly found guilty by omission when not in deed of the deaths of eight-hundred and four of our benevolent CoDominium's finest fighting troops, and further, having been sentenced by military tribunal to death for said rebellious, treacherous acts, the prisoners shall now, in full witness of Haven's citizenry, be hanged by the neck until dead. Their graves shall be unmarked, while their nefarious deeds shall be long kept in mind." He waved the sword again, and again caught, expertly, the light.

In thousands of eyes, a golden mote glinted for an instant, even as their attention turned toward the instruments of death.

A last few blows from a hammer sounded as the microphones flickered off; the eleventh gibbet now stood complete, ready. A generator somewhere received a kick, and found its rhythm again.

But this was just a tease, to add the drama of anticipation, which would sit like guilt on the shoulders of the crowd later, in their hovels. They'd berate themselves, having actually wanted the hangings to hurry up and happen, and that would make them prone to obedience, thinking themselves inwardly tainted. Or so read the manual on stage-managing public executions for conquered populaces.

The microphones came back to life, and General Lassitre said, "Your planet, having been accepted for full CoDominium membership, qualifies for consulate status, and a consul-general is even now being sent. In the interim, a colonial governor has been appointed by due process, and it is he who shall dispense with our unfinished business, for it is he who shall lead you those first few steps into a grand, profitable, and respectful future. Ladies and gentlemen, may I present a renowned businessman and politician from one of Earth's most illustrious families, your interim governor, Taxpayer Thomas Erhenfeld Bronson."

The claques must have passed around some pelf this time, for the applause was actually audible at the back of the stage. As Thomas Erhenfeld Bronson hefted his bulk to the podium in a slow gait, the condemned prisoners were taken up their final flight of stairs.

Nooses were snugged at the back and to one side of their necks, to ensure a clean snap, a quick and painless break. All the condemned except Naha and Castell wore black hoods of coarse cloth. All had their hands bound behind them, and their ankles, and their knees. As they stood accepting these indignities, Bronson gained the podium. "Justice be done," he said, in a low growl, unceremoniously as ever. He did not look at the podium, but instead glanced back at Cole, to whom he smiled.

That's when the guards knocked Ibansk over in their haste and grabbed Maxwell Cole, lifting him, pinioning his arms in grips strengthened by years of practice. The look on Cole's face was one of fury, fear and finality. As he was dragged past the podium, he yelled, so that the microphones caught and passed it on, "See Haven, then die."

The eleventh gibbet was Cole's. He clambered up beside the Reverend Charles Castell, who gazed over at him and said, "Peace is ours to offer."

As Thomas Erhenfeld Bronson made a short, sweet speech full of phrases guaranteed by researchers to affect the hearts and minds of the locals, Cole gasped as if he'd run a marathon, then felt his knees go weak. "I don't want to die," he said, almost crying.

The Reverend Castell said, "Seek Harmony," and was kidney-punched by a guard who strutted up and down behind the condemned as if he were the master of ceremonies.

The hangman, in black military hood, stood by the pole tied to the mechanisms holding the trapdoors shut. When he pulled the pole free, the doors would drop open simultaneously.

"A CoDominium Naval Base," Thomas Erhenfeld Bronson announced, to genuine cheers, and into those cheers he said, "and power sats, and food factories and all the earthly amenities by which a civilized world is known."

As the cheers rose, Bronson lifted one arm. He glanced at the gallows. Everyone fell silent. "But first, we must make room for such things."

His arm fell.

* * *

They'd been hearing the echoes from the loudspeakers and seeing the glow from the lights for some time, so Wilgar sent an irregular known for speed to see what was going on.

"Quickly," the ragged girl said, struggling to get her breath as she returned. "They're going to hang people."

Wilgar and Kev and the others ran the three or four blocks from lake to square, where they spotted a group of Harmonies huddled to one side. Someone at the podium spoke in a low, sulky voice. Sure enough, there were gallows, and a man was being carried up to the last of them.

Kev said, "That's Colin Maxwell, the spy from the miners."

Wilgar shook his head. "His name's Maxwell Cole, from CoDo Intelligence. Agent provocateur."

They found a distraught Saral slumped on the ground at the middle of the Harmonies. Acolytes and Deacons kept her grief safe from prying eyes, even as Beads patrolled the crowd nearby as extra security of a more physical nature. "They took him from me," she wailed, but as she saw Wilgar she reached up, joy and disbelief mingling in her feature.

Wilgar leaned down and hugged his mother, then extracted himself from her grip and backed off. "Be strong," he told her.

"They took the Reverend," a Deacon told Kev. "Said he was a rebel leader. What does it mean?"

Kev looked up. The sky, beyond the glare of the kliegs, was lightening. "It means we're on our own now," he said softly. With more urgency and an angry grimace, he added, "It should've been me."

The crowd cheered about something the speaker said, and then came the phrase, "...room for such things," and the speaker's arm fell.

The entire square fell silent, and even as the clatter of the trapdoors letting go echoed, a glint of dawn flickered in the sky. The stars went away, to be replaced by a rosy glow.

The condemned men fell as if in slow motion, and each pulled up short. Kev made out the Reverend Castell, recognizing the robes. "He collected bits of rope the way old people sometimes hoard ends of soap or bits of twine," he said, softly, apropos of nothing.

The ropes halted the falls, and necks cracked like distant gunfire, stirring the crowd to low murmurs. More dawn spilled over the planet's ecliptic rim. More darkness fled, and the klieg lights became, in an unexpected instant, redundant, then superfluous.

As the Reverend Castell's rope snapped taut, stopping his drop toward Haven's center of gravity, a flare of light flickered to life from within. The crowd gasped, and even as those nearby cringed back in amazement or fright, as the Reverend Charles Castell burst into bright white flame.

The Harmonies around Saral dropped to their knees, except Wilgar, but even he stood gaping, nonplussed. The few cads in the crowd who'd cheered the hangings fell silent now, too.

"He refused to curse the darkness," one of the Deacons muttered, crying openly and smiling through pain.

The Reverend Charles Castell's flames caused consternation, if not panic, among the VIPs on the stage, and for a few seconds pandemonium ensued as Marines scurried to douse the flames. The fire burned itself out long before anyone got to extinguish Castell, and then he, too, swung on creaking new hemp ropes, the same as the others, except for the fine coating of ash.

"I want his body," Saral said, and Kev gestured to a Deacon, who took some acolytes to try to claim it despite the threat of unmarked graves.

A man in Russian uniform eased up to Wilgar, then said, "Excuse me, but—"

"Ibansk," Wilgar said, surprise allowing him to stifle sobs.

The Russian said, "Don't call me that ever again." He glanced back at the stage, then all around himself, then lowered his voice and said, "When they grabbed Cole, I bailed out."

"But if you were up on stage," Kev objected. "then you're one of them."

Ibansk glared for an instant at Kev, who was crying along with all the other Harmonies and many of the crowd. He shrugged, then shook his head in disgust. "No, I was never one of them. But whatever I was, I think I'd like to become a Harmony now."

"He was one of Doxie's best contacts, when he could sneak away from Splashdown Island," Wilgar said, wiping tears and standing straighter. "Even gave us access codes so we could hack into CoDo computers." He touched Kev's arm. "He's Russian, and he knows all too well the kind of thing we're going through. He's a friend, he's helped us."

"Us?" Kev asked.

But Wilgar had already begun leading the Harmonies back to the Compound.

More Precious Than Rubies

By A.L. Brown

2060 A.D., Earth

Abdullah Hassan lay on the hot deck, gasping for breath. The air was hot, too, and offered little comfort. It reeked of many things—unwashed bodies, urine, the tang of rusting metal, and over it all, the cloying smell of bunker fuel. He felt feverish, and retched from time to time, but nothing came up. Abdullah was completely dehydrated and his body had no moisture left to spare.

He knew when he bought his ticket that there was no air conditioning in steerage on this ancient ship, but thought he could handle it. He hadn't realized that the ship would break down and that even the limited breath of fresh air from the vents on the deck would stop. Nor had he realized that the water would stop, too. He hadn't understood that there were people in the world who would let others die or how much he could grow to hate this vessel: hate the light green paint that had been used on the bulkheads, hate the yellowed paint on the ceiling he lay under, which may have been white in past decades.

It had sounded so romantic when he started out. Leave Boston, quit M.I.T., go to Somalia, find his roots, the family his father had worked so hard to leave behind. On to other parts of Africa, India and finally Pakistan. Then from Karachi, travel to Saudi Arabia, make his pilgrimage, the Hajj, to see Mecca. But after a long trip, even after taking odd jobs here and there to support himself, money was short, and steerage in this weather-beaten ship, the *Sidi Ferrous*, was the best he could afford. And now he realized that price had been no bargain.

All around him, other pilgrims were sprawled among their sparse belongings. Some were silent, many cried, others prayed, some moaned wordlessly. Most were resigned to accepting the will of Allah, but some still held hope that Allah's will would be to intercede and aid them. At first, as conditions in the below-decks area had worsened, Abdullah had tried to help the others, the youngest and the oldest that were first to fall. But soon he had no strength for anyone else, and eventually, no strength even for himself.

A scream cut through the still air, then shouting, thumps and crashes and the sound of metal on metal. When he heard shots, Abdullah struggled to his feet, and moved forward. The old man next to him tried to rise as well.

Abdullah put a hand on his shoulder. "Rest, pilgrim. I will find out what is going on." The Arabic he had spent a lifetime learning had become fluent in these last few months.

The old man nodded and sank back down, his head on a small pack.

He climbed a rusting stairway, stepped out onto the long covered walkway that ran the length of the ship on this level, and started for a ladder. He squinted as the burning sun overwhelmed his eyes. A body came tumbling down. It was almost on top of him by the time he realized what it was. He reared back in horror. It was a crewman—the man's throat was cut, and blood pooled around the body, the eyes already blank and vacant. A man leaned into the ladder well above him, and beckoned. "This way, boy." he snarled. "If you want to be any help at all, you will follow me."

So Abdullah followed him, up the ladder, then another and another, a mad corkscrew dash for the upper decks. When they reached the top deck the scene was pure chaos. The last few crewmen were on a ladder leading up to the bridge wing, holding rifles at the ready. At the foot of the ladder, pilgrims in their flowing robes gathered, armed with knives, axes and whatever makeshift weapons they could gather.

A burst of automatic weapon fire came from the crowd. The crewmen fell, and the pilgrims surged onto the bridge.ABdullah stared at the man, standing not too far from him, who had fired the shots. He was a large man with a thick red beard. His nose had been broken and there was a cruel scar across the right side of his face. He caught Abdullah's eye and grinned. There was no joy in that smile, it was more a feral baring of teeth.

Another man, a tall man in indigo blue robes, swept past them. "Follow me," he barked, and the scarred man immediately obeyed, as did other hard looking men in the crowd, all moving with a purpose. They swept up the ladder, into the bridge, and there were more shots, shouting, and after a hideous scream—silence. The tall man in blue stepped back out of the bridge and stopped at the head of the ladder. He was an impressive man, with a hooked nose, thick black hair and beard, and dark eyes.

"We have taken this vessel to prevent further suffering. Water, food and comforts will be distributed equally. Help us and you will live. Oppose us, and die. *Allahu Akbar!*"

His followers raised their voices in unison, "*Allahu Akbar!*"

The scarred man with the red beard came down the ladder. His weapon was held at waist level, but ready for immediate use. "You, you and you," he said, pointing at Abdullah and two others. "Follow me, we will find containers and water to bring back to the lower decks."

The next few hours passed in a blur. Abdullah saw great compassion, but also quick cruelty. Passengers who fought the mutineers were killed without mercy, while others were aided, given water, brought to cooler parts of the ship. The mutineers took everyone's phones, data devices, cameras, anything that would make a record of what had happened. Abdullah did what he was told, too frightened to think.

A man came by, calling, "English, English, we need someone who can speak English."

Abdullah raised his hand. "I can speak English."

"Then come with me," the man said, and they made their way to the bridge.

When they arrived, the man in blue turned to Abdullah and asked, "You speak English, African?"

"Yes," Abdullah said, "I went to school in America." He wasn't any darker than many of the other passengers, but his ancestors were definitely from sub-Saharan Africa. Better, however, to leave out the fact that he was American, let their assumptions stand. His nationality was not one that brought you friends in this part of the world.

The man gestured at the radio. "Tell me what they are saying."

Abdullah went to the radio, and translated as he listened. "They are talking about our ship, they have not heard from it. There is some sort of schedule for communications. There is talk of deploying forces, launching helicopters, sending a hovercraft."

"Who are they sending?" asked the man in blue. "Egyptians? Saudis?"

"No," answered Abdullah. "American Marines."

"The Great Satan!" the man snapped, and turned to his followers. "Weapons and any evidence over the side, along with bodies and weigh them down so they sink. If anyone who opposed us is still alive, kill them now. Spread the word among the passengers that we were attacked by pirates who came from a submarine, and have escaped. All of us are victims, trying to help those the pirates have harmed."

The man turned back to Abdullah. "You, follow me, I will have need of your skills with the language of the infidels."

*   *   *

Abdullah sat in the shadow of the white wooden barracks building, staring helplessly at the barbed wire that surrounded them. He was in Africa, but where, he had no idea. The Marines had turned them over to some sort of camp run by the CoDominium. The camp was near a spaceport, and day and night the huge lasers lanced up from the ground, igniting the fuel that launched ship after ship into orbit. The glare of the lasers pouring through the windows at night, and the roar of the ships, made sleep difficult.

He tried to take refuge in his faith. There were copies of the Qur'an available, he listened to sermons from imams who were among the prisoners, and he joined in the prayers five times a day. Because of his faith, he had often been the odd man out at home. But here among those of his own kind, he found he missed the diversity, the many viewpoints, the happy chaos of life back in Boston. He even missed baseball, and wondered how the Red Sox were doing. He tried to console himself that Allah would care for him, that he could trust that all was happening for a purpose, that his faithfulness would lead to fortune.

Abdullah knew more about the men he had been captured with. The man in blue was Tawfiq al Tabib, a noted Arab rebel, long wanted for violence against the Western forces that had meddled in the Middle East for over a century. The scarred man with red hair was called Barbarossa and was Tawfiq's principal lieutenant.

The U.S. Marines that had swept aboard the *Sidi Ferrous* met no resistance as they dropped from helicopters or climbed accommodation ladders. Tawfiq was the spokesman, and used Abdullah as his translator. The Marines listened to their story with skeptical glances among themselves, then they culled out all of the men who looked healthy enough to fight shackling them together. Their lieutenant was a hard man paying no attention to the rough treatment his men gave the prisoners. Abdullah kept his identity secret, telling the men he was African. He was afraid that if his fellow prisoners knew the truth, they would tear him apart.

When they reached the camp Tawfiq proved himself to be a force of nature. Abdullah had heard the term "larger than life," but this was the first time he had seen it personified. When Tawfiq found out Abdullah had some education he put him in charge of organizing classes, finding others among the prisoners who could teach things like history and mathematics.

Morning prayers were followed by an hour of calisthenics with another hour of exercising before supper. Work parties were organized to keep the camp clean. Sports leagues were organized with rugby becoming a favorite competition. There were also boxing and martial arts contests, and fighting techniques were among the lessons. At first, there was resistance to these new ideas from those who had been at the camp the longest. But Tawfiq and his lieutenants, by enlisting or beating down their strongest opponents, soon became the law

And so here Abdullah was, part of this group, but not *part* of it—trapped and alone. He had tried to talk to guards when he thought he would not be overheard, get them to listen, get them to understand he shouldn't be here. But they wouldn't listen, wouldn't believe him. Once he got a rifle butt across the side of his face, and perversely the welt brought him positive attention from Tawfiq's men. Anyone who made enough trouble to provoke the CoDominium was okay in their book.

One morning voices were raised and people began moving, heading for the parade field that lay in the center of the camp. There were no guards in the camp. Unless they entered in force, the closest they came was in the guard towers and by the gate where food was delivered. They crowded around the center of the field, where Tawfiq stood on a chair, his chief followers gathered around him.

He raised his voice, in both volume and pitch, obviously used to addressing crowds.

"I have been told what the CoDominium wants to do with us. They want to transport us, ship us to other worlds, send us away."

The crowd erupted in cries, shouts, questions, conversations. Tawfiq's lieutenants yelled for silence, while the man himself stood silent, waiting for quiet.

"They think that they are hurting us," Tawfiq continued, "But I say they are doing Allah's will."

The crowd erupted again, but was shouted back into silence.

"The infidels have destroyed this world, despoiled our homelands, made us slaves and lackeys. They took our oil, plowed under our crops, beat down our leaders. They think sending us away will destroy us. But I say that it will make us strong again. Let our struggle, our jihad, spill out across many worlds, throughout the universe. If they want to give us new worlds, let them. They also give us new chances, new lands, new resources. This would not be the first time in history that Allah has worked on the hearts of infidels to help his people."

A man cried out. "He is the Mahdi! The Mahdi has come in our hour of need to guide us."

The cry was taken up by others, and soon the whole crowd had joined the chant. "Mahdi! Mahdi! Mahdi! Mahdi! Mahdi!"

Abdullah was a Sunni, but he knew the legend of the Mahdi, the Shiite Imam who had disappeared centuries ago and was reputed to be waiting to return to lead the Faithful to victory. He stared up at Tawfiq surrounded by his lieutenants. They stood silently waiting for the noise to die down. They did not look like they had expected this and the men from the camp staring up at Tawfiq, who stood silently, dignified, firm. The entire crowd grew silent, and soon all were staring up at Tawfiq awaiting his reaction.

"If you want me to lead you, I will. I will lead you to the stars. As Allah wills. To the stars! As Allah wills!"

The crowd again took up the refrain. "To the stars! As Allah wills! To the stars! As Allah wills! To the stars! As Allah wills!"

*   *   *

After weeks of trying, Abdullah finally got an audience with a CoDominium Bureau of Relocation official. The man was fat and uncomfortable looking. A fan whirred on the table behind him, but despite the breeze, sweat still stained his shirt. A CoDominium Marine stood by the door, his eyes never leaving Abdullah looking bored but prepared for trouble. The official looked at Abdullah with disdain. He asked in Arabic, "What is your complaint?"

"I shouldn't be here," Abdullah protested in English, "I'm an American citizen."

"Your name?" the official asked.

"Abdullah Hassan, of Boston, Massachusetts."

The man typed the name into a desktop device. He scrolled through information, and his face hardened.

"No," he said, "I have your file and your picture here. You are Somali, and your name is Abdullah al Ibrahim. The file talks about your many attempts to claim the identity of a young American. It also talks about how you are in the inner circle of Tawfiq al Tabib, a murderer and troublemaker."

"I am not in his inner circle," Abdullah protested.

"But you were arrested with him," the official said.

"I was on the same boat as him, and when the Marines came aboard, I translated for them, I was trying to prevent more bloodshed."

"And you still stay in his company?"

"It's not like I have much choice," Abdullah replied, slumping back in his chair. "This is unfair, this is a mistake."

"Well, in the end it doesn't matter where you're from. Whoever you are, you were captured among enemies of the CoDominium. These files are clear and unambiguous. You are an associate of al Tabib and you will share his fate."

"And what fate is that?" asked Abdullah, his heart sinking.

"Transportation," the official said. "Your lot ships out in two weeks. To the planet Haven, I believe."

The official turned his eyes toward his computer, and Abdullah could see that the interview was over. He felt like he had been punched in the stomach. The Marine gestured toward the door and Abdullah rose and walked out unsteadily. He had left home to see the world, not to see worlds, not to be caught up in this nightmare, surrounded by people who scared him as much as the guards did. He would trade anything for a lecture from his father, to be called foolish, to be called a young idiot, to be safe at home in Boston. But it didn't look like there was anything his father could do; it was doubtful his father or mother would ever learn his fate. It appeared that Allah's will was leading him away. He was bound for the stars.

The day they were to depart, they waited in line to be loaded into busses long before the dawn, and were carried to another camp near the launch pads, this one austere, with only un-walled tents to provide shelter. There they waited in lines to be searched. Each of them had a small bundle of belongings which was checked three times along the way. They waited in lines for medical screening. They waited in lines to use toilet facilities, to get water and to get food.

Abdullah was kept close to Tawfiq in case any translating was required. The sun was low on the horizon by the time they reached the tunnels that led to the shuttles. There, at a holding area where low buildings without walls offered some shelter from the sun, was a scene of chaos. There were hundreds of women in burqas jammed together with children. And not just any women. There were shrieks of delight, shouts of joy, laughter and excited conversation.

Tawfiq barked to his lieutenants to find out what was going on. There were reunions going on all around him. Suddenly, Tawfiq stopped in his tracks. Two women ran towards him, one older, one younger. He gave a shout and fell to his knees, his face in his hands, weeping. The women fell to their knees beside him. He put his arms around them, and they hugged him back.

"What are you doing here?" he asked.

The older woman spoke. "Your call to go to the stars has gone out throughout the world. The CoDominium decided to accept petitions from families of men and women being transported for other worlds and is allowing us to come with you. To them, it is a good way to get rid of more of the Faithful."

"But the danger—" Tawfiq blurted.

"Oh my husband, you are still as naive as you are dedicated. Your jihad would be a short one without women and families. Do you really want your struggle to end after a single generation? What does our favorite proverb say about a good wife?"

Tawfiq answered, his voice husky, "She is more precious than rubies, my love, more precious than rubies."

Abdullah stood beside them, feeling awkward at the raw emotion of the moment.

The woman rose to her feet and looked at him. "And now husband, remember your manners. Who is this young man who accompanies you? I see many of your old cronies around us, but him I do not know."

"The African?" replied Tawfiq, standing up himself. "This is Abdullah. He speaks fluent English and has been translating for me. I plan to have him give English lessons during the journey, as part of our efforts to be ready for what faces us on the new world."

He turned to Abdullah. "This is my wife, A'isha. And my daughter, Faryal."

"Pleased to meet you," said Abdullah. A'isha was a tall woman, and even with the burqa concealing her, he could see that she was a strong woman, who carried herself with strength and dignity. The daughter was smaller, and her dark eyes, though full of tears, were very pretty. Her hands, clasped in front of her, were slender and delicate.

"It is good to meet you as well. My daughter and I will also receive your English lessons."

Abdullah looked at Tawfiq, who uncharacteristically shrugged. "You will learn, Abdullah, that there is one person in the world who feels free to give orders without looking to me for approval."

Around them, the chaos was beginning to subside. Lines were beginning to form again, the last lines they would stand in on this planet. It was time to go.

*   *   *

"You will teach me, my lieutenants, and my family, English." said Tawfiq. "But to the crew, you will know no English at all. The guards have told us that they want workers in the crew areas, workers to do the dirty work, like mopping decks, and washing dishes, they do not wish to do. So you will do this, and listen and learn."

The spaceship reminded Abdullah of the *Sidi Ferrous* in many ways. He slept with forty other men in a tiny compartment with canvas racks stacked four high. There were warrens of interlocking corridors and compartments, all with airtight doorways separating them. Many of the walls were even painted with the same hideous green that haunted his memories from those hot days on the Red Sea. The ship spun, so there was a semblance of gravity in most areas, and many of the passageways were curved in some manner. The galleys were simple and the food, often based on protein paste, nourishing but bland. The air was thin and dry with a metallic tang that never escaped notice.

The ship was somewhat shabby, with a crew too small to keep up with maintenance, and not well designed for all the passengers.

To help him gather information, Tawfiq made sure that Abdullah drew an assignment as a scullery worker in the ship's wardroom serving the ship's officers. Surprisingly, even though the transportees were controlled by BuReloc guards and officials, the ship they were on, the *Gettysburg*, was a CoDominium Navy vessel, and these were military officers Abdullah was serving. The ship was a military drop ship, its midsection lined with capsules designed to land troops from orbit.

After one of the first meals of their journey, as Abdullah was collecting dinner plates and serving dessert, the Captain made some comments to his officers that explained this mystery for Abdullah.

"Lift your glasses to *Gettysburg's* last mission. We stop in Haven long enough to drop off our 'passengers,' and then head to Makassar, where she will become an orbital base for the Fleet."

After the toast, a young ensign spoke up. "Why are we using drop capsules to deliver the transportees to the surface?"

"First," answered the Captain, "The Humanity League has complained that the settlers in the Dire Lake region have not been given enough support. The capsules are designed to be converted into barracks, warehouses and office space after landing. So they are our parting gift to our 'guests.'

"And second," he continued, "If you repeat this, I will deny I ever said it. There's a problem with the capsule system. When we dropped troops on Xanadu we lost twelve percent of them on the way down. There were many injuries, and even deaths, in the capsules that did make the drop. You can't deploy troops with a system that decimates the force before they even put their boots on the ground. The ship has been in service for over thirty years and is about to be retired. The Fleet decided to use the remaining drop capsules for one more mission, a mission where a few casualties won't bother anyone. It's a two-edged sword, but like I said, just one more parting gift for our guests!"

He raised his glass again and took a long drink as the room erupted with laughter. Abdullah kept his head down trying not to visibly react. His stomach muscles were tight, and he felt ill.

When he was not in the scullery, Abdullah taught English to large classes of Tawfiq's lieutenants and advisors. Another man, a Chechen, taught Russian. The focus, beyond basic vocabulary, was on the language of war. The students wanted to know the language of military weapons, tactics, the terms that soldiers knew. Abdullah cautioned them that he had never been a soldier, but did his best to satisfy their needs.

Tawfiq explained to him the importance of his efforts. If the people of Islam were to succeed on other worlds, they needed to press every advantage, turn their efforts toward self-improvement, pursue the inner jihad of self-improvement to serve the larger struggle. He made Abdullah feel good about what he was doing, as he did with everyone, his leadership turning the long months of being trapped on the ship into an opportunity to prepare.

But what Abdullah enjoyed most was his lessons for the women. Had there been a woman who knew English, he may not have been allowed to spend so much time with them. The harsh interpretations of social rules that fundamentalist groups like the Taliban had practiced around the turn of the century had faded. There was music among the Faithful, and even drinking, but no public dancing or displays of affection with unmarried men and women still leading mostly separate lives. Because of his knowledge, though, Abdullah spent an hour every day surrounded by the women some in traditional burqas, others simply in head scarves. He took pleasure in their laughter, and taught them to appreciate jokes and puns.

The women delighted in embarrassing Abdullah, pressing him to teach them the terms for body parts, for childbirth, medical terms that made him blush.

Tawfiq's wife A'isha was the acknowledged leader of the classes. Tall and dignified, she exercised the same natural leadership as her husband. The burqas that she and her daughter wore lent them an air of mystery. The daughter, Faryal, was a quick study, her hands always in motion when she spoke, swooping like graceful birds. Her eyes would sparkle when she was happy and Abdullah discovered he could tell when she was smiling simply by watching the corners of her eyes. He found himself leaving the classes relaxed and happy.

One day, after leaving the lessons, Abdullah saw a man moving furtively down a passageway. He was carrying a bundle in his arms. Abdullah recognized him, it was one of the men who worked with him in officer's country.

"Ibrahim," he called. "Where are you going?"

The man turned, and dropped the bundle, running away down the corridor. Abdullah opened the bundle, and found china, silverware and spices from the wardroom. He brought the bundle to Irfan, the lieutenant Tawfiq had put in charge of internal discipline. When he told him the story, the man's eyes narrowed.

"I will handle this," said Irfan. "You just go about your business."

The next day, a man came and told him to follow. They went deep into a part of the ship where Abdullah had never been before. In a gloomy, triangular compartment, he found Tawfiq, Irfan, Barbarossa, and between two guards the man Ibrahim who had dropped the bundle.

"Tell us your story," said Tawfiq. So Abdullah repeated what he had told Irfan.

Tawfiq turned to Ibrahim. "And now, tell us what happened."

"Why bother," snapped Ibrahim. "You wouldn't believe me anyhow. Not with your African so certain of his facts."

Tawfiq stared at the man for a moment, but that was all he would say.

"Very well," Tawfiq said. "We live at the mercy of the crew of this ship. Our success at the end of our journey depends on their success during the journey. They leave us alone to do as we wish and we want it to remain that way. This man does not deny his guilt. He deserves the punishment of a thief."

Ibrahim groaned. One of the guards brought out a cutting board and cleaver from the galley. As they pushed his arm down toward the cutting board, Ibrahim struggled, crying out, "Mercy, mercy for Allah's sake!"

Abdullah was horrified. "You can't do this. This is barbaric. It's not legal."

Tawfiq looked at him. "Are you retracting your statement? Did it not happen as you said? Are you saying my word is not law?"

"No. I mean yes, I mean, whatever this man did, does he deserve this?"

"This is the punishment of the Qur'an, and I am the leader Allah has set in front of you," said Tawfiq. "We must show that there are true consequences for actions. Harsh punishments prevent future infractions. There is too much at stake to be soft."

He glared at Abdullah. "And never tell me what I can do, or cannot do. Now, you will watch this, and consider the results of your own actions."

They put a tourniquet around the man's forearm, and the cleaver flashed. The clunk of the blade and the scream were nearly simultaneous. Abdullah realized that one of their doctors had been waiting in the corner of the room, and the man moved in and began to dress and stitch the stump. Tawfiq reached down, picked up the severed hand, and put it in a bag. He handed the bag to Abdullah.

"Dispose of this in the incinerator," Tawfiq said, "And think carefully of the consequences of disobedience."

*   *   *

Gettysburg was a huge ship, designed to deploy a Line Marine Regiment onto a frontier world that had no support to provide. The forward part of the ship was a giant ring that spun to create a semblance of gravity—vital on this journey, since Haven was about a year's journey from Earth. Along her central spine area, off limits to all until they reached their destination, were the five hundred drop capsules that would bring troops, vehicles, weapons and supplies to a planetary surface. Although, in this case, they had all been converted for personnel, two hundred per capsule. In the rear were the reaction drive motors that drove them through normal space, and the Alderson drives that twisted open paths to other solar systems. From the conversations Abdullah heard in the wardroom, he gathered that these Alderson drives were at the end of their useful life, and overdue for yard work. That, along with the sub-standard performance of the capsule system, was another reason *Gettysburg* was on her final voyage.

When he wasn't involved in teaching, or scullery work in the crew areas, Abdullah found himself in twice daily exercise sessions and combat training. He suspected that all this physical activity was not just to prepare the Faithful for arrival on the new world, but also to tire them out and prevent the restlessness, fights and friction that would otherwise result from too many people confined for too long in too small a space.

Abdullah had always been athletic and had even been a starting shortstop on his high school baseball team, but he hadn't been in a fight since the fifth grade when he took on a kid who had mocked his mother's head scarf. While there were many areas of Boston, mostly the Citizen enclaves called Welfare Islands, where fighting was part of daily life, the Cambridge school system was far more genteel. Here on the ship, he found himself in a fighting class taught by Barbarossa, the huge red-bearded military leader. He suspected this was deliberate and that Barbarossa, uneasy about a newcomer being so close to the inner circle, was taking his measure.

Abdullah found that he understood the theory of fighting well. He moved gracefully enough that he could evade a punch or kick, and move around a block. He was even able to adapt to the quirks of momentum that the ship's spin brought, the subtle differences between that and normal gravity. One thing that gave him trouble was the uncertainty of a fight. He had trouble guessing what his opponent would do next. He supposed it would come to him in time, like reading pitches when you were in the batter's box—trying to read the little quirks each pitcher had that indicated a fastball, changeup, curveball or slider was coming to you.

But his worst problem was being hit. It didn't always hurt, but it always rattled him, threw him off balance. And when it did hurt he really lost his cool. After one class, Barbarossa held him late to spar. The two circled around each other as the older man taunted him.

"Come on, book lover. Show me you mean business. Show me that you can be a man."

Abdullah came in fast, but the old man caught his legs, tripped him, and as he came down on his knees, put a fist in his stomach. Abdullah's breath whooshed out of him.

"Come on, get up. Kneel there panting in a real fight and your opponent will get a chance to finish you off."

Abdullah pushed himself upright, and took a defensive pose. "This time," he wheezed, "You can come to me."

"Good," answered Barbarossa. "You are learning, at least a little bit."

The big man came in fast. Abdullah countered one punch, but took the other in the ear. They circled around each other. Abdullah was sick of this, sick of the taunting. Barbarossa got him again, a hard blow to the shoulder. But this time, instead of pulling back, Abdullah moved in. He was able to land two blows to the big man's midsection before he took one in the chin that rocked him back on his heels. He caught his balance, and kicked out at Barbarossa's knee, or at least where the man's knee had been a moment ago. He parried a flurry of blows, and finally landed one right on Barbarossa's cheek. He grinned in triumph, but dropped his guard. A punch to his solar plexus took him off his feet.

Abdullah struggled to get up, but the big man said, "Enough for today. You are beginning to learn. To fight, you must learn to take punishment. If you cannot take pain, you cannot succeed. The Mahdi selected you for your learning, but every man who stands beside him needs to be a warrior. And in that, I will not let you fail."

After that lesson, Abdullah found that he did better and better. He learned to keep his focus in spite of blows, not to drop his guard ever and to always press his opponent. He would never be one of the best fighters in the group but he could finally hold his own with many of them.

Even Tawfiq would come down to fight. More interesting to Abdullah than his fighting style was the way he won even when he lost. When someone bettered him, he praised them, pointed out their value to their jihad and talked of putting men like them at his side so he would never fail. And those he did better always got an explanation, a lesson on how they lost, and how they could win another time. *Perhaps*, thought Abdullah, *he really is blessed by Allah*.

*   *   *

Abdullah was in the wardroom again, standing in the scullery, waiting to finish cleaning up after the Captain and Exec finished their coffee. He was daydreaming, thinking of a little joke Faryal had told, a joke that had the women's English class twittering like birds. She had a quick wit and a gentle way of poking fun at the silly things in life.

"Can I ask you a question?" the Executive officer said, his voice carrying into the scullery. Abdullah stirred from his reverie. The Exec rarely asked questions of the Captain. This might be something important.

The Captain nodded.

"This Tawfiq, this Mahdi, is a frightening man," the Exec said. "I've been watching the security cameras. He has the whole bunch back there training more fiercely than any CoDo Marine unit we ever carried. These people have a vision and a purpose; I don't believe it's one that is going to make anyone happy on Haven. I've been on that planet before and there's not a lot there, just a battalion of the 26th Marines and they're garrison troops, not line. These people could cut through our forces there like a knife through hot butter."

The Captain looked pensive. "We're dumping this bunch on the northern plains," he said. "Up above what the settlers in the Shangri-La Valley call the Atlas Mountains, and the Arabs call the Wall of Allah. Consul General Bronson has had problems with previous Muslim transportees and the Harmonies system of integrating transportees into their society has been overwhelmed by BuReloc in the past few years, so we'll be dropping them right on top of the mining area where they will be working."

"Shouldn't Bronson be warned?"

The Captain grimaced. "We won't be doing that," he said. "Not everyone in the Senate favors the Bronson family, and not all want them to succeed."

"But this won't just hurt a few people," the Exec said. "This could rip civilization apart. On a world where civilization is only a veneer."

The Captain rubbed his cheeks and sighed. He reached for his coffee and took a sip. "Let me repeat something. Not everyone in the Grand Senate wants to see the Bronsons succeed. Whatever happens on that moon," he said, "is not our problem." He looked sharply at the Exec. "And as far as anyone is concerned," he said, "our load is simply another group of transportees."

Abdullah hid a smile. Perhaps Allah had a plan for them after all. Perhaps the suffering he had seen in his travels was only a beginning for the Faithful. Perhaps Tawfiq was right and they were destined to succeed out among the stars.

The next day, Abdullah relayed this report to Tawfiq, who smiled and nodded.

"Sir?" asked Abdullah. "Could I ask you a question?"

Tawfiq nodded.

Abdullah swallowed, but pressed forward. "Does Allah speak to you?" he asked. "Are you the Mahdi?"

Tawfiq arched an eyebrow. "A brave question. But one you are wise to have asked me when we are alone. And my answer is for you alone, not to be shared with anyone." Abdullah nodded, while Tawfiq paused for a moment. "Allah speaks to me," he said, "in my heart, the same way he speaks to all men. And as to being the Mahdi, I do not think it is up to me to decide that, nor even my followers to decide. It will be up to history to decide that."

He looked sharply at Abdullah. "I will tell you one thing, however. I hope from the bottom of my heart, from the soles of my feet to the top of my head, that I am the Mahdi, and that I will lead our people to freedom!"

Abdullah felt his spirits soar. He had been ripped from his home, from everything he knew. But perhaps here, because of whatever forces led him to this place, to this point of his life, he would be part of something greater than himself, part of a grand journey.

As Abdullah left the compartment and went down the passageway, he heard a soft voice from a door, left ajar to his right. He entered, and found it was a storage compartment, full of mops, brooms and other cleaning implements. Faryal stood there beside him and pulled the door closed.

"We should not be alone," Abdullah said, feeling a thrill in his heart, which was much different than the one he had felt listening to the Mahdi.

"Yes, but I wanted to tell you that I like you and that is something I could not do unless we were alone. You are not like the other men I see. You are gentle and funny." She moved toward him, and lifted the veil of her burqa to uncover her mouth. "I find myself wanting to kiss you," she said, bringing her lips toward his.

Abdullah put his arms around her, and their lips met, hesitantly at first, but then more passionately. He felt her body against him. He had always thought of Faryal as a girl, but this curvy body he held was a woman's body. He stopped suddenly and backed away. Her veil fell back into place.

"But your father," he said.

She sighed. "Yes, my father. Always my father, always the goal, always the mission. Regardless of who my father is, I wanted you to know how I feel. You might not think so, many men don't, but how a woman feels is important. And while you worry about my father, I want to tell you another thing: My mother does not know I am here and would not approve of my actions, but she likes you, too."

She touched him briefly on the cheek, opened the door and went down the passageway. Abdullah fell back against a workbench, his head whirling. He had dreams like this, but this was no dream. It had been almost a year since he had been with a woman and now it appeared to him that he was cared for by a woman he could not possess. His life had suddenly become very complicated.

*　　　　　　　　　*　　　　　　　　　*

Abdullah clipped his harness closed and leaned back into the canvas jump seat. His stomach was knotted and his mouth dry. Even though he had used the head before boarding the drop capsule, he still felt like his bladder was full. He sat near the front of the capsule, his back toward the stern, and if he craned his neck, he could see the twenty people strapped in behind him. Along the floorboards (at least, what they hoped would be the floorboards when they landed), cargo and supplies were lashed to railings. Tawfiq was not in this capsule, instead, it was Barbarossa in the front row beside Abdullah. The Mahdi and his family were in another, as the leaders of the Faithful had scattered themselves among the different capsules to ensure continuity of leadership in the event a capsule was lost.

Abdullah couldn't stop thinking about the conversation he had overheard in the wardroom so many months ago. He had at least a ten percent chance of dying within the next hour or so. And a significant chance of being hurt or maimed by a rough landing. The crewman looked into the capsule, nodded to Abdullah, and shut the hatch. The wheel in the center spun, the dogs around the edges engaged, and Abdullah heard the thump thump of the man's fist, indicating that the hatch was sealed and ready to go.

There was a sudden bam as the docking lugs broke free. The capsule was underway. Abdullah felt the pressure of his body against his seat and the dull roar of rocket engines. Then there was a long period of silence, followed by a hissing noise and more pressure. They were entering the atmosphere now. The interior of the capsule began to get warm, which they had been told would not happen. The ride was not smooth, with lots of turbulence, and Abdullah was thrown around roughly in his seat. Then there was a strong yank, which would be the drogue chute deploying. When the main chutes deployed, there was a savage jerk on the capsule and cries of pain all around him.

"Shit," said Abdullah, in English. Then, as the capsule's motion smoothed, he was embarrassed. If there had been a problem, he would have died with that obscenity on his lips. They fell for what seemed forever. Abdullah found himself tensing, breathing shallowly.

When the impact came, he felt his spine compress, his neck crack and the capsule tumble, once, and then again. Gear broke free and flew around the capsule, as did a few of the people. There were cries, screams and shouts all around him. Then with a crunch, the capsule came to rest. Abdullah was sideways, the port bulkhead of the capsule now being its floor. There was sobbing behind him and excited conversation. Abdullah carefully unbuckled his straps, unable to prevent himself from falling when the final strap was loosened. He went to the forward hatch and turned the wheel. There was a hiss, and then a pop when the hatch unsealed, the pressure in the capsule being much higher than the air outside.

Abdullah clambered out. They were on a broad and rocky plain near the shore of a large lake. The weather was cool and breezy. They must have landed near their destination, because a few kilometers away from them was a dusty town on the shore of a river that ran from the lake. On the other side of the river, a crude fortress sat on a bluff, with another town before the fortress. Above him, the sky was a faded orange, with a small yellowish sun, and a huge striped planet filling a large part of the sky. The other capsules were hanging in the sky under gleaming white chutes, like seeds from a dandelion. Abdullah knew it was hundreds, but they looked like thousands. He finally looked down and saw there were plants among the rocks at his feet, none that he recognized, and an odd creature running from rock to rock for cover. He needed to take his eyes off the sky. This was his new home.

*   *   *

The losses among the capsules had been lighter than expected, perhaps because Haven's gravity was a bit weaker than Earth's. Out of the five hundred capsules, only forty-one failed entirely, mostly due to parachute or retrorocket failures. The injuries in the other capsules were light, many sore necks and backs, and a lot of sprains, but only a scattering of broken bones. Tawfiq, who Abdullah was pleased to see survived the journey, called it a blessing from Allah. Abdullah hid his further pleasure at seeing Faryal at her mother's side, safe and sound.

Nonetheless, the first order of business was burying the dead. The Qur'an was clear, this task could not wait. There were ceremonies all around them. With every body, they were already making the soil of this world their own.

The mining company, Dover Mining Development, sent out representatives, from the town beyond the fortress, the town called Eureka, flanked by large groups of well-armed CoDo Marines. They asked for a leader, and were pleased to find that the new arrivals were well organized. They told the Mahdi that they would begin providing rations from a nearby protein plant immediately. Water was available from nearby irrigation channels that ran from Dire Lake. They gave strict orders for sanitation. They asked for fifty men who would attend classes on Haven: How its days and nights occurred, its wildlife, its dangers, on the work the mining company had in store for the newcomers. They had two weeks to get themselves settled before three thousand men reported for mine work.

After they left, Barbarossa grumbled. "Are we slaves, to just stand and listen?"

"We have been over this," the Mahdi said. "Until I say otherwise, we listen, we obey, we watch and we learn. Strike before we are ready and

Allah will smite us for our stupidity."

The first morning brought a welcome sound, the sound of an imam echoing from the buildings of the nearer town, calling the Faithful to prayer. That was about the only welcome surprise they had for the next few weeks were filled with brutally hard work. They discovered that the nearer town, almost exclusively Muslim, was called Medina, and the fort overlooking the two towns was called Fort Camerone. There was also a bridge between the towns and they discovered that Muslims who did not have work or other business in Eureka, the town on the other side of the bridge, were discouraged from crossing.

The cool, thin air made things even harder and they panted for breath as they worked to lever the capsules into a more orderly array. They could not move them far, but at least they could align them in a way that would accommodate streets and other buildings in the future. They also set up tents, many tents, using the parachutes for material. The capsules held only two hundred people when packed tight.

Most unmarried men would be sleeping outdoors for the immediate future. Canvas seats were refashioned into canvas beds and people fanned out into Medina to find out what might be available for sale, what resources there were, where mosques were and which way to face when they prayed.

The land was barren and flat, with hills visible to the north and west of town, and a large mountain range on the far northern horizon. There were a few small farms in the surrounding area, mostly to the north of town, irrigated by water drawn from the river. But mostly the ground was rocky and the soil poor, with thin grass and a plant called bindle weed growing wherever they could. So most of the food came from a CoDominium protein plant located on the outskirts of Eureka.

Trees were sparse and odd looking; bottle trees with their thick trunks and tufts of leaves on top and squat fan trees with their broad but strange looking leaves. Domesticated animals were mostly Earth livestock, with mountain animals like sheep and alpacas heavy in the mix. Horses were in common use as were muskylopes. The only powered vehicles in town were those driven by mining company officials, and CoDominium Marine tanks and trucks.

Barbarossa, always thinking of military matters, obtained a number of wooden staffs, and also materials to fashion bows and arrows. The mining companies and Marines would not let the Faithful buy weapons, but Barbarossa refused to let them remain unarmed. He argued that they needed to be able to defend themselves, but also wanted to continue to hone the martial abilities the Faithful had learned aboard ship.

* * *

One truenight, a large man from Medina, with a thick, brown beard, reddish robes, and a dirty turban came to meet with the Mahdi. He had a gun on each hip, a large knife in a sheath stuck through his belt in front. He had four toughs with him, hard men, even dirtier than him, armed with pistols and assault rifles. He had asked to meet with the leaders of the newcomers, and Tawfiq had all his lieutenants around him, even Abdullah sitting in the corner quietly.

The visitor cleared his throat, looked like he wanted to spit, but then thought the better of it. "Are you Tawfiq?" he asked.

Tawfiq nodded.

"And you call yourself the Mahdi?" the man asked, in a voice caught between scorn and wonder.

"Some know me by that name," Tawfiq replied. "And you are?"

"I am Kabir," the man said, "and before you get too settled and set in your ways, we need to get some things straight."

"Continue," said Tawfiq, with an arched eyebrow.

"Well, first of all, we get five percent of what the mining companies pay everyone. I run a protective service, with roving guards, and it takes money to do that. And no one around here sells liquor without going through me, Or drugs, for that matter.

"And if you have the money," he said with a grin, "we would be happy to provide you whatever you need."

Abdullah looked around. Tawfiq had trained his lieutenants well. All sat quietly, as if this man were discussing the weather.

The man went on, "And I have a number of fine whorehouses, where you can find delights that would please any man. I am always looking for fresh girls, or young boys, and offer finders fees, if you know of any good ones who arrived with you."

At this, there was an audible but faint response, a kind of collective growl. Barbarossa looked pointedly at Tawfiq, his face red. Tawfiq sighed, and nodded, and his lieutenants erupted into action. Before the thugs could even get a shot off, they were overwhelmed and pinned to the floor. One whimpered from the pain of a broken forearm.

"And now?" Barbarossa asked.

"No mercy," replied Tawfiq. "These dogs will probably not even be missed by their wives. Make sure the bodies are buried deeply." He turned and stepped out of the capsule, as knives flashed, and the floor ran red with blood. Abdullah stared silently at Barbarossa, who wiped a bloody knife clean on the robes of his victim, a broad smile on his face. Abdullah trusted Tawfiq's intentions, but he wondered if the protective services, the drug and alcohol sales, the prostitution, would simply continue under new management.

* * *

One day, when Abdullah was away on errands for the Mahdi, a man rode into what had become known as Capsule Town, astride one horse and leading another, obviously a traveler, equipped lightly, but for a long journey. He was an infidel, but he rode into the camp of strangers with great confidence. Abdullah saw him pause a few times to question people, and when one pointed at Abdullah, he stopped to wait for the man.

The stranger was tall and lean and dressed in plain, dusty brown trousers and shirt, with high riding boots. He had a leather harness on, which except for its material, was similar to the belt and suspenders combination that CoDominium soldiers wore. From it hung an automatic pistol in a cross-draw holster, a large knife, canteen and a variety of pouches. A rifle was balanced across his saddle bow, an old fashioned bolt-action model, but well maintained, and ready for quick use. His hat was a broad brimmed brown felt, similar to those many of the infidels wore, but with its front brim pinned up.

The face revealed by this was weather-beaten, but young. The stranger had black hair and blue eyes, with a straggly attempt at a goatee making him look younger instead of older.

He reined in his horse, raised a right hand in greeting, and said, "Mornin'. They tell me you speak English."

"Yes," said Abdullah. "What can I do for you?"

"Well," the young man answered, "to get right to the point, I'm a scout, and I happen to be lookin' for work, and wonderin' if you folks might need my service. M'name is Patrick, Patrick Flynn."

"My name is Abdullah Hassan. Good day to you. Have you eaten?"

Patrick grinned, shedding any pretense of reserve, "Not yet today and I'm feelin' peckish. You know where we can get some food?"

Abdullah smiled back. The young man's name and something about his accent, made him think back to Irish friends he had back in Boston, a lost lifetime ago. "Follow me," he said.

They went to an inn made of adobe blocks and ordered breakfast. Abdullah usually settled for a piece of bread and a cup of coffee, but Patrick looked hungry, so he ordered rice, mutton, bread, cheese and coffee for both of them. Abdullah had used English to argue with CoDominium soldiers, government officials and mining leaders for so long, he had forgotten what a pleasure it was to use his native language for casual conversation. And Patrick seemed to have saved up a surplus of conversation in his lonely journeys.

Patrick spoke about his childhood as an orphan in Castell City, his mother having died during the year-long journey from Earth. He had ended up in an orphanage, under the care of the Church of Harmony monks who oversaw not only the orphanage, but also the training of newly arrived transportees.

He hadn't fit in well there, and always seemed to be getting into fights. One of the monks, Brother Miller, had taken a liking to him, and had arranged for him to be apprenticed to an old friend of his, Sam; a noted explorer, wilderness guide and hunter who lived in a small village in the hills north of Castell City. Sam's wife, Moira, ran a pub in the village, kind of a combination restaurant, bar and music hall. Sam and Moira had met in Castell City, and moved out of town just in time to miss the troubled years that started when the CoDominium governor set up shop. In fact, some of their friends ended up following them out of the city, including Brother Miller, who became the teacher at the village's school.

Patrick said Moira was Irish and loved to talk about the Emerald Isle, while Sam wouldn't talk about his life on Earth, only saying that he came to Haven for a fresh start. Even though they were starting a family of their own, they treated Patrick like a son. And starting when he was sixteen, Sam had started bringing him on his journeys, training him as a guide and scout. His wandering had taken him through the passes north of Lake Eden, and into the plains beyond, land he was eager to explore. He told Abdullah he would like it back home, the folks were all very friendly.

Patrick also mentioned that he was a baseball pitcher in his home town.

"They play baseball on Haven?" exclaimed Abdullah.

"Sure do," Patrick answered, "It's our favorite sport. People all through the hills come from miles around to see town teams compete against each other. The year before I lit out on my own, our team went to Castell, and we placed second in the World Series, playin' against teams from all up and down the valley. There are only six teams on all of Haven, but some of those players are top notch. I was our pitcher in the final championship game and gave up two runs, which was one more than I should have, and decided that would be the end of my baseball career."

Abdullah told Patrick about his own days playing baseball in Eastern Massachusetts, traveling from high school to high school in the springtime. He spoke of games in Fenway Park, seeing the best baseball players on any world. Abdullah found himself able to tell his whole story for the first time since leaving Earth: he spoke of his father, the Harvard professor, and his lofty goals for himself and his son; his mother, warm and friendly, but unable to muster the courage to say anything that might contradict her husband. He spoke of Boston, the excitement of city life, the challenges of school at MIT.

Patrick was amazed by all of this. So Abdullah took the luster off life on Earth, also describing the tensions between Taxpayers and Citizens, the erosion of liberties as the bureaucracy of the CoDominium encroached on the old United States government. He described running away to see the world, being swept up by the mutiny and into the Mahdi's movement.

"You sure have had an interestin' life," said Patrick.

"As have you," Abdullah answered. "Now, what kind of work are you interested in?"

"Well, I figured you folks, bein' new to the planet and all, would want someone to show you around, help you get the lay of the land. The CoDominium troops use a lot of local scouts, but my family has never had much use for those folks. And the mining companies have work, but they just make my skin crawl. I don't know much about you Arab folks, but I figure that anyone who doesn't get along with the mining companies and the Marines is okay in my book."

Abdullah said, "You found the right person. The Mahdi has been talking about sending out parties to explore the area around the lake and it sounds like the work would be right down your alley."

Abdullah's new friend was hired by Tawfiq and became a frequent visitor to both Medina and Eureka. He would often lead small parties of the Faithful out on horseback to explore the lands about them, returning after a few weeks eager for a good meal and friendship. He tended to avoid the company of what many thought were "his own kind," which drew comments from the Faithful. When Abdullah mentioned that to him, Patrick said, "If you knew a bit more about this planet, you would know that most people don't think of the mining companies, nor the Marines, as their own people."

He did sometimes take Abdullah into Eureka to a small pub that he enjoyed. There, a group of musicians played, not professionals just local people who played for the love of it. Patrick was dating a woman who played fiddle there and often sat in, playing his tin whistle. He found out that Abdullah had played some guitar in the past and, from somewhere, he obtained a small mandolin for him and taught him to play a few of the tunes. This brought Abdullah some acceptance among the townspeople who frequented the pub. The music had made him, in some small way, one of their own.

Tawfiq encouraged this. While many of his followers could not pass freely in Eureka, Abdullah, with his perfect American English and non-Arab looks, could move about with much less notice. He was encouraged to remain clean-shaven and wear trousers and a shirt instead of the traditional robes so many others of the Faithful wore. There were many blacks among the enlisted ranks of the CoDominium Marines and Abdullah struck up acquaintances with some of them. As always, the Mahdi was looking for intelligence and information that he could use to his advantage.

One day, Abdullah was walking past a field where CoDominium troops were playing a scratch baseball game. They had convinced a couple of Arab boys to come to bat, and then mocked them as they swung and missed, their robes tangling about them as they did so. Abdullah barked at the boys in Arabic and told them to come with him. The taunts at their backs continued as Abdullah lectured them about maintaining their dignity. The boys protested saying that they were just having fun, so he told them some of the things the soldiers had been saying about them in English.

The incident left Abdullah with an idea that he brought to Tawfiq. He spoke to him about forming a baseball team. "Let's show the infidels a thing or two by beating them at their own game," he said.

Tawfiq laughed, and dismissed the idea.

English lessons continued for Tawfiq, his lieutenants and others of the Faithful, whose work put them in contact with the infidels. Leaders among those who worked in the mines were chief among his students. They wanted to know what the supervisors were really saying about the mines, especially safety issues. DMD cared less about safety than profits and were constantly putting the miners at risk, and then blaming them for any problems that would result.

And there were still English lessons for the women as well. Many of the women just learned a little, and moved on, but the advanced class still held A'isha and Faryal. This class was still Abdullah's favorite, a special time in each day.

After one class, however, A'isha paused to speak to him. "You like my daughter," she said, without preamble.

Abdullah was caught off-guard. "Yes, I do."

"It shows. Too much. I like you, but do not overstep your bounds. She is a wonderful girl, but she is also the daughter of the Mahdi. Remember the stories of clashes between the descendents of the Prophet, blessed be his name, and think about what being with such a woman means."

She turned and walked away, leaving Abdullah gaping like a fish and wondering what had just occurred.

*   *   *

Days turned into weeks, and then months. Abdullah began to feel less out of breath. He wasn't struggling constantly to get enough of the thin air into his lungs. He began to get used to the odd cycle of days and nights on Haven, which repeated over the two hundred and sixty hours that made up a local week. Because it was almost impossible for people to adapt to Haven's odd patterns of light and dark, this was arbitrarily divided into eleven days that fell just short of being twenty-four hours long. So each day was different, and not divided into repeating periods of light and dark. Some days were "brightdays," with the sun up for hours. Some days were "dimdays," when only the gas giant planet, Cat's Eye, was above the horizon. And twice during the H-week were "truenights," a period where nothing but the stars appeared in the sky, nights that were piercingly cold on the hills and steppes surrounding their towns..

Every three or four T-months, the cry rang throughout the towns of Medina and Eureka, "Incoming!" This signaled the fact that splashships were arriving, amphibious craft that landed on Dire Lake, holding supplies and human cargo destined for the mouth of the river. They would pull up to the docks and off would stream a parade of transportees, mostly Muslim, who were herded to tents for processing. In return they would be loaded with ore for the trip back to the ore carriers in low orbit above Haven.

In warehouses lining the docks sat the gallium that had been mined and processed in the hills at the head of the Dire River. The cargo came down the river on rafts made from the wood of egg and steelwood trees. Upon arrival, the cargo was offloaded, and the wood was brought to sawmills to become building material for the ever-expanding towns. Along with each raft of hafnium came a crew of broken men, men who had washed out at the mines and had twisted backs and broken bones, or had lost fingers and limbs in mining accidents. The mining company blamed this on the men and their carelessness, calling them un-trainable. The survivors told a different story of lax safety procedures, sketchy preparations and outdated or makeshift equipment.

But even though the pay was paltry, there were few jobs on Haven that paid anything, there was always a steady supply of transportees and new workers riding the steam tugs back up the river.

When the gallium was loaded on the shuttles, they were fueled with liquid hydrogen and oxygen separated from the lake water. They then backed away from the docks, skittered across the lake until they became airborne and clawed their way back into orbit. This process would take days with shuttles arriving every few hours until all the transportees were offloaded and the gallium was in orbit. The towns would become a hive of activity with every business humming and every able-bodied man working. Spacers would spend a day or two in town, enjoying what rough pleasures they could find and buying some fresh food before departing for the next leg of their journey.

New arrivals were always a problem. The amount of supplies and equipment that came with them was pitifully small. The personnel needs of the mining companies had long since been satisfied, but still the transportees came. It made Abdullah think of a cartoon he had seen in his youth, where the young Sorcerer's Apprentice had summoned animated brooms to do his chores and draw his water, but then found himself overcome with too much help and drowning in far too much of that water.

It was obvious that the CoDominium didn't care about the local economy, as long as the mining operations continued. This was a dumping ground, a place to send the excess population of Earth, undesirables who were no longer welcome. The mining ships might as well carry something on their deadhead trips from Earth to Haven. Many of the newcomers arrived glad to be off of Earth and full of hope, but were cruelly disappointed to find that the Muslims of Haven were still an oppressed people and that the time of liberation had not yet come. The new arrivals found a land so chilly and barren that had it not been for the CoDo's protein plant in Eureka the local settlements would not have been possible. So they found what work they could in town, tried their luck at farming on the lakeshores around Lake Dire to the north or spread across the plains in a desperate search for someplace to eke out a hardscrabble existence.

* * *

One day, Abdullah was summoned to the presence of the Mahdi. He smiled at A'isha, as she led him into the room and at Faryal as she brought tea.

Abdullah nodded to Tawfiq, who gestured for him to sit.

"Pregnant women are losing their babies, and sometimes losing their lives," Tawfiq said.

Abdullah was surprised. Tawfiq usually asked about how he was doing; starting the conversation with polite chitchat, rarely getting right to the point.

"You are a learned man," Tawfiq said. "Talk to the people in all the towns. Find out what they know of this. Talk to doctors, and midwives. We must solve this problem. As my A'isha is so fond of telling me, a jihad without women and families ends after a single generation."

Abdullah looked at A'isha, and saw her hands knotted in her lap, her knuckles white. He looked closely at Tawfiq, and saw pain in his eyes. He realized that this problem was not just a theoretical one, the person

Tawfiq was worried about most was sitting in this room. His eyes must have widened, because A'isha caught them and nodded. He said nothing, because Tawfiq was a deeply personal man who would not want to discuss this with someone outside the family, even someone like Abdullah, who had become so close to them during their travels.

So Abdullah set out to research the issue. He found that the rate of successful pregnancies in the highlands above the Shangri-La Valley were less than four out of ten. And at least two or three out of each ten pregnancies led to the death of the mother. There were midwives in Medina who did their best with what was little more than folk remedies. The CoDominium Marine medics were useless, saying *female problems* were "not their department."

The mining company doctors in Eureka were more sympathetic, but offered little more than theories—something in the water, or the thin air, or diets or the odd cycle of days and nights. One of them, an older man, gave Abdullah access to his desktop computer, and Abdullah quickly realized how much he missed a world where so much information had been at his fingertips.

He spent hours in front of the computer, learning more than he ever thought he would about the subject. He interviewed women in the towns and would have gotten a reputation for being a bit odd had not A'isha put out the word that he was doing work for the Mahdi, work that would improve the chances of life for the children of the Faithful.

He did learn that some of the wealthier men in town sent their wives south through the Karakal Pass and Fort Stony Point into the Shangri-La Valley below. Success rates for pregnancies in the valley were apparently much better than they were here in the north.

In the end, though, he discovered his answer one night while taking a break, with his mandolin in his lap, and a pint of beer at his side. They were at the pub, and had just finished a set of reels, the "Banshee," and "Far From Home." *Far from home, indeed,* thought Abdullah as he took a drink.

"What ails you?" asked his friend Patrick, in town after one of his many scouting trips, his tin whistle on the table in front of him.

Abdullah explained the task that Tawfiq had set before him and how his research was hitting dead end after dead end.

"I know whatcha need," said Patrick. "A birthing chamber."

"A what?" asked Abdullah.

"A chamber, like in a hospital, where pregnant women go if they are having trouble."

"What do these chambers do? What do they look like?"

"I don't know what they do," answered Patrick. "But the doors look like the doors on those tin cans you folks came in. Except ya go through two of 'em, one after another. I saw 'em when I went to visit Moira, when she was pregnant with her third kid, and havin' problems. Made my ears hurt to go in and out, even though I swallowed hard, like they told me to. There aren't many of them, but people travel hundreds of miles to use 'em. Don't they have any 'round here?"

Abdullah's thoughts whirled. Two doors indicated an airlock, and what Patrick was describing was a pressurized chamber. He remembered reading about complications of pregnancies at high altitudes. He thought about their camp, with hundreds of capsules, each one a potential pressure chamber. He wondered if any of them had air handling systems that had not been scavenged for metal and parts. All along the answer had been right around them.

He whooped, and clapped his friend on the shoulders. He threw a coin on the table.

"Drinks are on me," he shouted, as he ran out the door.

The next morning, the hard work began. He'd had the one percent of inspiration, now came the ninety-nine percent of perspiration. He got Tawfiq to assign him assistants, an Afghan machinist, a Pakistani electronics technician and a couple of other men who were handy with tools. They surveyed the capsules and found a pair, fairly close together, that still had their equipment intact. These were occupied by senior lieutenants of the Mahdi, who were too well-off to need to scavenge and sell off components. These lieutenants soon found themselves moved to other quarters.

The capsules had been designed without airlocks, since they docked with their carrier, and were not designed to open until they reached the surface of a habitable planet. So there was welding and reworking required to fit each with a working airlock, and then he had the few men with engineering background design compressors that would keep the pressure inside the capsule and adjust the pressure in the airlock when it was used.

Abdullah found himself reporting directly to A'isha on this project and was surprised, but pleased, to realize she was not thinking just of herself, but also of other women of the Faithful. In fact, she said, if this would work, they could build more chambers, and make money from the townspeople.

He sometimes found opportunities to talk to Faryal after these meetings, stealing moments together in supply tents, having rambling conversations about everything except what was most important to them, whether or not they would ever have a chance to be together. He didn't dare tell her that he sometimes thought about running away, finding that place in the Shangri-La Valley that Patrick called 'real friendly.' She would never agree to leave her family, or her duties.

It took months, but finally, the chambers were ready. Midwives who had been trained as nurses went inside the chambers with women who were nearing their final trimester. In a few months, they would know if they were successful. A'isha herself was one of the first women to go into the chambers. It was hard to tell in her burqa, but sometimes, when the breezes swirled, you could see the bulge at her middle.

Tawfiq was bemused by all of this construction and activity. He didn't understand how the air pressure could make a difference, in fact, he seemed to worry that this experiment could do his wife more harm than good. But he trusted Abdullah, and he certainly listened when A'isha spoke to him.

"The prophet was a man," he once told Abdullah. "But he was born of a woman, and married a woman, and raised girls in addition to boys. And no man is wise who ignores the counsel of women."

*　　　　　　　*　　　　　　　*

One night, Abdullah was called to a meeting with Tawfiq and Barbarossa. There was a stranger there, a blond-haired man with a thin beard Abdullah was called upon to translate.

"I represent people who want to help you in your cause, Mahdi," said the man. He went on to describe how they could help with a stand alone protein factory, light and heavy weapons, ammunition, radios, radar. Barbarossa's eyes widened at this description, almost licking his lips at the thought.

"I am not at war," said Tawfiq. "Why do you offer me these things?"

"Because you do not wage war now," the man said, "that does not mean you do not desire to overthrow the current order of things. I suspect that is what you would do if you could find the resources to support the effort. When the CoDominium controls most of the food, and leaves you unarmed, you have no choice but to accept their boot heels on your necks."

"But why would you do this for us?" asked Tawfiq. "What is in it for you?"

"I represent those who want to see the CoDominium fail. We do not have the manpower to oppose them directly. But we do have the ability to help others who share our desires."

The man went on to invite Tawfiq to send a delegation to a meeting in the hills to the east. There they could meet their representatives, see some of the resources that were being offered and meet with others who opposed the CoDominium on Haven.

"Barbarossa," said Tawfiq. "You can barely contain your excitement over this development. You will go as my representative. Take our young African with you to translate and take the infidel scout, Patrick to guide you."

"And Abdullah," he continued. "You will help Barbarossa pick the young men for this mission. I want them picked based on their potential to play this game of baseball. Your idea of beating the Marines at their own game intrigues me. And even if we lose a hard-fought game, we will still gain advantage in their eyes. Train them on your journey."

Barbarossa objected that this would be a meaningless distraction, but Tawfiq was insistent, and so, before they left, Abdullah and Patrick taught the women how to make the necessary leather gloves and bought bats and balls. From his few possessions, Patrick took out his Red Sox cap for the first time since he had started his journey; the women used it as a pattern for other caps, and made uniforms. Abdullah and Patrick also presided over tryouts, timing sprints, measuring the distance of throws, watching people catch, watching them swing, searching for potential five-tool players among the Faithful.

* * *

That was how Abdullah found himself astride a horse for the first time in his life and wearing a pistol, an ancient revolver. The mining companies and Marines had banned sales of weapons to the Faithful, but enough of them had been obtained to arm the thirty odd men who rode into the hills. The horses had cost the Faithful dearly, both in treasure, and in talent. In addition to buying their own horses, the Arabs had shown themselves expert at breeding and had insisted they be paid for their services with mounts of their own.

This trip was going to be a long one, hundreds of miles to the northwest into a deep ravine in the Girdle of God mountains. Even though it was summer, the air was cold during dimdays, and downright frigid in the wee hours of the dark truenights. They rode through high plains, dry lands with scrubby vegetation and nasty creatures lurking among the rocks.

Provisions were not as much of a problem as Abdullah had expected despite the barrenness of the land. Thanks to Patrick's knowledge of the steppes, they were able to find and kill a wild muskylope on almost a daily basis, butchering them as a staple of their diet and saving their beans and rice for days when game escaped them. They were careful to share what passed for livers in these animals to get necessary vitamins, although the taste left much to be desired. Water was rare in the area, but Patrick had a knack for reading the land for signs of it and they kept their many water bottles and skins full.

Abdullah learned about saddle sores and that a horseman spent as much time walking, leading his mount, as he did riding. He learned to watch for the hazards of the land: Razorgrass that would open a horse's leg in an instant. Dens of land gators, vicious reptiles that could bring down a horse and kill its rider before anyone could ride to his aid. Vicious little lizard-like tamerlanes that hunted in packs like jackals. Rocks and holes that could trip a mount or a man.

Fortunately, the most common sight was simply the inedible reddish screwgrass that grew in patches on the low ground, made even more red by the light of the gas giant, Cat's Eye, that hung in the sky almost constantly.

Each day, during rest stops, they played baseball, awkward games at first. So Abdullah and Patrick had them run drills for fielding, catching and throwing. They tried everyone out as pitchers and catchers, searching for that elusive talent required for those two positions.

Barbarossa grumbled at first, but soon took an interest in the game himself and began to act as an umpire, calling balls and strikes. He always insisted, though, that they have sentries out whenever their games distracted them from their surroundings. And the blond man watched these proceedings with an air of amusement, keeping to himself as they traveled.

After weeks of journeying, they finally found the outpost they were looking for. It was set far into a mountain ravine and camouflaged with netting and tarps above the simple buildings. At the bottom of the ravine sat two vertical launch landers, also heavily camouflaged.

The blond man showed Abdullah and Barbarossa into one of the buildings and they sat at a large table with a group of men of varying nationalities.

"Before we proceed," said Barbarossa. "I need to know more about your organization. Who you are, what you want?"

A heavyset man at the head of the table nodded. "Fair enough," he replied. "We call ourselves The Brotherhood. The CoDominium is a marriage of convenience between two powers that do not trust each other, because they trust the other powers of the world even less. And this alliance brings out the worst in both nations. Now that man has moved out into the stars, power is shifting away from Earth, fragmenting among new worlds. Our organization does not want these new worlds to be united and dominated by the CoDominium. We want them to be free.

"So we support groups like yours of people who want freedom and are willing to fight for it. And in fighting for your own freedom, you draw the power of the CoDominium to many worlds, spreading their forces thin, thereby making them easier to defeat. We can also put you in contact with other friends who might want to aid your cause.

"So you see," he continued. "We help you not just to be generous. We help you because it serves our interests and furthers our cause."

"The enemy of my enemy is my friend," replied Barbarossa.

"Precisely," the man answered.

The discussions moved quickly. Soon, there were charts of the northern regions of Haven spread out over the table. They needed to find a base where their protein plant and military supplies could be delivered. They discussed how many men could move into the area to begin building the backbone of their military forces, how they could be trained, and deployed to fight guerilla actions until they had the strength for open combat.

These discussions went on for days, days Abdullah found tedious and unsettling. And even more unsettling was a statement from Barbarossa as they left one of the long meetings.

"This is my chance," he said. "To show the Mahdi that I am truly worthy of his trust. And to show him that I am the man to marry his daughter."

Abdullah's heart went into his throat. There was no man he wanted to hear those words from, least of all this cruel and powerful man.

Their trip back was quiet at first. The blond man stayed with his fellows, although two microwave line-of-sight transceivers traveled back with them on a packhorse. They covered many miles and Abdullah learned that riding a horse was something that got easier with time, as you learned to move with the animal instead of against it.

They were practicing baseball during a gloomy dimday when there were shots, and cries from the sentries. The ball players rushed for their weapons. A hail of arrows flew into the camp and there were howls of pain. A band of screaming men came charging in behind the arrows, wielding clubs and axes. Abdullah held his pistol before him in the two handed grip Patrick had taught him. He squeezed the trigger carefully and on his third shot, a man went down.

Beside him, Patrick stood like a statue, shooting as if this were target practice, his right hand smoothly working the bolt on each shot, an attacker falling with every round fired. Around them, both sides fought bravely, and it was soon hand-to-hand in places

One of the men tackled Abdullah and he fell back, the man's foul breath hot on his face, his hand around the haft of the axe that was moving toward his face. There was a crack, and the man fell against Abdullah, blood spraying from his nose. Patrick stood above them, the butt of his rifle bloody.

Abdullah nodded in thanks, but Patrick was already turning to look for the next threat. As he got up, Abdullah saw Barbarossa howling like an animal, picking up attackers and throwing them at their comrades. And before long, modern weapons overcame numbers and a pitiful few of the attackers fled over the rocky ground.

The attackers looked smaller as they lay on the ground dead and wounded, dressed in wretched rags.

"Who were they?" Barbarossa asked Patrick. "Do you recognize them?"

"Brigands," said Patrick.

"Who are brigands?"

"That's what we call men who go savage, head out on their own, form raidin' parties and live out on the fringes. They're prob'ly loyal to no one but their own band," Patrick replied.

"I hope you are right," Barbarossa said. He pitched his voice higher, calling out. "I want every one of them dead. Do not waste bullets, use their own axes on them."

As they went about this bloody business, Patrick whispered to Abdullah, "I hate to say it, but you folks're sometimes a bit too bloodthirsty for my taste." Abdullah was still catching his breath. He gulped, and nodded in agreement.

* * *

The Mahdi paced outside the door of the capsule like a caged lion, back and forth, forth and back. He growled like a lion, too. His lieutenants, some, like Abdullah, who had just returned from their long journey to meet with the Brotherhood, were gathered around him not wanting to face his wrath but wanting to be here with him. They did not know what to say, so they said nothing, gathering silently around a small fire in the dull glow of a dimday, drinking sweet hot tea. Tawfiq tried to ask Abdullah some questions about the upcoming baseball game against the Marines, but his heart wasn't in it and he paid little attention to the answers.

Abdullah could hear raised voices inside the capsule, muffled and indistinct. A couple of times, there were screams, and each time, Tawfiq flinched. Then they heard muffled cries and the wheel at the center of the hatch began to spin. The door opened and the midwife stuck her head out.

"The mother is tired, but fine. All went well. The child is healthy."

Tawfiq asked, "Is it a boy, or a girl?"

The midwife looked grouchy, as if this was a fact that made no difference.

"You are the father of a fine, strong son," she said.

"A son!" cried Tawfiq, and he turned and grabbed Abdullah, who stood next to him. "He will be called Nabil. A son, at our age! Abdullah, you have saved her life, and his life. You have saved my life! My name will not die with me. Truly Allah has blessed me."

Barbarossa raised a gun and fired into the air and soon Capsule

Town and Medina rang with gunfire. As word spread, they heard cheers in the distance. The midwife shook her head in disgust at this display, disappearing back into the capsule.

"Tonight, there will be music and drink! Tonight, we celebrate," cried Tawfiq. "I have a son!"

The party lasted far into the night. Abdullah was one of the first to succumb to the drink; it was something new to him, grain alcohol from a still on a local farm, tasteless but strong. He awoke to find himself lying on the ground, covered by a blanket, with a cottony mouth and a head that felt like it was filled with rocks. He heard gunfire nearby and couldn't believe people were still firing off rounds in celebration. A hand grabbed his shoulder and shook him hard.

"Get up, you fool," the man hissed. It was Barbarossa, who had been among the lieutenants at their outdoor party. "A'isha is under attack at the birthing capsule."

He shoved a revolver into Abdullah's hand, and they both ran toward the capsule. There were men running from all directions now. Whoever had attacked would find it difficult to escape. They ran up the wooden stairs that led to the hatch and swung inside. There were three men sprawled just inside the capsule and a nurse splayed against a bulkhead, her chest red with blood and eyes open and vacant.

"Check them," snapped Barbarossa, bending over the first man and pulling a gun from his hand, roughly looking for signs of life. "If they are alive, we want to find out who they are and who sent them."

Abdullah checked the second man, while Barbarossa went on to the third. The men were all armed and all dead. The inner hatch was open as well, and the capsule was un-pressurized. Barbarossa went to one side of the hatch, and motioned to Abdullah to stand across from him. Abdullah felt his stomach clench tight. He was afraid of what he was going to see in the inner part of the chamber.

"We have the capsule surrounded. Your only chance to live is to surrender now," Barbarossa yelled.

"I would hope you have the situation under control by now," a woman's voice snapped from inside the room. "I wish you had it under control a few minutes ago. Now, get in here."

Barbarossa entered the room, followed quickly by Abdullah. They were met by Faryal who was crouched behind a chair, an automatic pistol clutched in her hands, aimed firmly at the door. Her hair was tousled and her eyes were hard looking. On the bed behind her, propped up on one elbow was her mother, her bare face pale and drawn. She had her new son gathered in the crook of her arms.

"Has the danger passed?" Faryal asked.

"Yes," Barbarossa replied.

She sighed, turned the chair around and slumped into it. Faryal laid the gun on a table beside her.

"The nurse?" she asked.

"Dead," replied Barbarossa.

At that, she slumped a little further, making a small cry that pierced Abdullah's heart.

"What happened?" asked Barbarossa.

Faryal took a moment to compose herself. "There was a knock on the outer hatch. The nurse went to see what it was. I heard her scream and got my gun. When the hatch swung open, I was ready for them. I killed the first and might have died myself, but the nurse knocked over the other two men and their return fire was ineffective. She took one of the bullets instead of me. I was able to shoot both of them...and put extra rounds in all three to make sure. Then I took a defensive position in front of mother."

"You have a gun?" asked Barbarossa, his mouth gaping.

"Of course I do. I am of the Mahdi's family. We are all prepared to fight for him."

"Are you all right?" blurted Abdullah.

Faryal looked at him, and she smiled, "Yes, and mother and Nabil as well, praise be to Allah."

"Praise to Allah, indeed," sighed Abdullah.

"Your face..." Abdullah continued, suddenly realizing that he could see her face for the first time, not just her eyes. He saw her father's strength in those features, but softened. And beautiful. Her hair was long, dark and thick, a cascade of beauty. He smiled and her smile grew wider in response.

"Ahem." Her mother cleared her throat, reaching for a scarf, expertly twisting it over her hair and across her face. Faryal sighed, then went to a hook on the wall, took down her burqa, lifted it over her head and put it on.

Abdullah realized Barbarossa was glaring at the two of them with narrowed eyes, an angry stare that made the hair on Abdullah's neck stand up. A'isha also looked at them with an arched eyebrow, coolly appraising what the unguarded moment had revealed.

Two guards burst in quickly followed by Tawfiq. He laid a comforting hand on his daughter's shoulder as he passed her, strode to the bed, hugged his wife and picked up his son. He snapped at his followers to close the hatch and restore pressure to the capsule. As they took care of that, he heard the story again. He showed almost as much surprise as Barbarossa at his daughter's use of the handgun.

"You taught her to shoot?" he asked his wife.

"Of course, it's a good thing I did. Do I look like I am in any condition to defend myself?" A'isha asked fiercely. Tawfiq did not reply, just leaned down and kissed her. He turned to his daughter.

"I thought I was the father of a new lion," he said, with a smile on his face. "But I find that my family is full of lions."

*   *   *

A few weeks later, Abdullah woke up with thoughts of the recent incident and, of course, with Faryal's face on his mind. He had tried to see her again, but the extra security around the Mahdi and his family now made that impossible. He knew she was safer than she had ever been and wished there was something he could do himself to protect her. They were able to exchange notes which spoke more explicitly of their feelings, but that was all.

The mystery around the attack was not diminished by time. People were split on whether the object was murder or kidnapping. The guard who had been posted on the birthing chamber had vanished and people suspected that if he hadn't been paid off and fled, he was probably sleeping with the creatures at the bottom of Dire Lake.

There were some Muslims who felt, as did most inhabitants of Eureka, that someone within the Islamic community was vying for power. But most Muslims suspected, or were convinced, that the CoDominium was somehow behind the attack. Abdullah hoped that bringing everyone together on the ball field might ease the tensions, that a day of shared athletic competition would help the situation.

As soon as Abdullah had returned from his long journey, he had gone to the garrison commander and challenged the Marines to a baseball game. The request was met by laughter at first, but they finally agreed. In the weeks that followed, despite tensions caused by the attack on the Mahdi's family, excitement built on every side of town. No one thought the Muslim team, who called themselves the Faithful, had a chance, but they also knew the Marines would not have been challenged by the Faithful, if they didn't have something up their sleeves.

Abdullah rushed to the latrine, then back to his tent, changing into his new uniform. The trousers and cap were black, and the shirt was green. There were no numbers, but a white crescent adorned the left side of his chest. As he walked toward the field, he met the other players and Patrick. Soon they were at the head of a parade of excited people, some with picnic baskets, heading toward the game.

The field was no island of green grass as it would have been back home. They'd picked a wide flat area with hills behind it for the spectators. The bases were down, the base paths and foul lines limed, and a row of poles adorned with rope marked the limits of the outfield. The Marines were looking sharp and capable, dressed in white, with red trim on their uniforms, and blue hats with a red 26, the number of their Regiment. Abdullah and Patrick went up to the old man who had agreed to be an umpire. He was considered the fairest and most impartial umpire in town, and was known for keeping his officiating crew on a short leash. The CoDominium sergeant who led the military team was already at the umpires side and scowled at their approach.

"He isn't one of you," the sergeant said, pointing at Patrick.

"Well," said Patrick, "I ain't one of you either."

"You know what I mean," the sergeant said, "He's no Arab."

"Neither am I," replied Abdullah.

"You know what I mean, damn-it. Not a Muslim. Your team is called the Faithful, and your skinny friend doesn't look like the praying type."

Patrick grinned. "I may not be much for church, but I have faith in God and like these fellahs say, 'there ain't no God but the one God.'"

The umpire stepped between them. "No rules in this game about religions. If he suits up with them, he plays with them. Now, since you're both the home team, we want you to flip to see who has home field advantage."

The Marines won that toss and would have the last ups, already an edge in their favor. Their pitcher was good, and the first three batters of the Faithful went down swinging.

Patrick took the mound and made the first two Marine batters look like idiots, which he mowed down swinging. The third hit a weak grounder to short, which Abdullah scooped up and threw to first.

The crowd had split based on team loyalty, Marines and townspeople from Eureka on the first baseline behind their dugout, and the Faithful with the townsmen from Medina along the path from third to home. They cheered and clapped at every pitch, and both sides waved flags in their respective colors. Vendors moved among the crowd, smiling with glee at this opportunity to make a little extra money, nothing to be sneered at in this hardscrabble region at the edge of civilization.

First up in the second, Abdullah was able to get onto first with the next batter bunting him over to second. But the Marines turned a double play, and then a strikeout ended the top of the second. They also got a man on base when the third baseman couldn't get the ball to first quickly enough, but he was stranded on second.

There were a few hits, and a few walks, on each side, but the game remained scoreless until the fifth, when the Faithful's catcher, a stocky man who was still recovering from a brigand arrow in his thigh, clubbed a home run over the left field fence.

"I had no choice, I can barely run today," he exclaimed when he limped back to the dugout to be pounded by his teammates.

In the bottom of the seventh, the Marines began to get something going. With no outs, they got a man on first, another man walked, and their sergeant hit a double that brought both men home. It was now 2 to 1 in favor of the Marines.

Abdullah called for time and went to visit Patrick on the mound, motioning to the catcher to join them. Patrick was rubbing his arm, he was obviously tiring.

"I'm losin' velocity on my fastball, he said. "I'm gonna have to start getting tricky."

"But you'll blow out your arm," protested Abdullah.

"Hell," Patrick replied, "my baseball days are over, might as well leave it all on the field today."

And what Abdullah saw then was amazing. Patrick started mixing up his pitches and the Marines, who thought they had seen all his moves, were seeing a whole new pitcher. Abdullah realized that this might end up working to their advantage as Patrick was able to end the seventh by mowing three men down in order.

In the top of the eighth, Abdullah was able to get onto second on an error. The man who followed him hit a dribbler that got through the gap into center field and got on first. From the dugout, Patrick signaled for a double steal and on the next pitch the runners went, both diving into the next base.

As Abdullah came up on third, dusting the dirt off of his front, he realized that there were cheers coming from the crowds beside him and groans from behind first base. They had done it!

On the very next pitch, the man hit a high fly ball. But the Marine in center field was not able to get under it and it fell for a double—both Abdullah and the man on second scored. The crowd behind their dugout roared with delight. It was now three to two in favor of the Faithful. The eighth ended with no further scoring. Patrick let on two base runners in that inning, but both were stranded on base as their teammates struck out.

The Faithful tried their hardest, but the Marines were pitching to the bottom of their order with a fresh relief pitcher, a good one, and even Patrick went down swinging. Now it was the bottom of the ninth and it all came down to their defense. Patrick walked the first man, but the second hit a weak grounder to short. Abdullah flipped it to second while the second baseman relayed it to first for a double play. Only one out left. But the crowd was soon hushed as Patrick, who was losing his control, walked three men in a row. Abdullah looked out to him, but Patrick shook his head no. They had no real pitchers on their bench.

It was the sergeant who came up next, one of the best hitters on the team. Patrick got ahead of him in the count with two quick strikes, but then followed it with three balls for a full count. He gave the next pitch everything he had, right down the middle of the strike zone. The sergeant, a lefty, wasn't able to turn on it fully, but hit a solid grounder to third. The Faithful third baseman scooped it up and Abdullah screamed, "Home, home, throw it home." It was a high throw, but the catcher was able to get the ball, and dropped down to block home plate.

"Out," screamed the umpire and the Faithful bench exploded onto the field. Everyone converged on the pitcher's mound, and Patrick was hoisted into the air.

No confusion about who's the MVP of this game, thought Abdullah.

The Marines lined up, and invited every one of the Faithful team to shake their hands. "You did good," the sergeant told Abdullah. "I never would have thought you could beat us, but I guess on any given day...."

He and Abdullah grinned at each other. Abdullah left the field in a happy glow. Maybe sporting events like this could help ease tensions, bring people together. The path to the capsule settlement rang with gunfire as celebrants fired into the air. There was a huge party that went on for hours, a party that grew hazy for Abdullah toward the end.

A few hours later, he was shaken out of a deep sleep. The celebrations had turned ugly on both sides of the bridge between Eureka and Medina and there had been riots. There were dead on both sides. So much for the healing power of athletic competition.

* * *

The next few weeks were bad. The movement of people on the bridge between Medina and Eureka was almost completely shut down. Commerce ground to a halt. In better times the merchants would have complained, but now they feared losing everything in further rioting. There were skirmishes between both sides with toughs and rowdies taking advantage of the chaos to cause trouble, loot and even old scores.

Patrick pitched a tent on the edge of capsule town as he was no longer welcome in Eureka—even his musician girlfriend from the pub would no longer speak to him. He talked to Abdullah about it being time to leave. He said he had met some nice people and learned some new things, but a man like him knew when it was time to move on. Fall was coming and if he waited too long, it would be winter and too cold for journeying, especially on these high plains and through the mountains.

Patrick didn't say so, but it was obvious that Barbarossa's ruthlessness in dealing with the brigands had an effect on him. He talked about heading home, a three thousand mile journey, but a journey he now looked forward to. He had come to Medina by traveling north through the Atlas Mountains, down the Titan River and then via trade routes that crossed the hills and plains on their way to Dire Lake in the east.

This time, Patrick planned to take an easier path, down trade routes that led to the south and the pass guarded by Fort Stony Point. From there, he could enter the Shangri-La Valley and travel to the headwaters of the River Jordan, from there riverboat passage would take him close to home. He even suggested that Abdullah join him on this journey.

In their meetings to discuss the growing crisis, Tawfiq's lieutenants grew fractious. Barbarossa was chief spokesman for a faction that wanted war now and argued that the people were fired up and ready, while Tawfiq and the majority of lieutenants wanted to move much more cautiously.

There was no doubt that the Faithful would need to prepare for conflict which was what they had been doing before the riots. The recent hostilities had made that fact even stronger.

Abdullah thought of the friendships he had forged with Patrick and with people at the pub in Eureka, wondering if there wasn't another way—a way of peace. He wondered if armed conflict was the only way for the Faithful to further Allah's will. But he kept that unpopular thought to himself.

Barbarossa was authorized to send five hundred men to the new base that the Brotherhood was equipping for them, to prepare the way for a much larger force. Military training was stepped up and men went about the towns openly armed. Dover grew more difficult to deal with, continuing to blame problems on the workers, and threatening to stop food supplies, even to evict the Faithful from Capsule Town.

One afternoon, Abdullah finally found a chance to speak to Faryal. They were in a supply tent with two entrances and only a canvas wall in the middle. This was a favorite meeting place of theirs, a good place where they could have privacy, and enter and leave separately after their conversation. They spoke through a hole in the canvas.

Faryal said in a trembling voice. "My father spoke to my mother. Barbarossa has been asking for my hand in marriage." There was a catch in her voice. "Father thinks it might be a good idea, as it would bind Barbarossa's interest more closely to his and because I might distract him from his anger. Me, nothing but a distraction,"

She was openly weeping now. Abdullah thought about the look on Barbarossa's face, that day in the birthing chamber, and a chill went down his spine.

"Come away with me," Abdullah blurted.

"What?" she replied.

"Come away with me," he repeated, becoming more decisive as he spoke. "Patrick is thinking of leaving, we can go with him, to his home in the south. It's nice there, very quiet, with people of all faiths living in peace."

"And leave Mother?" she replied, "And everything I know? And ignore my duties? Oh, Abdullah, if only I could."

They spoke for a few more minutes, but Abdullah was unable to change her mind. He went to Patrick, and told him the plan. Patrick agreed to wait for a few more days to give Abdullah time to get through to Faryal, said it was the least he could do for a good friend.

Two days later, a note came to Abdullah from Faryal brought by one of her attendants in a sealed envelope. It simply said: "Yes I will go with you. Meet me at the corrals, a half hour before the start of the next brightday."

Abdullah rushed to Patrick, who told him to pack up, suggested he tell people he and Patrick were off for another scouting expedition. Their meeting was not for another nine hours. His packing took only a few minutes, as he had few belongings. He didn't dare draw a weapon from the armory, that would have required authorizations he didn't have. He spent the night staring at the roof of his tent, unable to sleep. He was up an hour before the meeting and spent his time sitting on a rock, staring at the two towns and fortress, so close to each other, yet so full of hatred.

He was excited to be leaving with Faryal, but now his thoughts began to turn to the future: Would they be safe traveling? How would he support her? Would they be accepted at their destination?

The time finally came and he went to the corrals. Patrick was not there yet. Instead, there was a stranger, a short, thin man with a thick black beard and a large dark turban on his head. The man was dressed in a coat and trousers and armed for travel, with two pistols and a rifle. He had a heavy pack on his back and a large wicker basket in his arms. Abdullah turned to walk in the other direction, but was halted by a loud whisper.

"Abdullah," the man said with a strange voice. "It's me."

"Me who?" he replied, confused.

"Faryal, you silly man. Now get over here."

Abdullah gaped. Yes, she was the right size, but hardly the right shape. She must have bound her breasts. And now that he looked more closely, the beard did not look very real. He gaped in surprise as she continued to speak in low tones.

"Here, take this chit to the stable master. It is for six mounts and saddles. For you, Patrick and me. My name is Jamal, if anyone asks. Take the chit now and get our horses. I am not sure how convincing this disguise would be at close range."

Just then, Patrick came up. "And who might you be?" he said to Faryal with a grin. He was obviously more quick on the uptake than Abdullah.

"Jamal," she replied and then turned to Abdullah, "Now, go and get our horses."

Off Abdullah went.

*   *   *

"Where is Faryal?" Tawfiq asked his wife as he strode into the capsule. "It is past time for breakfast."

"She is safe," A'isha answered.

"What do you mean, safe? Where is she?"

"I sent her off with Abdullah and Patrick."

"WHAT?" Tawfiq roared. "With the African and an infidel? Without a chaperone? Without troops to defend her? Sent her off where? How far?" He glared at her, his hands clenched into fists at his side.

"Calm down, my love, sit and have a cup of tea so we can talk."

Tawfiq's breath huffed out and he sat, although the tea she gave him remained ignored in the mug at his side.

"She loves him, you know," she said softly.

"Loves who? The boy?" Tawfiq asked. "What does love matter when we are moving toward war and moving more quickly than I would like?"

"She loves Abdullah. And it is precisely because of that coming war that I sent her away," A'isha answered.

"But my men, my generals, all of them compete for her hand as a reward. You know of Barbarossa's interest." protested Tawfiq.

"Our daughter," she answered sharply, "is not a reward. As parents, her happiness is our responsibility. If rewards are a factor, you should think about a reward for the man who brought us birthing chambers. More and more of the capsules are being converted, and more and more pregnancies are successful. We are even earning money from townspeople from Eureka who want to use them, in fact, people from across the steppes."

The mighty Tawfiq, heir to the title of Mahdi and ruler of the Faithful, began to bend to a higher power. "But Abdullah is just a boy. And although he is smart, and even brave, he is no warrior and no leader."

"And that is why he is a good match," she said. "He is young and so is she. She will be far happier with someone her age, than with one of those old bears in your inner circle. This is our struggle, not hers."

"And where will they go?" Tawfiq said as he slumped into the chair.

"They will be going to live with Patrick's family, in the Shangri-La Valley. From what he tells us, they are good people there with folk of many nations and many faiths, living together in peace. You see the friendship between Abdullah and Patrick. That will give them a strong ally in their new home. They can build a house, and live in peace.

"And," she continued, "they can keep our son safe."

Tawfiq sat up straight, his hands gripping the arms of the chairs like claws. "Nabil?" he whispered.

"Yes, I have sent our boy with him," she said, trying to be practical despite the tears that ran down her cheeks. "Think about this. If we succeed, you and I will know where to find them and can rejoin them. And if Allah does not will us to succeed—and he may not—our family will live on. That is the true mission of the Faithful, to survive from one generation to the next."

Tawfiq was silent for a long time before he replied quietly. "I would have liked to have said goodbye to her and my son."

"But would you have let them go if you knew?" A'isha asked.

"Perhaps not," he conceded. "And what you say makes sense. Worrying about the children would have distracted me." He paused for a moment.

"Perhaps you should follow them," he continued sadly.

She went over to him and knelt beside his chair, caressing his cheek. "That would be impossible, my love," she said quietly. "I could not live without you, nor you without me."

There was an urgent knock at the door. They rose to their feet and he kissed her.

"My duties..." he said.

"I know," she replied. "Go."

And he went.

* * *

Abdullah, Faryal and Patrick rode out of the camp at dawn, in single file, each leading their extra mount. The guards recognized Abdullah and waved him through without hesitation. Faryal's disguise was sufficient to get them through a cursory viewing, although Abdullah couldn't believe that it was sufficient to fool a careful observer. She balanced her large basket on her saddle bow, refusing to accept help from the others and refusing to let them tie it to the horse behind her.

They began their long climb into the western hills. They were now high above the towns behind them, not wanting to turn south until they were well away from civilization. There were thunderclouds forming over the plain and it looked like a rare day of rain was coming. They were high enough that the base of the clouds was below them, and the path grew steeper as the day grew longer. Finally, Faryal asked for a halt. "I can't stand this beard any longer. The glue is making my face itch."

They dismounted while she disappeared into the brush, still carrying her basket. Abdullah and Patrick disappeared to the other side of the trail to relieve themselves and share a small drink of water. When Faryal emerged a few minutes later, she was beardless but also had a baby in her arms. The empty basket was hooked over an elbow.

"What..." sputtered Abdullah.

"Surely," she said, "you recognize my brother, Nabil."

"Yes," said Abdullah, "but what's he doing here?"

He saw Patrick smiling, his hand over his mouth in an attempt to conceal his mirth. When Abdullah glared at him, he said, "Don't look at me, it's news ta me just like it is ta you."

"Nabil is here for the same reason I am," said Faryal. "My mother wanted him safe, wanted both of us to leave. So we gave him a draught to make him sleep and here he is."

"Your mother?" asked Abdullah.

"Yes, silly, how do you think we got these mounts and had such an easy time leaving? Do you think yourself so clever as to accomplish an escape like this so simply?"

Now Patrick was chuckling openly. Abdullah realized that she was right, realized that he had not given their escape as much thought as he should have. And then he realized something else.

"Your face," he said. "It's uncovered."

Now she smiled at him. "Yes, it is. And I plan to keep it that way. From what Patrick says, it is the custom in our new home. Certainly, he has seen enough women's faces that he will not be unnerved by it."

She took off her turban, and began untying her hair, brushing it back with her fingers. The thick, dark hair that had been in his thoughts ever since he had seen it. She smiled at him. "And certainly, a woman can reveal her face to her betrothed."

Now Patrick was laughing openly. Abdullah closed his mouth, although he didn't remember how it had opened. "Betrothed?" he sputtered.

"Yes, of course. Do you really think I would let you dishonor me by stealing me away without becoming my husband?"

Abdullah's head was swimming. This was what he had dreamed of from the very first time he saw her at the launch facility back on Earth. Her eyes had captured him and he now realized he had not been a free man from that day on. He smiled and began to laugh.

"Well," she said, a little sharply. "Do I have an answer? What are your intentions?"

Abdullah smiled back at her. "It will be," he replied, "as Allah wills."

"Good," she said. "You are learning already."

Patrick whooped and gave them both a hug.

Faryal fastened Nabil into a harness that snuggled him close to her breast, and Abdullah helped her onto her horse. She leaned down, grabbed the back of his head and brought her lips to his. He was blissful and could see that behind her sarcasm, so was she. Abdullah thought back to the words that A'isha and Tawfiq had shared the day he first met Faryal. Indeed, a good wife was more precious than rubies. He mounted his own horse.

"Now we must ride," said Faryal, "We have many miles to go until we reach safety, and the longer we can ride while Nabil sleeps, the better."

Behind them, the clouds began to flash with lightning. There were rumbles of thunder echoing through the hills. They turned their back on the storm clouds, riding toward their new future.

From the closed hearing by the Interior Subcommittee of the United States Senate, 1 September 2073.

Mr. Bendicks: Why, exactly, does the Administration want to cancel the treaties with the various Indian tribes and transfer the reservations to the public domain?

Sec. Pendleton: Seventeen years of free movement between national entities, ending in 2065, resulted in thirty-seven million foreigners, uh, extra-nationals, holding permanent residency permits within the United States. Fewer than six million of those persons have applied for citizenship, and according to figures of the INS, fewer than one in eleven is competent in the use of the English language. There are twenty-eight different newsfax publishing one or more times a day in the United States, in eleven different languages. Throughout the states, there are innumerable enclaves in which the principal languages spoken are other than English, notably Spanish, Portuguese, Russian, Chinese, and Arabic.

Mr. Bendicks: Mr. Secretary, one of us has obviously misunderstood the other. Let me repeat my question. Why, exactly, does the Administration want to cancel the treaties with the various Indian tribes and transfer the reservations to the public domain?

Sec. Pendleton: If the Senator will be patient, I'm coming to that.

Mr. Bendicks: Please do.

Sec. Pendleton: Not only the United States of America, but almost every other developed, industrialized nation on Earth, has such enclaves of unrepentant extra-nationals making their social and economic demands but unwilling to naturalize. This administration has gone to considerable effort and expense to absorb these non-American populations that make up more than eight percent of our total population.

Yet we have other un-Americanized enclaves of much longer standing. I refer to a number of the Indian tribes. In the first seventy years of the twentieth century, major progress was made in Americanizing these people. Some tribes lost their languages entirely. In most of the others, many of the younger people had limited or no ability to speak their tribal language. Then, in the last one hundred years, and particularly in the last seventy years, this healthy trend has been reversed. The children are taught the tribal language from infancy. Most tribes have modernized their languages for twenty-first century use by developing words from old roots, "adapting" American words by adding native prefixes or suffixes.

If we are to exert legal pressures on these recent immigrants to adopt the American language and culture, we must first eradicate these cultural regressions by the Indian tribes, who, after all, have been recalcitrant for a much longer time.

Mr. Bendicks: It's reassuring to know, Mr. Secretary, that we have you in there fighting to Americanize the American Indian. Now, let me ask one more time: Why, exactly, does the Administration want to cancel the treaties with the Indian tribes and transfer the reservations to the, public domain? I'd like you to state it explicitly, if possible, for the record.

Sec. Pendleton: Senator, the unfortunate cultural recalcitrance of these Indian tribes is rooted in the reservations. The administration has no argument with Indians as a whole. The number who live away from the reservations is five times the number who live on the reservations. Twelve times if we include those who identify themselves as Indian or part Indian and as having more than one-eighth Indian blood, so to speak. The majority of these are from mixed tribal stocks—Cherokee and Kiowa for example, or Jemez and Acoma. They speak only English, and essentially have been assimilated into the mainstream of American culture. To remove the Indian populations from the reservations would result in the completion of Indian assimilation.

Mr. Bendicks: Thank you, Mr. Secretary. I presume you're aware of the proposals by the Bureau of Reclamation for the large scale pumping of desalinized water to a number of the western reservations, and the establishment of urbanization projects on them. No doubt reservation land would become very valuable then. Who do you suppose would profit from this, if the land was first taken from the tribes and then made available for purchase from the public domain by developers?

THE COMING OF THE DINNEH

By John Dalmas

2074 A.D., Earth

The army landed at Lukachukai on February 6, 2074. Also at fifteen or twenty other places on the Navajo Reservation. It was a Wednesday. Not that February or Wednesday mean anything now; the calendar is more complicated here. But I remember those things because I am an old man. I forget yesterday, but I remember well what happened long ago.

My wife and I lived at Mescalero, New Mexico, then, but sometimes we did consulting, mostly on Apache reservations. Strictly speaking, the Navajo are Apaches. Were Apaches. The Spaniards got the name Apache from the Zunis, who used it for all the Athapaskan speaking-tribes that raided them. The Spaniards called the biggest of those tribes "Apache de Navajo," Apaches of the Fields, because they cultivated corn squash. The Spaniards never did conquer them.

If you know much about Indians, you might guess from my name, Carl Boulet, that I didn't start out as Dinneh, as Apache or Navajo. I'm a Chippewa-Sioux mixed blood. My great grandmother told me that the French last name came from one of Louis Riel's métis refugees from the Manitoba Insurrection in the 1860s.

But that's not what you want to hear about. You want to know what it was like to come in exile to this world, and what it was like here in the old days. I will tell you the best I can. I did not talk English for many Earth-years till you came here. Once it was my best language; I had three university degrees, and talked it like you do, better than Chippewa. Better than Mescalero. Now it comes forth differently, even though my words are English. That's because I have come to think differently, living as we do here.

The September before the army came to Lukachukai, my wife and I—her name was Marilyn—established a program in applied domestic ecology in several Navajo schools, on a trial basis. It is strange to remember things like that. I was a different person in those days. At the end of January, we went back to see how it was going. On February 6, she was at Window Rock while I'd driven up to Lukachukai the day before.

It was noon. I'd eaten lunch, and was in the gym shooting baskets with a couple of teachers. I have not remembered shooting baskets for a very long time. Then the principal hurried in. The army, he said, had just landed at Window Rock, and federal marshals had arrested the tribal government. Troops had landed at Tuba City and Dinnehotso, too; they'd probably landed at every town on the reservation that day.

Just then it was snowing hard at Lukachukai, which may have been why they hadn't landed there yet. The men I'd been shooting baskets with didn't even look at each other. They started for the door. Lemmi Yazd paused long enough to call back to me, "Maybe you better come too."

I hesitated for maybe a second, then grabbed my parka where it hung in the teachers' lounge and followed them outdoors. They scattered; I stayed with Lemmi and we trotted to his pickup; we got in, he lifted it on its air cushion, and we left the parking lot in a hurry.

"Where are we going?" I asked him.

"A place we've set up in the Chuskas," he said. "One of the places."

Instead of going northeast into the Chuska Mountains on the maintained road, he drove west a little way, then turned north on a small dirt road, not made by engineers but cleared through junipers and pinyons for their trucks. You couldn't see very far through the snow, which was fine with us. The snowfall thinned and thickened but never stopped. As we got farther north, the land grew higher, and the pinyon and juniper began to be displaced by ponderosa pine. And there the snow wasn't just today's new fall. There was snow left from before.

I worried about Marilyn. It sounded as if, at Window Rock, there'd been no warning. I wondered if I was doing the right thing to go with Lemmi Yazzi. But if she was interned at Window Rock and I was interned fifty miles away at Lukachukai... I turned the radio on in the pickup and got the tribal station out of Window Rock. It was playing *America the Beautiful*. In English. That made it real to me; the government had taken over.

We'd been warned, kind of. The summer before, a rumor swept the reservations all over the United States, that the government was going to start taking over and selling Indian lands and relocating reservation Indians.

Ten years earlier, hardly anyone would have taken a rumor like that seriously. But in 2172, the Soviets had begun rounding up some of the Turkic and Mongol peoples in Asia and relocating them by force to a world called Haven. It was scary to read about.

The CoDominium Bureau of Relocation had been sending immigrants to Haven for years, and once, out of curiosity, I'd read up on the planet. Not in the newsfax, but in technical journals. Haven sounded like a bad place.

Some tribes, the Mesaderos and Navajos among others, had set up unofficial committees of resistance. Not that we thought it would really happen, but just in case. Hideouts were built or dug in, in hidden places in canyons and forests, and supplies were hidden in them. It was to one of those that Lemmi was driving us.

We were the first ones to reach it. It was two hogans topped with a foot of dirt and twenty inches of snow, on one side of a shallow draw, shaded by pines and firs. The hogans would be hard to see from the air, with the naked eyes. Maybe an instrument search would show them.

Until that day there'd only been a rumor, and the Navajo Reservation hadn't seemed like the place where the government would start. The Navajos were the strongest and most populous tribe and most of their land was poor. The White Mountain and Mescalero reservations had much better land. And the Nez Perce; even the Pine Ridge. I suppose the government decided that if they took the strongest first, and relocated its people, the other tribes would lose heart and do what they were told. I used to wonder if that's how it worked out.

Within forty minutes there were ten of us in the two hogans. Everyone but me had clothes stored there, and boots, and a rifle. I was lucky to have worn boots that morning instead of oxfords; the weather forecast had given me that. And two of the pickups had rifles racked in them, so there was one for me. I didn't know who I would worry with an old .30 caliber Winchester hunting rifle. Two infantry riflemen had more firepower than the ten of us.

Of course, the idea wasn't to get in fights anyway. It was to make little armed demonstrations, get on the television and in the newsfax, and get the American people on our side. That had been the strategy of the Indian rights movement for more than a century. But the government was paying less and less attention to the people.

It stopped snowing that night. Meanwhile the government had shut down all the tribal radio stations and Navajo language programs on other stations, and banned any mention of what was happening. We tuned in Gallup, Flagstaff, Farmington, and Holbrook, and they never mentioned that anything was going on.

The guys I was with talked it over. They decided to sit tight and take it a day at a time. If we didn't hear anything tonight, maybe we'd send out pickups in the morning to visit the nearest groups. Maybe we could work something out.

No one asked my opinion; I wasn't Navajo. I wasn't any kind of Apache—any of the Dinneh, or Tindeh…the *people* in the Apache languages. I was originally from the Red Lake Reservation in Minnesota, where the country was soggy muskeg instead of timbered mountains or rough, stony desert. I'd married a Mescalero, learned the language, and done my Ph.D. research on them. Also I spoke pretty good Navajo. But I wasn't really one of them. Not then. I even had enough European genes to give me hazel eyes. But if they had asked my opinion, I'd have gone along with what they thought best. I had nothing myself to suggest. I was no chief then. I was an educator.

As it turned out, the army came to us, at about 3:30 in the morning. I suppose their instruments picked up the heat from our stovepipes, even though we kept very small fires. They'd have taken us entirely by surprise, except that I had awakened and had to urinate, so I pulled on my boots and went out of the hogan. And heard the soft, rumbling hum of landing craft settling into a meadow in the woods—what the Spanish and Anglos in the southwest call a *cienega*—a hundred or so meters down slope. I went into both hogans and woke everyone up.

We fooled them; we fought. It seemed unreal then that we'd do that. It seemed unreal to the army, too; that's why we did as well as we did. Some of us didn't even take time to lace our boots, just wrapped the laces around our ankles. The others strapped on snowshoes and went down the draw toward the *cienega*. I didn't have snowshoes; I just waded along the best I could in other people's tracks.

The troops were in no hurry. They were still in the *cienega*. They'd unloaded from the two light landers, I guess a platoon of them, and were forming up to move on us.

None of us had a night scope, of course, but the soldiers weren't wearing camouflage whites, and there was moonlight. With the snow cover, it was easy to see them. But it was too dark to use the sights on our rifles. We just aimed down the tops of our barrels and started to shoot from behind trees. We had time to shoot two or three rounds each before they started shooting back, but when they did, it was the most frightening thing in my life, before or since. It sounded like four hundred rifles instead of forty. I could hear bullets hitting tree trunks and rocks, and branches falling off the trees above and behind us. They fired for about half a minute, I guess.

Then they stopped, and started moving forward. Someone said later that they'd gotten orders through headphones in their helmets. They were to take us prisoner if they could and they thought they'd intimidated us; thought we were ready to quit, and I was. One or two of our people started shooting again though, so the soldiers did too, and then the rest of us did. I shot two or three times more before Lemmi yelled to cease fire and surrender. After a few seconds, the soldiers stopped shooting again, too. They came up and arrested all of us. A few started to beat us with their rifle butts, but their sergeants swore at them and made them quit. We'd shot a few of them—I heard we killed three and the rest were pretty mad. Five of us had been shot, and two were dead.

Another lander came down in the *cienega*, and they loaded us and took off. They didn't stop at Lukachukai. They flew us straight to Window Rock, where they'd set up a fenced compound with army field shelters, just for guerrillas, and mostly still empty. The other Window Rock internees were kept in the community college and high school auditoriums, and the livestock-judging pavilion.

The field shelters we were in didn't have any power cells in the heaters, so they seemed pretty cold, especially for sleeping. Especially when we lay on our cots in summer-weight sleeping bags, shivering and looking out through the transparent roofs, seeing stars through holes in the clouds.

Actually, most of us didn't know what it was to sleep cold. Not then.

The army let us know about our families—Marilyn at the school—but they kept us segregated. We were guerrillas. I never thought of myself that way, but we were. They kept bringing more people to the guerrilla compound, some of them women. This went on for several days. The

Navajo Reservation is bigger than some states—about the size of West Virginia—with a thousand canyons, a thousand ridges and mesas, and a lot of its people live out among them on isolated ranches.

The army didn't know who or where the guerrillas were. So they waited for attacks, and killed or rounded up the attackers, and checked out little ranches for groups of men with weapons.

Quite a few White Mountain Apaches had driven up from the Fort Apache Reservation—seventy or eighty at least—and maybe forty or fifty from the San Carlos, connecting up with the Navajos they'd contacted earlier, through the committees. The police and the army didn't try to keep them from coming. Maybe they wanted them to come and get rounded up; they probably thought that those who came would be the hardcore resistance on the other reservations, and they'd get them now instead of later. There were also twenty or thirty Jicarilla Apache, and nine who came all the way from Mescalero in a van, expecting to get arrested and jailed on the way. There was even a work van load from the tiny Yavapai Reservation, mixed-blood Apaches and Yavapais who spoke only English.

Those numbers are not exact. I've estimated from hearsay, and from how many ended up in the guerrilla compound. The nine Mescaleros are the only ones whose starting number I learned exactly. Four of the nine were killed or hospitalized, or maybe escaped to hide out somewhere; the other five were interned with us.

The compound got more and more crowded until, after eight days, more troops arrived. Not the U.S. Army this time, but CoDominium Marines. Russian-speaking. Someone said the army wasn't happy about having to do that job and that the whole thing had gotten out. Soldiers had told their families on the phone, also the newsfax and television, and the government couldn't pretend anymore that nothing was going on.

Then shuttles landed at the Window Rock airfield and they started loading us. I was lucky: I got a seat by one of the windows. After a few minutes we lifted, moving upward and outward till the rim of the Earth curved blue and white against black, and still outward till the curvature was strong. If I'd had a better view, I could have seen the Earth as a great beautiful ball. Finally, out beyond the outer Van Allen Belt, we docked with a converted freighter waiting to take us to Haven. I was feeling pretty bad; I thought I'd never see my wife again. But before they finished shuttling people up, they'd brought all the internees, Marilyn included, and we were together again.

2074, Luna

The *Alexei Makarov* was not a Bureau of Relocation ship. It was a tramp ore carrier on contract to Kennicott. They'd put in temporary facilities in the cargo holds, to take immigrants on the return trip. We slept in stacks of narrow bunks, used long common latrines, and ate standing up.

At the start there were 2,436 men and boys, and 1,179 women and girls, thirteen years old or older. There had been more than three hundred younger children with the internees, but someone in the government got them taken away before we shuttled up. The woman in charge of taking them said they'd be settled with people on Earth; that conditions on Haven were too extreme for young children. That didn't help the children born aboard the *Makarov*. And it wouldn't help those who would be born after we arrived on Haven. Or their mothers.

One of the first things Marilyn told me, when we got together, was that she'd started getting morning sickness when she was interned; we were going to be parents. She didn't know what that meant. I did—I'd read about childbirth on Haven—but I didn't tell her.

Meanwhile there were more than 3,600 of the Dinneh living in badly crowded conditions on the *Makarov*. I got the numbers from George Frank, the Navajo Tribal Chairman, who was the prisoner in charge of prisoners. He was the man responsible to the Marine Commandant for our organization and behavior. Bad colds broke out as soon as the Makarov left orbit. Practically everyone got one, and quite a few went into pneumonia. The Marine medics didn't have facilities to handle transportees, so only those whose condition was recognized as critical got taken to the clinic. Eleven died. We thought that was pretty bad.

George organized the Navajos according to clan, and the rest of us by tribe. Although I was only adopted Mescalero, the Mescaleros made me their spokesman because I could speak Navajo pretty well. From the start, most of the Apaches could pretty much carry on a conversation with each other, including the Navajos, each speaking his own dialect. But Mescalero is less like the others, and at first the Mescaleros had trouble understanding and being understood. And no one felt like speaking English; we felt betrayed by the English language government.

More and more, the Navajos included us in. All of us were Dinneh, George said—we were all "the people."

It was the Russian language that complicated things. Like all Americans, we'd taken Russian in school, and the Russian Marines and crew had all taken English, but not many on either side could understand what the other said very well. You had to talk very slowly and keep it simple. Marilyn was an exception. Her MA at the University of New Mexico had been in Native American Languages, but as an undergrad she'd had two years of Russian, on top of the three required years in grade school and a fourth year by choice in high school. So she was our spokesperson with the Russians, who liked her because she used their language so well.

Most of the Russians were all right. Whatever prejudices they had didn't include one against American Indians. But there wasn't anything they could do about too many people in too little space. It was always too hot in the hold. Water was rationed, and there weren't any showers. We could only wash once a week. After a while the holds smelled pretty bad. The food was poor and monotonous, but it nourished us all right, and on two meals a day, fat people lost weight.

To help pass the time, we'd sit in groups and tell stories. People would tell the stories of books they read, or movies they'd seen, or places they'd been, or they'd make up stories. At first only a few people would tell stories, but pretty soon more and more told them. Also we slept a lot. George set it up so everyone had a chance to do aerobic exercises once a day, in small groups. Most people did them—it was something to do—and it proved to be a good thing. But it did make it hotter in the holds.

Marilyn got to know the Marines' liaison officer, a woman lieutenant named Toloconnicov, who gave her a little book about Haven. It frightened Marilyn to read it. It didn't sound as bad as the technical articles had, but I didn't say anything. We'd find out when we got there. It might not be as bad as I expected.

Something more surprising came from her friendship with Lieutenant Toloconnicov. One day the lieutenant gave Marilyn an envelope and waited while she read what was inside: a formal invitation in English for both of us to have supper with the Marine commander, Major Shcherbatov. Marilyn told the lieutenant that we'd like to go, but we hadn't had a shower or washed our clothes for nearly five months. The lieutenant wrote us a permission to use showers in the sickbay, and said there'd be clean clothes for us there.

It felt good to shower and put clean clothes on.

The major had been stationed in eastern Siberia for a couple of years, and gotten interested in the Chukchi people there. From that he'd gotten interested in American Indians, so he had lots of questions about the Navajo. When he learned that not all of us were Navajo, he had questions about the other Apache tribes, and the Chippewa and the Sioux. We had supper with him twice, and talked for about three hours each time.

Marilyn asked him questions about Haven, but he claimed he didn't know much about it. I didn't believe him. He picked up his wine glass when he said it, which kept him from having to look at her. It didn't make me feel any better about what we'd find there.

It took the *Makarov* more than thirteen months to reach Haven. In that time we received four different series of shots, broad-spectrum vaccines to keep us safe from disease on Haven, as safe as possible. Also, Marilyn gave birth to a boy. We named him Marcel, after my grandfather.

The week before we entered the Byers System, George said he didn't feel qualified to be chief on Haven, and proposed Tom Spotted Horse, a retired marine master sergeant in his forties. The council agreed, so Tom was our chief. He organized us into squads, platoons, companies and battalions, and made sure we all knew what we belonged to. We picked our own officers and sergeants. That was tradition, and Tom didn't know most of the people.

A few days before we landed, Lieutenant Toloconnicov gave Marilyn a military topographic map of the district where we were supposed to land. Marilyn let me look at it before she took it to Tom. The latitude was subtropical; on a planet known for its cold climate, that was hopeful. The top half of the map showed the south part of a plateau that broke away into badlands. South of the badlands was a basin with the word desert on it. There were no towns or roads, but the plateau had a few thin broken lines with the words livestock driveway, and across it in large letters, the word *KAZAKHS*. The Kazakhs, I knew, were a people in Asia, and I remembered reading, years before, that a tribe of Kazakh traditionalists, herdsmen, had gotten the Soviet government to sponsor a Kazakh colony on Haven. This must be where it was.

An *X* had been marked on the plateau with a marker pen. The only reason I could think of for that was, we were supposed to be put down there. I went with Marilyn and told Tom what I'd made of the map; he listened, and then made me his technical aide.

The next day, forming up to load into the shuttles, most of us were feeling glad to be getting there at last. Even I was. At least I knew what we were in for. Instead of putting us down where the *X* was, they put us on a mesa isolated from the plateau by broken lands. Lieutenant Toloconnicov said the Major was responsible for that. He believed that if he lauded us at the X, the Kazakhs, who were armed, would attack us and make slaves out of the prisoners they took.

Then she marked on the map the mesa she thought we were on. I looked around. The ground cover looked a lot like bunch grass, shin high, with bearded purplish seed heads moving in a light breeze. Low shrubs were scattered around, mostly about knee high and stiff looking. It didn't look too bad.

We were told to unload some cases from the shuttles. Some were labeled *rations*, some *blankets*, and some *tents*. One small heavy case was unmarked. Lieutenant Toloconnicov said the ship's captain was going to keep the stuff, and not give it to us, but the Major was in charge of us, and didn't let him. She told us this was all that the government had sent along for us here. She sounded apologetic when she said it.

When all the people and cases were on the ground, Toloconnicov gave Marilyn a package. She told her, "This is a personal gift to you and your husband from Major Shcherbatov. It is not to be opened till we have left. I think the lieutenant knew what it was, but we didn't ask.

On the ground, Tom assigned some people to start opening the cases and counting what was in them. The rations were Marine field rations in individual packets, one meal per packet. The blankets were military, too. The tents weren't modern, individual field tents, but old, obsolete heavy squad tents. To carry them, we'd have to cut them up, if we could find anything to cut them with.

When the shuttles lifted for the last time, we all stood and watched them get small and disappear. It felt very final. We felt abandoned, which was how we needed to feel. The CoDo Marines had given us every treatment they had to protect us from disease, but the Bureau of Relocation had left us to starve or freeze, or be enslaved.

Tom's supply crew kept opening cases. The unlabeled case solved the problem of how to cut up the tents; it held 500 trench knives in sheaths. Only 500 knives for more than 3,000 people, but we were lucky to have them. Then, privately, Marilyn opened the major's gift package.

It held a big, 10 millimeter revolver in a holster, also a cleaning kit, and two boxes of ammunition, 100 rounds in all. That and a little kit for starting fire by compression. She gave the pistol to me.

There we were, 3,600 people, with blankets that still had to be counted, some old tent fabric for shelter, food for a few days, some knives and one pistol. There was no store to go to.

It could have been much worse. It was summer. Also, the ship's captain hadn't been allowed to leave us with nothing at all. Before the shuttles had brought down the last of the people, Tom had sent out scouting parties to look for water and anything else useful. They didn't find any.

And it was almost hot, warm enough to sweat. The things I'd read had emphasized how cold Haven was. But there was summer, a long one. And when the sun is up for more than forty hours at a time, heat can build. I thought it might be early afternoon. The sun was high, but not as high as it should be at noon in the subtropics.

I told Tom what I thought. He squinted at the sky, then looked at me. "Forty hours between sunup and sundown? There was something about that in the little book your wife showed me, but a lot of it was confusing. Do we get forty hours of night, too?"

I'd known people like Tom: Intelligent, but only what they saw around them was real. Information about space or other planets was just noise. "It's not that simple, I told him. "This world is a moon. The planet it goes around, Cat's Eye, is big and hot, hot enough to glow in the dark. When Cat's Eye is up, we'll get both heat and light from it. When it's up but the sun's down; we'll have what's called 'dimday.' It will get cooler during dimday, but not as cool as during truenight."

It also seemed to me that the sun would move around irregularly in the sky, because Haven circles Cat's Eye while they're both going around the sun. But I didn't tell him that.

He looked thoughtful, which was much better than if his eyes had glazed over. He was getting used to a new "here and now."

"It's complicated," I added. "We'll learn what we need to by experience." He nodded. Then the last of his scouting parties came back and told him they hadn't found any water. Nobody was surprised, up on a mesa like that.

"We'll go down into a canyon, he said to me. "If there's water to be found, that's where it will be. After we've found water, where do you think we should go? Down into the desert basin, or up on the plateau?"

"The plateau," I said. "We're going to need a lot of food, soon, and the Kazakhs up there are herdsmen. We need to steal some livestock from them. But they're armed, and they're supposed to be fighters. It will be dangerous."

His attention drew inward for a minute, then returned to me. "I'll send a raiding party to the plateau. Do these Kazakhs live in large bands or small?"

A raiding party. The Navajos had known about things like that, two hundred and fifty years ago. Now—Now I wondered. "I don't know," I answered.

"We'll have to go and find out," he said.

He told his scouting parties to find a way down off the mesa into one of the canyons that flanked it. A way that the women could hike. The canyon needed to have good water and be one that men could climb out of, up onto the plateau. When the scouting parties had left, he went to see how the crews were doing cutting up tents to make shelter pieces. I went with him.

It seemed to me we were lucky to have Tom Spotted Horse as our chief. He sized up problems, made decisions and gave orders like a marine sergeant.

The sun moved as slowly through the sky as you might expect on a world with forty hours between sunup and sundown. Tom's scouts had found two possible ways to leave the mesa. He selected one, then got the rations, blankets, shelter pieces and pieces of tent rope distributed among the people. They made packs out of them. Then he formed them up in their units and we started down the trail, with scouts leading the way. The sun seemed almost as high as when the shuttles had left, a little more than three hours earlier by my watch. There were eight rations for each person—that was all we had—and no one was to eat until Tom ordered a meal break.

It didn't pay to think too much about things; you could go into despair. We had to make a decision and do it, and handle the complications as they came up. Or lie down and die. The Dinneh weren't known for lying down and dying.

We didn't have nice backpacks from Wilderness Suppliers. We rolled up our rations inside our two blankets each, wrapped them in a piece of tent cloth, tied it all together with a piece of tent rope, and slung it over a shoulder. Also there were a lot of people—almost all the women—who'd been interned wearing street shoes. Their feet were soon in trouble.

Those who wore riding boots or engineer's boots were just as bad off. A few tried to go barefoot, but they put their shoes back on pretty quickly. Marilyn was wearing stout, low-cut walking shoes, but gravel and sand got in them. We took turns carrying Marcel. I offered to carry her pack for her, but she wouldn't let me. She said it would make her look bad to the Navajo women.

The canyon we worked our way down into was about seven hundred meters deep there, according to our map, and the way was steep, treacherous in places. It wasn't like hiking the Bright Angel or Kaibab Trails down into the Grand Canyon in Arizona. Those were surveyed, improved, and maintained—almost manicured; I suppose they still are. This was rough, untracked and uncertain. Much of it required scrambling instead of hiking. And we had people, especially women, who'd never hiked in their lives. Some weighed more than a hundred kilos, even after thirteen months on the *Makarov*. For them, the trail was hell; for some it was impossible. Twice we got cliffed out and had to wait while the scouts hunted for a way to continue. Then we all had to backtrack a ways before we could go on again. Once a scout fell to his death. We also lost eight people who fell when rock slid away beneath their feet and they couldn't stop sliding before they went over an edge.

All the scouts saw goatlike animals. One scout came face to face with something that looked much like a large mountain lion, with thick fur and a ruff—our first cliff lion. It backed away and disappeared when he yelled and threw a rock at it; it had never seen anything like him before.

The plants didn't look so unearthly either. I know now how strange some of them really are, but the strangeness wasn't conspicuous. It looked a lot like some canyon might in Arizona. There was a thing like grass with sharp leaves that cut when you touch them, and another with leaves that stung and burned like nettles, but quite a bit worse. Also there was something that gave people a rash; we needed to find out what it was, so we could avoid it.

The geology was different than I was used to. The rock strata seemed to be volcanic from the mesa top to the canyon bottom; there was nothing I recognized as sedimentary. Most of the strata were basalt; some were vesicular.

Even most of us who wore hiking boots had blisters by the time we reached the canyon bottom and buried our faces in the icy creek we found there. Lots of feet were raw, with bloody socks.

The hike down had taken us seven hours by my watch. I'm told some were still straggling in five hours later, and a few never made it, even with help.

Tom Spotted Horse was one of the first ones down. As others got to the bottom, he gave orders about sanitary practices, and had the people spread out along the creek. They could eat one ration each. During breaks along the trail, he'd had the platoon leaders find out who were the survival hobbyists—those who'd learned and practiced traditional survival skills. Now he sent them out to find material and make fire starters. Marilyn gave him the fire starter from Major Shcherbatov; it could serve to start fires till we had our own. She also gave him the little book about Haven.

Almost all of us took our shoes and boots off, and Tom had platoon leaders check on whose feet weren't too bad. All I had were a couple of blood blisters on the ends of toes, and blisters on the tops of my little toes, from walking downhill. They weren't very sore. Of the men with good feet, he assigned two hundred to be a raiding party. I'd shown him my pistol, so he made me one of them, assigned as an aide to Nelson Tsinajini, chief of the raiding party. Nelson and I already knew each other; we'd talked aboard the *Makarov*. He'd served in the infantry, making sergeant, and I'd done two years of ROTC at the University of Minnesota for the financial aid.

I didn't like to leave Marilyn and Marcel, but I knew if anything happened to me, they'd be taken care of. There were lots more men than women among us.

Nelson's orders were to go up the canyon, climb onto the plateau, find livestock and drive them down to the people. Even Haven's day wouldn't last forever, so we were to leave right away. No one knew whether it would be too dark to travel in the canyon after sundown.

No one knew if it was possible to herd sheep or cattle down from the plateau, either, assuming we were able to steal some. We didn't even know for sure that a man could get up there from the canyon. But we didn't have any choice. If we failed, the people would starve.

We started. The top of the plateau wasn't much higher than the mesa top, but the hike was uphill. Judging from what I'd read, the partial pressure of oxygen on top was probably about the same as at 5,000 meters on Earth. That made breathing about as hard as on the Tibetan Plateau. We'd all been living at 1,800-2,500 meters on Earth. One 1,830 at Mescalero, I remember—but we'd just spent thirteen months on a ship with the oxygen pressure about like on Earth at sea level. So we spent a lot of time stopped, sucking air through our mouths and sweating. When we stopped for real breaks, Nelson would ask questions about Haven.

The afternoon sun didn't get down into the canyon bottom, which ran pretty much north and south, so it wasn't very hot, but the hard work made us sweat. I was glad we had a creek beside us most of the way, to drink from. I was also glad that the gravity on Haven is only 0.91 Earth normal.

Most of us were in our twenties or late teens—I was almost the oldest at thirty-four—but even so, some of them got pretty sick, probably what they call altitude sickness on Earth. On top of that, a Jicarilla named Juan Cruz, up in front a ways, was charged and badly bitten by something that looked like a short-jawed crocodile. It would have killed him right there, but two Navajos started hitting it with big rocks. A couple of the rocks they couldn't have lifted ordinarily. Cruz's right leg was almost torn off at the knee, and he lost a lot of blood before we got it stopped with a tourniquet. He looked more gray than brown. Nelson assigned three guys who'd been having altitude sickness to take him back to the people.

It seemed to me he'd never make it. I'd read about land gators—that's what the first settlers had named them. They're a kind of hibernating, warm-blooded version of the komodo dragon on Earth. Usually if one of them bites you, you get blood poisoning.

It was dusk in the canyon when Nelson and I climbed over the lip and onto the plateau. We were damp with sweat, but the air was already getting cold. The sun was setting when the last men reached the top—the last of the one hundred and eighty-two that made it that day. There were others strung out behind for maybe a couple of miles, too sick to go on. It was pretty flat on top, and the vegetation was a little different than on the mesa; there was less grass and quite a lot of a knee-high shrub. Here and there were patches of a bigger shrub, chest high and with lots of thorns.

We had no way to make fires and a raiding party in unknown territory shouldn't have fire at night, anyway. So we paired up for sleeping, two guys huddled together, with two blankets and a tent cloth under us and the same on top. Nelson was my partner. Most of us had been picked up as guerillas and had gloves, winter caps and jackets in our bedrolls. We wore those too. I could have used some water, but the nearest we knew of was a mile and a half back down the canyon.

Nelson assigned sentry duty, two men on a shift, using watches that were either luminous or would light up. It gets dark fast at that latitude, especially where the air is so thin. It was already deep twilight when we lay down, and in spite of the hard lumpy ground, I was asleep in a few minutes.

The first time I woke up, it was with a leg cramp. I scrambled out of the covers and walked it off, careful not to step on anyone. It was dark and through the thin, clear air, the sky was beautiful. It was also cold and I was cold. When the cramp was gone, I walked out beyond where the men were sleeping, and urinated, then looked at my watch. I'd slept for two hours. That was the longest single, undisturbed piece of sleep I'd have that night.

The rest of the night I drifted in and out of dreams and half-dreams. Even asleep I was aware how cold it was, and while I didn't get another cramp, my legs felt strange. They wanted to squirm. Also my thighs and buttocks were stiffening up from the hiking. It was impossible not to squirm and jerk, and Nelson was as bad as I was; maybe worse. Huddling together for warmth, we were closer than Siamese twins, which made the squirming and jerking even worse. Add to that being thirsty.... We weren't used to being so cold and thirsty. It got worse as the hours passed, and I was awake more and asleep less.

Even so, dimday took me by surprise. I'd dozed, and slept through the rising of Cat's Eye. It made a kind of dawn, and the gas giant loomed above the horizon, looking big! A lot bigger than the moon does on Earth. It was a thick crescent of reflected white, and in the cradle of the crescent, the rest of it glowed a dull, banded red, about as bright as the coals in a campfire. I could see a long way across the plateau top now, though not details; it was a lot lighter than full moonlight.

I nudged Nelson Tsinajini. "Nelson," I said, "It's morning."

He grunted, uncurled a little, and half sat up to look around. "Some morning," he said, and shivered. "When does the sun come up?"

I looked at my watch; it was about ten hours since we'd laid down to sleep. "In about thirty hours," I told him. He swore in English; Nelson preferred English for swearing.

I could tell from the thickness and direction of Cat's Eye's crescent about where the sun was on the other side of Haven. It agreed with what my watch told me. "Is this as light as it's going to get till then?" he asked.

"It should get lighter," I told him. "Cat's Eye should pass through most of the phases before sunup. It ought to be pretty light out when it's full."

"Well shit!" Nelson growled. He folded back the covers, and got up stiffly. "We might as well get started," he muttered, and looked around. Then, changing to Navajo, he shouted, "Everybody up!"

It took a couple of minutes. When everyone was on their feet, Nelson made us all run in place to warm up.

It helped some. He took his knife and cut thorny stakes about a meter long from the pieces of shrub wood he could find and pushed them in the ground to mark where the trail was, out of the canyon. Then he had us roll our packs, keeping a ration out inside our shirts, and we started to hike again, away from the rim. He said we'd eat after we warmed up more. It seemed to me it must be near freezing and I suspected it wouldn't warm up much, if at all, till sunup; it was more likely to get colder After walking for about ten minutes—I remember that; I still had the white man's habit of looking at my watch—we came to a pool and Nelson called a halt so we could drink and eat.

He was quiet while we ate. When we were done, he called three squad leaders over. "I'm going to hold most of us here," he told them, "and send your squads out to explore, to see if you can find where the livestock is.

"Frank, I'm sending Carl here with you." He put his hand on my shoulder. "Carl is Chippewa, adopted into the Mescalero, but he talks good Navajo. He's reservation raised, in Minnesota. And he knows things about this world; he read a lot about it, back on Earth. He knows when the sun will come up. And he has a gun, a pistol, in case you run into trouble."

Frank nodded. Frank Begay was the only man in the raiding party who was older than me. He'd been a medicine chief. Too bad I would never get to know him well.

"Take another ration each," Nelson said, "but leave your bedrolls here. I want you back when it's time to sleep again. At the latest."

One squad went along near the rim toward the west, another to the east. Frank's squad, eleven with myself, went straight inland. When Cat's Eye is only a crescent, dimday isn't a good time for long distance seeing, but if there were sheep around, we'd hear them farther than we could see them anyway. We'd hiked for nearly an hour and a half when we came to another pool. It looked shallow, but was about a hundred meters across and around it were lots of tracks that looked like sheep tracks. As we walked around looking, we found pony tracks, too, and tracks as big as cow tracks, but longer and narrower, like young moose. I told Frank about muskylope, and that some people on Haven had learned to ride them and use them as pack animals.

We looked at the trail where it left the pool. Frank Begay had worked sheep all his life, and he said it looked like a big band—about two thousand. They were going east. We didn't see any dog tracks with them. Frank decided to split the squad. He'd take five men with him and follow the sheep. The rest of us would backtrack the sheep and find where they came from. We were to keep going till we either found the place, or for five hours, whichever came first. If we found it, we would learn as much as we could about it and then come back to the big pool. If both halves weren't back in twelve hours, the half that was back could go to Nelson Tsinajini and report.

He put me in charge of the half squad I was with. He said we were all Dinneh now, that the government had made us all one. And that Tom and Nelson both had confidence in me. One young Navajo didn't want to be under me, so Frank changed him to his half and gave me Cody George. Then we left.

I'd set my watch to zero on the stop watch mode and we backtracked the sheep trail for almost four hours when we saw up ahead what looked like a long wall or fence. By then it was lighter; Cat's Eye was still a crescent, but it was getting thicker. So we got down on our hands and knees and crawled; the low shrubs would make us hard to see.

What we'd seen was a fence made by uprooting and piling the big thorn bushes. On the other side of it were shaggy cattle. I remembered reading that the Kazakh colonists were going to take yaks with them. Yaks from the Tibetan Plateau, that could stand severe cold and thin oxygen. We followed the fence in more or less the direction we'd been going before, west, and pretty soon we could hear someone yelling up ahead, not an alarm, but as if he was yelling at the cattle. Closer up, I could see what looked and sounded like a young boy. He had a grub hoe, and seemed to be chopping some kind of plant out of the pasture. There was a gap in the fence, with only one big thorn shrub in it to block it, and when a cow would get close to the gap, the boy would yell and chase her away.

It wasn't just yelling; it was words. I was pretty sure it wasn't Kazakh. Kazakh is a Turkic language. This one sounded Indo-European to me. It reminded me of what Lieutenant Toloconnicov had said about the Kazakhs using slaves, and something I'd read about Balt and Armenian indentured laborers being shipped to Haven. If he was a Balt or Armenian, he'd probably learned Russian and English in school, so I could talk to him. He'd also probably not feel any loyalty to the Kazakhs.

I told my men to stay where they were and lie low, then moved to the gap in the fence and crawled through past the shrub that blocked it. Mostly the herd boy's back was toward it, so I crawled to him on hands and knees, slowly, easily, making no quick movements. When I got closer, I could hear him talking to himself, as if he was angry. The hoe was a kind of grub hoe and looked too heavy to be a good weapon, unless he was really strong.

When I was about forty feet away and he still hadn't seen me, I rose up and started for him in a crouch, still quietly, only rushing the last few feet. I don't think he knew I was there till I was on him. Then I hit him from behind, throwing him down and landing on him.

He didn't really struggle; I was surprised at how thin he was inside his cape.

"Don't yell," I told him, in slow, distinct English. "If you're quiet, nothing will happen to you."

He didn't make a sound.

"Come to the fence with me," I said. "I want you to answer questions about your masters." Then I let go my hold on his head and got off him.

He half turned over so he could look at me. And stared. "Are you—American?" he asked.

"I'm an American Indian," I told him, and watched his eyes get round. He must have seen old American movies back on Earth. "We don't have slaves," I added. "Those we admire, we adopt into the tribe as warriors."

I'd seen some of those movies too. Sometimes they weren't even all nonsense. He nodded, then picked up his hoe, and together we trotted to the fence, he kept looking back over his left shoulder as if for somebody coming. I looked too, and saw something I hadn't noticed before. I should have. By the light of dimday, I saw low buildings humped in the distance. They looked like a large set of buildings.

Crouching by the fence, I asked him, "What were you watching for?"

"Amud," he said. "It is his shift to keep watch on the herd. He just went to the—ranch, for tea. He'll be back soon, and if I'm not chopping puke bush, he'll beat me."

"We'll watch for him then," I said, and began to ask about the ranch and the people there. His eyes were gray and looked too big for his thin face, but they flashed with anger, and once I got him started, he talked without urging. All I had to do was steer. His name was Janis, he said. Most of the Kazakhs had left two truedays earlier—maybe 120 hours as I figured it. They had taken the sheep to summer pastures. The lambs were now old enough to be out during the cold of truenight.

Sometimes there was no truenight between truedays; there was just day, then dimday, then day again. Sometimes there'd be a short truenight, with dimday before or after. But now and then there'd be a long truenight and even in summer it would freeze hard then, the waterholes would freeze over and wet places would freeze on top like concrete.

There were fifty or sixty Kazakhs with this ranch. Fifteen or sixteen of them were still here at their year-round headquarters. There were also eight indentured laborers—seven Latvians and a Russian—whose contracts the Kazakhs had bought from the Bureau of Relocation. Indentured laborers were the same as slaves. Three of the Latvians were women or girls, and two of them were pregnant by Kazakhs. Their babies would die because the air was so thin, Janis said, and maybe the mothers. The Kazakhs didn't care enough about them to take them to Shangri-La for birthing. Besides, Kazakh women were supposed to arrive from Earth, later in the year, brides for the stockmen.

Of the Kazakhs still at the headquarters, three tended the cattle here in the pasture, one on a shift. Six tended the horse herd. The rest looked after the headquarters. Those not on duty would be sleeping or loafing.

And yes, they were always armed. They carried a short, curved sword and a pistol. Those out tending herds, like Amud, also carried a whip and a rifle.

That was as far as Janis had gotten when I saw someone riding out from the buildings. "He's coming," I said to Janis. Stay here. Pretend you're napping. When he comes over to beat you, I'll kill him. I have warriors with me. We'll kill the rest of the Kazakh, take their cattle and horses, and free your people. You can come with us if you want."

Then I crawled back past the gate bush and hid myself behind the hedge, to wait where I could see Janis through the gap. Two minutes earlier I'd felt confident. Now my guts felt tight and hot; it all seemed like a terrible mistake. Nelson had told us to scout; we were to learn, come back and report. What I was planning to do was kill fifteen or sixteen armed Kazakhs and steal their cattle and horses. With five men, a boy, and only one gun—three guns if we got Amud's. Maybe I could still change my mind, sneak away and go to the main force.

But Amud would whip Janis, and Janis would probably tell; he would feel betrayed. And— Did the Kazakhs have radios? Could they call in the crews from their outstations? Or police from somewhere, or Marines?

The Kazakh rode up on his shaggy pony and uncoiled his whip to wake Janis. I shot him in the chest, and he fell off his horse like a sack. The pony was well trained; he hardly moved.

I waved to bring my five men to me and we crawled through the gap. The sight of his dead ex-master didn't bother Janis; he looked excited. The Kazakh was armed, as Janis had said. I gave the boy the sword, gave the Kazakh's military rifle to a Navajo named Arnold and the pistol to Cody George. Then I told all of them what I wanted them to do, and nobody argued. They all looked as if they thought I knew what I was doing. After I'd put on the Kazakh's sheepskin cloak and cap, I got on the pony, helped Cody get on behind me, and told Janis to follow alongside. The others went back through the gap to do what I'd told them.

The ranch buildings were low and mostly oblong and their roofs were rounded. They were made of construction flex, but riding up to them, you couldn't tell, because thick outer walls of sods had been built around them for insulation, and thick sod pads had been laid on the roofs. Their windows were small and there weren't very many. Besides the finished buildings, there was almost a village of small round buildings nearby that weren't finished yet, for when the Kazakh brides arrived. The flex walls were up and there were piles of turf waiting to be set.

Janis was skinny but tough and used to the thin air. He'd jogged alongside me and had had breath enough to talk and answer questions. There was no radio at the headquarters, he'd said. That was hard to believe of volunteer colonists and I still half expected to see an antenna on a roof, but all I saw was a windmill. The breeze had died and the windmill wasn't moving. As we rode up, there was a smell I would come to know as the smell of dung fires. Somewhere a compressor was thudding; probably they had a power pump for water when there was no wind. I drove the pony with my left hand and kept my right inside my cloak, holding my revolver, in case anyone came out and saw that something was wrong.

As I rode in among the buildings, I could see a building with a lean-to on one side. A corner of the building was in the way, but I could hear a hammer clanging on iron; it had to be the smithy. The smith was Russian, Janis had told me, an indentured laborer whom the Kazakhs had given privileges. Janis didn't like him, perhaps because he had privileges, or maybe because he was Russian.

Janis pointed at one of the largest building, next to the windmill. "That's where the Kazakhs live," he said. Then he pointed at another: "And that is the horse stable." He started toward it, as I'd instructed him. His hand was inside his long cape, holding Amud's short curved sword; his job was to kill the stable boss, a Kazakh with an arthritic hip, and get his gun and sword.

A Kazakh came out of an outbuilding and crossed to another, not fifty meters away. He never paid any attention to Cody and me; I suppose he was used to everything being all right. Janis saw him too, and pretended he was going to another long building, maybe a lambing shed. Cody and I got off the pony just outside the door of the Kazakh bunkhouse and I looped the reins around a hitching rail there. Then we walked in.

The door opened into a fairly wide, shallow room with pegs around the wall for cloaks and wet boots. It would keep cold air from rushing into the rest of the house when the door was open. Then we went through the inner door, my eyes sweeping around. It opened into the main part of the house, which was mostly one big room with sleeping robes around the sides, and at one end a kitchen not separated by a wall. There were men sleeping, and three men around a blanket in the middle of the floor, playing some game. We started shooting at once, first at the men gambling, then at others as they rolled to their feet from their beds. The two women working in the kitchen were screaming. There were six men there, and we shot them all, right away.

"Cody," I said, "go outside and see if anyone's coming." I hoped no one had heard the shooting through the thick walls. While I reloaded my pistol, I walked over to the women, talking Russian at them the best I could. They'd already quieted. Both of them were naked—the Kazakhs kept them that way—and one looked about six months pregnant; I don't think she was sixteen yet. I'd read the Koran; these Kazakh settlers weren't very good Muslims.

"Where do they keep their rifles?" I asked.

Both women began talking at once, then the young one quieted. The older woman was pointing toward a corner of the building. In that room, she told me, also in Russian. One of the men we'd shot would have the key on his belt. Carrying a butcher knife, she went with me to look for the key. After we looked at a Kazakh, she would slash his throat, even if he looked dead. She was a little bit crazy.

We checked out the three by the blanket without finding the key. I took the holstered pistol from one of them and put it on my belt as a spare. Then I heard two shots outside, not loud at all through the sod walls, and I ran over and opened the outer door, just enough to see out. Cody was crawling out from under a big man in shirt sleeves, and there was a hammer lying on the ground. The blacksmith, I decided. Cody was having trouble getting free; it looked like one of his arms might be broken. Then a Kazakh came running around the corner of a building, and I shot at him and missed. He ducked back out of sight. Cody didn't come to the bunkhouse like I thought he would. Instead he ran into the building across the way, which would let him find targets of his own. There was more shooting, I couldn't see where.

From where I was, I could only see in one direction and it didn't seem like a good idea to pop out. Besides, one of us needed to be here and hold the armory with its rifles. Back in the main room, I saw the older woman opening the armory door. The pregnant girl had put on a pair of pants from a dead Kazakh and was buckling on his pistol belt. I could see a ladder fastened to a wall, and a trapdoor above it in the roof. From the roof I'd be able to see around. But first I needed to see the armory and get a rifle. I couldn't hit much with a pistol except up close; with a rifle I could reach out.

In the armory were rifle racks, one of them almost full. I took one, an obsolete military model and checked to see if the magazine was full. It was. I took two spare magazines from an open box, put them in a deep pocket in my Kazakh cloak, and went back out of the armory. The pregnant girl was standing by the inner door with a pistol in her hand, as if waiting for someone to come in from outside. I called to her to be careful, to kill only Kazakhs.

Then I went to the ladder and climbed it. The trapdoor opened below the roof ridge on the side away from most of the buildings. I could hear some shouting but no shooting, and crawled to the ridge on my belly. From there I could see across the buildings and into the horse pasture on the far side. One of the herdsmen on shift was just sitting on his horse about four hundred meters away about as far as I could make him out by dimday. He seemed to be looking in my direction. There should have been another one, but I couldn't see him.

That's when I heard three shots below, in the bunkhouse, two of them almost at the same time. I stayed where I was, hoping that the women would take care of things down there. There was more shooting from a building near the horse stable. A Kazakh ran out, around the corner of the door and waited, pistol in hand, as if he thought someone might follow him out. I raised my rifle and aimed as well as I could, given the distance and the light. Then I squeezed off a single round, and he fell. No one shot at me, and it occurred to me that if a Kazakh saw me, he might not be sure I wasn't another Kazakh.

Another one came trotting toward the bunkhouse, half-bent over, also holding his pistol. There was another advantage for us: Except for herdsmen on shift, probably none of them had a rifle with him. I shot him down, too, and someone shot twice in my direction, someone I hadn't seen. One bullet hit sod near my face and threw dirt on me, so I crawled back and rolled to my right a couple of meters, then moved back up just enough to over and see someone running from a shed and into cover behind another one.

It looked as if he was going to get around behind me. For just a second I thought about going back down through the trapdoor, but what good could I be there? I needed to be where I could find targets. So I stayed where I was. If someone did get around behind me, he wouldn't be able to see me from close up because of the eaves, and maybe he couldn't shoot well with a pistol.

One place I couldn't see at all was the ground close in front of the bunkhouse. Then I heard more shooting from inside. Right after that a window broke, as if someone wanted to get in that way. I knew the windows were double paned, because there was a sash at the outer end of the window hole and another one at the inner end. They'd be hard to crawl through. Then there was a shot from somewhere across the way, and I heard a yell of pain from in front, by the window. It had to be Cody that shot him—Cody with what I had thought might be a broken arm.

Right after that there were three quick shots from behind me, pretty far away—rifle shots, I thought. I didn't hear any bullets hit. From the corner of my eye I saw someone run from a building toward the Kazakh I'd shot near the stable. I didn't think it was a Kazakh; it was someone without a cap, someone baldheaded. He bent as he reached the Kazakh, just long enough to pull off his pistol belt and pick up his gun, then he shouted something and ran inside. I decided he must be one of the Latvians.

What happened next might have been from someone seeing my breath puff in the chilly air. There was a short burst of rifle fire, and one or more bullets hit just in front of me. One went through the sod, hit the flex below and glanced back up through the sod again to knock off the Kazakh cap I was wearing. Then I heard feet trotting as if coming to the bunkhouse from in front, so I rolled over the top, and with someone shooting at me again, I slid down the other side feet first, to drop off the edge. It wasn't a long drop, less than two meters. My feet hadn't hit the ground yet when I saw the two Kazakhs, and when I landed, I emptied half a magazine in their direction. They both fell, and I ran to the outer door of the bunkhouse, hearing more shooting and the dull thud of slugs hitting sod-covered flex.

I was in the cloakroom, panting as if I'd run a hundred meters, before I remembered the women. I called to them in English. "It's me! The American." But I still didn't try to go through the inner door. Instead I did some quick mental arithmetic. I'd killed a Kazakh in the cow pasture. Then Cody and I had shot six more inside. And I'd shot one near the stable and two just out front. And Cody'd shot at least one other. That made eleven, eleven of, say, sixteen. And there'd been other shooting. How many were left? Had the women killed any?

So I called out, "How many from outside did you women kill?" The answer came in Russian: "One." So there shouldn't be more than four Kazakhs left, it seemed to me. Just then there was more shooting outside, and I stood beside the door, listening for whatever would tell me anything. After awhile I heard someone, Janis, call out in English. "Indian!"

I answered without showing myself: "Yes?"

"I killed two, and I don't know where there are any more. Some of my friends have guns now. What should we do next?"

"What about the herdsmen with the horses?"

"We just shot one of them. I don't know about the other."

That might have been the one who'd been shooting at me. "Get his rifle," I called.

"We already did."

Janis said he'd killed two and then they'd shot a horse herder, unless Janis had counted the herder as one of the two. There could hardly be more than two Kazakhs left to fight here—maybe none at all. I'd just told myself that when there was a shot from inside the bunkhouse, then screaming, and more shots. I went inside to see. It was the pregnant girl that was screaming, lying on the floor, while the other woman was swearing—it sounded like swearing—and emptying her pistol at a window in the other side of the bunkhouse.

I turned and ran out, around the corner of the bunkhouse, then around the back corner. Behind, crouched below a window but looking right at me, was a Kazakh. I don't think he knew what was happening, even then; he probably thought it was all a slave uprising. If he'd shot right away, he could have killed me. Instead I killed him with another short burst.

I stood there panting and shaking for a minute, till my mind started to work again. Then I replaced the magazine in my rifle. Was there another Kazakh? Or had we shot them all?

I went back to a front corner of the bunkhouse and called out in Navajo: "Cody! Are you all right?"

He called back to me from somewhere. "All right except for one arm. It may be broken. The blacksmith hit me with a hammer."

Another voice called in Navajo. It was Arnold, the man I gave the rifle to in the cow pasture. "Boulet! Where are the Kazakhs?"

"Most of them are dead," I called back. "Shot, anyway.

"Maybe all of them. Have you seen any?"

"Just one. He's dead now. He rode past me without seeing me. It was impossible to miss."

"Janis!" I called in English. "I think we've got them all. Lets be careful not to shoot each other now. But keep an eye open, in case one of them is still running around.

Actually there were four still alive, all of them wounded and out of action. We dragged them into the bunkhouse to leave them there.

We had thirty-six horses and about eighty cattle. Yaks. I was only a fair horseman, but four of the five Navajos, all but one who grew up in Flagstaff, were pretty good and had herded livestock before. Four Latvians said they wanted to come with us. Another had been killed, and the pregnant girl had been shot in the chest. She'd gone into premature labor from the shock, and her breath came in and out of the bullet hole, making bloody bubbles that smelled bad. I was pretty sure she'd die soon and so was she. The older woman said she'd stay with her. I think she probably killed the wounded with her butcher knife, after we left. She really hated them.

None of the other four Latvians—one a pregnant woman—had ever ridden a horse. The Kazakh ponies were well trained, but thought that whoever was on their backs should know how to ride. Also, the Latvians didn't know how to control them, so the ponies took advantage of them, giving them trouble. Finally Cody made them double up, two to a horse. They saddled the ponies up and also made less for us to keep track of. It would be up to the Latvians to stay with or follow us.

We all had guns now, a rifle and two pistols each. We also put a saddle or pack saddle on all the spare horses. Three of the Navajos knew how to load a pack saddle; they loaded the spare rifles and pistols, and all the ammunition boxes and swords, on pack horses. Also we filled the waterbags and canteens we found there. Then, with Navajos running the show, we headed east, driving the cattle ahead of us. The spare horses trailed behind, tied in a string.

We went slowly. We didn't know how these cattle would act if we hurried them, and with Cody injured, and two of us not as skilled on horseback as we needed to be, there were only three men qualified to handle the herd. We'd traveled as fast earlier on foot.

There was time to think about the fight. How had we won at so little cost? The Kazakh's had outnumbered us and had many more weapons. But they had suspected nothing. Even after we began attacking them, they didn't know what was happening; probably they thought they faced only their slaves. It wasn't warrior skills that won for us, or virtue, although their own evil treatment of their slaves had allowed us to attack them and win.

If we had fought them in other circumstances, it would have been different. The Kazakhs had a reputation as a tough people, and those who went with the herds almost born on horseback. I remembered reading about the Kazakhs who wanted to be colonists: they were traditional herdsmen from the dry steppes around Lake Balgash. Probably they'd grown up in the saddle. I also remembered my reading on biogeography: wolf packs still ranged there; the herdsmen had probably grown up with guns, too.

Reading about them, I'd felt affinity with them. They had wanted to continue their way of life in freedom. Now I knew them and didn't like them anymore.

When we came to the big water hole where we'd separated from Frank Begay and his five men, Cat's Eye was swollen, gibbous and dim-day seemed about as light as a stormy day in Minnesota. I had not ridden for almost two Earth-years before and my buttocks were sore from the saddle.

We'd had water to drink, from canteens, but we stopped to let the animals drink. One of my men rode eastward on the trail, the direction that Frank and the others had taken, to see if he could find any sign that they'd returned before us. Then he came back, shouting that at the edge of vision, in that direction, he'd seen dust raised by animals. Either a herd was being hurried, or some Kazakhs were coming fast on horseback.

I took charge again at once, and told the men to get the herd moving toward the canyon. "Get them started, I said, "and drive them at a run! Get the pack horses there too! Nelson may need the guns."

The three skilled Navajos began at once; the rest of us helped as well as we could. Even the Latvians tried. They'd been keeping their seats better than at the beginning, but now, as we began to hurry, and to harry the cattle into a gallop, one of the Latvians fell off his horse, and the others seemed likely to. One of them, the baldheaded man, shouted in their own language, and they stopped their horses. All but one, the pregnant woman, got off with their weapons. Looking back over my shoulder, I saw the other three lie down behind bushes. Their ponies stood by till one of the Latvians got up and charged at them, shouting. Then the ponies wheeled and started after the rest of us.

It seemed that the Latvians were going to sell their lives to kill some of their ex-masters. It wasn't easy to ride away from them, but we had to get the herds, the cattle and horses, to Nelson Tsinajini, so he could drive them down the canyon to the people. We'd sell our lives afterward, if we had to.

As the herd began to gallop, they raised a cloud of dust. The Kazakhs would notice, and come after us. Probably they'd seen Frank and his men scouting their camp, and killed or caught them. None of Frank's people had more than a knife. Maybe the Kazakhs had even made one of them tell.

I dropped back a little and to the east, out of our dust cloud, to see better. I could make out the dust cloud the Navajo had seen, maybe a kilometer away now, or a little more. The horses would run faster than cattle; the Kazakhs would gain on us if they wanted to. And as they saw our direction, they could cut the angle and save distance.

I hurried and caught up with the others. Cody, riding with his one good arm, was leading the horse string past the cattle, with one of the other men harrying them from behind, to get the extra guns to Nelson. Behind me I heard gunfire, and for a minute I didn't know what it meant. They hadn't come to the Latvians yet. Then I realized: the Kazakhs had had prisoners with them, some of Frank's men, probably tied onto horses. And the prisoners were slowing them up, so they were dumping them off and shooting them.

How far had it been from the canyon break to the big pool? More than an hour and a half on foot through bunch grass and dwarf shrubs; seven or eight kilometers. Could we get there before we were caught? Surely the horses would, and the rifles, but would the cattle, and those who were driving them? I heard another flurry of shooting that quickly, increased. The Latvians! How many Kazakhs would they kill, the three of them? Would the Kazakhs stay long enough to kill them all, or were they exchanging shots in passing, hardly slowing? Did they know how important a few minutes were for us?

The other Latvian, the one who had tried to stay with us, fell off her horse. I saw her trying to get up as I passed; it looked as if she was injured. For a minute I thought of circling back and picking her up, but my horse would slow too much, carrying two, and I was needed. I felt guilty anyway. I slowed a little and looked back. She had turned, lying on her belly looking back down the trail. Her rifle was un-slung; she was ready for the Kazakhs. I speeded up again.

Soon the cattle began to slow. They were tiring. I told myself that I should have tried to rescue the Latvian woman after all, but by then she was a kilometer back. So I rode out to the side again, away from our dust, to see how close our pursuers had gotten. It wasn't as bad as I'd feared; their horses had been running longer than ours. But even so, they were more than a dust cloud now; they were objects. Soon, even by dimday, they would appear as men on horseback. I decided to stay to the side. If it seemed they would catch the herd, I would fall back and begin shooting at them from the flank. Perhaps I could lead some of them away.

But not yet. We still might reach Nelson Tsinajini before we were caught, and some of his men would have guns by then and be on horseback.

There were more shots, but they lasted only seconds. They'd come to the Latvian woman. Not long after that they began to shoot at us, just a short burst now and then. They could hardly be aimed, that far away in dimday, and there was little chance they'd hit one of us. It would be a waste of bullets to shoot back, and I'd have to stop. Or else shoot backwards, twisted in the saddle. I looked forward then, past the herd, and saw men coming on horseback. We were getting close; these had to be some of Nelson's men coming to help us. We closed fast and in two minutes they were passing us, four of them, with more in sight ahead. Almost at once the four began to shoot at the Kazakhs, veering off to both sides. The Kazakhs would either have to stop, or split up, or run a gauntlet of rifle fire.

Then I felt my pony flinch, stumble a little, and begin to limp. I didn't know if he'd been hit, stepped in a hole, or what. I reined him to a halt and jumped off. He stayed, obedient to his training, so I ran from him, throwing myself down behind some dwarf shrubs for cover.

The Kazakhs were coming up, maybe a dozen of them. Most would pass a hundred meters away, but one veered off toward my horse. He must have known I'd be somewhere near it. I shot at him almost face on, but his horse's head must have gotten in the way. It went down, and its rider unloaded from it even as it fell, landing on his feet but unable to keep them. He tumbled, rolling, and then I couldn't see him anymore. The others passed, paying no attention. I shot at the two hindmost, and one of them went down too, horse and rider crashing.

I started crawling to get farther away from my horse.

Three more of the people were coming. Of the four who'd already come, I could see none, only three horses standing, moving in little circles. The Kazakhs swerved toward those who were coming. There was a lot of shooting, and when it was over, those three of the people were gone too, shot off their horses. There were nine or ten Kazakhs left. It seemed as if they shot more accurately from a running horse than we did.

I had crawled some more. Now the Kazakhs looked as if they weren't going to chase the people anymore. They gathered in a loose group two or three hundred meters away, as if talking to one another. Then they separated, and went to round up the horses they could see standing around. I started crawling on my belly again, till I came to a couple of thorn shrubs. There I put a fresh magazine in my rifle. If one of the Kazakhs came close, I'd get up and shoot him, then shoot as many more as I could.

I got pretty cold, lying there on the ground. After a little while, when nothing had happened, I got to my knees. I saw the Kazakhs trotting off with some spare horses behind them. My horse was gone, When they were too far to see, I got up and went to look for the one whose horse I'd shot, who'd landed on his feet. I couldn't find him. I started walking toward where the people should be and the cattle herd.

They had left the small water hole and on horseback and foot were herding the cattle into the head of the small arroyo that grew to become the canyon. I was in time to help them. When all the cattle were in the arroyo, headed downward to where the rest of the people were, the armed men brought up the rear, in case some Kazakhs came. I was with them. Nelson saw me and we talked. He'd heard what had happened, heard enough of it to know I was responsible. He said I was truly one of the Dinneh, a spirit from the old times taken flesh again.

When we got to the main encampment, we kept going, taking the herd down to the desert basin below. The Dinneh followed. Eighty head of cattle were not enough to keep the people; we needed many more. Tom Spotted Horse was still the chief and he chose men to go back and get more livestock. Especially sheep—a big band of sheep that could be distributed to many people. I was one he chose. Half the horses and most of the rifles went with us.

The other horses were used to scout the desert while we were gone, and the people were told to explore, to taste every fruit, every seed, every root, every small animal. Quite a few people got sick and died. That was how we learned what was food and what was not. A few died the first time that truenight lasted forty hours, a night as cold as winter. Over the next few Haven days and nights, those who did not really want to live, died.

We brought almost fourteen hundred sheep down from the plateau. Pretty soon a force of Kazahs came to punish us and take back their livestock. They used the same canyon we had used, but we had left men behind with rifles, to watch from side canyons. When the Kazakhs passed by, they followed them, and when truenight came, they crept into the Kazakh camp from up-canyon. The Kazakhs had sentries out below but not above, so our warriors went in among them and killed some of them in their sleep with knives. Each time they killed one, they put his rifle in the stream.

By the time an alarm was raised, about a dozen of the Kazakhs were dead. The rest left, went back up to the plateau. By then they would have seen that we were many people and wouldn't know we had only the rifles we'd taken from them. Afterward we took their rifles out of the stream and cleaned them the best we could. The ammunition we had, we hoarded in case the Kazakhs came back.

After that we traveled for quite a while, slowly, driving our herds. Till the weather started to get colder. We wanted to be far from the Kazakhs and perhaps find better land. Meanwhile we learned to make bows and arrows, and spear casters, and bolos, and learned how to use them. We learned to drive muskylope into box canyons, where they were trapped.

Quite a few of the women who gave birth that first year died, and most of the newborn, but that was only part of it. We got so worried about the women that Tom Spotted Horse said only the men should eat unknown things. But that was too late for Marilyn. She died of a poison root. Then Marcel was killed by a tamerlane, and for a time, I wished to die also. In the first long Haven winter, more than half of the Dinneh died from cold and hunger—mostly men. The women were given more food than the men were and each woman was allowed to take more than one husband.

Tom Spotted Horse said we would not butcher more than half our cattle, or more than half our sheep. For the rest of our needs, we had to use what the land had to offer. Some of the Dinneh wanted to have a different chief, but the council said that Tom was right. They said that any group that wanted to leave could leave, and take their share of the livestock with them, but if they left, they could never come back. So no one left.

That was a long time ago. Tom Spotted Horse was killed in a rock fall, and I was named "master sergeant," which is what the Dinneh had come to call their chief. Me! A Chippewa-Sioux mixed blood, chief of the Dinneh! I have lived through fourteen winters on Haven, and I am old. There aren't many left of those who came here on the *Makarov*. I think we get old faster here. I remember reading that there are minerals in the water on Haven that gradually poison you. For a time it seemed that the Dinneh might die out, so many died and so few infants lived.

But some lived, and the yaks lived, and many of the sheep, which were also Tibetan.

The horses had almost as much trouble birthing as the women, and we learned to ride the muskylope. Now we number eight hundred and seventy-three, last count, which is up again, and our herds and flocks are large. We have found a lower valley where we take our women when their term is near, and mostly they live. Their mothers were ones who lived. The breed grows stronger.

The young people think this world is good. Except for the Kazakhs, years ago, you are the first outsider we've seen since the shuttles left us on the mesa. The CoDo Marines have never found us; I don't think they ever looked; I don't think they care. We may be here forever.

Business As Usual

John F. Carr

2074 A.D., Haven

Thomas Erhenfeld Bronson sat in his palatial office in the CoDominium Consul-General's Building. The CCG Building, also known as the Government House, was the largest and most impressive structure in Castell City; and, in fact, the entire planet since Castell City was the center of civilization—as it were—on Haven.

He had been appointed as Haven's first Consul-General eight years ago by the CoDominium Colonial Bureau. It hadn't hurt that his uncle Grand Senator Adrian Bronson had championed his commission. His primary job, as far as the Bronson family was concerned, was to see that Dover Mineral Development kept control of as much of the shimmer stone market as it could corner, as well as developing new mines to compete with Kennicott Metal and Anaconda Mining's hafnium mining operations on Haven.

Dover had had a good run with the shimmer stone monopoly since it had been a company held secret until 2052, when the shimmer stones were *rediscovered* in the hills outside Redemption by an Earth immigrant named Samuel Cordon. Once the secret of the shimmer stone's planetary location was revealed, there had been an exodus of miners and ner-do-wells from all over the CoDominium to Haven.

Even after their "discovery," Dover Development had continued to control the wholesale shimmer stone market until bootleg miners had formed their own association, the Haven Shimmer Stone Cooperative. Wholesale shimmer stone recovery costs had quadrupled since the late 2050s and this had not gone unnoticed at Dover HQ. Unlike ores and most gems, shimmer stones were rarely concentrated in clusters. They were produced by the heat and unfathomable pressures of volcanic eruptions and were rare in even the most productive veins.

The mechanism of gem formation required that a member of the species (now extinct) Giant Drillbit be buried in a burrow by hot lava. The teeth melted and reformed under the influence of an enzyme at the proper hellish temperature and pressure before turning into shimmer stones. This meant that they were rarely concentrated in the same place, and if so only in small numbers.

The best shimmer stone prospectors were diviners, with the same talents as dowsers, who could instinctively *divine* the stones' presence as they passed over the rocky areas where the shimmer stones were known to hide. Some used thin sticks to "locate" the stones, while others used complicated electronic and magnetic sensors whose design and reliability remained secrets with the diviners, like gamblers with their 'systems.'

To make things worse, Kennicott Metals had made a deal with the Harmonies that had squeezed Dover out of the southern Shangri-La Valley. Even though Haven was now a CoDominium Protectorate, much of its land was still owned by the Church of New Universal Harmony. After two failures in a row, anyone else—in other words non-family—

would have been out on the streets. However, what had saved Erhenfeld's bacon was the Company's discovery of the richest known gallite deposit in the CoDominium sphere. Gallium was a rare mineral that was necessary for microwave circuitry, infra-red applications and semiconductors.

As he poured over the latest production report from his Chief Mining Development Officer, Timothy Rice, he noted that gallium production had dropped precipitously. Since the metal melted at temperatures below body temperature it had to be stored in special refrigerated units and handled with care.

He looked up from the report when his intercom buzzed.

"Mr. Rice is here, Consul Bronson."

"Send him in," he replied.

Timothy Rice looked like a sheepish school boy reporting to a vice principal in charge of discipline. He had a ruddy face and a shock of brown hair that stuck up in back in a permanent cowlick. He removed his thick glasses and began to rub his eyes, a nervous tic that Erhenfeld had noted at their first meeting.

Rice paused for a moment to take a deep breath of the Earth-normal oxygenated air in Erhenfeld's office. "Your Excellency, I need to discuss the production slowdown at the Golconda Mines."

Erhenfeld laced his fingers together before replying. "I hope you've got some answers, because if you don't, heads are going to roll. Corporate's not happy about the delays."

"It's the drought, sir. It's been going on for three T-years. Its effects have been compounded by the fact that we're using large amounts of water for gallite mining and refining. Dire Lake, according to our Company Ecologist, is very similar to the Salton Sea in California: briny and, except at the head waters, very shallow with an average depth of ten to twelve meters. Since we began operations at Golconda, the lake has lost a third of its size due to drought and water depletion. If we keep mining operations at their current level, within two years there won't be enough water to land a splashship anywhere in the lake. That will quadruple our shipping costs to low-earth orbit."

Erhenfeld nodded. "I got all that from your report. What are your solutions, and I don't mean stopping the refineries?"

"One of our meteorologists, Professor Childress at Dover headquarters in Eureka, came up with the idea of pushing an ice comet or asteroid into a controlled collision course so that it would impact Dire Lake and provide a source of water."

Erhenfeld smiled. "Now, that's thinking outside the package. I like it. But how much is it going to cost?"

"There's already been some asteroid mining at Cat's Eye's Trojan Points, although not a lot since Haven's market for raw materials is small and out-of-system shipping is prohibitive, since our freightage charges—like the other mining outfits—are so high. But there's an independent company, that calls itself MineSearch Ltd. that has contacts with the miners. It might cost a couple million CoDo credits, but we'll lose that every T-week the mines are shut down."

Erhenfeld took out a cigarette from its pack and used the Quiklite to ignite it. After a couple of puffs, he said, "The *Sally Bee* is arriving in three T-days. I'll talk to the Captain and see what he thinks of this plan. He might even be able to do it himself and keep it in the Company."

"Your call, boss. The only potential problem is that when the asteroid lands it's going to cause some incidental reactions, like earthquakes and big storms, when the Dire Lake is momentarily vaporized—and who knows what else?"

"It's in the Northern Highlands, right? So, it's not going to affect the Shangri-La Valley, or is it?"

Rice was looking more and more uncomfortable, his head hanging lower. "Probably not, Consul-General; however, there are about two million Arabs and Muslims living in the Highlands, not counting all our own miners, and the Bureau of ReLocation keeps sending us more."

"What's the death of a few thousand towel heads going to mean to the Company, Rice? Are they somehow going to petition the Grand Senate and complain; hell, we're doing them a service. They won't live long without water. That's the spin we need to put on this; we're doing it to save the settlers from famine."

Rice looked up sheepishly. "They could petition the Humanity League or the Save the Planets people. I suggest we move everyone out of the area before we move the rock."

"Sure, but you don't have to pay for shipping, as well as food and board for ungrateful immigrants, either. Do you?"

Rice shook his head.

"Do you have any ideas where the Company can cache them for a couple of months, until the side effects die down? I suspect the Castell City Hilton could hold two or three hundred!"

Rice was pressed back so far it looked like his chair was in danger of tipping over.

"I'm not mad at you, Rice. You came up with a wonderful proposal; it's not your fault you're not mentally equipped to see it through. It's my job, to do the heavy lifting."

"Yes, sir."

"Now, what are the problems you mentioned with the miners?"

"It's work stoppages by the Muslims and their attacks against Company property. They're blaming the drought on us!"

"How many times have you people complained that the Arabs and Pakis are indifferent miners—at best. It is the Cornishmen, brought to Haven by the Company, who make up the bulk of the miners."

Rice nodded. "Yes, sir. But it was the Company who *suggested* that the Bureau of Relocation drop off all the rebels."

"That was a Corporate decision. No one took the time to ask how well a hot-climate people would flourish on a frigid world like Haven. They knew we needed miners and BuReloc needed to quell a local uprising. No one at Company HQ looked at the big picture, although I suspect some BuReloc bureaucrat got a good laugh at our expense."

"Yes, because those Arabs and Palestinians turned out to be the worst sort of miners. Well, some of the Pakis and Lebanese worked out, but for the most part it was a complete snafu. If it wasn't for the Cousin Jacks, we'd still be in trouble."

"Yes, and to think the Bureau of Relocation wanted to drop most of the Muslims off in the Valley."

Rice shook his head in wonderment.

Erhenfeld took the cigarette butt and mashed it out in a ashtray made from a fossilized cliff lion jaw. "What's done, is done. Now, we've got to get more water in Dire Lake before we're both sacked. As you know, when you get the boot on Haven there's no place left to go...."

POUND-FOOLISH

Charles E. Gannon

Cat's Eye, 2076 A.D.

As Nadine Przbylski opened the old-fashioned letter, she thought: *Gotta hand it to him, he's persistent.* This newest wrinkle in young Paul Nkomu's one-man crusade—the registered snail mail missive now in Nadine's hands—was an inspired innovation.

Its implicit brilliance was vested not in its content, but in its quaint, but shrewd, presumption of a well-mannered recipient. In the course of any single day, Nadine could, and cheerfully did, delete literally hundreds of emails, voicemails, vidmails and multifarious attachments from her commnode. But a paper letter—sent "signature of addressee required"—deftly sidestepped the oblivion of electronic communiqués. True, she could have simply refused to sign for it, but that was not merely an impersonal act of deletion; it was an act of personal rejection.

And from their modest prior exchanges, Mr. Nkomu had obviously—and correctly—intuited that politeness mattered to Nadine Przbylski, the Senior Energy & Fuel Administrator responsible for watchdogging Haven Hydrogen Generation And Servicing (predictably acronymized as H2GAS). She might be as inflexible as any other government administrator, but she was not rude.

Nadine sighed, opened the letter, and read:

> Dear Ms. Pryrzbylski:
>
> *Thank you for consenting to read this brief proposal for the establishment of a commercially viable ice-mining operation on the sixth satellite of Byers' Star Two, the moon known as Ayesha...*

She sighed. Paul Nkomu was nothing if not determined. The proposal was not much changed from the one he had delivered as a hypertrophied elevator pitch last month. Intercepting her as she descended the steps of Castell City's new (mostly pre-fab) Government & Commercial Annex, he had waxed eloquent and, alas, excessive about the merits of extracting ice from the moon Ayesha. Unfortunately, despite his impressive scientific and engineering credentials—awarded at the Bayerische Institut, virtually next door to where his shattered family had fled as members of Germany's latest wave of African *gastarbeiter*—Nkomu was a political naïf.

He had not considered the social and political requirements of his scheme. Had he gathered a base of provisional corporate support? His blank stare told Nadine he wasn't even sure what the term meant, much less why it was crucial. Had he given any thought as to how to phase out the current method of hydrogen harvesting—scooping directly from the upper reaches of Cat's Eye's turbulent atmosphere—and phasing in his proposed system? Why, no. Any plan for how to train or transition the current work force into the new operations? Again, no.

And so it went for six minutes, at which point Nkomu's technically shrewd plan had been hacked to pieces by Nadine's unrelenting practical critique of the hurdles standing between it and implementation. Like so many fine ideas that she'd seen in her time, it was doomed to fail not because it had flaws, but because it was a solution that no one wanted. Not the interface pilots, not the repair crews, not the tankage techs, not the ops directors, and certainly not the CEOs and CFOs of the consortium that had won the original fuel provisioning contract for the Byers' Star system, and later merged together to become H_2GAS. No, they were all inflexibly wedded to the notion of continuously sending their pitted harvester shuttles into the hydrogen and helium cyclones that comprised Cat's Eye's atmosphere. Despite mounting operational losses, Nadine knew it would take a genuine disaster to compel a rethinking of H_2GAS's penny-wise but pound-foolish dedication to the status quo . . .

*   *   *

"Status, Chabron?"

"Good to go, Avram."

Avram Meissen stooped under the wing of his gas scoop shuttle—a wide, flat lifting body design with swept wings—and saw at least half a dozen new dime-sized patches just aft of the leading edge. "Chabron, when are you going to re-coat and anneal these wings?"

"Soon as the frame has logged another twenty flight hours, fly-boy."

Avram sent a critical eye along the belly of his battered bird. "I don't like flying right up to the maintenance limits. It's not—smart." Avram had wanted to say "safe," but his pilot's pride would not permit even that oblique—and perfectly reasonable—intimation of fear.

"Yeah, well, tell the company fat-cats to let me re-hire the preflight techs I had to let go last quarter and we can return to a ten percent safety margin on operational maintenance. But until then, I can barely keep these birds flying at all."

Avram shook his head, and signaled the remote system to lower the cockpit module down from the seamless belly of his craft.

Fifteen minutes worth of preflight checks later, Avram grudgingly declared himself and *Cloud Scraper II* ready for flight. Klaxons wailed, red warning lights spun and air moaned out of the hangar into storage tanks. When the hangar read zero pressure, Claude Chabron, safe in the glassteel bubble that was the flight operator's booth, triggered the hangar door release. The immense bay-doors slid back, revealing a starfield, and the top quarter of a vast, milky sphere: Cat's Eye.

* * *

"You are sure about the paperwork?" asked a high voice behind Chabron.

"What paperwork do you mean?" Claude didn't turn to face his eternally cowering ops coordinator, Egon Klimczak.

"I mean, the old maintenance logs Ortiz found in the storage room last week."

"What about them?"

"There are considerable—discrepancies—between those maintenance logs and the ones in our online system."

"So?"

Egon tapped an index finger anxiously. "So, the Chief before you might have—well, 'altered' the data. As we have had to do."

"I haven't done anything wrong." Chabron was aware his comment had emerged in the form of a defensive growl. "I get orders, and I obey them."

"Of course, of course...but every time management increases or extends the maximum maintenance interval, they also order the logs rounded down for 'ease of tracking'."

"Yes...and?"

"Well, Claude, if that has happened before—if, as the logs show, the company has been steadily expanding the maintenance intervals—the shuttles could be dozens of hours beyond the currently indicated limits. Or more. Lots more."

Claude finally turned, which elicited a satisfying cringe from mousy Klimczak. "Look. I'm no design engineer and neither are you. So if the brain boys and bean-counters in the risk analysis division tell me that the old minimal maintenance requirements were too cautious, I believe them. And if they say it's safe to round down the old accumulated flight hours to the nearest hundred, I'll believe that, too."

Egon actually had the nerve to voice one last reservation. "What if this is not actually coming from the people in risk assessment? What if these numbers are simply fairytales spawned in management when the news from accounting is bad?"

"Maybe, but there's no way for me to know that, and nothing I could do, even if I did." Claude turned away, looked back out the hangar door at the distant delta shape now dwindling into Cat's Eye's roiling clouds. "Besides, those shuttles are fine. Just fine."

* * *

The commo channel from the trailing shuttle, Klaus Vebler's *Luft Fresser*, was scratchy and irregular in Avram's headset. "Turbulence up twenty percent. There's a lazy storm front receding from our equator-side. Our tail is clear."

"And polar-side?"

"Should be clear, too."

Avram heard the evasive tone. "Talk to me, Klaus: what's coming out of the cold top?" Cold, of course, being a relative measure, since even the equatorial cloud belts of Cat's Eye never went above a balmy -150 degrees centigrade.

"It's probably nothing, Avram. But I'm watching some top churn starting about 200 klicks polar-side." Top churn meant a problematic weather system lower down in the gas giant's murky atmosphere. Whether it would ever emerge at their cloud-skimming altitudes—or head in their direction—was, at this stage, wholly uncertain. Wholly troubling, too. But those were the risks that came with the job, Avram conceded philosophically. If Earth's ancient mariners had run home to port every time a cloud had troubled the horizon, humanity would still have been living landlocked and primitive. "Well, just keep an eye on it, Klaus."

"Understood. Time to form up for the scoop run?"

"Affirmative. But don't stay so far out on the trailing flank. Put a little more distance between yourself and that possible storm front."

"Avram, that will also put me too close to your wake turbulence. How about I boost up, cross over your jet wash, and settle in on your hot side trailing quarter, away from the weather?"

"Negative, Klaus. There's more water vapor in the hot side: if you shift over there, we'll bring back less H_2. That pushes up the filtration and refining costs. So you just stay alert and close the interval to twenty kicks. That way you can tuck closer and still stay out of my vortex."

"Avram, that's less than the minimum safe flight distance. A lot less."

"Yeah, but you're in more danger from a nasty weather surprise than from a chip of paint coming off of me. So close up and tuck into the cold-side sweet spot."

"You're the flight leader, Flight Leader."

Avram smiled at Klaus' wry communiqué. Klaus was a good pilot, but—as one might expect of an expatriate Schweizer—he was a bit overcautious, as well. And today's run was nothing special; just another day flying though a hell that made Dante's Ninth Circle of damnation seem positively balmy by comparison.

"Deploying scoops," Avram signaled, bringing the shuttle's nose up and matching its heading and speed to the prevailing weather patterns.

The scoops—rearward facing to minimize drag—opened, louvers rotating to create a vent in the lee of the upswept portion of the aft fuselage, where the shuttle's belly began winnowing back into the tail section. Vacuum pumps activated with a howl that Avram could not hear; he only felt it as a faint, thready vibration added to all the many other jolts, jostles, and hums that were his craft's customary operating cacophony.

Nearly pure deuterium started rushing in the vents, blasting through tubes into the cryogenic reduction and storage tanks. However, in the portside transfer tube, the tiny, high-velocity hydrogen atoms found thinner spots in the copper-lined conduit. Overdue for removal because of the constant "resettings" of its replacement date, the tube's one flexure had become partially brittlized: the passive but persistent assault of the mono-atomic gas at pressure had turned its once seamless molecular structure into the equivalent of cheesecloth. Slowly but steadily, small quantities of the hydrogen leaked into the surrounding safety sleeve.

The sleeve—a vacuum evacuation system—had a safety measure designed to purge any leaked H_2 out of the craft before it could come into chance contact with oxygen. However, this day, the left scoop's under-maintained primary intake compressor stuttered and slipped, unable to achieve more than marginal performance. Normally, this would have put a red light on Avram's system board, and would therefore have compelled him to immediately abort the mission.

But some weeks ago, during a software update of the shuttles' automated safety system, this cautious protocol had been replaced by a more fiscally prudent subroutine. Now, in the event of vacuum under-performance in the scoops, the system diverted a portion of the safety sleeve's own compression to the all-important task of sucking in more H_2—at the expense of timely evacuation of any leakage. And to keep the pilot from worrying too much, such a failure had now been re-designated as a notable, rather than critical, hazard. This change, along with hundreds of others—all coded with non-descriptive labels—had been part of the pilots' indecipherable, and thus, ignored, weekly update.

Avram saw a new orange light flicker into existence on his OpSys monitor board. The safety sleeve on the H_2 intake tube was acting up—or had exceeded its maximum service interval: either condition would trigger an orange light.

Which was nothing special: Avram stared sourly at the board, which was almost half covered by dull amber lights. He checked the H_2 inflow rate: nice and steady. Good. With a possible polar-side storm brewing, he wanted a short, clean run. To assure that it remained as short as possible, he edged the throttle forward slightly, attaining maximum safe airspeed, and increasing the slipstream back-suction under the shuttle, thus accelerating the speed at which the H_2 was entering his scoops.

The increase in thrust sent a slight shudder through the aft section of *Cloud Scraper II*, and a coupling in the safety sleeve gapped two millimeters. The traces of H_2 which had not been purged by the underpowered pumps rushed out into the fuel tankage compartment, where miniscule seal failures on the O_2 tank had allowed a small amount of that reactant to diffuse into the interstitial spaces of the craft.

The slight unevenness in Avram's acceleration further stressed the sleeve coupling. Which, brushing tight against one of the part-steel replacement struts, struck a single spark.

Avram felt no pain—indeed was not even aware—when *Cloud Scraper II* exploded in a bright yellow ball of incendiary plasma. Caught by the ferocious winds, the luminous sphere quickly elongated into a flickering amber smudge veiled in a growing swath of steam.

* * *

Klaus Vebler's quick pulse of panic manifested as a fleeting coronary twinge: the delta icon denoting *Cloud Scraper II* had flickered and then disappeared from his radar plot.

Suppressing an emotional wave that was one part horror and two parts grief, he flipped the toggle switch that would retract his cockpit canopy's weathered shields. Always a by-the-numbers pilot, Klaus was now in the one situation that demanded he no longer fly strictly by instruments: he had to make a visual confirmation of the catastrophe that his sensors insisted had befallen his flight leader. However, having flown *Luft Fresser* close against *Cloud Scraper II*'s air stream, Vebler was now at the outer peripheries of the debris cloud which had been Avram's shuttle.

A razor-sharp shard of *Cloud Scraper II*'s wing tip came corkscrewing out of the mists and punched a glancing hole in *Luft Fresser*'s blunt, shark-like nose. Riven upon impact, the wing tip shattered into a spray of fragments. One of the slenderest—resembling a spearhead but traveling many times faster than any spearhead had ever traveled—jabbed pointfirst into the front screen of Klaus Vebler's reinforced cockpit canopy and dug a divot out of the glass before tumbling away.

The atmosphere roared into the nose gash—friction heating and widening the hole like a blowtorch—while the same high-pressure atmospheric friction attacked the wounded canopy as Klaus fought to keep the mortally wounded *Luft Fresser*'s nose level. Relentless, the supersonic gust drilled further into the wounded glass, which crackled sharply, a star-shatter pattern instantly coursing outward from the failure point. A half second later, it blasted inwards, becoming a sleet-storm of supersonic glass needles and knives. Riddled, Klaus Vebler was dead before his flight helmet slammed back into the now-bloody headrest.

The gash in the *Luft Fresser's* nose yawned wider: the fuselage started splitting apart there, and the shuttle's nose dropped, pulling the craft into a rapid series of end-over-end tumbles that carried it down into the crushing depths of Cat's Eye.

* * *

Nadine reached out a slow finger to close the comm channel. She stared at the blinking cursor on her computer: What now? H2GAS's original refueling fleet of six shuttles was down to two, and one of those had been in the maintenance bay for three weeks and showed no sign of emerging any time soon. Replacement shuttles were neither available nor affordable. And pilot insurance was now sure to be unattainable at any cost.

Nadine's determined focus on the material losses of the disaster was selfish, she conceded, but necessary for now. She had had a brief, very energetic fling with Avram Meissen when he had first arrived on Haven about two and a half years ago. It had been a great lust, made easy by the big Sabra's companionable *bon homie*. The end had been as predictable as it had been emotionally effortless.

But that also had meant a complete lack of animus. So Nadine's memory of him was one of fond recollection. And on Haven—where the stuff that made happy memories was in short supply, any loss at all cut deeply. And so Nadine focused on the lost shuttles, not the film of mild but very desolate grief that seemed to settle on the world like a layer of fine gray dust.

So. Her heart was injured but not broken. However, the same could not be said for H2GAS's fuel collection contract or the company's fiscal viability. She did not have to wait for the actuarial analysis or legal announcement: H2GAS was irremediably bankrupt. And unless she was very wrong in her guess, the company would become the target of innumerable and well-deserved "culpable negligence" and "due diligence" investigations. Meaning, of course, that every H2GAS executive who could afford a ticket would be on the first outbound ship.

Prompt departure was not merely a way to flee prosecution but to stymie it; with almost all the principals out of range and out of reach, the nascent proceedings would die, stillborn for want of sufficient depositions and clear accountability. Yes, the rats would all jump ship together—and all survive, as a consequence of the simultaneity of their flight.

And realistically, their guilt and flight would quickly be eclipsed by the more pressing sequelae of today's disaster. The next CoDo ship to jump out of the Byers System would do so bearing news of the complete collapse of fuel production there. Word would spread: corporate shipping lines would become skittish; independent operators, reasonably concerned with becoming stranded in the system, would avoid it like the plague. Nadine could hardly blame them: located at the ass-end of nowhere, Haven was a backwater with only two noteworthy resources: shimmer stones and an almost infinite capacity to absorb a steady stream of refugees, rebels, and ruffians.

But the developed worlds could live without shimmer stones, which were simply a luxury—as was the cost of exiling, rather than exterminating, "social undesirables." Without a robust deuterium production facility, Haven's future would follow a course as clear and ineluctable as its own orbit: isolation, decline, die-off, extinction. As things stood now, nothing less than a miracle could save it—

—Or maybe, thought Nadine, Haven didn't need a miracle: just simple common sense. Her index finger wandered to touch the top of Paul Nkomu's proposal for a refueling station on Cat's Eyes' sixth—and second largest moon, Ayesha.

Comprised of rock and ice, its surface was ninety percent shallow, frozen seas. Extraction would be simple enough, and the byproduct of the electrolytic separation—oxygen—would not only provide the majority of the station's life support, but become a secondary revenue stream from passing freighters: without one-hundred percent self-sustaining bio-loops, ships needed to top off their O_2 and H_2O supplies, too.

A fusion plant would be the best way to power the operation, but cheaper stand-off solar satellites could, in the early phases, beam power to ground-based rectennae. After a few months of operation, revenues would make it possible to buy a brand new fusion plant, if Nkomu's decidedly conservative profit estimates bore any resemblance to reality.

Ayesha's gravity, while low, met the threshold that eliminated eighty percent of the physiological degradation caused by zero-gee. The rest of the effects could be offset by adding two compensatory technologies: a centrifugal exercise complex—a so-called "spin gym"—to the ground station; and habitation modules that would rotate around the tethered fuel head, which the crew would inhabit in two-week shifts.

The tethered fuel head was the new feature that Nkomu had added to his design. Responding to Nadine's initial criticism regarding the need for fuel shuttles to transport the deuterium from ground tanks to the waiting ships, Nkomu had put the tanks in low orbit, linked to the ground by a tether. The refinery output conduits now simply followed that cosmic leash up to a free-floating tank farm. The calling ships could now take on hydrogen directly, simultaneously reducing refueling costs and time.

So maybe, Nadine admitted as she reached out to put the hardcopy proposal directly before her in what felt like a gesture of commitment, a sane, sustainable energy plan might actually be able to transcend the tangled morass of Haven's otherwise corrupt and dysfunctional commercial politics. In this benighted junkheap of a system, it was often easier to believe that salvation required a fortuitous miracle, rather than basic common sense. But today it looked very much like common sense— which was anything but common—was finally in a position to triumph. Nkomu's ingenuity, insight, and skill would prevail after all.

But not without the timely intercession of the two co-dominators that truly ruled Haven: chance and blind-luck. Fortune had indeed smiled upon Paul Nkomu's brainchild—but only because it had turned its face away from Avram Meissen, Klaus Vebler, and the H2GAS consortium which had perched on their brave shoulders like a pitiless vulture.

Nadine sighed and pulled up the admin screen for initiating new project funding. Fingers poised above the keyboard, she reflected that while such perverse and ironic twists of fate could happen anywhere, they seemed oddly commonplace on Haven.

And as she did so, she typed; "re: commencement of funding for Mr. P. Nkomu's design for a deuterium harvesting station on satellite six, colloquially known as Ayesha...."

2078 A.D., Earth

The lights in the viewing room dimmed, and the officers from the Bureau of Relocation shared final satisfied looks with the executives of the advertising agency.

This screening was being held for their very special guest; seated in the center of the auditorium was Edgar Paulsen, the representative from the CoDominium Information Council. Paulsen was a pensive, ferret-faced bureaucrat who frowned a lot without ever telling anyone what was bothering him. Most people who dealt with him considered Paulsen an easily distracted, even absent-minded man, which was a very grave mistake. In fact, he was certifiably brilliant, and if his moods and expressions changed rapidly, it was because he routinely summoned up complex problems he needed to deal with, brooded a moment, solved the problem in his head and moved on to the next one.

Paulsen was here today to review the latest effort from the public relations department of BuReloc. Flanking him were Brian Callan, the junior BuReloc executive who had commissioned the ad spot, and Scott Saintz, senior partner of the Saintz-Raddison agency, which had produced it.

Neither man took the ad too seriously; BuReloc was not a public enterprise. As a CoDominium entity, its powers exceeded the constitutional authority of any nation where it operated, and it operated everywhere. Still, public resistance to BuReloc "excesses" was on the rise, and something needed to be done.

The result was the thirty second holo-spot being premiered today in its final form. The project had been arduous, since Paulsen's office had insisted on location shooting and complete physical accuracy. Over the past year, Saintz-Raddison's people had worked closely with BuReloc execs, traveling throughout the CoDominium for locations, and the two offices had developed good working relations. Today's screening was as much a wrap party for them as it was a presentation for Paulsen, and they were all looking forward to the celebration that would follow.

Paulsen blinked slowly and nodded to Callan, a signal that he was ready for the film to begin.

Before them, the screen shifted spectra from neutral blue to a star-field dappled black, onto which came the bulk of a sleek CoDominium cruiser. The narration began, just as the main thrusters of the CoDo ship came into view, and the camera angle swiveled around the gleaming ship.

"The new frontier."

Callan leaned over and whispered to Paulsen: "The narrating voice is performed by a computer-generated combination of three actors of the late nineteen-nineties; each voice was chosen for its qualities of recognition, sincerity and strength."

Paulsen nodded slightly and answered, as if speaking to himself. "It's like listening to the cloned child of Mister Rogers, James Bond and Darth Vader." Without knowing it, he was two-thirds correct.

"This is the challenge that awaits humanity here, today, at the dawn of this new age," the inhuman voice assured its audience. The sincerity aspect was important for the public, but it was wasted on the BuReloc and Saintz-Raddison people; they knew what was being sold here.

"Centuries of strife have ended, to bring this golden era of peace on Earth."

"Hasn't seen the tapes of the food riots in Tokyo this morning, has he?" another dark figure in the darker room asked. His companion chuckled.

On the screen, the camera's point of view had pierced the hull of the cruiser, and now moved down spacious corridors where people in coveralls moved purposely about undefined tasks, passing one another on opposite sides with crisp waves and cheerfully determined smiles.

A BuReloc woman in the audience snorted. "If this was shot on a CoDo ship, they used dwarves for actors."

"It was." The Saintz-Raddison beside her finished lighting two ganjarettes and handed her one. "And they did." Their laughter sparkled, their smiles in the darkness reflecting tiny red pinpoints of light from the smoldering tips held carelessly before them.

"And these are the people who will shape this golden era, the people who will make this age-old dream a reality."

"If they can ever learn to wake up without screaming," a Saintz-Raddison man said, and the room erupted into laughter.

Drowned out by the mirth, the narration continued: *"These are the men and women of the new frontier, whose bold spirit of adventure and dedication to the future will literally win worlds for them and their children."*

The camera's point of view had moved onto the cruiser's bridge now, and looked out a viewscreen that would make the one on which it was projected look like a postage stamp, had it ever existed. But it was pure fiction; the bridges of CoDominium cruisers were not built for the view. In the mythical viewscreen, a blue-green sphere loomed, graphic enhancements (and probably subliminal encoding) making it a hundred times more appealing than any tiresomely familiar snapshots of the blue-white old maid that was Earth.

"For this frontier is a place where all the old freedoms are alive and well." The voice paused, which was a mistake.

"Freedom to bleed, freedom to starve, freedom to die in childbirth, freedom to sell your daughters for scotch." The BuReloc woman was giggling as she counted off the points on perfectly manicured nails. Eventually she lost her composure, and her friend hugged her to stifle gales of laughter.

The camera pulled back to show a farmwork-hardened colonist straighten up over his hoe to stretch luxuriantly, and regard with pride the open fields, evidently his, that stretched on for miles.

"And where a man can have all the land he will ever need."

The entire audience, pushed to the brink by the past few minutes' comments, erupted into guffaws and howls of amusement.

"Yeah, a six-foot plot!" Callan couldn't help himself, the film was a huge success, and the party had apparently started early.

The camera panned up, into a starlit, indigo sky, and the Great Seal of the CoDominium faded into view, with the narrator's tag line:

"The CoDominium's Bureau of Colonization. Renewing the dreams of our forefathers, every day."

The lights came up as the laughter died down, the audience composing itself as its constituent members tapped out notes on datapads, chuckling to the person next to them.

"Oh, boy, that's great stuff." Callan pushed his glasses up on his nose as he entered figures for minimum police strengths required for the next days' round-up in London's Trafalgar Square. A rally to protest Britain's acceptance of Bureau of Relocation aid in various social programs would allow a vast number of English speaking colonists to be gathered and send a clear signal to the rest of the United Kingdom. The police would be CoDo, of course; had to keep it non-partisan. And best to draw them from the Russian half. It would do everybody good to remind the world that the old bear still had teeth.

He looked across Paulsen to see Scott Saintz wearing a pained smile as he listened to Paulsen.

"But, Mr. Paulsen," Saintz was explaining, "you must understand; our people spent a long time on those CoDo ships and colonies. They're just blowing off steam."

Paulsen was shaking his head. "I still don't see what's so funny."

Saintz's gaze flickered to Callan in a clear plea for help.

"Is there a problem, Mr. Paulsen?" Callan asked neutrally; he liked Saintz, but surviving unexpected disapproval by superiors was the hallmark of the successful bureaucrat.

Paulsen shook his head again. "There's nothing wrong with the film; it's an excellent piece of work. I'm just puzzled by the reaction of Mr. Saintz's people. And yours too, for that matter, Mr. Callan."

Callan had to choke back a laugh of his own.

"Ah, yes. Well, Mr. Paulsen, in any public relations venture, a certain amount of embellishment is always necessary, to—"

Paulsen cut him off "Embellishment?"

Callan's mouth was open; he shut it with an audible pop. What was Paulsen saying? That he believed conditions on all CoDo ships were like that? That all CoDo colonies were like that? Had Paulsen somehow missed the open secret—that those ships were, in fact, claustrophobic steel coffins bulk-freighting human refuse to backwater wastelands, pausing only long enough to jettison their miserable cargo, leaving them to scrabble for survival or die, and heading back to pick up another load of forced deportees?

Paulsen began closing up his own datapads and—an incredible anachronism—paper notebook. "It's a very good advertisement, gentlemen," Paulsen said. "Very good indeed. I see no reason to withhold Bureau of Information approval for its distribution."

Paulsen stood, looking down at them as he re-buttoned his jacket. "We've a lot of work ahead of us in the years to come. These riots and roundup measures are effective, from a bulk point of view. But the best colony worlds are getting the best citizens. BuReloc's getting the dregs of humanity, and that simply won't do if we're to build real worlds out there." Paulsen looked back at the blank screen, his smile almost wistful. "Something like this will encourage the brighter ones who can't afford citizenship on the better colonies to take a chance on the more marginal ones."

Callan was frowning, puzzled. "Excuse me, Mr. Paulsen; but what kind of person even remotely worthy of the term 'bright' would willingly go to a place like Tanith, or Folsom's World, or Haven?"

Paulsen shrugged. "Oh, someone who saw your ad and thought it a transparent lie. Someone who thought they could go to those worlds and organize a union, or form a political party." Paulsen smiled down at him, and the dithering bureaucrat's tone was so innocently matter-of-fact that Callan was chilled to the bone.

"You know the sort, Mr. Callan," Paulsen concluded. "Troublemakers. *Smart* troublemakers have always been the most difficult to deal with productively. But Professor Alderson's contribution to society has changed all that. My sincere congratulations, gentlemen," Paulsen shook their hands as he prepared to leave. "This film is going to be a big help."

Callan watched Paulsen walk up the aisle. Saintz was next to him, babbling in relief at his ad having been approved. "Boy, that was a close one," Saintz said. "I thought we'd lost the account for sure. Times are tough in the ad business these days; seems people change their agencies like they change their socks."

Callan nodded distractedly. "Everyone is expendable, after all. That's what BuReloc's all about."

Saintz didn't respond to that one, just excused himself to join the other celebrants. Callan looked at the blank screen for a long time.

POLITICS OF MELOS

By Susan Schwartz

It is desirable to be free if you can. It is natural that the stronger power will subject the weaker. These are not matters of right or wrong but of logic, cost and benefit.
The Limits of Empire, Benjamin Isaac (Oxford University Press, 1990).

2078 A.D., Earth

Maenads' shrieks from Lilith, dedicating a song to "brothers, sisters, and citizens!" tore through Wyn Baker's lecture yet again.

"You must think of the Fifth Book as more a dialogue than a history," she said. "Think of two speakers, a voice of Melos and a voice of Athens."

"Equality now. EQUALITY NOW" brayed from a bullhorn in the square below.

Eight thousand students disentangled themselves from bottles, *borloi*, and each other to bellow agreement. Then electronic guitars and keyboards clamored, and Lilith shrieked once more.

A few note takers, clustered near the front of the hall, recorded her statement. No doubt they were intent on grades, on winning scholarships they hoped would lift them from Citizens status to a post like hers: visiting scholar and Personage. Wyn was too well controlled to wrinkle her nose. She had, she knew, her tenured chair because her family had endowed it generations ago, long before people were divided into Taxpayers and Citizens. She had been born near the top of her world and had dutifully thanked God for that, for good health, and a powerful mind.

People like her might teach in a university in taxpayer country, fiscal and intellectual aristocrats. These days, the best a Citizen-turned-scholar might hope for was a position as major domo, a kind of nanny for adults who wanted culture on the hoof. And did she do well to encourage them?

"Awright, bros and sisters. We're gonna bring you a golden oldie from way-way-back-when. *'Be true to your school—'* For the People's University of Los Angeles!"

Another orgasmic scream from the students lying on the green four floors below. Hell of a way to have to teach. Her mind fleeted longingly to the dark wood and stained glass of Harvard's Memorial Hall.

Her colleagues would laugh at her if she gave up and went back in mid-semester. *"What did you think, Wyn?" That you could pretend you were doing settlement work? This is LA, not Phillips Brooks."*

No matter. It was her duty to teach them, and no Baker or Winthrop (her father had wanted two sons) shirked duty. "Think of it as Tri-V, in which two characters..."—she had wanted to say "disclose and reveal themselves" but she revised fast—"tell you how they feel." Her voice sounded reedy even to herself, lacking all conviction against Lilith's passionate intensity.

"Two voices," Wyn had lectured. "The voice of Athens, harsh, authoritative.... 'For we would have dominion over you without oppressing you, and preserve you to the profit of us both....' and the voice of

Melos, a lesser state threatened with war unless it paid tribute...paid a bribe not to be attacked. 'But how can it be profitable for us to serve?'"

Outside, an amplifier malfunctioned. The bleeding electronic scream forced a groan from the protestors. The students nearest the window flinched.

That did it. Never ceasing her practiced flow of speech, Wyn stepped down from her platform, stalked to the window—her soft-soled shoes and long, jogger's stride eating up the distance—and reached for the catch, which hadn't been closed (or cleaned) in years. In the grim surface, she confronted herself: tall, with what would have been a scholar's stoop if she permitted. Cropped, pale hair and an old suit that firmly resisted the Angeleno craving for the new and violently colored.

Wyn exerted the strength that forty summers of tennis and sailing had built into her arms and forced it closed. Amps, Lillith, and protestors faded to the sea-roar of a conch shell held to the ear.

She thought of black ships, armored Athenian marines landing at Melos and ringing it. Hopeless, hopeless, as the Melians knew; hopeless to lecture at these students; but she read out the passage anyhow. "Men of Athens, our resolution is none other than what you have heard before; nor will we, in a small portion of time, overthrow that liberty in which our city hath remained for the space of seven hundred years since it was first founded."—And more hopelessness in their counteroffer—"But this we offer: to be your friends, enemies to neither side."

To her surprise, the students nodded. But then, they knew from gang warfare: to be neutral was to be dead.

"Think of it as if it were today," Wyn said, her voice falling out of the trained, platform speaker's cadence she had learned almost as soon as she was allowed to join her parents at the dinner table or their friends when they sat at night and argued. "Of the people out there, who is Athens, and who Melos?"

The Sovworld? The CoDominium with its marines and its expatriates and its weight of distrust? Or her own life in the rearguard of privileged Cambridge? Answer that yourself, she ordered herself, and came up with no answer. She wondered what answers her students might have, if they dared to speak, or bothered.

Heads raised from the desks, and the note takers laid down their styluses and recorders. Attention flashed to the windows, then back to Wyn.

"I made a mistake shutting the window," Wyn told them. "You don't study history by shutting out the world. Go and open it again. Look out there, listen—and tell me! Who is speaking with the voice of Melos now?"

She saw the way their eyes kindled with hope, *Am I doing this right? Does this all mean something that I can understand?*

The boy nearest the window sprang up to obey her. Wyn felt a shiver as she always, did when her instincts told her she had caught a class's attention. The shiver deepened. The boy cried out in Spanish and leapt back as the window shattered and the building shook.

"Are you all right?" Wyn had run for years, but she had never moved as fast as she did then, brushing glass from her student (hers! how dare anyone touch him?) and blotting the blood on his hands with her scarf despite his protests that she'd ruin it. She comforted him in the Castilian she'd learned traveling with her parents.

Smoke and screams poured in the window. Beyond the square, a black column of smoke rose: the gate-control shack. Again, the building shook. Bomb or an earthquake?

The door opened, slamming against the wall with such force that two people cried out. Apologizing to the boy she held, Wyn strode toward the university rent-a-cops. Real police muscle stood behind them.

"Taxpayer..." An imperious flare of her eyebrows drew a snicker from one student and made the rent-a-cop correct himself. "Professor..."

"Ms. Baker," she identified herself crisply. In her world, everyone was a Taxpayer, and so many people were professors or had some such title that it was vulgar to use any of them.

"Begging your pardon, but we..."

"We've had a bombing. We're evacuating the building and moving our own forces in," said the policeman behind University Security, such as it was. He snapped up the dark visor of his helmet long enough that she knew it for a salute, then pushed it down over his eyes again. His riot shield and stick hung over his arms and belt.

"My students?"

"All right, any Taxpayers here...we'll see you out of the building."

"*All* my students, officer."

It was hard to stare down a black visor. She managed. "Where you want 'em to go, lady?" asked the cop.

"To their homes, of course."

A bark of laughter told her what the man thought of that.

"Then I will assume personal responsibility for them," she announced. She turned to face the students. "We are being evacuated," she told them. "I will see that you get home safely."

She walked between the policemen and her students out the door and to the stairs. Down and down and down the spiral stairs of the emergency exit they went. The Taxpayer students, fit from their exercise classes in garish health clubs, pressed at her heels. The Citizens, less fit and less well fed, panted. In the half-light, their eyes started and bulged with fear.

But I said I would assume personal responsibility, Wyn thought.

Troops—she could not think of them as security or police—waited at the vaulted ground floor and the great arched double doors, forming a cordon of flesh and armor. Flanked by security, the Taxpayer students were led quickly, in one direction.

"*Se ora,*" whispered the boy whose face she had wiped when glass had struck him, "You get the girls to safety. My friends and I..."

This was no time for a lecture about the backwardness of "women and children first."

"We *all* will leave safely," she told him. She edged up to the helmeted man.

"Do you have an escort for us?" she demanded.

"Will someone tell me why this overgrown pain in the ass thinks she's a privileged character?" he muttered at the rent-a-cop. "All I see is another Prof. Taller than most; snottier than any. Give me one good reason why...."

The man's eyes popped again. "Guest faculty. Professor Winthrop Baker from Harvard."

"Big...fuckin'...deal. Got an attitude out to there."

The rent-a-cop hissed, drew him slightly to one side. As clearly as if she had a mike turned on them, Wyn overheard. "My God, do you know who her brother is?"

Her brother, Putnam, or as he liked to be called, "Put & Call" Baker, who managed her family's money and a good chunk of her university's.

The helmeted man shook his head. "Jeez. Just this once...just this once."

"Fire! Look!"

Adrenaline spiked, leaving Wyn calm and observant. She threw out her arms in a warding gesture, as if she could shield her students. Those who do not learn from history are destined to repeat it, Santayana had said. You can tell and tell a Harvard man, but you can't tell him much. Well, she was a Harvard woman, and these were her students, and no one was going to tell her she wasn't going to protect them.

Least of all a rent-a-cop charged with getting them all out safely.

Amps and instruments twanged as musicians raced to shut down their equipment and escape. A blue tide of security, bearing the university president in its wake, flowed out from patrol cruisers onto the green. Bullhorns blared and interrupted each other. The president's eyes bulged. His cheeks puffed as he tried to make himself understood. Beads of sweat stood out on his bald head.

The building rocked from another blast. Across the green, flame shot from windows, licking the pink marble facade black. From the roof a man jumped. There was fire equipment nearby, but none in place to catch him. Wyn heard the crack as his bones broke. Behind her, a student dropped retching to his knees.

"Someone hold his head," she ordered in an undertone. She had to watch. Police cruisers landed, the whirring of their airpads shrieking, then quieting as they touched down. More blue and armor marched onto the green, wielding nightsticks with a passionless precision that made her think of martial arts and weapons practice. Two techs stood a cruiser, hoses at the ready.

A civilian in bright clothing—"Target!" screamed some damn fool and hurled a bottle that a policeman deflected with a blow from his shield—climbed to the roof of the cruiser and began to read.

"We got to get out of here," muttered one of Wyn's students.

"May they leave?" she asked the policeman quickly.

"What about you?" one student, astonishingly enough, asked her.

"I'll be fine. And we'll have class next week. I'll post a..."

"Outtahere!" the policeman jerked his chin. The girls in their midst, they fled.

The students on the green screamed down the negotiator, tried to rush the cops, and found themselves pushed back, back toward electrified barriers set up on two sides of the square.

Wyn saw her students caught up and engulfed. "No!" She cried, "No! Help them!" A nightstick came down on the head of the one with whom she had spoken Spanish. He toppled, blood pouring from his nose.

Wyn grabbed the policeman's arm. It was like grasping an industrial robot. "You promised they'd be safe! Go help them!"

"Go out in that, lady, and no one can help you. Sorry." He wasn't.

Four technicians drew hoses from a cruiser. As the police advanced, they shot foam, gray and slimy over their heads. It splattered on the feet of the advancing rioters. Where it fell, so did the protestors.

Again, clubs rose and fell. Wyn pressed forward. "Get her *out* of here," ordered the cop.

"Come on lady. Move it, Professor." Forming a wall between her and the battle on the square, they forced her out a side door. She was breathing in gasps, forcing herself not to weep, not to swear. She had seen blood on the faces of students. Her students.

And she was powerless to help.

Around back, she saw President Kerr-Truman, still sweaty, pale now as he realized that his East Coast trophy had damn near been a casualty in this stupid private war of his.

They bundled her into a van, carefully unmarked with the University's crest. It sped down side streets, careful to avoid the press.

She waved away the offer to go straight to University Health or straight to LAX and back to Boston-Logan Airport and the refuge of her Cambridge home.

All she wanted was a bath, a drink, and a chance to do some thinking.

Even at dawn, blood and smoke still tainted the air. Jogging in place, Wyn Baker glanced about, surprised at her own wariness.

The gray college Gothic buildings of Los Angeles University's central square looked as if some inept army had tried to fight a rearguard action and lost.

Splashes of paint stained the walls, the bars, and the shattered glass of the narrow windows. Lower down were splashes of slimy white foam and other things she preferred not to remember.

Hard to believe how silent the square was now, the quiet broken only by the high whine of bugs and birds on a May morning that would kindle into torrid noon. Charred earth and blackened grass marked where students and trespassers from the nearby Welfare Island had kindled yesterday's bonfire.

She had come out prepared to fight. Around her neck hung her panic button. All she had to do was press it, and a signal went out, alerting a private security force that charged a no-doubt sizable fee for being at the beck and call of security-conscious Taxpayers like her brother, who had insisted she wear it. Her account statements revealed a hefty monthly charge for its use. Studying it, she saw other companies bought into her account: McDonnell-Nomura, Kennicott Metals, tax-free municipals from some government resettling organization or other (they all sounded alike). She supposed she had the prospectus for it somewhere. She was more interested, though, in the balance her statement showed: enough and more than enough in the month's income statement to sustain her for a year. She could well afford to post bail for her students.

Statement, ID, and debit card lay in her beltpouch along with a map, the location of the police station carefully circled. Best go in now, she thought, post bail quietly and get her students out. She had some notion of bringing them back to her on-campus house for breakfast.

Better not, she told herself. She might as well tell her colleagues and her dean, accept the escort of however many university lawyers they would probably unleash, and, dressed in her most formal suit, drive ceremoniously to the station. Where, no doubt, things would take forever if they happened at all. She had suspicions that the lawyers would express "grave reservations" and other such language designed to stop her from doing what she thought was right until her brother could be called.

A campus cruiser whirred slowly toward her. Jogging alongside was a cleaning crew in coveralls and sun visors. *Workfare recipients?* she thought. They ran in step, without the sloppy individualism of the Welfare Island denizens. Almost, she thought, as if they were programmed. Their coveralls bore the University seal. One lifted his visor to wipe his brow. His face was very young, his eyes blank. Students had an ugly word for the maintenance squads: campus nulls. No one knew where LAU found so many of them. Student myth insisted they had defaulted on their loans.

She ran by them, noting from the corner of her eye the rent-a-cop's surprised look. Damn! He'd probably call that in. She turned a corner, looking down as her running shoes sent broken glass cracking and scattering, and scuffed through stained, torn paper. Legs and feet assumed the rhythm of a thousand morning runs on the streets by the Observatory or on the beach by the big old family place at Manchester. The smells were painfully different—urine and fear instead of clamshells and the salt sea.

She began to perspire, and her thick old gray sweatsuit settled into its familiar folds. She passed a broken shard of glass and saw the same lean woman she had seen reflected yesterday in the helmet of a hoplite's riot gear: sandy-colored, rather than vivid, but wholly resolved. The street narrowed here. The station...that turn, or the next?

She stopped and drew out her map.

"Yo!"

Wyn crumpled her map with one hand. With the other, slowly, she reached for her panic button.

"Not gonna hurt you, lady. " It was a boy's voice, reedy despite the tough street cadences. "What you doin' here? Ain' no place for you."

"I'm trying to help out some friends," she answered before she thought. *Don't let him know you have money, not him, and not whatever friends he's got with him.* "They were...got caught in the riot yesterday."

"You the teacher?"

"What?" She jumped at the voice and unfamiliar presence that questioned when she had expected threat. Something about its tones reminded her of her student she had come out to rescue, and she replied in Spanish.

"Speak Anglo, lady, *por favor*. I need to learn it good and blow this fuckin' Island like *hermanito mio*. An' I don' understand your kind of talk."

"Your brother?" Eyes and voice and face flickered as the boy rose from behind a scribbled-over, rusted dumpster.

"In your class. How you think I know you?"

"Want to go with me to the station?" Wyn asked. "He was arrested in the riot, defending some of the other students. I'm going down there now to bail him—"

"No WAY!" cried the boy. "You stay clear. He's gone now, you gotta think of him as gone.... I'm telling you the truth. Get outta here fast."

"It is the law," Wyn said firmly, "that a Citizen—not just a Taxpayer, mind you—but any Citizen may post bail and be released unless he's done something for which bail is, denied. It is the *law.*" Echoes—*we honor the laws, and we honor the laws that are above the laws*—rumbled like thunder in her mind. Or maybe that was the junker that clattered by on malfunctioning airtreads, forcing Wyn and the boy against a stained wall.

"Law don' work for us." The street-crawler's whine came back into the boy's voice.

"There is *always* law."

"For you, maybe. Rich lady. WASP lady. You go and talk, and maybe they give you coffee, maybe they call you 'ma'am.' But it won't do no good." The boy scrubbed a fist across his face. "They're gone. Gotta think of it that way. Even our mama, and she cry all the time. Don't go, lady. You don't want them to know who you are."

"He's your brother," Wyn said. Her voice went high and reedy. It nettled her: here she was, prepared to go bail out her students, and this child warned her away. His own *brother*, for pity's sake.

The boy looked down. "He's gone. And you're off your turf." He shifted from foot to foot, uneasy.

"People coming?" she asked, arching one eyebrow up. "If we stand here too long."

"Walk me to the station," she suggested. The longer she stood here, the less she liked the walls with their smeared graffiti and windows covered by broken boards or the way they pressed in on her, or how old-style dumpsters provided the sites of a hundred ambushes. "Get me there, and then take off."

He thought about it, glanced around with a sentry's wariness, then nodded as if he were making an enormous concession. "Part way," he grudged. "Gotta get home. Don't want them to see me."

He turned his face away, but not before Wyn saw a dark flush of shame.

She was used to precinct houses that aped the Georgian brick of her university, to police who nodded to her and called her ma'am. She was not used to the boy's unease at approaching a police station or at the bunker that squatted between a garage and a locksmith's; and she did not approve, either of the fear or the reasons for it. Booths heavy with Plexiglas and metal loomed up before it, well before it. The men and women in them stared down, not out. Wyn's guide hesitated. "They know we're here. Sense our body heat or something like that."

His feet shuffled, a strained, uncomfortable dance.

What would be the point of giving him a reward? They were being watched: if not by the police, then by his friends or his enemies. No point.

"I'll be fine from here," she said over a deep breath that made the lie believable.

"They're coming!" The boy's voice cracked. At Wyn's gesture, he vanished more quickly than she would have believed.

"He bothering you, lady?" The officers who edged up to her wore gear only slightly less formidable than the visored helmets and shields of their riot equipment. One held a bell-mouthed weapon Wyn identified with some amazement as a sonic stunner: For me?

"He was giving me directions. He was trying to help." She raised her voice, hoping the boy would hear her.

Their eyes raked her suspiciously. She wished for the protection that a car, a university escort, or the careful panoply of a dress suit might give her. She held her hands prudently away from the pouch at her belt.

"I'm from the University. Wyn...Professor Baker, on leave from Harvard." She managed not to wince as she brought out the seldom-used snobberies. "Classics department. Some of my students got caught up in yesterday's disturbance. I came to bail them out." And, seeing their disbelieving eyes on her gray sweatsuit and tousled hair, "I have ID and credit on me."

They gestured her to precede them into the stationhouse, a move that had everything to do with caution and nothing to do with courtesy. Her shoulder blades prickled every time she thought of the sonic stunner, of being clubbed down by a wave of inaudible noise, blinding, sickening dizziness.

She was sweating as if she'd run the Boston Marathon by the time she moved through the metal detectors and stated her business, first to a uniformed receptionist, whose flat eyes blinked, once, skeptically at her, then widened as she produced ID and platinum card. The sudden respect in her voice made Wyn tighten her lips, and tighten them further as the officers who had brought her in escorted her past the barrier. Her show of money and ID made them more respectful, but only slightly.

A flickering monitor and a bored officer faced her as she stated her business. She knew her voice had taken on its most glacial New England snap as she stated her business.

"All students who claimed Taxpayer status have been released to their parents. Unless, of course, they face additional charges." His stubby fingers hit the keyboard with bored efficiency.

"And the Citizens?" Wyn asked. "Several of my students had Citizen status only. I have their names and IDs ." She laid her list, culled from student records, on the man's desk. He gestured it away.

"Lady..." at her indignant eyebrow-lift, "Professor Baker," he corrected himself, "don't waste your time. All these...Citizens have been remanded to the proper authorities."

"Who are these 'proper authorities'?" she, asked, her voice frosting over.

"The Bureau of Relocation," he told her. "They'll be supplied with jobs, new homes, outside the urban infrastructure. It will give them new purpose and productivity." His jargon came out pat, by rote, designed to reassure and, if not to reassure, to intimidate. She might not know much about BuReloc but she recognized a pacifying-the-tourists spiel when she heard it.

"They were my *students*," she insisted quietly, "They had perfectly appropriate jobs and purposes in life. I wish to restore what they had. How much?"

For a sick instant, she feared the duty officer might take that as an offer of a bribe.

"They're out of my jurisdiction, Professor. Why don't you go on home?" *Go back to your library*, Wyn heard. She flushed with anger.

"I understand. Very well, then, officer. How do I contact the Bureau of Relocation?" she asked.

"Lady, you don't. And you don't understand what you're letting yourself in for. Now, you look like a nice person who just doesn't understand the rules. So, I'm telling you: go home. Smith, Alvarez! Lady here can't go back to campus on foot; it was crazy a thing to come out here at all. Give her a ride back, will you?"

She could just imagine turning up on Faculty Row in a patrol car and having to apply CPR to half the cowards on campus.

"I'd rather have you escort me to the Bureau of Relocation," she told them.

"Lady..." One man laid a hand on her elbow. She jerked it away.

"Professor, you're upset; you've had a scare; you're not used to this. Why don't you let us take you to a doctor...."

A nightmare vision of an outside physician, a diagnosis of nervous, over-privileged woman, a regimen of too many tranquilizers, blunting not just her anger but also the keenness of her mind, tore through her thoughts. She was afraid, more afraid than she had been as she jostled through the wrecked streets.

She spun away, backing against the wall. They came at her as if they were trying to tame a spooked horse. Their out-raised, weaponless hands... she remembered hands like that on clubs, hurling her students down, hauling them here, then tossing them to the Bureau of Relocation....

"Stay away from me," she demanded.

They kept advancing. Her back touched the wall. Her fingers touched the poli code and, as their hands fell upon her arms, she jerked one hand free and pressed the panic button.

She had just exchanged jailers, Wyn thought as she sat in the soft leather First Class of what she considered an unnecessarily luxurious LAX/Logan shuttle. Muscle from the private security firm her brother had engaged to protect her—or keep her from making a fool of herself—sat guarding her. A woman sat on one side; across the aisle was a male guard.

Even now, she didn't like to think of the scene that she had caused by pressing the poli code. A jurisdictional war between private security and the LAPD was only the least part of it. As the lawyers screamed, she had been hustled out of the station and back to campus. The dean's hysteria, her brother's outrage at what he called her recklessness, a veritable feeding frenzy of reporters...in the end, packers had been called in, and she had been whisked off-campus and onto the first available transport for

Boston.

Her brother had wanted to charter a plane. For once, she had managed to overrule him on something. But a car would be waiting. She winced at the expense, at the needless, ostentatious care, as if she were some rock star or new rich who needed a vulgar display of paranoia to establish her importance. Her male and female companions seemed more captors than companions, and they muttered about her brother with the respect that a priest might use for a captious deity.

Glancing over at her escorts for what was, essentially, permission, she reached into the carryall they had allowed her to bring with her. A few books, some tapes...there was her financial statement. She pulled out the prospectus for the BuReloc bonds and began to read.

A very important and long-lasting anger smoldered within her. "Go back to your library." Most recently, her brother had reinforced that order, which was right out of her infancy. "Don't play with the children in the street. Stay in your own garden."

But there was blood on the roses. Even if she'd thought lifelong she wasn't good for much else, she had to wash the blood off those damn roses.

She looked down at the transaction record on her statement, found one of her guards watching, and turned the paper over.

Something about those bonds...a name on the prospectus...surely she had seen that name before. She turned to the description of a limited partnership, of which her brother had made her a silent, but voting partner. Sure enough...she recognized one name as a judge, another as a congressman. She remembered a dinner table conversation about a few court cases; that is, she remembered hearing a few names—Bronson, Niles, Tucker—before she had turned her attention from what she had always thought sarcastically of as Important Business Affairs to faculty gossip.

Foolish, wasn't she? Her lips formed a silent whistle, and she recalled what one of her keepers had said. *"It's a wonder they let her out without a leash."*

A wonder indeed, if she wandered about with her eyes and ears sealed by ancient history. What was that sanctimonious stuff about law she had told the street kid?

The kid had known enough to run. But she wasn't a scared kid, she thought. In that case...if she could find a conflict of interests, a bribe or some knowledge of inside information, which (she now recalled) had dealt one of the blows to the world's economy from which it had never recovered...It would never occur to Putnam to think she would know that.

And for once, she would have a weapon in her own hands. She thumbed on her hand comp. It was a small unit, more used to writing than to database searches. She had always been a good researcher. By the time she landed at Logan and was hustled into a waiting car and the indignation of various family members, she had what she thought was a clue, a weapon and an end to her naiveté.

Over iced tea and poached salmon, her brother lectured her on discretion, security and what she owed the family. Wyn disagreed.

May sunlight shone through the familiar, beloved ugliness of Memorial Hall's stained glass windows. It stained the old floor, hollowed by footsteps, with the color of blood; and blood was in the air.

In the year since her eviction from Los Angeles, Wyn had been through enough Welfare Islands to know when someone was being stalked. The pack was gathering; the hunt was on; and she was their prey.

She shrugged one shoulder, adjusted the strap of the old-fashioned green book bag, and entered Sanders Theatre. Briefly, the smell of the ancient, polished wood overpowered the scent of blood. For more than a century, someone had taught the introduction to ancient literature here. She wondered how long it would take Harvard and the Department to name her successor—or if they would bother. Already, she had heard rumblings that the subject material was not just irrelevant to learning how to run a business or treat a cancer, but subversive. *Look what it did to Mad Wyn Baker.*

This sort of thing happened in the best of families. They used to shut the strange ones up in attic rooms, or let them rove about the big old country houses. Now, of course, there were drugs and rest homes.

She wondered what excuse would be found when whatever was planned actually happened. Because no threats had been made, no protection orders could be issued. "They don't mean squat!" one of the women in the Dorchester Project had assured her about such orders.

It had been a mistake to inquire about her students, now long vanished. She knew that her inquiry had been reported where it would do her the most harm, in those carefully, lavish offices where her brother and his aides compiled a dossier on Professor and Doctor Winthrop Baker and her troubled state of mind. *Did she seem...composed when she pressed her police call button? Did she perform her duties in a satisfactory manner upon her return? Would you call Professor Baker's involvement in the Literacy Programs at the Welfare Islands characteristic behavior? Did you notice any...uh, behavioral quirks when she was arrested on charges of civil disobedience?*

Even her housekeeper had been questioned: *Does Professor Baker appear cheerful? Does she keep irregular hours? Has she ever said...?* The poor woman had reported the questions and her answers to Wyn. When she realized how her answers might be used, she had broken down in tears, and Wyn had to dose her with her best brandy.

She suspected they would use her as another example of how professors shouldn't interfere in business, much less politics. Probably the excuse would be the usual one for a woman and an intellectual. She was working too hard, poor thing. And then she started poking into business and wasn't up to the stress. What could you expect?

Actually, she figured her brother would try to prove her incompetent. That meant a rest home—a country club with guards for wealthy, neurasthenic, or otherwise inconvenient people. She hoped the one they'd probably park her in would have a decent library. Maybe tranquilizers wouldn't be too strong, or she could spit them out.

Well, the rest home could just wait. She had one last lecture to give.

Wyn climbed the platform, arranged notes she knew she would not use, and looked out at the students waiting for her to speak. Faces pink and assured, with the familiar chin or browlines of distant cousins, come to hear lecture or scandal as they absorbed the academic airs and graces suitable for the heirs of rulers.

There were ghosts in the room, too. Floating above empty seats at the back (which were the places they would probably have chosen) were other faces, the olive skin and dark eyes of the students who had vanished because they were Citizens, to be engulfed by BuReloc. What would they have made of Sanders Theatre and this university Wyn had called home for most of her life? Could they see it for the tainted thing it had become?

Her voice rang out over the room with its pine and sun scented echoes. Aristocrat speaking with aristocrats, she could invoke references and languages that would have lost and shamed her LAU students. "We have been reared," she told them, "to admire *Realpolitik*. Consider, for example, the ways of Thomas Hobbes and his Leviathan. But must life, as he formulated it, be 'nasty, brutish, and short' to be considered 'real'? I find it interesting...."

There, she had used first person; that ought to bring her students' heads up. They must know: she would be detained today, taken away, whatever euphemisms they chose. No wonder Sanders had filled the way it did when elder professors were retiring.

"...that Hobbes chose to translate Thucydides's *Peloponnesian War*, which contains Pericles' funeral oration. That speech is perhaps one of the most moving formulations of belief in an ideal code that we have from the ancient world, and the Melian Dialogue...Book Five, which is a debate between such an ideal code and a rather cynical *realpolitik*.

"I cannot quote Hobbes to you at this point. The book is out of print and I"—Wyn paused to let the irony sink in—"lost my copy in California last year. It is strange, however, how one recalls phrases in and out of context. For me, the most chilling phrase from Book Five comes not from Hobbes but from another translation. For all I can recollect, it may have been one of my own, done many years ago. 'For the strong do what they will, while the weak suffer what they must.'"

She could see the smiles, evoked by her mention of the California riot that had brought her back prematurely to the East Coast, altering to nods of approval. "We are used to agreeing wisely with such statements. To disagree, these days, marks us as naive, foolish, sentimental, especially those of us who plan to enter the more active fields of law and commerce. And yet, to have these words spoken by a people who had earlier declared that they honored the law and they honored the law that was above the law is to hear a chilling moral progression. Or, as I see it, a moral deterioration.

"As students, we are not just entitled to make such judgments."

She paused.

"We are required." Shock on those scrubbed, smug faces. Had she ever looked so sure, so jolted out of her composure? Memory shocked her: the day before the riot.

Disappointed at hearing ethics when they had hoped for scandal, her class was glazing out again. Perhaps only a riot outside the windows would convince them of what she had seen. But no such riot would taint the Yard if she could help it. More than enough blood had been shed on any campus.

"Why you goin' back there if you knows they gonna take you?" Her brother had been very, very right. Social work, settlement house work hadn't been the answer. But students in Harvard's "adopted" schools in the Dorchester and Mattapan Welfare Projects had received her. Primarily, because they had no choice. No Citizens turned down help from a Baker from Harvard. Then once the newsgrids had shut up and the Welfare rumor mills had a chance to spread the word, they had bothered to listen. Warily at first: like all the people who came into the Projects when anyone in her right mind knew the only thing to do was get out as fast as you could, this professor had to be crazy. But maybe, just maybe, she was their kind of crazy.

And maybe, just maybe, she was theirs.

It had been strange at first to teach basic reading rather than Linear

B or Homer. It had been stranger yet to make home visits to grandmothers younger than herself but pregnant once again. And strangest of all to find herself learning more from them than they could from her.

Abandoning generations of "keep it in the family" she had asked their advice; and they had warned her. "*They'd* never *do that!*" she had protested to faces, black, white, and brown, old and young, all wizened from the same street wisdom and the street fights that erupted when that wisdom failed.

Was she expecting trouble? What kind? Given tough licensing laws and the penalties for illegal weapons, she'd better not pack a weapon. So her book bag held books and papers, nothing more dangerous. A first-aid kit rode in one pocket. She had even sewn some simple jewelry and coins into the seams of her bag. With luck, the nurses in whatever rest home she was bound for could be bribed.

"You're pushing it, Wyn. I'm warning you." Sure enough, Wyn could hear the minatory singsong in her brothers' voice. For years, it had been second nature in the family to yield to him when his face turned red, and he waved his finger at her as no teacher beyond the elementary grades had the ill grace to do.

She had held the statement out to him, the statement of her holdings and the records she had found. Saying nothing. Letting the record speak for itself.

"So, you're blowing the whistle? Do you want to disgrace us all?"

"This illegality has done that already," she had retorted. Tactical blunder. She should at least have looked as if she were ready to deal.

She had tried to hire a lawyer the next day—not a Family member. The lawyer had sweated, hedged, gabbled of consequences that made him sweat through his shirt until even the silk of his tie hung limp. Ultimately, however, Baker money—even after it was besmirched by old Put & Call—convinced him to accept a retainer. And her instructions. She wondered if he'd stand tough if...when...she disappeared.

Subpoenas were delivered; the newswires went ghoulish with "need to know" and the implication of famous prey. But "you haven't heard the last " her brother had promised. The elaborate contra-dance of bail, hearings, and indictments began.

So did the careful, cautious "it's for her own good" of her brother's people's investigation.

Carry money and small valuables. Wyn's Welfare Project friends warned her. *Don't stick to fixed habits. Watch yourself.*

But what about her life?

"Lucky if you keep it." She had herself seen the boy who had been set on fire when he refused to run *borloi*; the woman whose boyfriend had slashed her face; the ex-gang member whose brothers stayed with him, as if on guard—and those were the lucky ones, who got to go on living.

"You stay here. We hide you."

She assured them she was protected, that she played a game circumscribed by law.

"You step on his turf he get you. You stay here."

She hadn't listened. And she hadn't run. She had no great faith in her ability to hide, in any case. And some bravura notion of being arrested at her work, taken from her classroom had pushed her back from the Welfare Projects to Cambridge and this final lecture.

After all, it was her students in California who had vanished quite literally off the face of the Earth, bound—as she knew now—for interstellar Devil's Islands like Tanith or Haven. They couldn't afford the luxury of grandstanding: she could.

He sayin' you crazy, her friends from Welfare, her students there, had told her. Gonna put you away. Even after two girls had dressed up like cleaning crew and raided the dumpster behind her brother's lawyers' office for shredded transcripts, Wyn had found it hard to believe that he would turn on her.

You turn on him!

She never had persuaded them of the difference between crime and revenge, had she? But, assuming he said she was crazy and tried to have her committed, she was hardly the first over-privileged woman to be that way for the crime of disagreeing with her family. How bad could a rest home be, after all? She had meant to ask her aunt Dorothea, who had spent twenty years of her life in and out of them. Old now, and lucid on the days she bothered to stop drinking and dress to come downstairs; Dorothea had watched her as ironically as the women in Mattapan.

No point in thinking of that now. *What's done is done.*

Where was she in her lecture? *That was right. Shake them up a bit with their own weakness. They only think they're safe, prosperous: what if someone stronger comes along and decides to take what they have?*

"...It is a sign of our own deterioration that we need to ask 'who are the weak?' Are they, those who live in Welfare Islands, those who have turned their back upon our nation and our world for the dubious loyalties of the CoDominium? Or are they, those who do not ask? The unexamined life, Socrates said, is not living. And we have failed to examine our own lives.

"It is thus we who are the weak..." Wyn let the statement drop gently into the sunny, civilized theatre.

"...For we have forgotten. And we have forgotten to ask."

She had not forgotten, she protested as she moved into the final section of the class. A century or so ago, there had been a great classicist, a Jew, who had fled Germany. He came to a checkpoint and was stopped by a young soldier who searched his baggage. With the instincts of the hunted, the scholar *knew* that the soldier recognized him, knew him for a Jew and a fugitive. He waited for the man to lay his hand upon his arm and shout the words that would herald the start of his arrest and death. The soldier indeed spoke. "*You have a copy of Horace in your bags Herr Professor.*"

And so the professor had spoken of Horace, had lectured, risen on the wings of fear and eloquence till he taught as he had never taught before. And when his mouth dried, his voice broke, and his throat almost closed with weariness, the soldier again. *"Danke schon, Herr Professor,"* he said. And stamped his papers and sent him on his way to freedom and to life.

Heads turned to stare out the blurred glass of the theater's windows.

Wyn's head went up. Again, the copper spoor of blood dimmed the air.

"Prowl car," muttered one student to his seatmate. His ruddy face paling. "It's white."

Psycops? No security but Harvard's own has ever set foot in the yard. Were they going to make her out to be a dangerous lunatic?

Wyn's belly chilled, and her mouth dried. Her voice went hoarse, but she forced breath up from her diaphragm, and her voice rang out with a strength that surprised her. *Could she turn back?* she wondered. Even at the last, Antigone had been offered a choice: recant, retreat. She had not—and she had died. Too rigid, people called Antigone these days.

Like Antigone, Wyn had a brother who had betrayed his family. That had to be set right as best she could.

Perhaps Wyn should have been more discreet. She could not have been less foolish. Not when she knew. And she knew other things too: that there was always a payment for knowledge.

Now, she spoke to the kids who would never see this over-civilized room. The faces that she saw only in her imagination—the blackened eyes and bloodied mouths—seemed to relax as she spoke, then fade as if they were ghosts she had assuaged. Then, to faces leached by unaccustomed fear of their confidence, she spoke of the students they would never meet.

"They were dispossessed, you see, being weak; being only Citizens. You say that you are safe, being Taxpayers? Taxpayers you are; Taxpayers we are; and yet I tell you, when a government like that of Athens turns first upon its principles and then upon the people who still espouse them—as if ashamed before them—anyone can become the weak. And in that situation, one may only hope one has the strength to endure. If you take one thing from today's class, I suggest it be this: the *Gedankenexperiment...* Einstein's term, which translates as thought experiment.... Assume that you have become 'the weak.' What will you do now?"

Pause to draw a long, much-needed breath and meet the eyes that challenged hers.

"You're quite right, of course. The question cuts both ways. What would I do?"

She looked down into those faces and nodded, a minute bow of conclusion.

"I should hope to be equal to the ordeal."

For a moment, she stood, catching her breath, assembling her papers and stowing them in her book bag. To her astonishment, the students cheered her as if she were Lilith. Their red, opened mouths reminded her of students in the first riot she had seen and how their mouths bled as they fell.

She forced a smile and a rueful, modest headshake. Then, with a last look around the wooden vaults of the old theater, she slipped out a side door. Memories died as quickly as the sound of old applause. She wondered who would forget first: her students or the kids from the Welfare Districts.

It took all the strength she had to leave Mem Hall and begin her usual leisurely stroll toward the Yard and her study in Widener Library.

"Professor Baker?" Outsiders, then, not to use a social title. They didn't call her "doctor" either: that would be reserved for medical types. So it was the rest home, was it? And so soon! She turned and eyed the two men and one woman as she might size up freshmen. Their tailoring was good enough to let them pass for Taxpayers, yet loose enough to let them move freely. She wondered if she could outrun them; she was certain it wasn't worth trying.

She inclined her head, then continued on her way. "Could we talk with you?"

"I have office hours in the Library."

"We would prefer some place more private."

She kept on walking. Quick steps sounded behind her and someone laid a hand on her arm. Wyn spun around, the arm holding her book bag coming up in pathetic defense.

Two students strolled past. More emerged from the iron and brick gates that opened into the yard. Could she appeal to them?

The woman in the group had a hand in her breast pocket. Wyn

wondered if she would produce sedatives or a weapon.

"Not here," she said. "And not in front of them." She gestured with her chin at her students.

They nodded, relaxing visibly now that she was proving reasonable. That should be in her favor at a sanity hearing.

"This way," said the man in the lead. His voice held the deliberately soothing tones of a psychiatrist, though Wyn had never met a shrink who moved as if he led katas every morning. He took her arm—just a friendly meeting, wasn't this; and *smile* for the innocent kids, why don't you?

Past the Science Center. Past Mem Hall again. Past the dreadful ersatz Georgian of the Fire Station and onto the street. A white van, bare of logo, idled. *Psycops indeed*, Wyn thought. Might as well announce in the Freshman Union that she had run mad. The door was opened for her.

"I suppose," she said cautiously, "There is no point in talking you out of this?"

"Please get in."

No students were on the street. Wyn spun on her heel, preparing to run into the street, to shout; but the hand was on her arm again, urging her toward the car. And a lifetime of civility, of restraint blunted her willingness to make the scene that might have saved her. *We are the weak.*

The door whined shut. There was no release mechanism on her side of the vehicle. The car rose on its hoverpads and sped down Cambridge Street, out of the city, beyond Boston into the manicured exurbs where only the wealthiest Taxpayers lived. No one spoke to her.

"Damn!" the exclamation forced a grunt of surprise from the man who sat beside her as lights and sirens erupted behind them.

"Why dint y'stay inna the speed limit?" he slurred as he hit his chin on the Plexiglas dividing driver from passengers.

"I did," protested the driver.

"Keep on going."

"You keep on going, Taxpayer." The driver said, "It's not your license they'll lift, and then what do I have?" A quick trip to a Welfare District." He pulled over.

A prowl car pulled up. "You have custody of Professor Winthrop Baker? This warrant authorizes us to demand her release."

A flood of warmth, of gratitude, washed over her. Bless her lawyer and his timing!

"That's not a good idea," replied the psychiatrist. "She needs medical intervention..." His voice, so assured when dealing with Wyn, trailed off as he saw the sonic shockers that the newcomers held. Now he was "the weak." She wondered what punishment he would face?

He took the papers, leafed through them, and exclaimed before he could control himself. "But we—"

"Apparently, someone had second thoughts about security."

The psychiatrist eyed Wyn. "For *her?*"

Both men shrugged. "Whatever else you can say, he's thorough."

The man from the prowl car gestured at Wyn. "Out." The door opened. Wyn slid out. Her book bag lay on the seat. When she bent to retrieve it, someone waved a shocker at her.

"Let her have it"

Wyn seized its strap before anyone could countermand that.

"Whatever she's got in there, she'll need it where she's going."

The prowl car pulled round. Now Wyn could see the panel on its door. Bureau of Relocation.

She had been out-plotted and outfoxed. Her fingers rose to her throat, tightening convulsively on her poli code that would call out to a force of her own choosing.

"Cancelled. Get in." The absence of even a pretense of civility chilled her. Dispossessed and disenfranchised like her students. And now she would learn what they had endured. She heard an appalled whimper, flushed with fear and shame, and began desperately to run....

A wave of sound rolled after her and struck her down.

Antiseptic and old pain were in the air. Wyn turned her head on what felt like a paper sheet on a too-worn mattress. *I am not going to ask "where am I?"* she vowed. She knew she was some place medical: had to be, seeing that her last memory was of taking a sonic shock.

You have been to the wars, haven't you? she asked herself, astonished.

She was determined to sit up and was astonished at how weak she felt. What felt like the grandmother of all migraines glittered and stabbed in her eyes.

"Coming around?" asked a man in a white coat so worn that even the red staff and crossed serpents of his profession were frayed. RYAN said the badge on the coat. His eyes were blue, and his hair was graying. His face bore the reddish patches of skin cancers, cost-effectively (if not aesthetically) removed. To her surprise, Wyn heard a South Boston accent. *A contract physician?* He was a long way from home. The tones were efficient, kind and blessedly familiar. She felt her eyes fill as he propped her up and handed her a disposable cup.

"As soon as you can think straight, I have to talk you. There's not much time."

She gulped the bitter analgesic. The spikes into her brain seemed to withdraw, and then diminished to a bearable level. Light from warped overhead panels: no windows.

Damn all, had they taken her to a state institution? She'd never be found, much less sprung from one of those rat-holes!

"I don't have time to break this to you," the physician told her. "You took a hit from a sonic stunner. You're at the BuReloc station in Florida. When I finish processing you, you'll be put on the first ship out."

If she started laughing, she knew she would never stop. Emigrants, forced or voluntary—wouldn't do for them to die in droves aboard a starship, now would it? And what was *she* doing here?

"May I make one call, please?" she asked. Her lawyer...her family... could she reach their Senator's staff? It would be a waste of breath, even if she could. They probably all knew and assented.

"What good do you think it would do?" Ryan asked her gently. "Records have you down as a political." His hand went up, blocking Wyn's sight of the scratched data screen.

Wyn allowed herself to chuckle once, briefly. "So the son-of-a-bitch got to his Important Contacts, did he? Got named guardian of his crazy sister, the dangerous radical. No civil rights. And off she goes."

She shook her head to clear it of the ghosts that threatened to storm her sanity: Hecuba wailing before the black ships; Andromache in a cart; Melos burning, the men dead and the weak led away into slavery.

"Nothing I can do?" She couldn't take that. She jumped to her feet, looking for the exit. She was taller than Ryan, stronger, probably, from years of all that good Taxpayer nutrition and exercise. She could push her way past...

"For Christ's sake, don't try it, Ms. Baker!" The sincerity in that shout brought her around.

"This is kidnapping," she told him. "You know that." She paused to catch his eye, to underscore his awareness that they shared a hometown.

"In the name of God," she whispered, "could you make some calls for me?"

It was hopeless. Already, he was shaking his head. Wyn met his eyes. *I'm not throwing my life away the way you did.* Astonishment and fear that she had had chances he could barely dream of, yet had blown them all showed in his face. He was half afraid of her, half angry.

"Sure, you've been shafted." He spoke too fast, his face now turned away. "Ms. Baker, five more years, and I reach Taxpayer status, and my kids with me. We'll never have what you threw away, but we'll get by. You think I'm going to risk that? We're just little people. Look: I can make sure you're fit to ship out. But I'm not ruining my kids' lives for you."

He paused, and his face, already pocked with the scars of skin cancers flushed dark. "I'm sorry, Professor. But it wouldn't do either of us a damn bit of good.

"And you can hate my guts all you want. Damned if I care. I don't have to do this, you know. There are people out there who'd be grateful if I spent more time with them."

Wyn bowed her head, fighting panic. I'm not equipped for this, she thought. *Read, listen, stay at home; why join the rat race?* She'd been told all her life. Her family was too old for people like her to go haring around the universe. Space travel—she tried to recall what she knew of it and was embarrassed she knew so little.

She wasn't going to live through this, she thought abruptly. But other exiles had survived. If she were weak, if she let her life slip away, she only let her brother and his trained slaves win that much earlier.

Listen, remember; try to keep alive.

"Now, you've one hour, one hour before you ship out. It's going to be rough. And if you're as smart as your records say"—incredulous head-shake—"you'll help me prepare you to survive."

I don't believe this. I just don't believe it. She shook her head, waving away the offer of a trank. This was one nightmare for which she had to be conscious.

"Go ahead, Doctor," she said in the crisp voice she would use with her own specialists. "Maybe you could start by telling me what I face."

"First, Luna Base, then out-system. Tanith, maybe, or Haven." Coerced, perhaps, by her tone, he tapped in an inquiry on the computer, muttering under his breath as it beeped and sputtered. "There's a ship bound for Haven scheduled to leave Luna Base. Cold weather world. I can make sure you're not dropsick, that your immunizations are up to strength and that your circulation is in as good a shape as it can be."

I'll live, Wyn vowed to herself. *Living well—living at all—is the best revenge. And I'll get back....*

He shook his head. Compassion replaced his earlier defensiveness. "Something else," he said. "I need your permission to inhibit your fertility."

Wyn burst out laughing.

"At my age?" she demanded. "Whom—or what do you think I'm going to meet on Luna Base...."

"Lady, you listen to me. You're still at risk. And there's damn few contraceptives on board ship, and those'll go to the younger women—if they're lucky. If they're damned lucky. You *don't* want to be pregnant when a ship Jumps, believe me. Not with what they've got for medical care on board if you miscarry...."

Wyn raised her eyebrows at him. "Doctor, I am not sexually

active."

He shook his head at her. "Dr. Baker, you've got to understand. This trip's *long*. And it makes steerage look like a yacht. You won't be Dr. Winthrop Baker on board a BuReloc ship. You won't be much of anything except a female body. I can't tell you what to do with your own body. But if you've got any sense, you'll take the implant. It'll suppress menstruation, too. And believe me: you want that."

Ultimately, she did. Feeling vaguely queasy, she slid down off the examination table and dressed in the coverall he handed her, a coarse thing of greenish gray. *Ship issue?* she wondered and wondered even more to find herself curious.

"Better move it," said the medic. "But before you do…" he handed over her book bag. "Your things are packed in it. I wouldn't let anyone handle that, if I were you. I added a few more medical supplies. You'll need them."

"Why?" she asked bluntly. "And how much?"

"I haven't sunk that low. Yet." He flushed, and the scars of his surgeries for skin cancer flushed darker than the rest of his face. "Guard this stuff; it's all you have. Your money's been impounded, you know," he told her. She hadn't. She was not surprised. "God bless. It's time."

She drew herself up and walked to the door, then whirled back to shake Dr. Ryan's hand. She forced him to meet her eyes, to see the respect—reluctant but genuine—in her own. She was glad his face brightened a little at it.

"Good-bye, Doctor," she said. "And thank you."

There was blood in the air. And the stinks of sweat, of packaged food gone rancid, sickness and babies too long left unchanged assaulted Wyn, backing her against the stained white concrete walls of the processing center. She gagged, drew a careful breath, and then another.

Two CoDominium Marines walked by, careful of their weapons and of the crowd of families awaiting processing as if they were criminals instead of willing immigrants. They walked right by her, their glances dismissing her: a middle-aged woman, tired, scared, and shabby—in other words, no threat and virtually invisible. Given the wailings and babblings all about her, she doubted if they'd even hear her.

Cold from the concrete spread into her back as she stared at the panels in the ceiling. Past her flowed the crowd: with screaming children; brothers and sisters huddling together; here and there a solitary man swaggering toward the ship that would take him into exile; the occasional woman, blowsy or terrified, shrinking against the walls: people angry, frightened or numbed by what they faced.

Dr. Ryan's shabby office seemed like a paradise of reason and care by comparison. Hard to believe she had ever sat in a chair, been treated and thanked someone like him in a cool, civil voice as if she had a right to care, without appreciating the privilege.

"Move it, sister." A trusty gestured to her.

Wyn moved it; her book bag with her pathetic few supplies and her clothes, the jewels still sewn into the seams, bumping on one shoulder.

It was really happening. It was happening to her. Ahead of her, someone sank to his knees, moaning and was shoved back to his feet and on ahead. No: no use in collapse, then. She walked toward the wire cages that held interviewers enthroned behind battered metal desks for processing. Her footsteps took on a rhythm that, gradually, she recognized. One of the Herald's speeches, she thought: *March to the ships of the Achaeans whenever the commanders of the army sound the shrill note of the echoing trumpet. March into exile. March into slavery.* Euripides had written that after Melos; and all the Athenians, blood upon their hands, had wept. She would have wept if she could find her tears and if they would do any good.

"Baker," said the trusty seated at the desk. His coverall, the same gray as the guards wore, was too tight and stained by food. He glanced down at the screen built into his desk. "Political." Wyn drew breath to make some sort of last appeal.

"Move it."

She stared at him. *What about the records checks and the checks for medical clearance—?*

"Move it, traitor bitch, or I call the guards."

He glared and gestured. A Marine ambled over, the bell-shaped muzzle of his sonic stunner gleaming, Wyn moved it.

The trusty pushed a button. A door opened in the wall and Wyn went through, into a maze of narrow white corridors and then into the blinding yellow sunlight she would never see again. She drew a deep breath of air blessedly free of the taints of blood, filth and old sweat. Moored at the end of it wasn't after all one of the black ships out of a Greek tragedy, the blue eye warding off evil at its prow, but a huge-winged landing ship.

Ahead of her stretched a narrow gangway, crowded with guards and transportees. "Get a move on it," muttered a guard, gesturing at her with a prod and a whip. "Haul ass!"

Wyn moved it. Five more steps and she would be at the end of the gangplank where it fed into the ship. The Florida sun was warm, almost a benediction on her aching back. Before she entered the ship, she turned and took a hasty, hungry look at the violent crimsons and golds of the last sunset she would ever see on her world.

Moments later, the hatches clanged shut. She was shoved onto a padded shelf and secured like merchandise. The screams of the other transportees rose about her. Then the shrieks of the ship's engines drowned them out and seemed to hurl them all on top of her.

Wyn staggered in the unfamiliar, blessed weight of Luna Base's one-seventh gravity. Not much, but it would suffice to anchor the vomit, assuming her fellow prisoners had anything left in their stomachs. From acceleration to zero-G, the trip to Luna Base had been a horror. Not just the stinks and the slime, but the closeness. She had never thought of herself as overly fastidious and had daily worked up a good sweat running, but now she realized how much she needed space. Here, instead of elbowroom, she had cubic room. And precious little of it.

And this was the dream of space that she'd heard a few old-time physicists lament? Still, there had been that one glimpse of the Earth from space.

They've taken the dream and broken it. And it should have been ours, she thought. She had never cared to think much about it before.

Plato, she knew, had written of space, as had the Neo-Platonists. Dream visions, all of them. All out of fashion. In the last gasp of this century, intellectuals had made it a fashion to spurn the idea. Her too, though she had never considered herself as subscribing to fashions in thought. If you surrender control of something, *someone* will seize it, she told herself. Of all her sins of omission and commission, she feared that abandoning the dream of space, the control over the ships that flew through it, was one of the things that had brought her to Luna Base a convict, rather than an eager student.

Unsteadily, she walked down the corridor of this new prison, painted the gray-green of Luna's rock. An intercom crackled over the straining air vents, ordering groups to this side and that. She saw a crowd of men young enough to be her students herded in one direction. Then the order subsided. Indecisive, the crowd from the shuttle milled. A few sat on the now-filthy bundles they still carried with them.

Their faces as expressionless as if they wore bronze helms with only slits for eyes and nose; the CD Marines in blue and scarlet stood guard.

Enlisted men. Wyn met officers at this dinner or that. If these men had been officers—*what makes you think they wouldn't tell you that you got precisely what you deserved?*

The crowd waited so long that even the CD Marines began to shift from foot to foot. Finally, the intercom crackled to hasty life.

"ALL HAVEN-BOUND..." Static drowned out the rest of the message, but not the shouts that followed. "Rest of you, down there! Step lively, now."

Trusties in gray coveralls emerged from side doors. They had sonic tinglers; not as bad as the stunners, but nothing Wyn wanted to be hit with. Swearing, waving their weapons, with orders blaring so loudly overhead that it too felt like an assault, they herded Wyn and the other prisoners from the shuttle into a huge room, subdivided into pens. Doors—no, a port—began to slide shut as motors whirled and whined, building up to....

Was this the ship? No processing, no questions, no explanations: Had they just been herded on board?

She closed her hands to conceal the trembling in them. She had hoped that Dr. Ryan was wrong. Around her rose the cries and stinks of poorly tended children. It was like something out of the Trojan Women: herded onto the black ships, helpless and afraid.

"You come in with us, honey," came a voice. Wyn nearly wept for gratitude. Men, women and children, thugs and citizens they might be, all lumped together. She had hoped, at least, that convicts would be separated from...from what? Law-abiding citizens? *Wyn,* she told herself, *up here we're all convicts.*

Then, the screaming started.

A girl, her mismatched skirt and jacket almost shredded, darted through the narrowing port, pursued by red-faced trusties. Unused to the gravity, she stumbled and fell, still screaming in two languages.

"They put him out! They threw him out the lock! Out *there!*" Her sobs doubled her over, and she gagged and retched.

Wyn started forward, but not before a shorter, much plumper woman grabbed the girl, raised her, and smacked her face sharply. "Quiet! You want to follow him? You want it all to be wasted?"

She gulped, drew breath for another scream, and the woman slapped her again. "Shut up! Or we'll all be in for it."

Wyn threaded through the crowd and knelt beside them. "What's wrong?"

"What's it to you?" The woman's eyes were ancient, suspicious, though her face bore the too-taut look of many plastic surgeries.

"We're not rats in a trap," she snapped back. "Was she...?"

"Probably," said the older woman as she soothed the hysterical girl with the absent skill of too much practice. "Someone tried to protect her. They put him outside."

And when Wyn's face went blank, the other jerked her thumb. "Out the airlock."

Air bubbling, lungs bursting, blood freezing and boiling. Wyn fought to breathe and not to gag.

"Don't tell me you're gonna be sick on me, too. Keerist, I thought at least I'd stopped baby-sitting."

She bent her head, murmuring over the girl. "You're called Nina? Pretty. Come on, little girl, you gotta show us you got guts, you gotta make sure the bastards don't get you, you can live through this, I've seen a hundred girls like you, and they all ended up rich and sassy...you'll see...."

She glared at Wyn. "Do something!" she hissed.

Like what? She could see the men who had chased Nina into the hold, pushing this way and that. Only the crowds kept them from finding her thus far.

Wyn rose and forced herself to draw a deep breath.

"All right, you over there. Hide them!" Her coverall was stained. She needed a bath more than she had needed anything in her life, probably including air. And here she was, snapping orders.

Incongruously, people obeyed. "You—" she gestured with her chin at a compact man surrounded by his family... "See if you can't get the attention of the Marines."

His wife raised an immediate protest.

"Why..."

"Shut up!" snarled the woman who comforted Nina. "See what happened to her? It can happen to you family broads, too. Raped and your man breathing vacuum... All right, you men, turn your backs on the poor kid. She don't need to have men staring at her. Listen to the lady. She told you to get moving."

"Just do it," Wyn ordered. And when the man hesitated, "Please...if we don't hang together, they'll hang us separately. It could be your wife, your daughter...."

The man went. Wyn turned back to Nina. One filthy hand fumbled in a pocket and drew out a phial.

"Good stuff," approved her ally, recognizing the brand of trank.

"Save it for emergencies."

"What do you call this?"

"A real pain in the ass." She took the drug anyhow and fed it to her patient, "Now swallow, or I'll rub it down your throat like I would a dog," she threatened, but her hands were gentle.

Nina obeyed. Wyn wasn't surprised at that or when the strong sedative hit her like a sandbag at the base of the skull.

Wyn looked up at the people who stood between Nina and the men searching for her. "You have to stand up to them," she told them. "This time it's her. Next time, who's it going to be? You? You? The little boy over there?"

"You think you can take care of your own family?" the other woman asked to mutters of "*puta*" and other words Wyn didn't catch. "When they have stunners, and you have what? Good hearts? Better you should have brains."

"We have to work together," Wyn repeated. "Make a start now. Even trusties have to sleep sometime, and they know it. And if there's a riot, they won't be trusties for long."

That drew feral grins from the men standing about. As if glad to turn their attention away from the girl now dozing on the deck, they formed a ring about her, their wives, their daughters, and the three women in the center.

A stir in the crowd announced the arrival of CD Marines, the bells of their weapons shining as they were pointed in Wyn's direction. In their center marched a midshipman, barely old enough for his freshman year, but a man and an officer already.

"What's going on here?"

The group opened up, looking at Wyn. *I won't speak from my knees like some wretched Hecuba!* But already, she had learned wisdom: she held her hands away from her body and rose, carefully.

"This young woman was raped by two of your...two of the trusties," Wyn said. "They followed her in here. She claims they, spaced someone..."

"My father!" wailed the girl, much to everyone's surprise.

A fierce scuffle broke out too close to where they stood. "I'll get you all, you bastards!" someone shouted thickly, as if he spoke through a mouthful of blood and teeth. The midshipman gestured, and two Marines fanned out. Shortly thereafter, the whine of a sonic stunner made her flinch.

A freshman would have blushed and looked down: not this young officer. He took names, numbers, what details he could extract from Nina, to whom he spoke with such detachment that the girl could reply without sobbing. Then he turned away.

"Sir!" Wyn called at his back. He pivoted and faced her, impatient, but polite about it.

"What will be done now?"

"I'll have them in a pen before they're an hour older," he said. She could see the "Why am I bothering to answer *her*?" take shape on his face and pressed in with her next question fast.

"And the girl? She needs medical attention."

He shook his head. "Ma'am"—the title slipped out—"this isn't a passenger liner."

She held her eyes and raised a brow. He had the grace to flush. Behind her came fearful murmurs, and she looked away. *What if he checks my records? God only knows what sort of thing my brother's put into my files.*

Deliberately, she let her shoulders sag, lowered her head, just like most of the other women present. *One of the crowd. Just another convict. Don't notice me. Please.*

His eyes went back, the interest, the respect extinguished. Then he was gone. The pen doors slammed shut.

"We made ourselves some enemies," a man said. "We better stick together and watch out."

There were nods all around. A few men patted each other's shoulders, then turned, reassuringly to their families. The women murmured agreement.

"Hoo-boy, that does it!" announced…? Wyn looked in vain for a name on the woman's coverall. *She looks like a pro*, Wyn thought.

"First time decent family types have done more than spit at me. Usually, they throw out the loners. This might not be so bad. Well, I always was up for new experiences."

Wyn raised an eyebrow and gestured. The woman laughed extravagantly.

"Well, not *this*, exactly, honey. You political?"

Wyn nodded, mildly shocked. She had supposed that prisoners would consider it…well, ill-mannered to discuss how they came to be on board one of the BuReloc vessels.

"Lady, aren't you? From back East."

"Boston." Her voice almost broke on the name. "I'm Winth—"

"Don't have to give me your name. 'Boston' will do fine. Call me Ellie. You get in wrong with some political stiff?"

"My brother."

"If it's not money, it's men. I've seen enough of both in my life."

The pause drew out, and Wyn knew she was supposed to ask about the person she was talking to. She thought she could guess. The silence grew demanding.

"What about you?" Wyn asked.

The woman sat back on her heels and laughed. "Boston, honey, you wouldn't believe it, but I'm a political too. Didn't pay taxes on my…if you want to be nice, we can call it an escort service." She wiped at her eyes. "Tax evasion! I've been pushing it, or watching my girls for twenty years, and they get *me* on lousy tax evasion."

To her surprise, Wyn laughed too. At Ellie and at herself, all New England righteousness companionably chatting with a madam. Ellie watched her narrowly.

"Yeah, sure," she said. "Even here, you're a lady and I'm…well, what *am* I?"

"Brave, I'd say," Wyn retorted. "Besides, it's happened in the best of families." Hadn't one of the Philadelphia Biddles made a vulgar stir and dined out on it for years?

Again, Ellie laughed. "Boston, you kill me, you really do."

"God, I hope not, Ellie," Wyn found herself saying. "You're the first person I've met since the world caved in on me who hasn't bored or scared me to death."

"Shake on it?" asked the ex-madam. "It's not like I'm asking you to work for me, you know. I mean, you do know?"

Wyn laughed again and held out her hand for a brief handshake that Ellie broke off to warn Wyn about not showing off whatever it was she had in "that tacky green bag."

Wyn never learned the name of the ship. Once it had been a CoDominium vessel—the *Gdansk*, she thought from seeing the name stenciled on a bulkhead. Now, decommissioned, turned over to BuReloc, it might as well be called the *Botany Bay*. Or, she thought, *the ship of fools*.

The days turned into a litany of grumbles. "Clean" became a myth; Wyn looked back even to visits to Welfare Islands as trips into a vanished Eden. Even the rickety bunks were scarce; the younger men traded shifts, so that the narrow beds, in stacks of four, were always in use. That provoked a rude snort from Ellie that Wyn ignored. A few people showed signs of gambling away bunk time: A meeting of the people in their bay stopped that and instituted a schedule of regular cleanings for their deck and for the inadequate refreshers that served them and, for all they knew, half the other convicts. After all, you couldn't expect Marines to clean up after prisoners.

It was like, Ellie announced one day, perpetually having cramps and PMS—and you didn't even dare scream or throw things. Not even Nina, who turned thin, silent, and jumpy. Every day Wyn expected her to burst out screaming so the Marines would come and remove her, but she never did.

She didn't bleed either. In these close quarters, they'd have known if she had. Ellie's question, too blunt to be embarrassing, brought the answer: the medics had worked on her before she left Earth. Wyn was profoundly relieved.

What the women did who had not inhibited their fertility, Wyn didn't want to think of. She struggled against a claustrophobia that threatened to drive her frantic. Given no space and no activity and the bulky starches of convicts rations, she felt herself sagging. Even the isometrics she began to work at with almost a religious fervor brought her little relief.

Day after day, the ship sped toward Jupiter. Day upon day was a nightmare of heavy gravity, bearing down upon the rickety welded bunks until, one ship's "night", some buckled, trapping a family beneath them.

The bunks were cut away, and Wyn tried not to retch at the stink of burning flesh when someone was less careful about the cutting than he might have been. Then the people beneath them were taken away, too.

She never saw them again. And when she tried to ask a Marine, Ellie—whom Wyn had privately considered nerveless—flashed her a glance of such fear that she shut up. When a few men slipped out on work assignments about the ship and returned with steel pipe to reinforce the bunks, she helped them conceal it from the Marines.

From the one broadcast Wyn had watched years before while recovering from the flu, she knew that Alderson Jumps were instantaneous; transits from point to point were what occupied the days and weeks and months a ship actually spent going from one star to another. They had not yet left Earth's system, and Haven was more than a year away. Wyn wondered how she would stay sane that long.

At the orbit of Jupiter, the ship paused. After a nightmarish interval in which the low spin gravity failed as the ship took on fuel from the immense scoopship tankers waiting nearby—as "near" was reckoned in space. She knew that they had reached the point of the Alderson Jump when the alarms howled. People had time to scream once before everything blurred and stayed blurred for a long time.

After a featureless eternity of first lying on the bunks or the bulkheads, then of sitting staring at scratched, dirty hands, Wyn forced herself to move.

"At least with a hangover you can throw up," Ellie moaned.

There were people all about them who had not reached the sitting, staring or moaning stage. Some never would. Later that day, CoDo Marines herded trusties in to remove the bodies before people started to panic.

Thereafter, bunks were not at all scarce in Wyn's bay.

The broadcast Wyn had seen on BuReloc showed men and women going earnestly about the business of rehabilitating themselves and making themselves fit colonists. She wondered who dreamed that one up.

She thought she could understand the convicts who suddenly began screaming and hurling themselves against the bulkheads. Certainly, she could understand the man whose wife died and who, next time the call came for work crews, went out and never came back. Either he'd run wild or—and Wyn hoped this—he'd seized the chance to enlist in the CD forces.

The filth, the uncertainty, the threats of violence, even the "days" and "nights" that passed, perceptible only by a diminution of the light from scarred panels mused her first into fury, then into a frenzy that she could not express. The woman in the bunk beside hers had foul breath; Wyn lay awake one night plotting how to suffocate her.

Ostensibly, a prison ship was just that—bare bones. In actuality, if you had money or valuables, you could buy almost anything...or anyone. Mindful of Dr. Ryan's advice and Ellie's street smarts, Wyn guarded what was in her book bag, doling it out to the men on work crews to trade for medicinals, even an occasional treasure of food or drink, anything that would make her life and the lives around her a little less bleak.

She tried to rough out articles she'd never write, even a chapter of the book she had started before her arrest. But she would forget critical words in the Greek texts she had known by heart since she was a girl and, overpowered by the confinement, the stink and the hopelessness, her arguments raveled and faded into apathy. She began to think she had enough tranks left, perhaps, to kill herself: better so, perhaps.

"You think you're fooling me, Boston?" Ellie asked. "I've seen it when a girl gets like you. She's thinking of cashing in. And you know what I tell her?"

Let the old whore babble, Wyn thought. *Maybe it would tire her out and she'd let everyone alone.*

"I tell her to live long enough to spit on the bastards' graves, that's what I tell her. And what I'm telling you. You've done good here. We got a kind of law in this bay, and we all know it's you. If you check out, what's that mean to everyone else?"

Wyn raised a heavy eyelid. "What makes you think I care?" she asked.

"Boston, you're full of shit. 'Course you care. You got 'good citizen' all over you."

Wyn glanced down at herself. She had gotten very thin in the past months; that happened when you gave away your rations most of the time. "What I have written all over me is dirt," she snapped.

"Then clean up your act, will you? Thin as you are, how you going to survive the next Jump? And you got some graves to spit on, remember?"

"That's a long way back," Wyn objected.

"Then, you're going to have to be in shape to make the trip."

There was no way back. Wyn had known that in her bones from the time she had boarded. But Ellie's mouth wobbled, and she—*My God! She was even crying.* No one had ever cried over Wyn before. And now that she thought of it, she realized how quiet it was around where she lay, as parents kept their children quiet around her, hoping she would make the turn away from despair and back to them.

Wyn sighed and levered herself up. It seemed about a light year to the head, where she traded a gold pen for the chance to take a brief, blessedly hot shower. Thanks to a man released from cleaning detail, she had ship's chow from the CD galley and ate it with more appetite than she'd had for weeks. It gave her the strength to stomach ordinary rations the next day and all the days afterward. As soon as she could walk about the bay without staggering, she forced herself to do isometrics and to increase the time she spent exercising in the days that passed.

Another Jump, and she survived it. Now, she found herself restless, as she had in her first days on board. After prowling about the bay so often that people were heartily sick of it, she hacked her hair short and volunteered for cleanup duty.

It wasn't as if women were exempt from "volunteering." Usually, the Marines recruited female convicts for galley work or for cleanup in a place where they needed someone small, with a lower center of gravity. What else the women did in some cases was a matter of rumors—plus, what Wyn personally considered the fairy tales of Marines and even officers falling for a particularly pretty girl.

With her hair cut short, scrawny as she was, her face pallid from long confinement, Wyn didn't think she was a sight to break the heart of some hapless CoDo officer, while midshipmen were a whole lot likelier to run the other way.

It was a relief to leave the bay, to thread through corridors and passageways she hadn't seen, but that she marked in the too-keen scholar's memory that even despair hadn't taken from her. The bite of antiseptics came as a positive pleasure and so did the warmish water and watching the grimy bulkhead gleam beneath her scrubbing hands.

She grinned at the other woman and the men of her crew. As they scrubbed, they spread out, glad of the chance for at least the appearance of privacy. What a wonder it was not to have ten people crowded around you! Even the Marines seemed to have disappeared. No doubt they'd decided that a middle-aged woman was a damned unlikely candidate for running amok or storming the bridge.

She was kneeling on the deck, rubbing away at a particularly tough smudge when a kick from a boot sent her sprawling.

"Can't believe my luck!" came a voice Wyn had last heard thickened by blood after he'd been punched.

She levered herself up from the deck, murder in her eye, and the boot kicked her flat again.

Where had she seen that face before? Above a coverall...smeared with blood. That was it. He'd been a trusty, one of the men who'd spaced Nina's father and raped her.

Pretend you don't recognize him. Lie your way out, she told herself.

"I said I'd get ya. Never thought I'd find you alone though, and on your knees. Good place for you."

Wyn glanced down the hall. To think that a moment earlier, she'd been glad the Marines were nowhere in sight. She drew her breath for the loudest scream of her life, but the man pounced forward. A needle-thin knife flashed before her eyes as he grabbed her coverall with his other hand. The wet, flimsy, fabric ripped, and Wyn gasped.

"Quiet, bitch! You're coming with me."

"What do you think you're doing?" she demanded.

"Getting some of my own back. You cost me a soft berth. Now you owe me, gotta make it up to me."

"That's stupid. You were breaking the law," she snapped. "What good does this do?"

"Good? Because I *can*. Like I could with the girl."

Adrenaline washed through Wyn. "Look at the man," she mocked. "Too bad they didn't space you, too."

He backhanded her and she spat blood at him as he dragged her down the corridor.

Wyn struggled, trying to stamp on his instep, trying to bite the hand that held her, to pull free so that she could scream and run, but always, there was the knife in front of her face. It wasn't death she feared, nor being cut, it was her eyes! What if he blinded her! The fear made her tense her muscles so her bladder wouldn't give way.

A port was coming up, and he shoved it open onto what was little more than a closet. Long enough, Wyn found, for her to fall full length onto the deck, and for him to fall upon her. He barely kicked the door closed.

His breath was foul. If he—God, if he even tried to kiss her, she was sure she'd vomit in his face; and then he'd kill her. She hoped. In the end, that was about all he didn't try.

The strong do what they will. The weak suffer what they must. She told herself in an attempt to achieve distance from the spasms and grunts on top of her, the pain as he thrust into her unprepared and wholly unwilling body. She would not be weak. She would refuse weakness. Her hands balled into fists and she struck his back, brought up her knees (regretting that for the leverage it gave him), then trying to buck him off her body.

He was on his knees in front of her face all too soon thereafter, his knife in one hand in case she had any ideas about biting him where it would do the most harm. When he pulled out, she spat at him.

He slapped her, then rolled her onto her belly. *Beware of Greeks*, some fragment of Wyn's mind gibbered at her. This could do real damage, if he didn't kill her when he was finished. He'd have to kill her; she had seen him, and he had to know she wouldn't hesitate to report him. She heard something clang on the deck and felt her legs forced apart. Despite the horror, the metallic sound registered. He was using both of his hands. He had dropped the knife.

And there it was, about a meter away. It might as well have been a light year away unless she could grab it. A desperate plan, complete the instant she saw it, seized her mind and body. With what she hoped would sound like a hopeless moan, she collapsed onto one arm, and curled up into a ball, as if that pathetic maneuver could stop the painful invasion of her body.

But her left hand snaked out and seized the knife, bringing it beneath her toward her stronger hand, the right.

You want to die, you could fall on your sword right now, her mind warned her. Ellie's "spit on the bastard's grave" rang in her head. She jerked with her shoulders and thrust her hips up, as if fighting the man off. When he hurled himself back onto her, though, she was ready with the knife. And a lifetime's reading of the Iliad showed her exactly how to drive it into his chest below the sternum and twist it so the blood gouted out.

Again and again, she stabbed him. His blood splashed her, hot, though she thought she never would stop shaking.

If his buddy was around, she was dead meat; she knew she couldn't force herself, to retrieve the knife. She retched herself dry, spat on his body and staggered out of the tiny room.

Please God, this was no time for the Marines to come charging up! Instead of the Marines, she got a scared midshipman whose voice squeaked on the "ma'am" he shouldn't be calling a prisoner.

"In there," she rasped from a throat bruised from the grip of the dead man. Whom she had killed. She doubled over with dry heaves. "He fell on his knife," she willed the midshipman to believe.

The boy walked to the closet, opened it, then backed away. His eyes flicked over her half-naked and wholly bloodied body. No one could tell how much of the blood was hers.

"Terrible things, knives," he agreed with a maturity that stunned her. He moved in to support her. Boy though he was, she recoiled.

She didn't want to go to what passed for a Sick Bay on this sick, sick ship. No one ever returned from Sick Bay. She would get back to her bunk, and she would ask Nina how you lived with this.

"Just let me get back to...I have friends there, they'll help me... No, no need to. I can walk on my own."

When the worst of the shuddering had left her weak, but quite calm, she retraced the corridors to the prison bay that had the feel now of a refuge. Her legs wobbled, and her groin burned, and she blessed Dr. Ryan.

She was no distant goddess now, no lady, no scholar to be spoken to with respect and touched not at all. Just a female body. She hit the buzzer and leaned on the port.

It slid aside.

Ellie was not the first to see her, but she was the first to guess.

"Jesus *wept!*" she said and started forward.

Nina reached her first and flung her arms around her. Ellie joined her, taking her face in her hands to examine the swollen, split lips, before steering her expertly toward her bunk.

"Come on, honey... Baby, you fetch me my little bag, will you?" she told Nina. "You take this cloth, wet it good..."

Feet padded off fast. Wyn wanted to sag against Ellie's reassuring, female bulk, wanted to hide her face. If she'd been more cautious....

"Not your fault!" hissed the other woman. "It's not."

She guided Wyn through the ranks of cots. Men sat on many of them, but they turned their faces away as the women passed, granting them the respect of privacy.

She didn't want to be tended and cleaned, but Ellie was quite inexorable. With antiseptic salve on her, face, antibiotics and painkillers in her system, and her groin bound up in soft cloth—Ellie must have traded for a diaper from one of the mothers—Wyn was put to bed and covered with the least smelly of the blankets they were issued.

"I spit on his grave," Wyn whispered to her. "He had a knife and he dropped it...."

"*Good* girl, Boston. You're a champion." Ellie hugged her. A tear splashed down her face and onto Wyn's.

"Damn-it, you think I'd have seen it all by now. Here...." She reached behind her. "Drink this."

To Wyn's surprise, it was whiskey. She pushed it away.... "What about the painkiller?" She hadn't been raped and committed murder just to die because of an alcohol/drug problem, damn-it.

"This stuff doesn't react with alcohol. Don't worry about it. Just you get stinking drunk and we'll take care of you."

"Bring my bag," she muttered. She still had jewels sewn into its seams. She had to pay Ellie back.

Ellie pushed her back down. "Y'know, Boston, you can be a real asshole sometimes. Shut up and drink."

The whiskey burnt the cuts in her mouth, then seared as it went down. Field surgery used to use alcohol as a painkiller and cleaner, Wyn knew, and it was working now. After awhile, the lights dimmed. When she was certain no one was watching her, Wyn cried silently, her face buried in the shabby blanket. After awhile, she drifted.

A little after she woke, the ship Jumped. Her last thought before the Jump and the first one thereafter was that it was a shame that the ship couldn't perish in the antiseptic heart of a star.

* * *

The cuts and aches faded. After awhile, so did the nightmares and what Wyn came to regard as a deplorable tendency to flinch from men's voices. Boredom replaced weakness and fear. At one point, she even tried to teach Ellie Greek.

"You're outta your mind, Boston, you know that? Strike a deal with you. I don't tell you about my business; you don't teach me that stuff."

Ellie's business: clearly, she intended to resume it once they landed. "Hey, stands to reason this Haven they're sending us to is no garden spot. They've got miners there; and where there's miners, there's girls. Now, I'm way too old to start turning tricks again, but I'm a damn good bookkeeper...work my way in and work up to a share in the place."

"Is that all you want?" Wyn must have been half stupefied by boredom or the question wouldn't have popped out.

"What I want? I *want* to have enough credit so I don't have to OD on pills and booze when I get too old to work and the food runs out. I want to be my own person. You need money for that, in your own name, under your own control."

Wyn could see the wisdom in that. She only wished she were as certain of her future as Ellie.

What would await any of them on Haven? What awaited her? She knew convicts worked and worked hard. They were charged for their passage. They were charged for their life support. They were charged for the wretched coveralls they wore and the food, even when they didn't get full rations. Charged at rates, she suspected, she wouldn't pay for luxury travel.

It might be possible to repay all that by some form of indenture ranging from apprenticeship to slavery, depending on the employer/owner. And then you'd have to start all over to save the money for passage back to Earth.

No, that wasn't even a possibility. She had known that from the start. Her exile was final.

If she were going to survive, better not regard it as exile, but as a new life. How would she manage?

A glance about the bay showed her fellow exiles in a new light. The strong ones—casual labor. The other politicals—maybe they could be used as clerks. The wives and daughters arrested with their men? Women's work, the answer occurred to Wyn immediately. In a low-tech society, cooking and cleaning would no doubt be handed right back to them. Even the children: she recollected that even in the Plymouth Colony that had become her home state, indentures started young.

It looked as if she was about to suffer from her own ancestors' management tactics. She wondered if she were up to it; she'd lived off Baker wealth, Baker fame and Baker connections her whole life and counted herself lucky. At the same time, she knew, she had inherited the Baker conscience—*a double portion, since my brother clearly didn't get any.* And that conscience had a bad way of surfacing at inconvenient times to reproach her or, as it had this time, get her kicked off-world.

So now you get the chance to prove yourself, Wyn. Just what is it you think you can do? An interesting question, wasn't it? What kind of trade could a displaced aristocrat with a talent for languages take up in middle age?

Anyone on Haven need a butler? A nanny? Sure, she could teach. But with "political" written large on her dossier, would they trust her within five parsecs of a school? What *had* her brother paid to have written into her files?

She feared she would soon learn.

A few more Jumps and gravity shifts, and the intervening weeks and months passed. Atrocious as their rations had been, they became shorter. They began to sleep more, waking to eat and invent new versions of old curses on the purser, who pocketed the cost of their food. They shed the unhealthy bloat that comes of eating too much starch, became thin, then gaunt as they stinted themselves still further to make sure that the children, at least, had enough.

Haven would be too rough a world for children stunted by malnutrition, she had told one woman, the mother of three, and the word had spread.

One last Jump. One last interval of sitting in a daze. The variable gravity wobbled sickeningly, then steadied at a level that made her ache in every joint. To Wyn's surprise, gossip helped her identify this as mercy.

Then, one ship's "night," while the prisoners were groggy and disoriented, crew and CD Marines burst into the bay and ordered them out. *Now.* On the double, if not faster.

"My God, just smell them! Like pigs, these convicts," muttered one Marine. The ensign overseeing the transfer didn't silence him.

Wyn scarcely had time to grab her precious bag before she and the rest were herded to landers. She staggered a little in the unaccustomed G, then sucked in her breath as if someone had kneed her in the belly as the lander broke away from the ship in which she had spent more than a year of her life and whatever illusions she had brought on board. Zero-G brought her empty stomach flip-flopping perilously close to her mouth, and then Haven s own gravitation and the lander's braking rockets took hold: she was heavy, heavier than she had ever been; and her vision blurred. It wasn't fair; she was going to burst, and she hadn't survived the trip just to explode in reentry because the pilot poured on the G's. There were no hatches; she wouldn't even see the sky in which she would die.

From the lander's cockpit came a steady drone of affirmatives and static: "Beginning final burn...mark...Splash Island coming up on the horizon..."

My God, were they going to land in *water*? Wyn forced herself not to scream, to unstrap herself and claw at the nearest bulkhead: not to be trapped, not to sink in this steel trap, plunging further and further till it burst asunder, and her lungs...

She wanted to scream a protest, but "uuuhhhhh!" was all that came out, more breath than pain.

And then they were down.

In the water.

On whatever Haven this world might be.

*   *   *

The stench of steam and overheated metal rose about the port. Clutching a bag that felt heavier than any suitcase she had ever packed in her life, Wyn tottered toward the port. A blackened metal ladder led down from it to boats that bobbed in the black water far too much below. Even as the ship floated, she could feel Haven's gravity, heavier than the ship's. It felt heavier than that of lost Earth, though she knew otherwise.

Her feet trembled on the rungs of the ladder; the boats crew steadied her as if they hated touching anyone as filthy as she was. *Could they smell it through the steam and the traces of this new world?*

It took forever for the launch to fill. The thin crying of hungry children rose in the alien air.

"Where are we going?" she asked.

To her surprise, she was answered. "Splash Island," replied a man with a twisted arm. He grinned and pointed across the dark, dark water. Lights gleamed from translucent sheds on that Island.

"There's Splash Island. Pro-ces-sing..." he sounded the long word out. "Over there"—a sweep of his arm—"you got Docktown. And beyond it, The City. Castell City."

A combustion engine roared into fetid life, then backfired so loudly that at least two people screamed and the launch jolted dangerously. The ferryman laughed, exposing broken teeth.

"You don' wanna fall in. *Believe* me. We can't fight what's in there, and I ain't goin' back for ya. Keep your arms inside the launch."

I haven't a coin for the ferryman, Wyn thought. In the next instant, she realized she was wrong. The coin shone in the night sky, dominating it, more crimson than copper, baleful as the eye of a cat. Another shone upward, reflected in the opaque water.

Ship's rumor called Haven's bloated primary the Cat's Eye. Funny: on Earth, it had always been the dog who had been sacred to Ares. Cat's Eye and its reflection glared at each other. It was a world of War, Wyn realized at that moment; and this Charon, this convict who'd served out his life here, ferried her across the water to start a new life.

Haven's gravity took her as she climbed out of the launch, and she stumbled to her knees. Her hands scrabbled, then filled with mud. *Dear Earth, I do salute thee with my hands,* the mournful pentameter from

Richard II rang in her thoughts. Wrong again. Haven's ground was dirt, soil: it never would be *earth*.

"Why are we so heavy?" wailed a child. Its cries were quickly hushed as if it knew Haven were no planet for weeping.

And yet, with the Eye above and the reflection below and the lights of Docktown and Castell City shimmering over the water, it was beautiful.

Moving like invalids their first day out of bed, the convicts shuffled toward the Processing Center.

"God, I am too damn old, for this," Ellie moaned. "Feel like I got lead boots on. All over me. Or maybe that's just crud."

"Men on one side...women on the other...all right, move!" came the order. "Kids with the women."

Men and women clutched each other, dismayed. They had all been together for so long that separation came as a threat. Down long, shabby corridors they were herded. Wyn noticed that the women guards hustling her and her friends along were unarmed. The corridors opened into a room that smelled, blessedly, of clean steam and water, dripping from nozzles set into the ceiling.

"All right, everyone strip. And scrub good!"

The soap they found in squeeze bottles nearly took off their outer layer of skin, and Wyn had never felt anything as good. Steam billowed about them, mercifully hiding their bodies. But at that moment, she wouldn't have minded if they hadn't separated the men and the women.

Tugging a fresh coverall (for which she'd no doubt be billed, too) over damp skin, Wyn caught sight of herself in one of the cracked, water-beaded mirrors still clinging to the walls.

"Look like a New England schoolmarm," she muttered to herself. In fact, she reminded herself of the frayed sepia photos of her Great Phoebe, who helped found a girl's school in India, then went on to China to fight against footbinding.

She wasn't as much slim as lean now, starved down into endurance. And at some point during the journey into exile, her eyes had traded a scholar's abstraction for a veteran's wariness.

"Not bad," Ellie shook her head. "Don't know why you act like you're ready for an old-age home."

"You're not recruiting me for your line of work, are you?"

Both women laughed, a little raggedly. After decontamination would come Processing, and then Assignment. But what contamination had her brother put in her file? They wouldn't let her anywhere near students, would they? She might be lucky to find herself hauling scrap in a mine until she collapsed.

Medical processing rid her of fears she'd contracted some disease from the man who raped her. Her arms were sore from immunizations when she was Processed—identification, classification interview, and a battery of tests. She identified them as out-of-date aptitude and personality evaluations, plus an ancient IQ test. Practically meaningless; and yet whatever future she might have could ride on them. Her palms began to sweat, and she pondered each answer as carefully as the girl next to her.

For deportees to survive on Haven, matters were simple. Someone had to buy their contracts for work in town, in the mines, on farms, or wherever: almost anything was better than going it alone. The only other options were farming—usually with inadequate supplies and equipment and in Haven's outback—or to become one of the walking dead who loitered around Docktown seeking casual work or a quick deal.

Further down the hall, Ellie squirmed in her chair. Wyn knew the woman was thinking, I'm too old to go back to school.

As the tests ended and they were returned to holding pens, Nina turned to her. "Boston, what are we going to do?"

"We have to wait to be assigned," Wyn said. She just wanted to sit down and rub her temples. How many years had it been since a test had psyched her out?

Nina came close to her, dark eyes wide with terror. "I heard...there's mines here. A place called Hell's-A-Comin' and I'm afraid, Boston. Where there's mines, they need girls, and..." The big eyes overflowed.

Wyn put her hands on the girl's shoulders. She glanced about helplessly. Ellie was nowhere in sight. What would Ellie say to this girl? She could practically hear her, "*Boston, no way I could make a working girl out of this one.*"

So many lives had been broken. Against that, what did the life of one girl matter? Plenty: Nina had been Wyn's shipmate and she looked to Wyn for help. Wisdom from the Welfare Projects blurted from her mouth.

"We're probably being watched," she whispered. "Mess your hair. Slouch. Act anti-social."

"Anti-social?" Oh God, now she had to give examples.

"Drool or pick your nose or do something that's a real turnoff. Damn-it, don't *laugh*! And, Nina, you want to do me a real big favor? When you start this little act, turn your back on me, okay? I don't want to watch."

Wyn sat alone in the detention pen, wondering who would emerge from an inner office to claim her. Everyone knew, when applying to graduate school, on about what day the letters of acceptance or rejection would be delivered. And everyone waited for mail that day for the precious thick or damning thin packets delivered the old-fashioned way. She had sat on admissions committees since then and knew how candidates were discussed. How were her new...her new masters discussing her?

The door slid open slowly and a guard entered. Wyn rose, quickly enough for deference, slow enough to preserve her own illusions. "This way," the guard said.

No statement that Mr. so-and-so had bought her contract? She started to raise her eyebrows, then thought better of it.

She was brought to a tiny room. In it sat a man dressed in rugged, all-weather clothes conspicuous only by the shimmer of the gemstones he wore on one hand and on the slide about his neck. She had seen such a stone only once, when her niece Caroline had wed that improbable Texan and Shreve's had had to set the veritable boulder he gave her in platinum. It had been vulgarly large, but the stones this man wore as baubles made it resemble a seed pearl. The man rose as she entered. Her eyebrows did flick upward at that.

"Ms. Baker?"

She inclined her head.

"I've been studying your file. Oh. I'm Dan Carmichael, private contractor, at the Kennicott Mines over Hell's-A-Comin' way."

She froze. She had always been able to identify euphemisms. And from her days working in the Projects, she recognized this man. *I know a pimp when I see one.*

"I said I'd get ya. Never thought I'd find you alone, though, and on your knees. Good place for you."

Her callused hand went out to brush the back of an empty chair, and she shut her eyes against the pain, the violation and thereafter, the feel of her hand driving steel into flesh and hot blood spurting over her wrist.

He was aiding her to sit; in an instant, he would shout for help, she knew it. She summoned strength from the core of rage she had learned to nurture—"spit on the bastards' graves"—and shook her head.

"I am too old to...I believe you call it, 'turn tricks.' Not to mention my lack of other attractions."

He stared at her. *I'm not going to faint.* When he seemed to be sure of that, his laughter rattled the flimsy partitions of the room.

"Varley owes me a favor. He said I ought to meet you, that you were likely to wind up near the top. It stands to reason. The Consul General flags all the politicals; and hell, lady, you're something special even in the way of politics. Can't think of a job I could offer you, unless it would be teaching... My gals tend not to have kids. Down the road, though, it's sure going to cost plenty to send the ones they do have to Company schools."

"I would hardly think so," Wyn murmured.

"Some of 'em do, though. And sooner or later, they'll need schools. Well, that's down the road...."

Frontier schoolmarm. Wyn you are going back all *the way—at least, if you're lucky.*

"You might tell me something, though. That little girl, the one who talked to you, then started...ugh! That's all an act, isn't it?"

Nina had cried in her arms. The urge to protect her like a student made Wyn shiver.

He can check to see if you're lying, her good sense told her.

"She was raped at Luna Base. When her father tried to help her, they spaced him. She won't earn back your investment," she said crisply. Then, inspiration struck.

"Sir..."

"Lord, you speak fine!" He shook his head at her.

"Sir, if you have access to the BuReloc files, you should know that there is one woman..."—How could she phrase this appropriately?—"in your line of work. We called her Ellie...."

Wyn slid forward on her chair. Sure enough, built into the computer panel on the table was a screen for observing the prisoners awaiting assignment. There sat Ellie. Obviously, she had finished processing later than Wyn. "That one."

The man's fingers tapped on the keyboard. A guard emerged and shepherded Ellie out of the holding pen into the cubicle. One quick glance, and she had sized up Carmichael. A grin, a pass of her hand across her hair and coverall, and she looked younger, flushed, even pretty. Wyn blinked. So that was how a real pro did it.

"Damn-it all, Boston," she blurted. "I thought you said you didn't want my line of work!"

"Ellie..." It was Wyn's turn to flush as she realized that she had never known her shipmate's last name, "I would like you to meet Mr. Daniel Carmichael, who manages...."

What *was* the proper way to introduce people in their line of work? Apart, of course, from the obvious. Aha! What had Ellie called her business when they'd met back on Luna?

"...an escort service at Hell's-A-Comin'."

She glared at Ellie, willing her to hold out her hand first. The lady always indicated whether she wished to shake hands.

Ellie shook her head, then Carmichael's hand. Only then did she start to grin.

"Thank you, Ms. Baker," Carmichael intoned, his voice hollow with laughter.

"Boston, you never told me your name was Baker," Ellie said. "One of *those* Bakers? And you let me. Hoo-eee! I'm surprised you even spoke to me."

Wyn shrugged. Both Ellie and Carmichael watched her with growing amusement.

"Is that how you learned to keep a straight face? You ought to come to work with us…make you the standup comic."

Wyn smiled at her. So few words, and it was all arranged. *I ought not to approve, she thought. But there is Hell's-A-Comin', and the brothels are real; and no question, the women in them will do better with Ellie to look out for them.*

"Or I could play the piano in the parlor," she said slyly.

"Got a keyboard instead," Carmichael said. His face reddened as he lost the struggle against a great shout of laughter. "Sure you won't reconsider?"

Wyn smiled. "I'll take my chances."

"Ya know, Boston, you can be a real asshole sometimes," Ellie said.

"I'll be fine," Wyn assured her with more confidence than she felt. "You'll make so much money up at the mines you probably won't even recognize me next time you see me. Or want to talk to me."

"You'll still be respectable. Still Boston," Ellie said and hugged her. The next instant, she was all business "Where's those papers?" she demanded. "Isn't there someplace I got to sign? You want it in blood or what?"

More keystrokes, and the contract whirred out of a slot in the console. Tongue between her teeth, Ellie signed and handed the papers over to Carmichael.

"Ms. Baker, I thank you," he said. Then he hesitated. "Here's for luck. The way you're thinking, you'll need all the luck you can get on Haven." He lifted the slide with its glowing gem, a tiny replica of Haven's giant moon, from about his neck and threw it over to Wyn. "Will you get a move on it, Ellie? We open for business at 2000, and we need to find you a decent dress."

Ellie followed her new employer out the door. "…gave away a fortune, and you ought to see the stuff she's still got hidden in that green thing she carries.…"

Silence. The tiny room seemed suddenly cold, echoing. Wyn was relieved when the guard escorted her back to the holding pen. Quickly, she stuffed her new lucky charm into the green bag. At some point, she might be able to sell or trade it. And there was no sense in being a walking target.

There were no windows in the pen. It smelled like every other pen in which Wyn had been deposited with a grunted "wait here." It shouldn't, Wyn thought. This was an alien world; somehow, she had expected it would look and feel different. She wanted out, to fight for whatever future Haven might offer her; she wouldn't get that future sitting here.

"Ms. Baker?" Not a guard this time, but a man dressed almost drably, in what Wyn was suddenly sure was "solid citizen" clothing. Once again, she trotted down the hall to the interview cubicles.

"Ms. Baker, I am Richard DeSilva. He waited for her to acknowledge his family name and to take the hand that he—a vast concession—held out to her.

"How do you do?"

"I assume that your trip here was rather trying."

Wyn inclined her head and nodded again when DeSilva waved her to a seat. A DeSilva of Kennicott here on Haven? Must be from a minor branch of the family. Not old enough to be a failure, shipped out to the frontier; not young enough to be an heir, proving himself. Probably just old enough to be desperate to make one last push to better himself here, if not lift himself off-world.

"The Consul General alerted me when your file crossed his desk. Yours was marked for two reasons: politics and high intellect."

"The charges against me were false," Wyn said levelly "All of them except terminal folly." *And you can't file an appeal back on Earth for that.*

"Most unwise to launch a frontal attack against entrenched authority."

He steepled his fingers. Recognizing the tone of Official Pronouncement from many dinner parties, Wyn nodded: *You expert; me, unworldly professor. So tell me, Mr. DeSilva, have you bought my contract? And what do you need me to do?*

"I would not do it again," she said.

"So you have learned from the experience?"

"A very great deal, sir," she said. She had learned to study those in power, to figure out their weaknesses and survive by playing upon them. She had been a trusting fool, and then she had been helpless. She would not willingly be helpless again.

"It is your knowledge of Earth that I could find useful...."

"My knowledge of Earth?" Wyn allowed herself to smile. "Mr. DeSilva, I left Earth more than a year ago on what I fully expected to be a one-way trip. And I think neither of our families would say I knew much about the real world when I lived on it."

"Still," he said. "Your family's contacts. Your education, the way you speak."

She glanced at his hands. He wore a wedding band. That told her: *outpost mentality.*

"Do you have children, Mr. DeSilva? School-aged children perhaps? And the local schools—are they adequate to those children's needs?"

Years of faculty/parent conferences and student advising made him easy to read. Shipped out from Earth or maybe born here: an early marriage to a local woman unable to keep pace with his ambition or supply their children with whatever polish he thought they ought to have.

He'd bought her contract for politics. But teaching them could be her insurance policy once he'd mined out her few Earth names and networks.

His face lit. "I have taken up your contract."

Wyn inclined her head.

"Please think of it merely as an employment contract. My children, of course: and we could use an executive assistant, discreet, cultivated."

In short, a major domo, their resident status symbol from Earth.

You won't get a better offer, she heard Ellie's voice.

No doubt, he would pump her for details of Earth politics, out-of-date as they were. No doubt, he would mine what connections he thought she had about as thoroughly as Kennicott went into the hills by Hell's-A- Comin. And in return?

Maybe, just maybe, I can strike back.

The idea did not provide the angry pleasure it once had. She had learned something, after all. If DeSilva was a power here and relied on her, she too would have power of a sort, even a chance to shape a place that was not already hopelessly corrupt.

Even her tie to Ellie and Carmichael at the mines might be worth something. Exiles made what choices they had to: anything to cease being "the weak" Anything they could stomach. Ellie's and Carmichael's work might be cleaner than the game she was offered.

She thought she could manage. Life on board a BuReloc ship toughened her to the point where she thought that maybe, just maybe, her ancestors—who had *not* been pampered aristocrats—might not find her a weakling. She was well up to this game, she thought. In fact, even if DeSilva could produce passage back to Earth, she thought she would spurn it in favor of the promise she saw for herself on Haven. She would not always be "the weak," fated to suffer what she must.

It was not often a person got a second chance. Hers sat across from her, folding up the contract of her indenture and tucking it into his jacket.

DeSilva rose, and she rose with him. "We would be obliged if you would begin at once. Tonight, we have an important dinner.... You will, of course, join us." He looked pained. "There is the matter of suitable clothing...."

Hadn't Dan Carmichael said the same thing to Ellie? No, Wyn didn't think she'd stop speaking to Ellie.

"When I earn it," Wyn said. She had a sudden crazed vision of stripping open the seams of her faithful green bag, extricating the pearls she had sewed within it, and wearing them with the coverall that was the convict's badge.

He flinched. "Consider it a condition of employment. You must appear…presentable. One of the Hamiltons will be there."

Well, thank you, sir! She was a Baker; of course, she was presentable. Then she thought about what else his statement might mean. She intended to teach. But there was always that other way. Marry one's way up and out.

At her age?

Why not even that? After all, when Great Aunt Phoebe had gotten thrown out of China, she'd come back to Boston and she'd married (*which branch of the family was it?*).... But DeSilva was waiting for her reply. Wyn copied Ellie's, even to the downcast look and the breath held long enough to let her blush.

Decent clothes, fabrics that didn't chafe. And chances to stop being "the weak." She could hope. It was dignified to hope.

Count no man happy until you have seen the hour of his death. She recalled the old caution from Herodotus.

But don't write him off till then either. Or her.

DeSilva escorted her through the Processing Center and onto the launch bound for Castell City. A light snow was falling, and the fresh air filled her with new hope as she gazed at the huge, feline primary reflected in the water. When the launch docked, DeSilva made half the dockyard stare by handing her, dressed as she was in convict's gray, down from the boat. She nodded thanks, then followed him out into her future.

* * *

"And the town being now strongly besieged, there being also within some that practiced to have it given up, they yielded themselves to the discretion of the Athenians, who slew all the men of military age, made slaves of the women and children, and inhabited the place with a colony sent thither afterwards of five hundred men on their own." (Thucydides, *The Peloponnesian War*, translated by Thomas Hobbes, University of Chicago Press, Book 6, page 372)

Atalanta

Don Hawthorne

Bureaucracy
Luna, Co-Dominium Offices: 2073 A.D.

After twenty minutes of preamble, Maldonado, the Minister for Sports, was framing his closing argument as any good bureaucrat would: In the form of an opening statement.

"The problem, Mister Chairman, is that the whole justification for holding the games at all is at risk of being invalidated."

Chairman Vladimir Serafimov of the CoDominium High Council had been listening to his guests for nearly twenty minutes and his boredom threshold was, by his own estimates, about three sentences away and closing fast.

"I disagree," came the rebuttal from Voorhees, representative from the Colonial Athletics Committee and appointed to serve as an advocate of his colony world of Sauron and its participation in the CoDominium

Olympic Games. "If one colony fields superior athletes, it should stimulate the other worlds to increase their efforts on behalf of their own sons and daughters to rise to the challenge."

Voorhees turned to Serafimov and addressed him directly. "It is neither Sauron's fault, nor its responsibility, to accommodate the other colonies' lack of commitment for an event to which Sauron's young people dedicate themselves for years beforehand."

"Mister Chairman," Maldonado said, "in the decades since the CoDominium nationalized the Olympics, they have steadily regained their stature and dignity as contests of amateur athletics held in a spirit of comradely competition."

"Sauron's athletes *are* amateurs," Voorhees interjected in an icy tone, "They receive no state funding or support whatsoever, and the CoDominium Olympic Organizing Committee verifies this on a yearly basis. A rather insulting process, in fact, which, I hasten to add, no other colony is required to undergo."

Maldonado clenched his teeth. "By the very nature of Sauron's militaristic governmental structure," he began, but never finished.

Serafimov raised his hand, a gesture he rarely used. Anyone who had ever dealt with him in the political arena soon came to regret seeing it. "That is quite enough from both of you." He leaned forward, interlaced his fingers and held the silence for a moment, regarding both men carefully.

"This has gone from a tedious debate to a rather ominous allegory about nationalism. I would remind you both that when the Olympics were confined to this world, my own country often received the same criticism being leveled at the Sauron System. That's one of the very good reasons the Olympics are not held between nations any more, but between colony worlds, each of them far more varied in their cultural composition than any one nation of Earth ever was.

"Now," he sat back and looked at his desk clock, "I require that you, Minister Maldonado, come to the point and make your proposal. Representative Voorhees, do not interrupt." He nodded to Maldonado.

"Proceed."

Maldonado sighed. "I wish to bring a proposal before the CoDominium Olympic Organizing Committee that Sauron be banned from future competition in the CoDominium Olympics."

Voorhees opened his mouth, but Serafimov stayed his words with the barest lift of a palm in his direction.

"On what grounds, Minister Maldonado?"

Maldonado spread his hands. "On the grounds that in previous Olympics, Sauron athletes have consistently increased their medal winnings at a steady rate, until the last Olympics, when Sauron took medals—gold, silver, or bronze—in *all three hundred and eighty-six events!* In addition, virtually all CoDominium athletic records are now held by Saurons! Given the trend of Sauron dominance of the games up to this point, there is every reason to assume that within forty years, every medal will go to a Sauron!"

Voorhees did interrupt at that. "You refer to our athletes as 'Saurons', not as 'Sauron citizens', not even as 'people from Sauron'… aren't they human anymore, Maldonado?"

"Only Sauron's government could answer that, Representative Voorhees," Maldonado's answer was a condemning hiss, and the silence following it was long and ugly.

"That is a despicable thing to imply, Maldonado," Voorhees finally declared in a low voice. "Even for you."

Maldonado shook his head. "It is no secret how I feel about Sauron eugenics policies, and if they are willing to oversee marriages with genetic screening, who can say how far they will take such practices on a larger stage?"

Serafimov decided he had had enough. "Minister Maldonado," he said, "You may see fascist, racist regimes hiding under every bed, and you, Representative Voorhees, may be excused for your passionate advocacy of your colony world in the face of perceived insults to its character. But I do not have time to provide you two with an audience while you try to drum up support for your silly games."

Both men stared.

"Yes, you heard me correctly. If either of you had the slightest idea of the problems we face in administering the day-to-day *survival* of the CoDominium and its colony worlds, to say nothing of just keeping the government in operation, you would hang yourselves in shame for having wasted my time on this petty nonsense.

"We are witnessing something like the first period of real stability the CoDominium has ever known, and already it is being threatened by renewed nationalist factions that have forgotten why the CoDominium came about in the first place. That stability is precious, and crucial to the continued peace and the very survival of life on Earth. I will not have it jeopardized by the likes of you two turning a frivolous sports party into yet another divisive exercise in colonial issues to further erode CoDominium authority."

Serafimov took a deep breath.

"So. Here is my solution to your problem, gentlemen. The colonists on Sauron have proven they can field the finest athletes in the CoDominium—be quiet, Minister Maldonado. Therefore, having nothing left to prove, the Sauron colony is heretofore banned from competition in the CoDominium Olympics until such time as further review by CoDominium officers *at their convenience and discretion* deem otherwise."

Serafimov turned his gaze to a white-faced Voorhees. "Since the Sauron colony has proved herself to be capable of such unequalled expertise in these matters, all CoDominium Olympics judges will be drawn from—and solely from—the Sauron colony, with citizens of the colony assigned by their colony senate to such duties based on their expertise in the individual events of the CoDominium Olympics, until such time as further review, etcetera." He glanced sideways toward his secretary. "Have that written up for my signature and distributed appropriately for the next colonial diplomatic disbursement."

Serafimov turned back to his guests. "Now, gentlemen, I have to deal with food riots in Omaha, Kiev, Lebanon and half a dozen other cities—some of which are rumored to have suffered outbreaks of cannibalism—before I authorize the forced colonial relocation to some wretched rock at the back of beyond for approximately twenty-two thousand luckless wretches from Afghanistan. I hope this helps you both appreciate the amount of time I have spent on your *crisis*." The last word was greasy with contempt.

Voorhees and Maldonado rose in stiff coordination, thanked the Chairman for his time and left the office. The two men were marched side by side down the long corridor of the CoDominium's offices on Luna, toward the launch bays where they would board shuttles to vessels which would return them to their respective homes; Maldonado to Earth, Voorhees back to Sauron system.

For a brief moment they stood on the platform alone together. Neither man looked at the other.

"So," Maldonado finally said, "That went well."

Voorhees did not nod, but agreed: "Better than expected. The funds will be in your account by the end of the week. Geneva, as usual?"

Maldonado sighed. "Where else? How anyone can claim to live a civilized life on those colonies is beyond me."

Voorhees' shuttle pod arrived first. He turned and smiled as he entered it. "Yes", he agreed, making a frank appraisal of Maldonado's portly form. "I'm sure it is."

The pod doors closed on Maldonado's reply.

Voorhees hailed a private car, sealed himself in the back and activated a small device in his case that would scramble any surveillance equipment. He checked the time; he would be early for his meeting with the Sauron colony's representative in the CoDominium Senate, but he would put the extra half hour to good use.

He began opening cascade-encrypted files and reviewing the status reports of an operation he had initiated almost two decades ago, and today he could report to the Senator that he, in turn, could inform the Sauron High Council that the operation was on schedule.

The file name read: Project *Perseus*.

THEOCRACY

Haven, Royce Farm, Northern Pasture: 2081 A.D.

Becca Royce concentrated on controlling her breathing, no mean feat in the thin air of Haven, even at sea level, and she was well above that now. The fingers of her right hand twitched as they moved in tiny, tickling probes over the surface of the rock beneath them, seeking purchase. Finally, she felt just the right texture beneath her fingertips and dug them in, gripping the rock with such force that small puffs of dust rose from beneath her hands. Only when her grip was secure did she pull herself up, one-handed, toward the ledge above. Beneath her dangling fifteen-year-old legs, three hundred feet of daylight separated the soles of her shoes from the rocks below.

With one last effort, Becca pulled herself onto the ledge, twisting round to sit next to the terrified lamb that had fallen from the meadow above but, miraculously, no further.

"Well, baby," she said, stroking the lamb's head to calm it down, "Some view, huh?"

Becca had crawled down and around to reach the ledge, and after securing the lamb in a sling and the sling onto her back, she returned the way she had come: twenty-five feet straight up an almost sheer rock face overlooking the Shangri-La Valley to a meadow above, where the rest of the herds grazed, one dam bleating in sheepish befuddlement over her lost offspring.

Becca trotted over to the dam and returned her offspring, oblivious as it sought its mother's teat, then went to get her tools to repair the fence around the meadow's perimeter.

Becca wasn't even aware that she ran everywhere she went. Despite the barely-tolerable altitude in Haven's already thin atmosphere, she wasn't even out of breath.

"Good trueday, father," she said as she entered the tool shed. Her father was standing at his workbench, working on a new leather harness, big powerful hands twisting the leather, the great curved needle pulling the lacings through and back, through and back.

"Harmony, daughter," her father Emil offered in the way of their faith. Becca's forebears had been among Haven's first permanent colonists, members of the Church of New Harmony, who had petitioned the CoDominium for colonization rights to Haven when it was just one more unlovely, unloved little moon, another speck of non-terrestrial real estate that no one else had wanted.

Led by Church Founder Charles Castell, the Harmonies had come here to live and worship as their new faith guided them, far from the prejudices of those outside that faith, and the interference of CoDominium laws.

For years the Church had flourished and, given the doctrine's few material needs and Haven's meager resources, had even prospered after a fashion. Haven was just slightly more than survivable, but more important to the Harmonies, it was isolated, and it was theirs. And for a while, it was large enough to accommodate the Harmonies and the rare Bureau of Relocation shipload of forced-emigration refugees without the groups ever bumping into one another, except for the fairly common converts to the faith who found the doctrine amenable…or at least preferable to death by starvation or freezing.

Those idyllic first few decades had only lasted until some of those refugees had started mining the little moon; Haven, as it turned out, was rich in several odd but commercially valuable minerals. Now the Church was locked in battle with the mining consortiums over Haven's future and who would shape that future, and by extension the surface of Haven itself.

Emil was a member of the church council and this made him a target for all sorts of attention from the mining interests, none of which he welcomed. But today, it seemed they had changed their tactics; today their agents had approached him about his daughter.

"Had a pair o' discos up to the house looking for you, child." Emil used the contracted version of one of the Church's casual term for those outside of their faith. As *Harmonies* sought to live in harmony with the universe, those who did not were known variously as *tinears, deafs* or *discordants*—"discos" for short.

Becca's heart rate went up significantly for the first time all day. Whatever her father and the Church thought of the non-Harmonies on Haven, to Becca they represented opportunities she would never have without them.

"Yes, father?"

"Summat 'bout your schooling in the town," Emil went on as he continued working on the harness he was fashioning. The "town" was Castell City, the largest metropolis on Haven. Originally the small trading center of the Church of New Harmony's original settlement, in recent years the mining corporations and the CoDominium's policies had spurred its growth into an unrecognizable sprawl. But to old timers like Emil, it would always be "the town". He looked up at Becca—the girl was already taller than he—and met her eyes. "They tell me you ran, daughter."

Becca looked at the floor. "Yes, father."

Emil studied the leather lacings in the sunlight coming through his workbench window. "Schooling in the town, you wanted. Your mother wanted it for ye, too, and I give in, so long you kept t' the Harmony Way and no wildness."

He put the leather down and rubbed his hands. Becca could hear the joints grinding inside his flesh, the arthritis getting worse by the year, but her father didn't even wince. "An' ye been true to your word, daughter, an' never did you give us cause to regret letting you go." He smiled, and Becca felt her father's love for her like a warm breeze. "I'm proud of ye,

Becca; these discos say you're the smartest in your whole school. But this running thing…." Emil's frown was one of concern, not of censure. Even so, Becca could not stop herself from interrupting her father.

"I've not run overmuch, father, never in competition; only the regular health class courses…it's just…." Becca blushed and quieted, aware of her disrespectful behavior.

Emil was quiet for a moment.

"Mm-hm. I know. They make all the youngsters do their fitness trials. Want t'be sure ye're fit for their militaries, if need be… as if just livin' t' fifteen Earth years here on Haven wa'n't proof enow of how hale and hearty a child is, an' has to be." Emil's voice dropped.

Becca's mother Thora had lost two daughters and a son to Haven's thin air and harsh climate, and Becca's own robust—even amazing—good health did nothing to relieve her parents' worrying over their eldest and only living child.

"Anyway," Emil changed the subject and the tone, "These two discos come t' ask your Ma an' me about your future schooling. Asked if ye planned on goin' t' th' University in town, like your Mother did."

Becca's eyes met her fathers. "I want to, father." she admitted. "I've never made secret of that."

Emil nodded. "Ayuh. An' you still want to go for the same thing, yes?"

"Veterinary sciences, father, yes. For the farm."

Emil's heart swelled with pride at the iron in his daughter's tone. He and his wife Thora would have no more children, and Becca would hold the farm in her name when she came to wed. It would not pass to her husband; Emil had already seen to that when he filed his daughter's marriage contract with the Church Elders. With luck, Becca's husband would be a neighbor boy, making the farm she one day left to her own children even larger and more prosperous. The man who married Becca would share her wealth, but he'd best have no illusions about taking anything away from her; Harmonies might now and again fail in strictly adhering to Church Edict, but Emil had never known Becca's will to bend.

"Well, then, they say they want ye to come try for those colony games the CoDo people run. If ye want to, they think ye might go as part of Haven's group of young people. An' if ye'll do that, they say y'can attend University fully paid for by the Redfield Foundation."

Becca was confused. "Colony games? The CoDo?" For a moment she couldn't understand what her father was talking about, then: "Father, do you mean they were talking about the CoDominium Olympic Games? They want me to try out for a *spaceontheHavenOlympicteam, oh, father!*"

Becca was a devout Harmonite. She was ferociously intelligent and iron-willed and usually very serious, but she was also fifteen-years-old. She threw her arms around her father's broad shoulders and hugged him with almost all her strength, and then Emil *did* wince.

"Now daughter, "he managed to gasp out as the last of the air was crushed from his lungs, "Ye may run and jump all ye want," Becca heard the sternness in his tone and stepped back. Emil put his hands on her shoulders, keeping his astonishment off his face as he held her gaze; *by Old Charlie Castell's Beard, the child was as strong as a tamerlane!* "But ye may not wrestle. It's unseemly. Are we agreed?"

"Yes father," Becca agreed readily, and meant it. She didn't care for wrestling, in any case.

It was too easy.

AUTOCRACY

Earth, The Kremlin, Russia: 2082 A.D.

When the latest CoDominium Olympics began, few citizens of the colonies, and almost no one on Earth, had ever heard of Haven. By the end of the first week of the two-weeks of the games, "the little moon that could" was all the news.

Haven athletes had medaled in a third of the events and excelled in so many others that the standings, normally dominated by the Sauron System athletes, had been completely thrown off due to upsets and displacements of Sauron's competitors by Haven newcomers.

Compared with the day-to-day workings of the CoDominium—where striving to keep a star-spanning civilization functioning in the face of economic chaos, burgeoning corporate power and a resurgent nationalism among the countries of Old Earth and their colonies—it was hardly an important event.

But in the corridors of power of that same CoDominium, where nothing that might prove a fulcrum or a pole ever went un-noticed, un-examined or un-used, the advent of an obscure moon-colony into the forefront of inter-colonial competition was noticed, examined, and its usefulness discussed and pondered with great interest.

The term of office of the Supreme Chair of the CoDominium Council alternated every two years, by law, between American and Russian appointees, with neither country allowed to place the same person in the office within the same ten-year period. Americans were used to revolving-door bureaucrats, but the Russians liked their leaders to proceed directly from supreme power to divine judgment and a peaceful transfer of power that was actually held to a schedule did not sit well with them, at all.

So, as they had always done with every other law that got in the way of what they actually wanted, the Russians simply ignored it. For the last eighteen years, whatever the name of the Russian appointee who happened to actually hold the Supreme Chair, the person who actually held the reins of power was the General Secretary of the Communist Party of the Reformed Soviet Union: Sergei Yevgenievich Volkov.

Volkov was of medium height and build, with a pronounced potbelly and a bulbous red nose that gave him the appearance of a hard drinker. In fact, he routinely substituted water for vodka in nearly all political meetings and every social event; one more way he maintained an edge over anyone in his immediate circle who might be probing him for weakness or maneuvering to replace him.

American intelligence was fond of referring to him as "The Wolf", the literal translation of the Russian root word of his name, *volk*. Volkov was aware of this and despised the Americans for it. This was his only indulgence in emotions toward anyone except his son's daughter, Illyana, and on her, he was a doting grandfather.

He was doting now, reading the reports of Illyana's dismal standing of twenty-third in the track and field events on the likewise humiliated Earth-sponsored CoDominium Olympics team.

"Who is this Becca Royce person?" Volkov asked as he read the newspad with his morning coffee. The Olympics were being held in Rio de Janeiro, and the images made him think of blue water, white beaches, golden sunshine and round, tanned asses, all of which on most days would normally put any Russian's mood over the moon. But not Volkov, and certainly not today.

He looked up at the Supreme Chairman of the CoDominium Council, Mikhail Utkin, who stood before Volkov's desk with his hands sweating, his feet aching and his back doing both.

Even so, Utkin was prepared. His own staff was charged with maintaining Utkin at a high level of usefulness to Volkov, and they had briefed him about the Secretary's tendency to focus on his granddaughter's achievements, or lack thereof.

"A Havener, Comrade Secretary," Utkin answered. "Qualified for her colony's team last year, excelled in training at the colonial University. Haven is a small colony moon, nominal American protectorate status, no representation in the CoDominium Senate, prime relocation site for undesirables from all over Earth. Originally an independent body colonized by religious fanatics, then received corporate sponsorship by an American mining consortium, and Haven soon became—"

"*Eb tvoi mat'*, Utkin, what are you, the fucking Encyclopedia Britannica?" Volkov looked back down at the newspaper and flipped the page; Germans were starving in Berlin and the redistribution was sparking food riots in Rome. *Two cheerful pieces of news in one day*, Volkov mused, distracted. He hated Germans and Italians almost as much as he hated Americans.

"Utkin, I don't give two shits about some capitalist dumping ground for CoDo trash, I want to know *who is this Becca Royce bitch?*"

Volkov had finished with a shout, now he lowered his voice. "One of yours?" he asked in a conspiratorial tone.

Utkin knew what the Secretary meant; anyone who had worked with the pig would know. He let out an even breath. "I don't believe so, Comrade Secretary."

Volkov looked up from beneath shaggy white eyebrows. "You are sure? 'Becca'; that's short for Rebecca, I think. Isn't Rebecca a Jewess' name? Don't all you kikes stick together?"

Utkin had spent his life in the Soviet bureaucracy, had risen to a position of power in the Party sufficient to be appointed to the Supreme Chair of the CoDominium Council, even if only as a cat's-paw to this two-legged dung heap seated before him. Utkin had not lasted so long nor progressed so far by having a thin skin, but rather a smooth one that kept him moving along in a survivable if oily fashion, in and out of the labyrinth of insults and suspicions and betrayals and disappearances and purges that had always furnished all Russian halls of power, Czarist or Communist.

"I believe the Royce girl was raised in a cult known as the 'Harmonies,'

Comrade Secretary. They were the original settlers of the Haven moon. No clear relation to any Earth-based religions, though some parallels with Buddhism have been noted."

Volkov snorted. "Whatever," he mused. "This Royce girl is giving every other colony fits. She's breaking records right and left, she passes every drug screening with flying colors—I don't think this brat even drinks tea—and she's doing it all for the benefit of some outer space gulag I wouldn't bother to piss on if it were on fire."

Finished with his tirade, Volkov tapped his finger on the desktop as he collected his thoughts, and resumed.

"Well. She's a farm girl and she's not an American, so that is enough for me to forgive her for being any stripe of mytho-religious nut-job. Christian, Buddhist..." He looked up at Utkin and grinned. "Even a Jew."

Volkov's smile froze at Utkin's obvious lack of appreciation for his witty remark. "Oh, now, don't pout, *Mischa*, we're all comrades in the glorious Reformed Soviet, I'm just busting your balls."

Volkov closed the paper, sat back and looked up at the corner of his office ceiling.

Utkin waited patiently for whatever instructions Volkov was about to impart.

"Okay. So." Volkov said, and leaned forward again. "All this other business of the CoDo Council this week, you handle that on your own. You know the status of our operations, what we want done in our Antarctica developments and the relocation quotas we'll need for workers for the St. Ekaterina colony. Get those handled as first priority when the CoDo Senate reconvenes.

"But this week, I want the CoDo Olympics Committee to throw a party in the Olympic village. Make sure all the athletes attend. If the games have to go on an extra day, that's fine, too; the Brazilians can use the extra money. And make sure the entire Haven team attends, but especially this Royce girl."

Utkin was about to ask why the Secretary General of the Communist

Party of the Reformed USSR, one of the two most powerful men on fifty planets, would bother himself with a party for a sixteen-year-old girl from a backwater, relocation-hellhole moon. A moment later, he had his answer.

"Get an agent to talk to this girl, a good-looking one. Have them talk to her parents if they are with her, her chaperone otherwise. Let her know we'll set her family up with a *dascha* and a farm in Yalta if they want one, or an apartment in Moscow if they'd prefer. Or both, I don't care. I suspect they won't, either, once they have the opportunity to come and live on Earth instead of staying on that rock, that… what did you say it was called?"

"Haven, Comrade Secretary."

Volkov rolled his eyes. "Whatever. If the weather in Rio has seduced her utterly, then we'll make them the same offer for living in Cuba, but she stays on the Russian Olympic team for the next eight years. She can compete for St. Ekaterina colony." Volkov looked at Utkin and squinted, thinking.

"No," he said finally. "No agent."

Utkin waited until Volkov completed his thoughts as Utkin knew he would.

"I think I'm going to get some sun," the Secretary said as another blast of snow scoured the windows behind him.

PLUTOCRACY

Earth, The White House, United States: 2082 A.D.

"So Haven colony comes out of nowhere, kicking ass and throwing off all the odds, and suddenly betting on the Olympics is fun again."

"But still illegal, sir." The Secretary of State replied as a Navy orderly poured more coffee into the boss's 16-ounce mug with the ornate eagle-emblazoned seal.

"Oh, yeah, Keach, illegal as hell," agreed the President of the United States. He grinned. "Which of course makes it more fun." He tossed a soft foam basketball across the room into a net over one window of the Oval Office. "Nothing but net," he mused aloud.

"Any of your people at State talk to her, yet, Adam?"

"Only at the reception. I'm told she's a nice kid, tall for her age. Strong as an ox."

President John Holt glanced back at the newspaper with the picture of a young athlete from Tabletop colony at the finish of the women's 100 meter. The kid looked like a goddamn skinned antelope, every muscle and tendon looking like it was lasered out of bronze and sprayed with oil; she was sweating like a racehorse. Gasping for breath, her features were stretched in a rictus showing enough teeth to reinforce the racehorse simile. Half a meter ahead of her, Becca Royce' nicely-developed bosom was parting the tape at the finish line; she almost looked distracted.

"Media has started referring to Haven as 'The Little Moon That Could'," Holt said, and shook his head. "Jesus. Does *anybody* in the news have *any* shame anymore?"

"I have to wonder about genetic manipulation," the President continued. "But if it was going to come from anyone, I'd have expected it from Sauron colony. But they can't compete in the games anymore, so who? The French? Or the Russians? Hard to believe a backwater like this Haven place would have a eugenics project we didn't know about."

Secretary of State Adam Keach shook his head. "Very doubtful, sir. Haven is a poor colony. Smaller GDP than Puerto Rico. Since it hit the CoDominium Eminent Domain list, a lot of forced relocation has gone there. Just last year the Russians dumped about 20,000 Afghans in the mountain regions."

"Afghans", the President said under his breath. "The Russians were messing with them before you and I were born. When I was in grade school, they were our problem. Now the Russians have them back again." He looked up at Keach. "Seems they're taking the opportunity to settle a lot of old scores."

Keach shrugged. "Better them than us, sir."

"Well. Be that as it may. Do we want this kid?"

Keach frowned, thinking. "It's a safe bet the Russians do. The Sauron colonial government was always a huge embarrassment to them; an American colony with a home-grown socialist model that's run by capitalists where everybody works and everybody is wealthy. Having a bright young Communist athlete around to break all the Sauron records in future events would be just the sort of thing that appeals to them."

The President scowled. "Saurons may embarrass the Russians, but they just plain piss me off. The Sauron colony is rich, arrogant and too independent by half. Did you know they get full autonomy at the end of the decade?"

Keach knew. "That was your predecessor's idea, John. Several other colonies do, as well. Not your fault and it won't be your problem. You'll be opening your Presidential Library by then."

Holt gave him a look that disagreed. "I'll still have to live in a world where Planet Skinhead has a vote in the CoDominium Senate."

"That's not really fair, John. The Sauron colony is almost as racially diverse as Earth."

Holt almost guffawed. "Sure, as long as we don't talk percentages.

And the ethnic diversity of the place is melting very quickly into what our people are already calling 'Sauron ethnicity.' They can't quite pick and choose their genes, not yet. But their whole culture revolves around *suitable matches*; arranged marriages, fetal genetic screenings, state-mandated gene therapy and quietly-but-firmly 'state-advised' abortion.

"Keach made a conciliatory gesture. "They can rightly claim zero birth defects and the lowest infant mortality rate in the CoDo."

Holt nodded. "That's true. But the way they're getting those numbers would make a certain German chicken farmer of the twentieth century very proud."

"Mister President, what do you want to do about the Royce girl?"

Holt thought a moment. "Haven's one of ours, isn't it?"

Keach looked uncomfortable. "Well… not exactly, no. The Church of New Harmony bought initial settlement rights. It was pretty much left to fend for itself ever since. First the mining consortia strong-armed their way onto Haven; that factionalized the place badly enough, but when the CoDominium created that Bureau of Relocation and started forced deportation to any world that couldn't prevent it with CoDo Senate votes, the mining groups welcomed the potential for cheap labor with open arms. Now, 'Haven' is quite possibly the most inaccurately named colony in human history."

"Hmm. Sounds like they could use some foreign aid. Have our people on the Hill look into a stimulus package for Haven. See what it needs and send a bunch of it in U.S.-licensed transport. If Haven is breeding people like young Miss Royce, we might want to look into taking this "Little Moon That Could" under the good old Eagle's wings."

"With Utkin running the CoDominium Senate this term, getting CoDo Navy assets to carry American aid to a neutral colony is bound to meet with some resistance," Keach warned.

Holt shook his head. "Then we won't try. Use all United States vessels. Nothing goes aboard CoDominium Navy transports. That reminds the Russians *and* the CoDo that we can afford this sort of thing with or without the CoDominium. And besides, I want something the American people can see as being all their own government's doing."

Holt pulled another foam basketball from a drawer in his desk and set up his shot.

"We're all getting a little tired of this 'one world' stuff."

TECHNOCRACY

Earth, Olympic Village, Brazil: 2082 A.D.

The host city of Rio de Janeiro had constructed the Olympic village around a central hall built to accommodate news conferences, interviews with the athletes, and speeches by the directors of the Interstellar Olympics Organizing Committee. Inexplicably and with no mention of it in the events calendar, midway through the games, the entire hall had been given over to a sort of "Family of Humanity" celebration. Since the Sauron System no longer sent competitors, but instead oversaw every aspect of the games, most of the attendees had only seen citizens of Sauron colony in their official administrative and largely humorless capacity, so not much was expected in the way of entertainment or cuisine.

But the event was sponsored by the CoDominium, which was this year chaired by a Russian. Few of Earth's cultures could put on a feast like the Russians, and nobody in the entire CoDominium could throw a party like the Brazilians. The combination made for a memorable evening, and a delicious one.

Arlen Cavor was a third-generation Sauron colony citizen and the Activities Director of the games. An expert in logistics, Cavor's was the guiding hand behind the flawless progression of every event that occurred outside the purview of his associate, Aishya Broome, Athletic Events Coordinator. Broome was also old-family Sauron colonial, and while Sauron dominance of the games had barred either of them from ever having competed, there were few events for which they could not have qualified, either in their youths or even now.

They stood together in the Host's Box, an elevated room overlooking the floor of the hall, and watched the proceedings below.

"Do you miss it, Arlen?" Broome asked as they looked down on the room filled with the physical cream of two dozen colony worlds and moons.

Cavor shook his head, then shrugged. "Well, I miss the parties." He smiled at her. "Not that there were ever any girls there who were prettier than you."

Broome gave him a friendly but cautionary smile. "We're not supposed to be married, Arlen."

Cavor's eyes made an almost imperceptible roll. "Please. I haven't seen a single young man here yet who was worth your time. Besides, the days when we had to gather genmat that way are long gone." He looked at his wife. "Not that I'd deny you the recreational aspect if you were so inclined."

Broome almost shuddered. "Please. There is nothing 'recreational' to having one of these—stud horses—lurching above you for thirty seconds and thinking he's the greatest lover in the universe because he 'bagged a Sauron'. I did my part in four sets of games; two winter, two summer. That was enough for the Genetics Ministry and more than enough for me." She bumped into her husband in a way that no observer would suspect meant all that it did to the two of them. "I much prefer the exclusivity of my contract—and the children I've had—with you."

Cavor's expression was almost pained. "*Stud horse*...in their wildest dreams they would not warrant the dignity of such a title. They're more like...I don't know...." he searched for the right label. "Cattle?"

Broome nodded. "I'd say that's a perfect word."

"Oh, I don't know that they're as bad as all that," a voice spoke up from behind them.

Broome and Cavor turned and nodded greetings to Commissioner Larson Voorhees, director of the IOOC since Sauron colony had been given sole responsibility for the games four years before. Voorhees' family was among the initial colonists of Sauron, commonly referred to as "Firstholders." But that would not have been enough to secure him his position had he not combined his heritage with an organizational genius of the first magnitude. Since Sauron had begun running the games, and with Voorhees at the helm, the Olympics had grown in popularity and even turned a consistent profit.

"Good to see you, sir," Cavor shook Voorhees' hand and Broome kissed his cheek warmly. Both were longtime friends and close confidants of the Commissioner. "Although I think I'll have to stand by my assessment. With the obvious exception, of course," he gestured toward the crowd below in a way that indicated they all knew who he meant.

Voorhees collected a glass of champagne from a nearby table and joined them in their review of the festivities.

"It's been a genetic goldmine for us, sir," Cavor said. "Twenty Earth nations and thirty colony worlds send athletic teams to the games. We've been able to collect genetic data from every one of them for the last twenty years. Congratulations, sir. Really; well done."

"Indeed," Broome raised a glass to Voorhees and Cavor followed suit.

"You are both very kind," Voorhees accepted the praise gracefully. One did not demur in Sauron society; if the truth was praiseworthy, it was to be acknowledged, just as one acknowledged responsibility for failure. And Voorhees' manipulation of the CoDominium Olympic Games was no failure, but a triumph of political maneuvering and scientific research."

"It's been a great pleasure to see the work progress so well. The broad spectrum genetic samplings have provided us with tremendous advances. But the real benefits will come from the samplings we collect this year. Of the fifty Perseid embryos implanted throughout the CoDominium, twenty-two are in that group of young people gathered down there today."

Broome and Cavor were stunned. Broome was the first to find her voice: "Sir," she said, "That is, in a word, wonderful."

Voorhees nodded. "It is. Though it is hardly surprising that such physically advanced specimens should find their way into athletic pursuits on their worlds, even we could not be sure so many would be chosen by their home worlds to compete in the events that would put their genetic material, quite literally, back into our hands."

"Then this will be the conclusion of the Project?" Cavor asked.

"I should think so. The other thirty-eight embryos failed to come to term, or died young, or have already been eliminated in arranged accidents on their worlds." He sipped his champagne and reassured Cavor and Broome: "Needless to say, our agents acquired sufficient tissue samples from the bodies immediately upon each individual's death, natural or otherwise."

"A shame we could not have arranged for all the survivors to be here at these games." Broome mused.

"Well, we only have so much in the way of assets to invest in political manipulation, Broome," Voorhees admitted. "I too, would have liked to use those assets to force the various colonial legislatures to send all forty-seven Perseids to these Games. However, it is a tremendous effort to maintain our covert support of the nationalist movements growing on Earth. The sooner America and Russia disavow the treaties that created their CoDominium and return to their provincial squabbles, the sooner Sauron and all the colonies attain independence. Once Sauron is free of CoDominium oversight—and with it, Earth's meddling in our affairs—we can begin to build the kind of world that is best for every human, everywhere."

"Hear, hear," Cavor agreed.

Broome was looking at the mass of Olympic athletes. "What I find fascinating is that, by definition, every one of those young people is an exceptional specimen. Yet, once you *know* that there were twenty-two of them who are superior even in that rarefied group, a trained eugenicist can pick them out of the crowd."

"And of those twenty-two," Cavor added, "One stands out above all the rest."

"Yes," Voorhees agreed. "I see she's become something of a sensation in the media. Not to mention the young 'stud horses' here at the party." He directed the latter comment to Broome with a smile.

The three of them looked down at one of the buffet tables. A mass of young and handsome athletes from all over the CoDominium was gathered in a swirling circle, and at the center of this hurricane of testosterone was Becca Royce of Haven.

"If she is not yet a great beauty," Broome commented, "that time is not far off."

Haven's thin air meant a higher exposure to ultraviolet radiation, and its inhabitants had adapted accordingly in just a few generations. Becca tanned quickly in the warm rays of Earth's sun in Rio de Janeiro. Bronze skin, golden hair and her mother's deep grey eyes had every male who saw her asking who she was and whether all Haven girls looked like her.

"The reaction of her fellow athletes is to be expected," Voorhees said, "What about her response?"

"Not so much as a flirtatious smile, Commissioner," Cavor answered. "Then again, this is a farm girl, and farm girls learn at a very early age how young males act around young females. And why."

Voorhees smiled. "There is a Greek myth about a young girl who was suckled by a she-bear and grew into a fantastic athlete and huntress. She was the first to wound the monstrous Calydonian Boar and was even counted among Jason's Argonauts on the quest for the Golden Fleece. She vowed never to marry any man who could not beat her in a footrace; she only lost because of trickery and divine intervention." Voorhees pointed at the young woman below. "I believe she stands there in the flesh."

"Acquisition Branch has been diligent, Commissioner," Broome said.

"Particularly with this one," Cavor added. "In fact…" he called Voorhees' attention to one of the wait staff below; no sooner had Becca Royce put down her glass than the waiter swept it up and into a pocket in a single gesture.

"The saliva samplings provide a wealth of detail about her gencodes," Cavor went on, "but we are still taking great pains to acquire as much actual live tissue as possible. We were hoping she'd be menstruating during the games, but according to the monitors in her quarters, there's been no sign of this. We do, of course, have blood samples taken in the normal course of drug screenings and other tests."

"I suppose it's too much to hope that she might be sufficiently injured to put her in hospital for a few days?" Voorhees mused.

Broome did not look hopeful about that, at all. "That, Commissioner, would require that she actually injure herself—or at least be in a position where an injury could be inflicted without drawing too much attention. Both are problematic given her skills and talents as evidenced to date."

"It's not all bad news, sir." Cavor said. "The preliminary examination of her codes bears out your hypothesis that Miss Royce is, in fact, a mutation of the Perseid Embryo, and by all appearances a thoroughly stable one. The lack of menstruation supports your conjecture that she is infertile, which means that the potential for exploiting her genomes can be monopolized by Sauron."

"The Russians can't perform directed genetic modification and the Americans won't." Broome's tone was simultaneously contemptuous and pleased.

"Idiots," Voorhees declared. "A universe waiting for the hand of Man to reach out and grasp it and they twaddle over their absurd moralities and labor to keep human science in the dark ages with the suppression of scientific research. All because they think it will prevent a war that is, in fact, inevitable."

All three were quiet for some time.

"They're really going to do it, aren't they?" Broome asked. Like all Sauron colonials, Broome was of North American ancestry. Her family tree had transplanted wholly to Sauron and, while it no longer had any significant branches left on Earth, loyalties ran deep in Sauron's young culture The lack of a clear lineage did not make Broome indifferent to the fate of the twelve billion people still living on what even the most independence-minded Sauron still thought of as the Home World.

Voorhees's expression was unreadable. "For the first time since the Great Exodus, people on colony worlds are seeking to return to Earth rather than escape from it. The greatest number of returnees have been from colonies settled by the former states of the old European Union: Churchill, Bismarck, Nueva España, Beau Monde…but even Tabletop and St. Ekaterina have lost reactionary elements who have returned to the Home World to 'renew their allegiance' to the U.S. or Russia, as it were. Publicly, less than half a dozen colonies have voiced any criticism of the nationalist sentiments that have been sweeping Earth for a decade."

"And those openly in favor of the movements all think their "mother nation" could run things better than the Russo-American CoDominium," Cavor said.

"Well, I suppose they wouldn't be *nationalists* if they didn't." Voorhees sighed. He turned to Broome. "So, yes, Aishya, in answer to your question, I believe they are 'really going to do it'. They'll have their war, the war they've been preparing for ever since China died and the Russians re-created their Soviet Union from the remains. America and Russia simply cannot co-exist; it's not in their cultural natures. One world isn't big enough for them, and dozens of worlds only make them more keenly aware that who rules Earth rules all worlds."

"Do you think their war will spread to the colonies?"

Voorhees shook his head. "Doubtful. The political balance is shifting toward increased power for the CoDominium Senate; and the stronger the Senate becomes, the weaker it makes the Russian and American coalition that created it. Earth's nationalist movements are accelerating this process. Their war will fully establish the CoDominium Senate as the uncontested authority over human affairs. Even if the colonies objected to this—which they will not—a Russo-American war on Earth will be over before the colonies can participate in any way. Given the time constraints of Alderson Jumps, it's likely such a war will be over before most of the colonies even know it has begun."

"Either way," Cavor said, "The CoDominium will be too busy to meddle in Sauron's internal affairs."

"What trickery?" Broome suddenly asked.

"Hmm?" Voorhees turned to her.

"The young girl in the Greek myth. What was the trickery used to get her to lose the race and marry against her vow?"

"Ah. I wondered if you'd catch that." Voorhees finished his champagne. "A young suitor appealed to Aphrodite, the goddess of love, for a way to defeat the girl and win her hand. Aphrodite, being generally opposed to vows of chastity, gave him three golden apples of irresistible beauty to cast in the girl's path during the race. Thus distracted, the girl stopped to collect each apple, falling further and further behind the boy, who won the race and her hand in marriage."

"He didn't win much of a bride if she was such a flighty creature as to be distracted by baubles," Broome observed.

"Oh, don't be too hard on her," Voorhees said. "The apples were enchanted, after all. And solid gold, something of a commodity in the ancient world."

The three friends laughed.

"I think I know that story," Cavor spoke with a dawning realization. "Wasn't the girl's name—"

"'Atalanta,'" Voorhees answered with a nod.

"So that's where you got the name." The tone of Cavor's voice had gone from respectful to awed.

"Yes," Voorhees admitted. "I changed it right after you two were brought in. The original 'Perseus' code name for the project seemed inappropriate once I learned of her gender and her exceptional attributes."

Cavor frowned. "Too bad they can't be allowed to return home," he said with real regret.

"No," Voorhees answered. "It would hardly do to release such breeding potential back into their general populations, beyond Sauron control. Besides, what really matters about them, their genetic potential, will be preserved and perpetuated through Sauron."

"It occurred to me," Broome said, "That the conclusion of this project will create an entirely new field in Sauron's social organization."

"Indeed?" Voorhees asked.

"This data will require an entire branch of professional eugenicists who will be dedicated solely to overseeing the genetic database of all

Sauron citizens now and into any foreseeable future. They will have to be a highly trained caste, an authority unto themselves. Masters of breeding, as it were."

Voorhees nodded. "Yes. Quite right, Aishya. We shall have to think of something to call them...."

Cavor stiffened. "Look. The Supreme Chairman of the CoDominium is talking to the Royce girl. Getting his picture taken with her too, I see."

"And the American Secretary of State is right there with them," Broome added, smiling. "I wonder what they are promising her? Golden apples, perhaps?"

"The world, no doubt." Cavor said.

"But which one?" Broome asked lightly, and they all laughed.

"If I were her," Voorhees said, "I should hold out for the golden apples. I don't think the other offer will amount to much in the long run."

MERITOCRACY

Earth, Olympic Village, Brazil: 2082 A.D.

Despite having grown up on a farm and making many trips with her parents to Market Days in Castell City, Becca thought she had never seen so much food in one place at one time in all her sixteen years.

In the past year of schooling and training for Haven's Olympic team, Becca had gained seven pounds and an inch of height, by the Church's Old Standard measurements.

She was neither distracted nor tempted by the many young men who worked so hard to impress the young girl from the colony moon no one had ever heard of.

She was, however, very distracted by the food.

Becca was frowning at a miniscule ear of corn, wondering why on earth anyone on Earth—hungry, hungry Earth—would ever bother with growing such a nonsensical waste of effort. She shrugged, popped it in her mouth and reached for a strawberry.

"Those won't mix well," a voice at her shoulder warned.

Becca turned to see a tall man about her father's age smiling at her. He wore a steel-grey suit and a deep red tie. Medium brown hair and steel-rimmed glasses completed the image she had seen on so many newspads: Mikhail Utkin, the Supreme Chairman of the CoDominium, himself.

Becca had stopped with the strawberry halfway to her mouth and realized she was doing a fair interpretation of one of the family's musky-lopes: Staring, slack-jawed, unblinking and just about to make a sound that would come out like something between a cow's low and a snore.

Utkin smiled and put an arm around her shoulders, turning them both to smile for a conveniently close photographer.

"Smile, Miss Royce," another voice said. Becca saw he was equally well-dressed, sporting a pin in his lapel that was a perfect miniature replica of the flag of the United States. "We have lots to talk about."

And talk they did, until an ever-growing crowd of news people began to press in on them all and Becca actually managed to break away into the crowd of athletes and some semblance of anonymity. She never noticed the three members of the serving staff who had culled her from the photographers and the squabbling statesmen. The Sauron waiters had culled her from the herd as artfully as wolves isolating a young elk calf.

Becca found herself in a mix of young men and women closer to her own age. All fit, all glowing with vibrant good health, and all of them apparently happy to see her.

"Hey, it's the golden girl," one of the girls said, smiling. Her jersey showed she was an athlete from the American-sponsored colony of Tabletop. Becca thought she was the most exotic creature she'd ever seen. Golden-hued skin, bow-shaped lips and black eyes that actually slanted, like a cat's! All framed by hair so straight and black it might have been painted on.

The girl held out her hand. "I'm Bao-Yu Colson," the girl announced. "Equestrian, Tabletop."

"Becca Royce," she said, shaking hands. "Um, Track and Field, Haven." The others had formed a semi-circle and regarded her with expressions ranging from polite interest to positively grim resolve, though all had smiled or laughed when she had told them her name and events.

"True enough, Becca," a boy in New Hibernia colors asserted with a grin, "We *all* know *your* events!" he too offered his hand, though he'd been one of those whose expression showed that he was somewhat wary of meeting her. "Bruce Ede, Boxing, New Hibernia. *Och*, and I am going to be in *big* trouble when my girlfriend finds out I spoke to you. Ye're nae exactly her favorite person in the 'verse right now."

Becca smiled at his funny accent; all his *r*'s sounded like little motorboat engines, but his smile was warm, his handshake was just enough beyond brotherly to be flattering and his eyes were very, very blue.

"Sara's not your girlfriend, Bruce; you've only known each other for three days and after the games end next week you'll probably never see each other again." A lanky young man with ebony skin and golden eyes clarified Bruce's relationship status, much to the other's dismay. "I'm Ronnie Nwosu; Ronnie's short for Badrani. I'm on the Panafka swim team."

And so it went 'round the circle of athletes, only two of whom were competing in Women's Track and Field. Not surprisingly, these gave Becca the coolest reception, but in a few minutes, both had warmed up to her, as well.

One of them was a pretty girl with short, dark hair and eyes like old ice, a Ukrainian girl named Illyana Volkova who was competing for the CoDominium. She said she was relieved that her standing had not put her up against Becca in any events, but Becca noticed that Illyana's nails were raw and bitten down to the quick.

As she spoke with and learned about her fellow athletes, Becca remembered a story from Sunday school when she was a child. It was about a little boy with a voice so beautiful the other children resented him for it. The boy wanted friends so badly he stopped singing in church, lowering his voice more and more each week until finally he was only mouthing the words. One day all the other children were sick and the Priest asked him to sing, only to find he had been silent too long, and the gift he once had was gone forever by his failure to use it. 'Those who excel at anything must accept the responsibility to do so,' the lesson ran. 'An aria is not meant for a chorus.'

Becca reflected that as friendly, as kind, as good as all these people were, above all else they were here to win. Each was the very best their country or their world had to offer, and each felt the overwhelming burden of their obligation to their country or world to excel. It made her feel humble and proud at the same time.

They talked about home, friends they had made, plans for life after the games. Bruce Ede's 'girlfriend' was from Tabletop; she was the girl who had come in a distant second behind Becca in the Women's 100-

meter. She arrived a few minutes later and, despite Bruce's misgivings, hugged Becca warmly. "God, you're fast!" she said, and nothing more was said of the race.

And so the evening passed, pleasantly, in good spirits. On the field, in shared events, these were all mortal foes, but they could never be enemies. Whatever the differences of their nations or colonies, the enemies for these young people were a missed step, an off-stroke, a hundredth-of-a-second miscalculation, and always the ever-present specter of a crippling, or even deadly, injury.

They spoke of how short life was, feeling themselves very wise and lucky and immortal. The oldest among them was nineteen.

Around them, the wait staff collected glasses, and napkins, and unfinished bites of food. Occasionally one would offer a comb to a preening young man, or deftly pluck a strand of hair from a girl's jersey. None of the athletes noticed any of the wait staff. Most of them were, for all intents and purposes, invisible.

All of them were Saurons.

ETHNOCRACY

Sauron, Autonomy Day: 2112 A.D.

"Citizens of Sauron; today we celebrate the thirty-fifth anniversary of our entry into the community of independent nations as a free and autonomous world, and a full member of the CoDominium Assembly.

"Our independence was not won in battle. We were not cast out from colonial forebears. We did not tear asunder the bonds of kinship, of culture, of loyalty from the nation which first sponsored our struggling colony here on Sauron, or from the Home World of Earth which supported us as we grew to our own maturity.

"No, we did not gain this state through violence; rather we have earned our place in this universe by the fruit of our own labors. We have worked to make our world wealthy. We have strived to make our culture rich. We have suffered to make our people safe. And we have dreamed, to make all our efforts worthwhile.

"It has been nine years since the Great Tragedy that devastated the Home World in a nuclear fire of wasted ambition and petty, nationalistic squabbles. We of Sauron are all descended from that Home World, and while we forever grieve for the loss of Earth, we resolve too that we shall never embrace the twin follies that destroyed her; provincialist nationalism coupled with an unwillingness to see the greater destiny that awaits the human race in the vast expanses of the galaxy."

Voorhees was sitting in the back of a diplomatic limousine, listening to a recording of the Autonomy Day speech by First Citizen Kallas of Sauron.

Not a bad speech, he thought, *although it is a terrible name for a holiday. And whatever speechwriter came up with that "provincialist nationalism" phrase should be sterilized.*

Contrary to the First Citizen's avowal, Voorhees did not, in fact, grieve over Earth's fate. On the one hand, he felt such grieving would be hypocritical; his own agents' role in supporting the Russo-American nationalist groups had certainly been part of America and Russia collapsing into the nuclear war that had rendered large portions of the Earth a poisonous, mass grave. And, while unfortunate, Voorhees did not consider the 'Great Tragedy' either especially great nor even particularly tragic; extinction was a part of life, after all. It was merely an example of what one of his professors had described as "evolution in action".

In any case, today Voorhees had a flight to catch.

He had wanted to make this journey for some time, but he had been simply overwhelmed with work, especially in the last four years, since the Exodus of the CoDominium Fleet from Earth. Sauron had received millions of survivors, all of whom required screening and approval for—or rejection of—asylum on Sauron.

Sauron had dutifully accepted its quota of Earth refugees; almost none of whom met Sauron's standards of genetic acceptability.

However, sterilization was absurdly easy to implement and even easier to blame on the refugees. They had simply been exposed too long to the increased levels of radiation on Earth; such a shame, Sauron offers her condolences, etcetera.

With the bulk of that work behind him, Voorhees had finally decided to take the time to book the many inconvenient Alderson Jumps it would require to reach the little backwater moon where lived the Mother of his Atalanta; who was destined also to be, in many ways, the Mother of Sauron's Supermen.

He wanted to tell her many things, about his triumphs, about her part in them. She who had been the only willing participant in the Project that he had re-named because of her daughter.

Because of our *daughter*, he amended.

He had lied about Becca Royce being an infertile mutation. It was the only way to allow her to return safely to her mother on Haven.

Now, after more than fifty years, Voorhees too would finally return to Haven, to see the only two women that had ever mattered to him.

Only to find he had come too late.

EPILOGUE

Haven, Royce Farm: 2113 A.D.

Becca Royce Jeffries Parmenter held the last note of her mother's favorite hymn as the voices of the other mourners faded into silence. Then Becca, too, finished the measure, and released her mother's spirit to join the great song of the Universe.

Becca's sons and daughter, along with her grandchildren, stood on either side of her as the Church elders filed by to tender their condolences and offer their respects. They were followed by friends and neighbors, a few tradesmen from the town of Redemption, but no one who had to travel more than a few miles.

Becca didn't blame them. Nobody traveled very far from home, anymore. Things were very bad on Haven, these days. Earth was dead, and the CoDominium was overextended everywhere, trying to maintain some cohesion among worlds which had overnight gone from colonies to the sole remaining preserves of the human species. Across the human-inhabited universe, people withdrew, retrenched, and awaited the storm they feared might come and destroy them any moment.

Which was why she was surprised to see a mourner she did not recognize, standing by the bier after everyone else had left.

"Do you know that man, Mother?" her daughter Bao-Yu asked. Bao-Yu Jeffries was curvaceous, blonde and blue-eyed; the physical antithesis of her namesake, a friend of her mother's who had died in a Jump Catastrophe over thirty years before.

"I do not," Becca admitted. The mourner was looking calmly at Becca, but had not stirred from his place by the gravesite. "But I believe I will go and say hello."

Becca was something of a local legend. She had buried two husbands—the second only last year—and today, her remaining parent. She was a successful rancher and had been Professor of Veterinary Medicine at Castell University until it had closed four years ago. At fifty-seven and a mother of four, she looked no older than thirty and was still regarded as a great beauty; there were several unabashed suitors who were checking off days on their calendars until they could approach her at a respectable distance in time from her latest bereavement.

"Good trueday to you, sir," Becca addressed the man. "Were you a friend of my parents?"

The man standing before her was tall and slender, obviously very athletic in his youth and still appeared quite vital despite a cane he apparently needed, if only at intervals. He looked to be in his early seventies, perhaps a bit older, but Becca knew from her own experience that such appearances could be deceiving.

The man nodded. "In a way. I knew your mother when she studied at the University." He stepped closer to Becca and extended his hand. "My name is Larson Voorhees."

Becca felt sure she knew the name but could not place it.

"I am sorry, Mister Voorhees, but my mother never mentioned you to me." She became aware of a mild sense of apprehension; this man was looking at her with a great, and progressively unwelcome, intensity.

"I would not think she would. We only met briefly. I was working on a research grant at the time. Your mother was a student volunteer, the only one who—" he stopped.

Becca frowned. "The only one who what?"

"The only one who was also a medical student," Voorhees continued smoothly. "It gave us a common ground to talk about. She could fully appreciate what I was trying to accomplish here on Haven. Her...contribution...was a great encouragement. We were more friends than colleagues, but I daresay I could not have succeeded in my research were it not for her."

"Well, my mother never finished college," Becca said, wishing to end the conversation. "She married my father in her second year, and I was born in what would have been her third, so I don't know how she could have given you much help with your research, but I'll take your praise as a compliment to her and thank you for it."

She felt an immediate and unreasoning dislike of Voorhees, but being unable to explain the feeling did not mean she was prepared to ignore it.

"Please do; I meant it sincerely as such." Voorhees nodded in farewell. "I just wanted to see you and speak to you briefly." He looked past Becca's shoulder to where her children were waiting, two of them holding children of their own. "An excellent family," he said, and turned away.

Becca watched him go, trying to remember where she had seen him before. Years ago, and only briefly, at some gathering. Becca had only attended one gathering in her youth, and suddenly she remembered. It had been just before her return to Haven.

"Mister Voorhees! You were with the Olympics in '82, on Earth!"

Voorhees turned and smiled. "I am flattered you remember me, Mrs. Parmenter."

Becca's lips thinned with anger. "It is not a happy memory, Mr. Voorhees." Becca took two long steps toward him. "It was at the memorial for the athletes. Twenty-two young men and women died. I survived only because my ship was late because trips to and from Haven were so infrequent in those days. I missed the ship to Wayforth that carried almost all the other athletes."

"A terrible tragedy, Mrs. Parmenter," Voorhees agreed.

"Yes. One I have had to live with every day for the last thirty years. I had friends on that ship, Mr. Voorhees. People I had only known a fortnight, but with whom I shared bonds that have lasted my entire life." Becca could feel the blood pounding in her ears; thirty-five years of anger and grief trying to burst forth.

"I share your grief, Mrs. Parmenter, but I do not understand your apparent anger," Voorhees was trying to be conciliatory, but something inside Becca told her that both his statements were lies.

"I am angry, Mr. Voorhees, because those young people—my

friends—were on a *Sauron* ship, a ship which you, too, were supposed to be on. At the memorial you mentioned a 'cruel trick of fate' that detained you at the last minute. But for some reason, I never believed you." Becca felt tears on her cheeks. She had not cried for her mother today. She had never cried for her friends, not in thirty years; but now she cried.

"But what could a sixteen-year-old girl do? Nothing. Nothing but go home; live, marry, raise a family and try to forget her pain and her suspicions."

Voorhees was silent for a long time. "I don't know what you expect me to say, Mrs. Parmenter, so let me say this: Living, raising a family and forgetting one's pain is the sum total of human existence." And suddenly, Becca saw a gleam of revelation in Voorhees' eyes, as if he only now was seeing the truth of his own words.

"You could say they are the 'golden apples' of our lives." He nodded again and turned away, walking back to a car where a driver opened the door as he approached; on the door was the State Seal of Sauron. "Goodbye," he said.

Just before he reached the car, Becca called after him. "What exactly was the research you were doing that my mother helped you with?" she asked.

Voorhees turned and favored her with a smile of paternal love.

"Obstetrics."

The car door closed, and the vehicle slid down the hill and out of sight.

The End